"Kade, w

He halted

"Fine. Duly no

"No." She frowned. "It's not fine. I accused you of something horrible, and I was wrong. I'm sorry."

Shit. Tears were filling her eyes again.

"I think it's wonderful that you help out the Humane Society."

He did more than that, but he wasn't about to enlighten the crazy woman. "Thanks." His tone gave away his less than sincere thoughts, but he didn't care. He was ticked off. *Damn high-n-mighty Pennsylvanian.*

"Why are you so sensitive? I said I was sorry."

"Why indeed." He stepped closer then stalked the frustrating Yankee when she backed up. "Tell me, Ms. Wyne." He didn't stop until her back hit the front of a stall. "There are several other people who live on this ranch, did any of them cross your mind as being the culprit?"

Eyes round, she swallowed and slowly shook her head.

Kade bit back a curse. "Figures."

He stepped away, and then changed his mind. Grasping the spokes on either side of her head, he pulled himself in and stared into her widening brown eyes. "Just what the hell is your problem with me, lady?"

What they're saying...

About Her Unbridled Cowboy:

"I love Ms. Michaels' voice and she knows how to hook her readers in from the very beginning. I love how she develops her characters and makes them so believable that you feel as if these are real people you could become friends with. I highly recommend this second novel in the Harland County Series and I'm eagerly looking forward to book three and four. Don't pass this series up!"
—**Night Owl Reviews,** *Reviewer Top Pick*

About Her Fated Cowboy:

"As always, this author perfectly blended an amazing storyline, which contained characters you just can't help but fall in love with and she worked her magic in creating a masterpiece of the heart. I even enjoyed her sense of humor sprinkled throughout, which was placed in all the right places. This is one story I highly recommend and one author I just can't read enough from. Since this is the first book in the Harland County series, I'm eagerly looking forward to the next book."
—**Night Owl Reviews,** *Reviewer Top Pick*

About Cowboy-Sexy:

"A blend of military man and cowboy …ohh my. The connection between these two is electric. This book is full of real life struggles that military couples face. These details give the story a lot of depth and heart. Yet despite the difficult topics tackled, the upbeat dialogue makes this a fun read. Readers will race through this story and then preorder the next book in the series to see what is in store for outrageous Brett."
—**RT Book Reviews, 4 Stars**

Dear Reader,

Thank you for purchasing Her Uniform Cowboy. This is the third book in my Harland County Series. *Unruly cowboys and the women who tame them.*

In this story, I've incorporated a few similarities to my life. The hero is in the National Guard, like my husband, and the heroine deals with the same thyroid condition I have for years. I thought it was time to put both in a book. ☺

Kade Dalton has been on several deployments with the Texas National Guard. The tough, handsome sheriff, a consummate helper, doesn't realize he also needs help. It takes a strong, understanding 'cowboy tamer' to stand by him.

Brandi Wyne is the perfect match for the cowboy guardsman. Diagnosed with hypothyroidism, she's had weight issues and boyfriend issues, and needing a clean break she's hoping to build a new life in Texas—without a military presence. But her friends' matchmaking parents have other ideas.

When their need for each other becomes too strong, soon Kade and Brandi are in a relationship that heals as well as frightens, pushing them each to face their demons, and discover, together they can overcome their past.

Another hot, heartfelt, sexy read, this story also includes some of the other characters in the series. I'm also creating a spin-off series-*Citizen Soldier Novels*-set in the Poconos of Pennsylvania, featuring Brandi's National Guard brothers briefly introduced in this story.

Thanks for reading,

~Donna
www.donnamichaelsauthor.com

Also by Donna Michaels

~Novels~
Captive Hero (Time-shift Heroes Series-Book One)
The Spy Who Fanged Me
Her Fated Cowboy (Harland County Series-Book One)
Her Unbridled Cowboy (Harland County Series-Book Two)
She Does Know Jack
~Novellas~
Cowboy-Sexy
Thanks for Giving
Ten Things I'd Do for a Cowboy
Vampire Kristmas
~Short Stories~
The Hunted
Negative Image
The Truth About Daydreams
Holiday Spirit
~Do-Over Series~
Valentine's Day Do-Over
Valentine's Day Do-Over Part II: The Siblings

UPCOMING RELEASES:
Cowboy Payback (Cowboy-Sexy Sequel)
~Time-shift Heroes Series~
Future Hero—Book Two
~Harland County Series~
Her Forever Cowboy (Book 4/Kevin)
Her Healing Cowboy (Book 5/Jace)
~Citizen Soldier Novels~
Wyne and Dine (Book 1/Ben)

Her Uniform Cowboy
Harland County Series
Book Three: Kade

By
Donna Michaels

HER UNIFORM COWBOY

Harland County Series/Book THREE: Kade

Copyright © 2013 Donna Michaels
Cover Art by JT Schultz © 2013
Excerpt from *Her Forever Cowboy* Copyright © 2013 Donna Michaels

ALL RIGHTS RESERVED. No part of this book may be reproduced or transmitted in any form whatsoever without written permission from the author—except by a reviewer who may quote brief passages in a review to be printed in a magazine, newspaper, or on the web. For information, please contact the author via email at Donna_Michaels@msn.com

All characters in this book have no existence outside the imagination of the author and have no relation whatsoever to anyone bearing the same name or names. They are not even distantly inspired by any individual known or unknown to the author, and all incidents are pure invention.

ISBN-13: 978-149472010
ISBN-10: 1494742012

Print edition December 2013
Book Three in Harland County Series

Dedication

To Harland County fans, and my wonderful street team, my minions, I hope you enjoy the story of Connor's best friend Kade, the helpful, haunted cowboy/sheriff and his tough journey.

To my husband Michael, my family, the HOODS, and my cp JT Schultz. And to Jinny and Kelly, and my editor, Stacy, for their help and appreciation for this series.

Chapter One

He left behind a fiancée and six-month old little girl...

Try as he might, Kade Dalton couldn't get that fact out of his head. He'd lost a soldier during his last deployment with the Texas Army National Guard. And that soldier had had dependants.

He failed.

Grumbling a curse, he slammed his mug on the counter and strode for the back door. Just because he was up before the ass-crack of dawn, didn't mean he had to wake the whole ranch. Not that the household wouldn't be up in a while anyway. His cousin, Kevin, usually left early for his commute to Houston for his vice president job at McCall Enterprises. Jen, Kevin's sister, would be up soon too, thanks to her four-year old son, Cody. And her husband, Brock, had Shadow Rock, the Dalton family ranch to manage. But even though they would all be up soon, Kade quietly closed the door before heading to the stables. He had no desire for his family to realize how poorly he slept, or worse, to start his day with a lecture.

Yes, he knew it wasn't his fault the soldier had died.

He was just doing his job.

These things happen.

It's unfortunate, but a part of war.

Well, not on his watch. Not during his three previous deployments. Christ. He was the First Sergeant on the last two tours. He was responsible for the soldiers under his command. *Therefore, I was responsible for the man's...*

Kade closed his eyes and inhaled while he worked to get his mind out of Afghanistan and rejoin his body back in the states. The scent of dirt and manure mixed with the fragrance of roses from a nearby trellis.

Home.

Still somewhat cool, the early June morning air felt good on his heated skin. Another deep breath rushed through his lungs. He was home where he belonged. In Harland County, Texas. On Shadow Rock Ranch. His Guard family—minus one—was home where they belonged. He had people here who depended on him. Animals that depended on him. A community that depended on him.

Every morning he told himself this.

Every morning he got out of bed and went to work.

Every damn morning he felt like screaming.

And that...Pissed. Him. Off.

He wasn't weak. Hated being weak. Almost as much as he hated being on edge. And he was on edge. Ever since that damn day.

Gravel groaned a muffled protest under his two-hundred pound stride. Keeping busy was the key. So, he helped out around the ranch. Worked with the horses. Went to auctions discerning which would make good stock horses. And being on edge was the main reason he'd agreed to take over the sheriff's position when the former one had approached him with the offer to finish out the man's term.

Harland County Sheriff?

Not something Kade had ever aspired to be. No. He liked horses and ranching and giving up one weekend a month and two and half weeks a year to Uncle Sam in the Guard. Never had Kade ever thought about being a sheriff. Yet, here he was, decked out in the tan uniform, weapons belt, badge and hat. Been that way for the past month. Harland County was fairly quiet, mostly rural, not much crime going on. Still, the extra job helped with his edginess.

So did sex.

Hell yeah. But his mutually agreed upon one-nighters had ceased once he'd accepted the badge. Didn't seem right. And looking for a relationship was out of the question. He wasn't about to stick some poor woman with his sorry ass. Hell no. Not until he got through some issues. Besides, relationships involved sharing more than a body, and his heart was off limits. Closed off. Locked up tight. In fact, no woman had ever reached his heart in over two decades. If it wasn't for the way he felt about his family and friends, Kade would question if he even possessed one.

Bypassing his truck, he headed for the stable on the far right. The quiet stable. The one which housed the abused and abandoned horses. Currently, there was only one. Thank God. That meant most of his fellow Texans were taking their ownership responsibilities of the magnificent creatures seriously. Horses weren't toys you could ride whenever you fancied. They weren't pets you paid attention to occasionally. They required work, maintenance, human touch and…

Son-of-a-bitch, he was edgy again. Nothing pissed him off more than a neglected or abused animal.

Stepping inside, he sucked in air heavy with the smell of more dirt and manure, but this time laced with the sweet scent of hay. The combination instantly calmed, took off some of that damn edge, and he headed to the first stall.

For several years now, he enjoyed working with the local vet to nurse the horses in this stable back to health. He'd made it Shadow Rock's practice to volunteer the stable to the Humane Society. It was a project of his, one he hoped to expand in the future. Now that he was more than likely home permanently, he needed to draw up plans to—

Sweet mother of Texas...

He stopped dead at the entrance.

...that is a beautiful sight to behold.

Bent over, lightly rubbing down one of the horse's legs was a local designer. A beautiful transplant from Pennsylvania. God, she was curvy and hot and he wondered if she felt as soft as she looked. Something he would've discovered within the three months he'd known the woman if it weren't for two things. One, Brandi Wyne was not a one night stand, and two…she had an aversion to the military.

The fact she was the only woman to spark part of him to life with just her mere presence didn't sit well with Kade. Hell no. So you'd think he'd be able to order his legs to slowly back out of the stall before being seen by the sexy woman whose big brown eyes, full of warmth and understanding, sucked him into a false vortex of hope. But no. Instead of retreating, he stepped forward like a complete idiot.

Seems his legs took orders from a body part due south of his brain.

Without his permission, his gaze ran down to her battered boots then back up, noting strategic creases in her well-worn jeans where they hugged her long, lean legs and mouthwatering ass.

What he wouldn't give to be those jeans...

About the same time that thought flashed through his fogged mind, the designer stiffened and slowly straightened. Awareness zinged around them, overloading the air with so much energy the poor horse shifted her stance in agitation.

Damn. The last thing he wanted was to spook the abused mare.

Intending to ask the woman to step away from the horse, he got as far as opening his mouth, but not a damn sound came out when she turned and glared at him, gaze full of pure venom.

He was the one to take a step…backward.

"You," she snapped, jabbing a finger at him while she marched forward, hair bouncing around her shoulders in a flurry of sun-streaked caramel waves. "How could you? I would expect this kind of behavior from someone irresponsible. Not you. Wow. This…this is unforgivable."

Stopping in front of him, she inhaled, her rant obviously not over. And damn, he wished he knew when he'd lost contact with his tongue because it was not taking orders from his brain at the moment. No, the only part of his foolish body responding was still in the southern region.

"You know what? I'm calling the police." She shoved a hand in her pocket and came out with her phone. "Oh, wait…" Snorting, she turned in a circle, arms flailing. "Can't do that. They'd only send me you!"

He watched as the phone made its way back into her pocket with an angry thrust before the designer advanced closer. Kade backed up, leading the crazy woman out of the stall and away from the nervous horse. Half of him wanted to set the beauty straight, the other half wanted to set her against the wall, press into her luscious curves and put her delectable lips to better use.

He did neither.

"Well?" she asked, hands jammed on her hips, head tipped back, chest heaving.

His gut took an invisible blow. Damn...the woman was gorgeous.

"*Well?*" she asked again. "What do you have to say for yourself? This is inexcusable. How could you? Did it make you feel like a big boy, treating such a beautiful creature that way? Huh? Did it? Seriously, who do you think you are?" the banshee continued, not giving him a chance to speak. "You think because you're in the Guard or because you're the sheriff you can do what you please? Well, you can't. You're not going to get away with this. You hear me? You're accountable for your actions just like everyone else, mister." She pressed closer, her heaving chest now brushing his in tantalizing bursts with each indrawn breath. "Well? What do you have to say for yourself?"

He cleared his throat and managed to get his tongue to cooperate. "She's not mine."

Okay, not the best of explanations, but hell, he didn't owe any.

"Of course, you'd try...wait...what?"

Brown eyes blinked up at him, confusion clouding the fire.

"The horse isn't mine," he repeated. "The Humane Society brought her in yesterday."

More blinking.

"Oh." Her shoulders relaxed. "You're housing her?"

He nodded, anger starting to heat his blood. "She'll be here until she's healthy again, and the vet releases her."

"That's so sweet."

Tears filled the woman's eyes before she flung herself at him and crushed his body with her curves. The beauty's about-face made his head spin.

On any normal day, he would've been pleased, damn pleased to have her fulfill a fantasy that had been running through his brain for months.

Him.

Her.

No air between their bodies.

But this morning was far from normal, and he was far from pleased.

Grasping her shoulders, he set her away from him. "Yeah, imagine that, a National Guardsman *and* sheriff who's sweet. You must be mistaken." He released her, fished the reflective sunglasses out of his shirt pocket and shoved them on his face. "Good day, *ma'am*."

Warm fingers curled around his bicep and pulled hard.

"Kade, wait. Look, I'm sorry. I really am."

He halted and turned to face the clinging designer. "Fine. Duly noted."

"No." She frowned. "It's not fine. I accused you of something horrible, and I was wrong. I'm sorry."

Shit. Tears were filling her eyes again.

"I think it's wonderful that you help out the Humane Society."

He did more than that, but he wasn't about to enlighten the crazy woman. "Thanks." His tone gave away his less than sincere thoughts, but he didn't care. He was ticked off. *Damn high-n-mighty Pennsylvanian.*

"Why are you so sensitive? I said I was sorry."

"Why indeed." He stepped closer then stalked the frustrating Yankee when she backed up. "Tell me, Ms.

Wyne." He didn't stop until her back hit the front of a stall. "There are several other people who live on this ranch, did any of them cross your mind as being the culprit?"

Eyes round, she swallowed and slowly shook her head.

Kade bit back a curse. "Figures."

He stepped away, and then changed his mind. Grasping the spokes on either side of her head, he pulled himself in and stared into her widening brown eyes. "Just what the hell is your problem with me, lady?"

She drew in a breath, her luscious mouth opening as if to respond; the action brought their bodies in contact in a hell of a delectable way. And son-of-a-bitch, if his body didn't overrule his mind and take over the interrogation. Tightening his grasp on the bars, he pressed closer, rejoicing in her hitched breath and the way she trembled against him.

"Well?"

"I…" She swallowed, blinked a few times, then asked, "Wh-what was the question again?"

Damned if he knew. Christ, he was lucky to remember his own name with her soft curves brushing him, pulling him out of himself, busting his restraint, making his need a number one priority. And he never put himself first. Ever.

But when her hungry gaze dropped to his mouth, all bets were off. He had to know. Had to taste her.

With a curse on his lips, he bent lower, his attention pulled to the mouthwatering cleavage peeking out from the rounded neck of her brown T-shirt. Absently noting how the color matched her darkening gaze, he was about to finally get a taste of her sweet lips...

The loud snorting of a horse broke through his fogged brain.

Glancing through the bars, he caught sight of the skinny mare shifting its weight on sadly neglected hoofs. The same horse the woman melting into him accused him of abusing not ten minutes earlier.

Shit. With a jerk, he released the stall and stepped back.

What the hell was wrong with him? His lack of self-respect was disturbing. The designer, although sexy as sin, was off limits. *A no-touch zone.* Her opinion of him was too poor to ignore.

Setting his shoulders, he stared down at the blinking woman. "I have work to do."

Not waiting for a reply, Kade stepped around her and into the stall with the female that needed him, and away from the one his body mistakenly thought *it* needed.

Brandi Wyne had come to accept she had good days and bad days. Today was starting out to be a bad day. A very bad day. Dammit. Why did her brain take a hike whenever Sheriff Kade Dalton appeared? Was it his strong, can-do, capable attitude? Thickly lashed, mesmerizing gray gaze? Tall, broad, deliciously muscled body? Lips that curled when he smiled? The sexy hollow between his square jaw and high cheekbones?

Oh, I don't know. Hello...maybe all of the above?

Turning, she sighed and grabbed the bars still warm from his touch. Maybe it was his voice. She watched as he carefully approached the nervous mare, talking softly but firmly while he reached out to gently stroke the creature's neck.

Brandi shivered. *Yeah, definitely his deep, sexy voice.*

The horse stepped closer to the sheriff/cowboy/soldier and gave a soft whinny. Was it wrong to wish she could change places with the mare and be the one his big, strong hand currently stroked?

Another shiver raced to her toes.

Well, if she'd stop stuffing her mouth with her foot whenever the gorgeous guy was around, then maybe she'd have a shot at replacing the horse. Or at the very least, avoid tripping and falling on her face, making a big fool of herself.

Okay, she may be stupid, but she wasn't dumb. Before the debacle at the Harland County Fair back in April, she'd received many interested glances from the cowboy. Many. And she'd returned every last one.

Even now, her heart raced at the thought of enjoying one of her friend's stuffed strawberries with the man. Kerri Masters had handed her the decadent dessert while Kade's best friend, Connor, had called him over to help her share the confection. A whole swarm of mutant butterflies had invaded her stomach, and she'd been so excited to finally kiss the sexy, gray-eyed cowboy she'd been flirting with for weeks.

Until he'd approached wearing a National Guard uniform.

It'd felt as if she'd stepped on a rake. A really big one. With both feet. At mach speed.

Still, there'd been many a night she'd lain awake imagining what it would've been like to lick strawberry juice from his sexy bottom lip.

Great. Now she was hot in all the right places. But for the wrong guy.

Her gaze took in the horse-whispering man. Why did he have to be in the military? Wasn't owning a horse ranch *and* being the sheriff enough? Okay, that wasn't fair. Kade, no doubt, made a great First Sergeant.

One thing she'd observed over the past few months was how the man helped anyone, no matter how big or small the problem. He always put others first. And now that she had a moment of clarity, she realized how utterly stupid it had been to accuse him of animal abuse. He was a good man. A good sheriff. And despite what he may think, she really had nothing against the military. Heck, she wouldn't have joined the Guard at eighteen if she had, and if it weren't for…

She gave her head a quick shake to dispel the worn-out thoughts. That was the past. And unimportant. Only the here and now mattered. New job. New state. New friends. Brand new beginning, and Brandi was bound and determined to do the things *she* wanted to do. And she was, *and* enjoying life for the first time in far too long. No more taking orders. She was in charge now.

Bringing her mind back to the present, she refocused on the sexy soldier-sheriff still whispering to the now, much calmer mare. Big hand still slowly stroking, voice soft and low, the man could calm a charging rhino, especially of the female persuasion.

As she continued to inspect the lean, broad man, one thing became abundantly clear. No matter what uniform Kade Dalton wore, he sure could fill it out. The tan shirt stretched across muscles rippling down his back and arms while the pants fit his hard form like a glove. A tight glove. A lucky glove. And yes, the man was hard, all of him, as their 'pressing' confrontation had recently confirmed.

All her good parts were tingling.

Again.

Dammit.

She didn't want to be attracted to the man. He was a soldier. And off limits.

Before moving to Texas from the Poconos back east, she'd made a vow. Service men were no longer on the dating menu. From any branch. Been there, done that…had the scars. Every boyfriend she'd ever dated had been a soldier. How could they not be? Her stepdad was a Major in the Pennsylvania Army National Guard, and all four of her stepbrothers were Guardsmen. There was never a shortage of good-looking recruits coming in and out of her house while growing up. She'd always been surrounded by soldiers. Still, not all the soldiers she'd dated were bad. Just the last one. And he was bad enough to cure her of her attraction to any man in uniform.

Her gaze lingered on the Texan, straightening up, giving the mare one last pat, lean forearm flexing in the process. As her mouth dutifully dried, she began to question that cure. Maybe the sheriff uniform cancelled out the soldier uniform. Yeah, that had to be it. That had to be why she lusted after the cowboy and hated herself for breaking her vow.

Still, that was no reason to take out her frustration on him. It wasn't his fault she was weak. She chanced a peek at his face. Maybe he wasn't mad anymore.

Silently exiting the stall, he secured the door, then turned to her. "Ma'am," he said with a curt nod, before striding out of the stable.

Nope. Still mad.

Good going, Brandi. Way to piss off the local sheriff.

And who could blame him? The man obviously adored animals, and she had to go and accuse him of neglect. Hell, she might as well have accused him of harming baby seals. Good thing she hadn't, though, or those cuffs jangling just above his fine ass could've been on her wrists right about now.

Was it wrong for that thought to heat her from the inside out?

"...Not at all."

Brandi jumped, then twisted around to find Kade's cousin standing in the doorway wearing a sharp, black pinstriped suit. "Oh, Kevin...you startled me."

Striking blue eyes lit when he grinned. "Sorry, darlin', didn't mean to."

He touched the brim of his black Stetson, and she wondered if all the corporate vice presidents in Houston wore one. Maybe it was a requirement his boss, Cole McCall, implemented. After all, she knew both drop-dead gorgeous men wore similar attire. Sort of a CEO cowboy thing. Her friends back east would drool a new lake if they were here.

Of course, Cole McCall was no longer on the market. Nope. That handsome cowboy had recently gotten married to Jordan, one of the two sisters she'd become fast friends with while working on their restaurant a few months back.

But Kevin, oh he was most definitely single. He loved women of all shapes and sizes and they loved him. Tall, dark hair, bright blue eyes, easy-going nature...yeah, he had women falling at his feet. Literally. She'd seen it happen on more than one occasion. Silly girls faking a fall just so he'd reach out and catch them. At first, Brandi thought the women pathetic, until she found herself fighting the urge to do exactly that with his cousin. What did that make her? A hypocrite?

No. Pathetic.

"I thought you heard me approach," Kevin remarked. "My apologies."

"No worries," she reassured. "But I'm afraid I didn't hear what you were saying."

He shrugged and gestured with a nod toward the now empty doorway. "All I said was not to mind Kade, not at all. Abused animals make him hot, you know, in any angry way. Unlike you, darlin'."

"Me?" Brandi laughed, body warming for some unknown reason. "No. I'm pretty sure I made him hot in an angry way today."

"Oh? Really?" The handsome vice president raised a brow, gaze twinkling as he leaned against the stall, apparently more concerned about what transpired between her and his cousin than getting dirt on his expensive suit. "Do tell."

She shrugged. "Not much to tell, except I kind of…sort of accused him of…that."

Kevin's gaze followed her finger, his blue eyes widening when he glanced at the mare. "Nooo!" He straightened from the wall, ripped the Stetson from his head and slapped it against his knee. "Oh man…I *knew* I shouldn't have bothered with that second cup of coffee this morning. Damn, I missed everything." His gaze shot back to her. "Tell me. I need to know. What happened? What'd you say? What'd he say?"

Brandi laughed again. She couldn't help it. The cowboy's enthusiasm was funny. "Well, it all started when I heard the mare as I was walking past the stable to go ride my horse." Her morning routine. She stopped by most mornings to ride the horse she boarded here at Shadow Rock, and it was always without incident. Until today. "I peeked in, saw the poor thing and got really angry."

"Yeah, how anyone could neglect their horse is beyond me," the handsome cowboy said as he set the Stetson back on his head.

"I agree. And you could imagine how disappointed I was to find a neglected animal on this property. I mean, you Dalton's aren't the type."

"Yet, you accused Kade."

She sighed, more than a little disgusted with herself. Okay, a lot disgusted with herself. "Yes, I did. But in my defense, the mare is practically all skin and bone."

"True."

"And on your property."

"Also true," Kevin agreed. "But why in the world would you think Kade, of all people, could be responsible?"

Good question.

She lifted her shoulders again. "He was the first person I saw in the stable, so I guess I assumed the mare was his."

"Ah, so it had nothing to do with the fact he's in the Guard?"

"What?" Brandi reeled back, shock rolling down her spine. "No, of course not. What does that have to do with anything?"

"You tell me."

She studied the handsome man. The crazy handsome man. He was off his rocker. "There's nothing to tell."

"Come on, Brandi. Everyone knows you did an about-face a few months ago...the very second you discovered my cousin was in the military."

Heat raced through her body and settled in her face. Mostly because it was true. Dammit. She just hadn't realized everyone else knew. Not a comforting fact. Neither was the thought that maybe that really *was* the reason she'd assumed the horse had belonged to Kade and not the other three adults living at Shadow Rock.

Shoot. She leaned back against the stall. Just because the last man she'd been attracted to was in the Guard, and a cruel ass, didn't mean the handsome sheriff suffered the same affliction.

"Look, I realize you're new to Harland County," Kevin said. "But you have eyes. I think you've been around my cousin enough to see he's a fair and just guy. He would never stand by while someone or something needed his help. He's the first to rush in…well, actually…" The cowboy snickered. "Now that Jordan's back, he may be second."

Brandi smiled in agreement. The former L.A. cop possessed the same attributes the VP just mentioned. Come to think of it, Jordan and Kade were very similar. First to spot a problem. First to offer a solution. First to offer a helping hand. The kind to stand up for those who couldn't stand up for themselves.

Heroes.

And she'd just accused one of animal abuse. *Way to go, Wyne*. She would never have accused Jordan of such a thing. Brandi wasn't sure what that said about her, but she knew it wasn't good.

"Ever since we where kids, Kade always had an affinity for animals and hated to see them abused. I think it was because of his upbringing."

Brandi's heart dropped. "He was abused?"

"Not exactly," Kevin replied. "Neglected, well, actually more like abandoned."

"How awful." Her gut twisted tight.

Kevin nodded. "Since it's common knowledge I see no harm in telling you about it."

Stop him. The sane thing would be to stop the guy. She was not interested in Kade, therefore had no real reason to hear or care about the sheriff's childhood. And yet, her mouth remained clamped shut as her head moved up and down in concurrence.

Stupid head.

"Kade's dad and mine were brothers," the cowboy in a business suit began as he leaned back against the wall again. "My uncle was a Marine, and when he died in the first Gulf War, Kade's mother—and I use the term loosely—moved to Shadow Rock with Kade. A few weeks later, the woman took off with a rodeo clown, and the two were killed in a car accident."

Air funneled into Brandi's lungs and her heart instantly ached for the little boy. To lose both parents so young and so close together was just tragic. "That's horrible. How old was he?"

"Eleven."

Her stomach clenched tighter. Only a year older than she had been when her mother married her stepdad. It had been a lonely, confusing, scary time. Young Kade surely had felt the same way. At least she'd had her mother for a little while longer. Not much, but she was grateful none-the-less.

"But Kade loved it here. He took to the ranch as if he'd been born on it, and enjoyed helping my father out no matter the chore. When my dad died in a freak ranch accident, Kade was as devastated as all of us, if not more."

"I'm so sorry. How old were you?"

"Thirteen, Jen was nine and Kade was fifteen," Kevin replied. "He stepped into my father's boots, so to speak, and took over as many of my father's chores as he could, doing them before and after school. I helped, too, of course, but it wasn't enough. The ranch began to suffer both physically and financially. So, I got a job at Foster's Creamery in town, and when he was old enough, Kade joined the Guard. The extra money made a big difference." He shrugged. "Along with a loan from the Masters and the McCalls. They originally wanted to pay off the debt, but my mom didn't want charity, so it was turned into a loan, on the condition Kade, myself and Jen went to college."

"Oh, how nice of them." A smile tugged at Brandi's lips. She could just picture her friends' parents making that stipulation so the young Dalton's had a bright future.

"Yes, it was." Kevin nodded. "We got degrees, paid off the loan, and we're all doing what we love. Jen takes care of the books, I create software with my buddy the bossman, and my cousin loves the Guard, this ranch, and animals, especially those that are tossed aside or abandoned."

Closing her eyes, she dropped her head in her hands and groaned. "And I just accused him of doing that very thing."

A warm hand patted her shoulder. "Like I said, you aren't from around here, how could you have known?"

She opened her eyes and sighed. "Yeah, but…deep down, I did know. I knew he was a helper."

"Well, don't you fret none, darlin'," Kevin said, slipping an arm around her as they started to walk out of the stable. "My cousin not only has a thick head, he has thick skin to go with it."

Whether that was true or not, Brandi wasn't going to sleep at night until she did a better job of apologizing to the man. And the sooner the better. So, not only did she have to put the finishing touches on the Garnett living room make-over, stop by the Masters' to pick up a check for the patio job she was starting at the end of the week and meet with Jordan at her restaurant to discuss the preliminary design of her master bedroom suite, Brandi now had to track down a thick headed, thick skinned, sexy-as-sin sheriff and make amends. Today.

God, she hoped the restaurant had a full pot of coffee on. She was going to need it.

Chapter Two

Kade should've clued in. Judging by the encounter in the stable this morning, he should've known today was going to suck. Now, a false alarm and two nuisance calls later, he finally pulled up in front of the station for the first time that day.

Situated between the post office and the fire hall on Main Street, the Sheriff's Department faced the ocean in a fairly new building constructed after the historic one had become a casualty of the last Gulf hurricane.

The hospitality in Harland County never ceased to amaze him. Everyone had rallied to help those who could be helped, and raised money for those who needed to start over. Now the Sheriff's Department was as hurricane and tornado proof as possible with state of the art equipment. The two-story building was rather large considering there were only three staff members—him, a pubescent deputy and a secretary/dispatcher. But it was what it was, and he'd make do. He always did.

Shifting the jeep into park, he was about to cut the engine when his cell began to pound out an AC/DC ringtone. Grateful the call was on his phone and not the radio attached to his dash, he glanced at the caller I.D. and breathed a sigh of relief. Connor McCall. His best friend since grade school. The way his day was going, he half expected it to be work related, or the Readiness NCO calling with a problem about the upcoming drill weekend. At least this was a social call. He could use a quick break.

"Hey, Connor," he said into the phone. "How's the cattle treating you?"

"Better than your horses, buddy."

"What do you mean?"

"I heard there was a report of abuse in your stable this morning."

How the hell had he heard? Brandi and Connor's fiancée, Kerri, were good friends, but he didn't think the designer would mention the incident. Especially since *she* had made the mistake, not him.

"Kevin told Cole and me all about it this morning."

"How the hell did my cousin know?"

"So, it *is* true."

"What? No, it's not true." Kade blew out a breath. "Look, I don't know what that woman has been saying, but you know damn well I'd never abuse an animal."

"Calm down, buddy. Calm down. Of course everyone knows you wouldn't do any such thing. And no, Brandi wasn't blabbing. Seems your cousin ran into her in the barn this morning. She told him about her mistake and how bad she felt. So, of course Kevin had to gossip like a little girl."

She felt bad? Good. She should. Maybe the woman actually possessed a little shred of conscience after all.

A deep chuckle rumbled through the phone. "You sure have a way with the ladies, Kade."

"Shut up."

Another deep chuckle met his ear. "Can't. It's just too funny. Too absurd."

"True," he replied, feeling a bit calmer. "Anyone who knows me knows I'd never neglect a horse."

"That's not why I'm laughing."

"Oh?"

"No. I'm laughing because you are so whipped and you just don't know it yet."

His head jerked back. "You don't know what the hell you're talking about."

As Connor's laughter increased, so did Kade's frown. He was far from amused. He wasn't whipped. He was in perfect control of his life. *Perfect* control.

"Oh, man…" Connor sobered. "It wasn't too long ago the roles were reversed in this conversation."

His mind instantly flashed back to a Skype conversation he'd had from Iraq with his buddy, right after Thanksgiving last year. One where he'd correctly summed up Connor's relationship with Kerri.

He smiled. "Yeah, but in that one, I was right."

"As I am now, buddy. As I am now," Connor repeated. "But I'm going to take pity on you and drop it."

"Good, 'cause I was about to drop the call."

"You are such a baby. Why don't you grow a set?"

"And you're a big pain in my ass, McCall."

"Then my job here is done," Connor stated. "You still meeting me for lunch at the pub in an hour, or do you need more time to compose yourself?"

"Now you're just getting bitchy. And yeah, I'm still meeting you, provided I'm not sent out on another stupid-ass call. They've been one right after another today. Was there a full moon last night?"

Connor snickered. "No, but it is Monday."

"True." Kade sighed, running a hand through his short hair. "Only thirteen more hours to go."

"Then I'd better let you get back to it. See you later."

"Yeah, later."

Kade hung up the phone and shoved it back in his pocket. He had just enough time to tackle the morning paperwork before lunch. His least favorite part of the job, although given the way his morning had gone, it was a task most welcomed. Now if he could just get through the next hour or so without—

"Mr. Sheriff Dalton, sir…"

His young deputy's voice crackled through the radio on the dash.

He closed his eyes and sighed. Well that wish got shot to hell. Opening his eyes, he grabbed the mike and responded. "Yes, Donny, go ahead."

"I'm out at the old Blackwell ranch on a disturbance call and could use your help, sir."

Adrenaline instantly washed away Kade's pity party and straightened his spine. "All right. Stay put. I'll be right there."

The kid was barely out of his teens with less common sense than most, but a whole lot of heart, and a damn good crack shot. Still, the only reason Donny Royal was a Harland County Deputy was because his daddy was on the town council. Of that, Kade had no doubt.

Six minutes later, he turned off the highway and onto the dirt road leading to the Blackwell ranch. Live oak trees whipped by in his haste. He hoped to God Donny listened to him and waited. The last thing he needed was the young pup walking in on a burglary in progress.

With the rash of random break-ins going around since before he'd taken over as sheriff, this call could be one of them. Money, electronics and tools had all disappeared from houses and ranches in unrelated locations. No one had been home at the times. Thank God. But sooner or later, that was bound to change. He had no idea how dangerous the perp or perps were and hoped to apprehend them before ever finding out.

As the ranch came into view, he relaxed a little at the sight of the young deputy leaning against the back of his squad car, clothes and hair a little rumpled. Well, what do you know, the kid listened for once. There might be hope for him yet.

That thought instantly nose-dived the second Kade stepped out of the jeep. The unmistakable odor of skunk filled the air, emanating from the young, frowning deputy.

Okay, so this wasn't a burglary.

He stopped dead, eyes already beginning to water, and he was still a good ten feet from the kid. Even though he could hazard a guess, he had to ask, "What happened?"

The deputy shrugged, glancing down at the dirt on his boots. "Old man Blackwell called in about a rustling in his barn. I'm sorry, sir. I found them in the south corner. I…I thought they were kittens. They were cute and furry with white spots. They didn't have the usual white stripe on the back. Honest."

Doing his best not to laugh—or hurl—Kade cleared his throat and nodded. "Some western ones have spots, Donny. So, let me guess…" He waved a hand at the kid. "Momma wasn't too happy you got close."

Donny nodded, brown hair flopping into his eyes. "Yeah, she came out of nowhere, hissing and rushing me like a banshee."

He could relate. Even though Brandi smelled a hell of a lot better, she did have that banshee move down pat this morning.

"Did you call animal control?" he asked, stepping upwind, trying desperately to suck in a clean breath of air.

The kid nodded, swiping the tears from his face. "Yeah, they're on their way now."

"I'll wait for them," Kade said. "You go on home and get acquainted with some tomato soup from your mom's pantry. It won't do much good, but it's better than nothing."

He knew this first hand, thanks to Cole and Kevin. Several times throughout their youth, he and Connor had been at the wrong end of a skunk.

"Thank you, Mr. Sheriff Dalton, sir." The kid practically tripped over his feet to get to his door.

He shook his head. "Donny, what did I tell you about calling me that?"

"Sorry, sir…I mean, Sheriff."

"That's better."

"Yes, sir."

Kade resisted the urge to close his eyes and groan. "And, Donny?"

"Yes, Sheriff?" The boy looked up at him from the front seat.

"Burn the uniform."

"Yes, sir." The deputy shut the door, started the engine then drove off, kicking up dust in his wake.

It was going to be months before that squad car didn't reek.

Brandi's morning flew by. After a less than gracious start at the Dalton's, her day continued to stink. The couch she'd special ordered for the Garnett's living room, the final piece of her masterpiece, arrived right on time…in a plaid pattern of bright pink. She was on the phone for a half-hour getting that mess straightened out. So much for finishing the job today. It was going to take another forty-eight hours before a replacement would arrive and she could finish the job.

As if the Kade debacle and Garnett fiasco weren't enough, she ran out of gas on her way to the Masters'. Thank God Jordan had been visiting her parents before work. Her friend had found her on the side of the road and drove back to retrieve a can of gas for the mower from her father's garage. It had been enough to get Brandi to the Masters'.

She parked, then set the empty can near the garage. Too bad her truck decided to share the fuel with her shoe. After she met with her new client, she'd head to the nearest gas station and fill up, then go home and clean up...if there was time.

Right now, she needed the nearest bathroom to wash the gas off her hands. She glanced down at her foot as she rang the door bell. Unfortunately, a bathroom wasn't going to help her shoe. Not hardly. Soap and water were no match for the gas-coated black pumps.

Why couldn't she have run out before she'd changed for work? Better yet, why couldn't she have remembered to fill up when the damn light had dinged on her exit from the Dalton's? Oh, right...probably because she'd been too preoccupied with thoughts of her encounter with Kade. Yeah, she was just full of brainpower today.

"Hi, Brandi. Come on in." Mrs. Masters smiled as she opened the door wide.

She returned the smile. "Thank you. I put the gas can by the garage like Jordan told me. Would you mind if I washed my hands?"

"Of course not, dear. Go right ahead. You know where it's at."

Her Uniform Cowboy

A few minutes later, she joined her friend's mother in the great room where she sat having coffee with Mrs. McCall.

"Hello, Brandi, dear," the other woman said. "You look like you've had a heck of a morning."

So much for trying to mend her appearance. Apparently, she'd failed. Miserably. "Yes, it has been one of those days."

The petite woman, looking cool and collected in a sleeveless blue dress patted the couch. "Well, sit down, and have some coffee, dear."

"Yes, coffee always makes things better," Mrs. Masters stated with a grin, already pouring a cup before Brandi could stop her.

"Thank you," she said, reluctantly sitting down. She didn't want to stink up the house. "I can't stay long. I have a few others to see." *And a sheriff to track down.* "I just want you to look over the ideas one last time before things get started this Friday."

She pulled the electronic tablet out of her purse, called up the plans and set them on the coffee table.

Her host leaned forward and scanned the screen. "Everything looks perfect, Brandi. Oh, I can hardly wait." The woman slid the tablet back along with a check. "Thank you so much for fitting us in. I know you're getting busy."

"Yes. Business is starting to pick up," she replied, slipping the tablet and check into her purse before reaching for her cup. The amount of work Harland County was beginning to supply her was quite a pleasant surprise.

"Word of mouth will do that." The older woman pushed a strand of graying-brown hair from her eyes and winked.

Mrs. McCall turned to her and frowned. "Was work good in Pennsylvania?"

Music wise, great. Designing, nonexistent. Mainly because she hadn't been allowed. Too bad she couldn't say the same for the coffee. It not only existed, the beverage went down the wrong way, and she was now choking on the brew.

After coughing and making a big spectacle of herself—because she never did things in a small way—Brandi wiped her mouth with the napkin Mrs. McCall had shoved in her hand.

"Sorry, thanks." She drew in a breath and forced a smile. "I worked a lot back in PA."

At least that wasn't a lie. She had worked a lot, just not as a designer. After years of pleasing others, doing what they expected of her, she'd finally had enough. Who knew answering Jordan and Kerri's ad would've led to her leaving her job, her home, her father, her brothers, her nephew…Ed.

"Well, I for one am glad you decided to come down here and work," Mrs. Masters said. "And dare I be as bold as to say a certain sheriff was, too?"

"Kade?" She coughed, then coughed some more. Would've been smart to swallow before speaking. Another napkin found its way into her hand. She wiped her face, and cleared her throat. "W-why would you say that? We're just…friends." She used the term loosely. *Very* loosely. Especially seeing as the guy kind of hated her at the moment.

"Oh, it's just the way he looks at you sometimes," the woman in blue answered, a knowing smile curving her lips while the other nodded.

Her pulse hiccupped, but she shook it off. "He probably has indigestion." The ladies were nice, but really needed to have their eyesight checked.

"Oh, I don't think so," Mrs. McCall insisted. "Mark my words, he likes you."

Butterflies decided to take up residence in her stomach. That was new.

"He's a good man." A warm hand covered hers. "You should give him a chance."

Okay. Yeah. No. Time to put an end to the tag-teaming. "I'm sure he is, but I didn't come to Texas looking for a boyfriend. I came to work. I enjoy working, and look forward to getting started on your project."

Her host squeezed her hand one last time before releasing. "And I'm so excited for your design to come to life out back. Nate and I can't wait to use the hot tub."

Brandi smiled, having initially been shocked by her customers' request. But after observing the couple, and seeing how much they were still in love after being married for over forty years, the request made perfect sense, and she'd gladly worked in a five-person hot tub.

"Neither can Alex and I," the tiny woman added, a pretty blush covering her cheeks.

"And I can't wait until it's done so you can all enjoy it," Brandi said, placing her cup down before rising to her feet. "I'd better go and double-check to make sure everything and everyone is all set to get started bright and early this Friday." She turned to her host. "You're sure you don't mind workers here over the weekend?"

"Not at all," her new client reassured. "I'm eager to get started. I know it will take a few weeks."

"No more than two." The job was big, but not huge. She'd allotted a ten day time frame, two weeks should the weather turn uncooperative.

The women exchanged a glance.

Mrs. Masters turned to her and smiled. "Whatever it takes."

"Okay, then I'll see you at the end of the week." She shouldered her purse and nodded. "Thanks for the coffee."

Both women were smiling as they walked her to the door where she said goodbye before climbing into her white truck. They were sweet. And content. She'd seen the matchmaking gleam in their eyes, and understood it was because they wished that happiness for everyone. Of course, pairing her with Kade was a complete waste of time. A dead issue. But her friends' mothers were nice, and she knew they did it out of the goodness of their hearts.

As Brandi drove down the drive, she couldn't help but wonder if her mother would've been that happy, and that happily married, if she'd still been alive.

"Well now, maybe getting Kade and Brandi together won't be as hard as my sons," Leeann McCall exclaimed, walking back into her friend's great room for another cup of coffee.

Hannah Masters followed close by. "I don't know. I get the impression Brandi has just discovered her backbone and is not going to be so easy to budge."

"True," she said, retaking her seat on the couch, smoothing a hand over her blue dress. "But we've faced adversity before, and prevailed. Twice."

Hannah sat down across from her and nodded. "So we have." Her friend lifted her cup in a salute.

"Brandi is in for a big shock if she thinks we won't give her and Kade a little push," she said, pouring coffee into her cup. Her sons were a lot more stubborn, and a lot harder to handle, although Kade had a much tougher childhood than her boys.

Her best friend set her mug on the table and sat back. "If we managed to help Jordan along, there's no way we can fail Brandi. Jordan's stronger willed than a bull."

She hoped that were true. In the short time they'd gotten to know the designer, Hannah and her husband, and she and Alex were all in agreement. Brandi was a good-hearted woman who liked to help others, and was loyal to a fault. Exactly what poor Kade deserved. Besides, anyone with eyes could see the two were attracted to each other. They just needed a push. *That's all.* A bit of a push.

"Of course, there is a problem," she felt inclined to point out. "Your daughter readily admitted she loved my thick-headed son practically from the get go. Both Brandi and Kade are closer to the opposite."

Her friend nodded. "Kind of like Kerri and Connor were in the beginning."

"Except I think Kade will be a lot harder. The poor guy was left behind by everyone he loved. I fear he won't take a chance." Her heart ached for the boy. Always had. Ten years ago, she'd made a vow to Sarah Dalton, his dying aunt, that she'd make sure Kade, Kevin and Jen were looked after, and she was not about to break it.

"Well, we'll just have to help him," Hannah stated with a firm nod.

Exactly what she'd been thinking. They'd helped her son, Connor, who was too stubborn at times to get out of his own way. And her son, Cole, who'd practically been unreachable. No. Getting Kade and Brandi together was definitely doable.

"You're right," she said, several plans forming in her head. "And I know just the couple to help."

A half hour later, Brandi's gas tank was full, but her stomach was empty. She pulled into the Texas-Republic lot hoping to rectify that and talk business with Jordan at the same time. Parking next to a familiar red pick-up, she smiled. Connor McCall was no doubt there to have lunch with her friend Kerri—his fiancée.

She turned off the ignition and sat back. Since she seemed to have left her house without her smarts that day, she was now faced with the dilemma of her shoes. Which was worse? Going into the restaurant barefoot, or with gas on her shoes? Neither seemed sanitary or acceptable. She glanced around her truck. Nope. Nothing. An empty, low-cal snack wrapper was not going to work. Her cottage wasn't too far away; maybe she could just run home quick.

The muffled buzz of her cell phone jarred her thoughts, and she quickly pulled the vibrating device from her purse.

Where are you?

Sighing, she answered Kerri. *Outside. Was just about to go home to change shoes. Pulled a Lucy. Spilled gas on shoe and don't want to come inside restaurant with it.*

No, meet me upstairs.

Kerri used to live in the apartment above the restaurant. Though she now lived at Wild Creek with Connor, maybe her friend still had a few things upstairs.

Okay.

Ten minutes later, Brandi walked into the restaurant with Kerri, wearing the only thing they could find. A pair of pink bunny slippers with big ears. Yeah, fashionable.

Went well with her white, short-sleeved silk blouse and black pencil skirt. Which would've been only mildly embarrassing if it was just Jordan, Kerri and Connor in the pub. But sometime during her rummaging session upstairs, another costumer had arrived.

The Harland County Sheriff.

Chapter Three

Just kill me now…

Brandi's day just kept getting worse. Of course the guy was here. It wouldn't be the day from hell if he wasn't, now would it? Having learned long ago to roll with the punches, she continued to walk next to Kerri as if wearing normal, big girl shoes. Which, of course, she wasn't. No. Her feet were shoved into bright pink, fuzzy slippers with a smiling, white, over-sized bunny head and large pink ears leading the way.

"Way to rock the slippers, girl." Jordan winked, giving her two thumbs up from the table where she sat with Connor and Kade.

The tall cowboy rose to his feet, along with the silent sheriff, and looked from her feet to her rapidly heating face as she approached with his fiancée. "I want to ask…I really do…but I won't."

She smiled despite herself. "What? You don't like my big bunnies?"

Well, his fiancée's bunnies. After all, they were Kerri's slippers. And it was somewhere in between that thought and the men's widening eyes that Brandi realized what she'd said. Then blushed accordingly.

"I…um…I'm sure your *bunnies* are just fine, darlin'," Connor drawled, slipping an arm around his fiancée's shoulders and drawing her near. "But I prefer Kerri's."

"Actually, they are hers. She let me borrow them because I spilled gas on my shoe," she babbled.

"Okay. Makes perfect sense," he said with a laugh that signaled otherwise. "Why don't we all have lunch? I'm starved."

She chanced a glance at the sheriff. Amusement flittered through his eyes, turning them a light gray. An emotion she hadn't seen there in quite a while. Her heart did that stupid rocking thing in her chest, so she quickly turned her attention back to her friend. Rocking was dangerous. The sheriff was dangerous. Dangerous to her pulse. She didn't need danger in her life. No. Calm, strong and steady were more her speed and what she sought in the new lifestyle she'd worked hard to achieve. Entertaining thoughts about the sheriff was hazardous.

"You're always starved," Kerri said, patting Connor's stomach as she looked adoringly up at the cowboy.

Watching the pair interact, Brandi noted their relaxed, confident demeanor exuded strong and steady. Not normally one to envy, she felt the faint tug just the same. Kerri and Connor had the strong and steady, but also managed the dangerous. The two had taken risks, put it all on the line for the other, and had come out on top. Not a common feat. Although, from what she'd heard, Jordan and her husband Cole had risked it all, too. Twice. Married twice. Lost a spouse and found the courage to take a chance again.

Brandi wasn't that strong. She couldn't do it, and she'd never even lost a lover in that way.

The tall cowboy displayed his trademark lopsided grin. "Of course I'm starved. Especially when I know I'm about to eat *your* delectables."

"Okay." Jordan stood, coming to the rescue of her blushing sister. "On that note, I think it's a good time for the three of us to go fetch lunch from the kitchen. Excuse us, gentlemen."

Looping an arm through hers and Kerri's, the former cop ushered them out of the dining room with lightening speed. Which was a real feat considering Brandi's skirt only allowed baby steps. She had the feeling she wasn't the only one glad the Texas-Pub didn't open to the public until four in the afternoon. Embarrassment could've had a much larger audience.

"Alrighty." The dark-haired beauty let go once safely inside the kitchen. "While my sister heats up the lunch she made for everyone, you and I can sit at the table in the corner over there and discuss my master suite."

"Sounds good to me," Kerri said, face a nice shade of crimson as she headed for the stove, not looking either of them in the eye.

With a wink and a smile, Jordan motioned toward the corner table. "Shall we?"

Brandi nodded, an answering smile forming on her lips as she took a seat and pulled a notepad from her briefcase/purse. She knew her friend's house was under construction and scheduled to be completed within the month. And she also knew her friend was eager to start her life alone with her husband in their own place. "Is Cole joining us, or did he give you a list of things he wants?"

"No." The woman shook her head, still smiling. "He's working, but I know what he wants."

Okay, she was not going to touch that sentence. Clearing her throat, Brandi looked across the table at her friend. "Why don't we start with what you both want, then we'll schedule a walk-through so I can take measurements, and in a few days, I'll draw up a tentative plan and we can tweak from there."

"Great," Jordan said, setting her folded hands on the table. "I know Cole would like a stone fireplace, the chimney's already in place. You might be able to use some of the rocks we've excavated on our land."

"I'll check them out. That would save on your budget."

Her friend nodded and continued. "We'd also like a stand up shower, a soaker tub big enough for two, double sinks, long counter space, his and hers walk in closets...which are already framed out."

"Oh really? Again that could save on your budget. Provided the walls are in the right spot and don't need to be moved," she added.

"Sweet." The former cop smiled. "Even though Cole says money is no object, I can't just spend and spend. That isn't me. Not by a long shot."

Brandi couldn't agree more. That was one of the things she liked most about the Masters sisters, one of the reasons they'd become fast friends. They held the same ideals she believed in. Spending time with family was more important than spending money. Helping others instead of helping themselves.

And whatever it was Kerri was stirring in the pot on the stove... Damn, it smelled like heaven. Her stomach dutifully growled, echoed by Jordan's. They looked at each other and laughed. Kerri's ability to out-cook anyone and satisfy her stomach while keeping the calories low enough for Brandi's hypothyroidism was an extra bonus.

"I hope that's ready," Jordan said. "Because if our stomachs are grumbling, I shudder to think what's happening with those two strapping men out there."

Kerri snickered as she spooned out five dishes. "Yeah, it's ready. Brandi, I hope it's okay that I put the stroganoff over rice for you? It's around four hundred calories."

"Yes," she replied. "That's great. Thanks, Kerri."

To have something that smelled that good be under her five hundred calorie meal limit was sweet. Her stomach rumbled in agreement. There were times when keeping her metabolism going was a chore, especially when she had to eat every two to three hours, yet stay under fifteen hundred calories a day or she'd balloon up. Yeah, meals like the one Kerri was making made life so much easier for Brandi. And today, she was all about easy.

Jordan turned back to face her. "Did you need anything else from me?"

"No," she replied, jotting down a final note before slipping the pad back in her purse. Even though the general rule of thumb was to never do work for family or friends, she knew this was going to be a fun job. She'd worked for Jordan on this very restaurant and looked forward to having her friend as a client again. "We just need to set up a time for me to come out and look at the rooms and discuss an appropriate budget once I do a walkthrough."

"What's good for you? Is tomorrow too soon?" the brunette asked as they stood.

"Tomorrow's good. How about around noon?"

The former cop smiled. "Perfect. Now, if you don't mind helping my sister, I'll go out and get the drinks so the cowboys don't wither away."

"Sure thing," she said, turning to her other friend placing dishes on two trays. "What do you need me to do?"

The pretty cook pointed to the food. "Just carry one of these."

Tray in hand, Brandi followed Kerri out of the kitchen, and applauded herself for making it to the table without tripping. Given her day, it was a true miracle. One she didn't dare question. It wasn't until the others took their seats that she realized she'd been forced to occupy the spot across from Kade. Of course. Why would fate start behaving now?

That the sheriff was silent through most of lunch was no surprise to Brandi. The others, however, kept giving them strange glances. Okay, not Connor. No. The handsome cowboy just wore a constant smile. Even while eating. But Jordan? Kerri? Oh, the Masters sisters were blatantly curious. Their brown eyes were bright with interest. It was eating them alive.

Too bad.

She had no intention of enlightening them. Although, she would like to try to apologize to the sheriff again. Just not with an audience. So she remained quiet and ate.

As she slipped the last mouthful of deliciously seasoned meat, carrots and rice into her mouth, disaster struck.

"Brandi," Jordan said, placing her fork down. "I just realized I forgot to mention we want something bigger than a bench seat in the master shower, for…you know…when we do more than shower."

Rice really stuck to the back of the throat when swallowed the wrong way. Kerri slapped her back. Connor chuckled. Kade…no way in hell would she look.

"And at least one sturdy wall that isn't glass," her soon-to-be-dead client added.

Brandi continued to cough. Kerri continued to pound. Connor continued to chuckle. And Kade...she still wasn't going there. But the good sheriff did hand her a glass of water. Which she sipped and sputtered, but eventually she gained the upper hand on the stray piece of rice.

Feeling obligated, she nodded briefly at him, then turned to Jordan. "Okay," she croaked while wiping her eyes with a napkin Kade also pushed her way. Another sweet gesture considering their early morning fiasco.

"I'm sorry," her friend said, brown eyes dark with concern. "I didn't mean to make you choke."

She shook her head. "No worries. It just went down the wrong way." *Due to your blatant request and my inability to curb a reaction.* She would've asked more about the shower design, but Jordan's phone rang.

"Excuse me, I have to take this, but I also have to go. Thanks for lunch, Kerri. Bye, everyone," the woman said in a rush, already halfway to the door before anyone could respond.

"You know, darlin'..." Connor smiled as he brought Kerri's hand to his lips. "I think my brother got that shower idea from the one in your apartment."

A picture of her friend's shower flashed through Brandi's mind. The cowboy was probably right. The master shower in her friend's old apartment was very similar to what Jordan had requested. And she had to admit, would be big enough to have sex in. Several ways.

Heat rushed through her body, and increased when her gaze found its way to the still silent sheriff with smoldering eyes.

Wait...*smoldering?*

She blinked, her mouth bone dry. A second later, the blaze was gone. Had she imagined it? Maybe. Yeah.

Probably. For goodness sakes. Mrs. Masters and Mrs. McCall planted that darn seed and she fell for it. *Idiot.*

"Could be, sweetheart," Kerri said. "I miss that shower."

"Me, too." Connor glanced up at the ceiling, presumably to the apartment above, then to his fiancée, a grin tugging his lips.

But Kerri shook her head and waved a hand in Brandi's direction. "Forget it, cowboy. Now is a good time to do some asking, don't you think?"

Confusion flittered through his mocha eyes before it cleared and he straightened in his seat. "Yeah, you're right. Now's the perfect time. You go ahead, darlin'."

Kerri nodded, alternating her smiling gaze between her and the sheriff. "Brandi. Kade. We'd very much like you both to be in our wedding."

The request shocked the hell out of Brandi. Not that they'd asked Kade, but because they'd asked *her*. She was new to the county, and their lives. Despite her lack of history with the couple, she did consider them dear friends, but...

"Of course I would," Kade said, surging to his feet, and they all followed.

He went to shake his friend's hand, but the tall cowboy pulled him into a back-slapping embrace, then stiffened.

"Ah hell. What'd you do, buddy? Bathe in skunk today?" Connor grimaced as he drew back.

Kade rolled his eyes. "No, but my deputy got a good soaking. Sorry, I tried to stay upwind of the poor kid."

She hadn't noticed the smell until they all stood. The slight odor did nothing to detract from the sheriff's sex appeal. Damn him. She turned to the smiling bride-to-be.

"I'm so very happy for you both," Brandi said, hugging her teary-eyed friend. "Thank you for asking me to be a part of your special day."

Kerri's hold increased. "You were there for me on many occasions, Brandi. It'd mean the world to me to have you in my wedding."

Okay, now the tears were dripping from her own eyes. Dammit. "I'm blessed to be welcomed into your circle of friends."

Although she had lots of family and friends in Pennsylvania, Brandi never truly felt the peace she'd encountered here. Not like in Texas. No. She felt a oneness with Harland County and its residents, especially the dear friend in her embrace.

She'd barely stepped back when two big, strong arms surrounded her and pulled her in. "You are a good friend, Brandi Wyne," Connor said. "Thank you for taking care of my girl when I was an ass."

Her face brushed the soft T-shirt covering the cowboy's broad chest as she chuckled. "My pleasure, but I do appreciate that you've kept your *ass*-tendencies to a minimum."

"And I'm glad you're finally going to make an honest man of him, Kerri," Kade said.

She stepped back to see the sheriff hug the blushing bride-to-be.

"Yes, it's a tough job, but someone has to do it," her friend replied with a grin.

They all laughed as they retook their seats.

"Have you set a date?" she asked, pouring water into her glass.

Connor nodded, draping an arm around his fiancée's shoulders. "October eighteenth. It's after the fall cattle drive, plus it's not too damn hot out that time of the year."

"It's also not too cold," Kerri added.

It also didn't give a lot of time for preparation. "That's only a little over four months away," she felt obligated to point out.

Her friend turned to her and smiled. "I know. But we don't want anything huge, and I've coordinated a few of these so I know with your help, and my sister's help, it'll be fine."

"Hey, what are we? Chopped liver?" Connor drew back, brown eyes twinkling with fake disdain.

"No," Kerri replied. "You're guys."

"What?"

Brandi had a tough time holding in the laugh bubbling up her throat at the cowboy's raised brows.

"You know what I mean." Her friend waved a hand at him. "You're all fairly useless when it comes to planning parties. But, of course, if you want to help…"

"Nope. No, darlin', that's not necessary." Shaking his head, her fiancé held up his hands in surrender. "You girls can have all the fun."

Brandi glanced across the table at Kade and caught his amused gaze.

"That's what I thought," Kerri said, regaining her attention.

The cowboy nodded. "You thought right."

"Good, then you can help me with another thought."

Interest sparkled in his dark eyes. "Sure, darlin'. Anything."

"You can help me clear the dishes."

"Ah, and here I thought it was something good," Connor joked as he stood to stack their dirty dishes on a tray before he followed a grinning Kerri into the kitchen, leaving Brandi with the sheriff. Alone.

The perfect opportunity to apologize for the second time.

She turned her attention to the silent man again and watched as he poured coffee from a carafe into his mug. He took a sip, and she absently wondered how he could drink it without the aid of milk or sugar to soften the bitter taste. But, it was fitting. The man was a no-nonsense type of guy. Setting his mug down, he sat back and raised a brow.

Yeah, okay, perfect lead in. She cleared her throat and, as always happened when the gorgeous man looked at her with those amazing gray eyes, she forgot her thoughts.

"Something wrong?"

"No…I mean, yes," she stammered like the idiot he'd reduced her to. "About this morning, I want to apologize."

He stiffened and all light disappeared from his expression. "You did. It's in the past."

"No." She shook her head and leaned forward. "I apologized for accusing you."

"Like I said, it's done. Forget it."

"No," she said again. "I'm trying to apologize for accusing you."

He blinked. "Well, that's different then."

Smart ass. She laughed despite her frustration at not being clear. "It is, you goof. I got to thinking about what you said. You were the first person from the ranch that came to my mind when I saw the abused horse, and that isn't right."

He didn't move a muscle, just sat there staring. Maybe he didn't hear her.

"Look, Kade, I'm sorry you were the one that came to mind. It wasn't right. Heck, I'm not even sure why that happened." But she had the feeling that wasn't true. Okay, she *knew* it wasn't true.

So did he. She could tell by the disbelief curling his lower lip. His scrumptious lower lip. The urge to capture it with her teeth and soothe with her tongue hit Brandi with an unexpected force that held her immobile.

"It's because you hate the military."

She reeled back. Apparently, no longer immobile. "What? I don't hate the military."

He muttered something under his breath before bringing the cup to his lips.

"I don't," she insisted. "But I'm not fond of the last guy I dated, and *he* was in the Guard."

Kade set his mug down, never breaking eye contact. Again, he remained silent, but something in his gaze compelled her to continue. And tell the truth.

"Ed was an ass, and I think maybe you're right. I may have transferred my negative feelings for him to you because you're also in the Guard." She sat back and grimaced. What an awful thing to do. She really didn't know Kade, which was completely her fault, but necessary and not something she wanted to change. Still, he did deserve an explanation. "You are not like him."

"I should hope not. Especially since we've established he's an ass."

She smiled. "Right."

"So…what am I?"

The only man to make my panties wet with just a look.

Okay, not something he needed to know, but he was looking at her, studying her with that damn unreadable gaze of his, waiting for a reply. She'd have to fudge it.

"The sheriff."

Now he laughed. And heaven help her, laughter looked good on him. Real good. His tight features relaxed, making those incredible smoky eyes sparkle with life, and his tempting lips curve in an even more inviting way.

"Thanks for pointing that out," he said quietly.

"Glad I could help."

They stared at each other, and soon, the amusement warming his gaze shifted into something hotter, stealing her breath, heating her from the inside out. Brandi tried to swallow. Which was a problem because her throat was dry. Very dry. Parched to the point of crumbling into dust.

In desperate need of regaining control, she ordered her body to retreat. To sit back, keep a respectable distance. So, why in the world did she find herself leaning closer to the man leaning across the table toward her? The edge cut into her ribs. That didn't stop her. She drew near, until their breath mingled, and heat coursed through her body, tingling all her good parts to life. Lord knows those parts had been dormant for far too long. She was afraid they'd gone on a permanent vacation.

Nope.

Everything happily tingled for the sexy sheriff and his commanding presence.

Then his gaze dropped to her lips. Holy hell. That was it. She was done. She stopped breathing altogether. Her whole body vibrated in anticipation. This was nuts. This was crazy. Something in the back of her mind nudged and prodded, and she knew it was a warning to stop. That she shouldn't be doing this. That she didn't want to do this. But, oh, yes. Yes, she did want to do this. She wanted very much to kiss this man with lips so sensual, so damn tempting her toes were already curling in her pink bunny slippers.

Correction, *Kerri's* pink bunny slippers.

Kerri…

Nothing like a fake animal bringing you back to reality. Brandi sat back in her chair so fast it moved an inch. Holy smokes, that was close.

A weary gleam entered Kade's eyes.

"What are you afraid of?" he asked, settling in his seat, his gaze back to unreadable.

Before she could answer, or deny, the kitchen door creaked, signaling they were no longer alone.

"Sorry to leave you so long, but we, ah, had some dishes to do."

Dishes…right. Judging by the blush in her friend's cheeks, the couple disappeared to do more than just dishes.

"No problem," Kade said, transferring his attention back to her. "Brandi was apologizing."

"Apologizing? What for?" Kerri's frowning gaze shifted between them as she sat down.

Unwilling to allow the bugger to reply for her, Brandi opened her mouth to speak, but he wasn't the only one she had to worry about.

"Well, darlin', it seems Brandi came across an abused horse in Kade's stable and thought it was his."

Now *she* was frowning. At Kade. What the heck? Didn't take him long to blab her mistake all over the county. Disappointment soured her gut, killing the last of the butterflies.

"Oh, he would never do that," Kerri said, placing a hand on her arm. "He loves animals."

"So I've heard." She turned back to the man. The man whose good looks were clouding her judgment. "I never took you to be the loose-lipped kind."

His chin rose, and gaze hardened. "I'm not."

"It wasn't Kade," Connor rushed to say. "Kevin told me and Cole when he came by the ranch to pick up my brother for their commute."

Oh...

Now she owed the man another apology. Just friggin' great. Maybe if her brain cells didn't play dead whenever the darn guy was around, she'd have an actual clear thought. Cripes. It was maddening.

"Sorry, it's been one of those days." She held the sheriff's unwavering, sterling gaze. "I think my brain stayed in bed this morning."

He rose to his feet and glanced at the happy couple. "Thanks for lunch, but I have to get back to work."

And without a word to her, or a glance, Kade Dalton left the restaurant.

"Don't mind him," Connor said with a wave of his hand. "He's just being a little girl today. Must be the skunking."

Brandi nodded, and even managed a smile, but she knew that was not the reason. Heck, no. *She* was the reason. Her and her big, fat mouth.

Yeah. She did it again. Managed to piss off the sheriff. She really needed to work on that.

Kade hadn't been in the best of moods lately, and he refused to believe it had anything to do with a certain designer and her ability to jump to the wrong conclusions about him. Several days ago she'd accused him of animal cruelty and gossiping. What a joke. The woman had a real high opinion of him.

He sipped his third black coffee of the day and decided he wasn't going to let it bother him. She was just a woman, of which there were plenty. So, why this one got under his skin and crept into his thoughts with her sun-kissed hair, warm brown eyes and beautiful smile was a complete mystery.

And pissed him off.

His mug hit the desk with a thud. He didn't like mysteries or surprises. Everything was better on the up and up. Hell, he'd had enough surprises and disappointments to last him a lifetime. Several lifetimes.

Sure, his job was a mixture of routine and surprises. He knew that going in. The Guard was a mixture of routine and surprises. Again, he knew it going in. But Brandi Wyne? Christ, the woman was a walking, talking, sexy contradiction capable of twisting him into knots. A complete mystery. Hot and cold. Interested, not interested. What the hell? Several years ago, he would've been up for the challenge. But now?

Now, he was just weary. Tired.

As if to concur, he yawned and stared at the clock on his office wall. Eleven fifteen. Still morning. And a quiet morning, thank the Lord. Paperwork he'd put off for two weeks finally managed to end up in the 'done' pile on his desk. One less bothersome chore.

"Mr. Sheriff, sir, I finished cleaning the car out again," Deputy Don announced, right before he tripped over his size thirteen feet and took a header into the desk.

Muttering under his breath, he surged to his feet to steady the boy. "You all right?"

"Yes." The deputy nodded, eyes rounding as he stared over Kade's shoulder. "But…ah…sorry, sir."

The sinking feeling in the pit of his stomach increased as he turned to find the completed paperwork soaking in a coffee bath of epic proportions…because Deputy Don did nothing in a small way.

"I'm really sorry, Mr. Sheriff, sir. I'll clean it up," the kid stammered, swiping a folded T-shirt from a stack of physical training clothes on a nearby bench before Kade could stop him.

So much for running after lunch.

"Don. Don…Donald!" He had to use his First Sergeant tone to get the kid to stop.

The poor boy jumped a foot before turning to Kade, eyes wide, shoulders hunched. "Y-yes, sir?"

"Let it be. It's all right. I'm more concerned about you," he said, grasping the kid by his upper arms and checking him over. "Did you hit your head?"

"No, sir," Donny replied. "That was my shoulder you heard. I'm fine. Honest. And I'll get this cleaned up, and print out what I can. And what needs typing, I'll type. You'll only have to sign—"

The ringing of the phone in the outer office cut through the kid's babbling. Kade exchanged a look with his deputy before releasing him to head to the doorway.

"Okay, Mr. Haggerty," the secretary/dispatcher said into the phone.

The middle-aged mother of three was the most organized person he'd ever met. A real asset to the team. Too bad she was only part time.

Too bad she didn't have a permit to carry.

"Someone will be right out there to help you round up Old Charlie."

Ah hell.

He turned to Donny and cupped the boy's shoulder. "I'll handle this. You take care of that paperwork."

"Yes, sir, Mr. Sheriff." The kid nodded, already reaching for the wet papers.

Kade sighed. "Donny, what did I tell you about calling me all that?"

"Sorry, Sheriff."

"Don't be sorry," he said, unlocking the drawer where he kept his firearm. Old Charlie was harmless, but general rules stated he couldn't leave without his issued piece. "Just save yourself a mouthful."

"Yes, sir, Sher—...I mean, sir," the deputy stammered.

Kade nodded. "Better." Now, if the kid would just remember that two minutes from now it would be a miracle. He secured his belt, grabbed his hat and headed for the door.

Old Charlie, Mr. Haggerty's aging horse, could be a good mile from home by now, with not much chance of finding his way back. For as clever as he was at getting loose, the old trooper had lost his sense of direction and most of his sight, and often wandered for miles. Luckily, everyone knew the gentle giant and always brought him back.

But if the horse made his way to the highway, it could be trouble for all involved. Kade had seen more than his share of accidents involving wild horses or burros running into vehicles to last a lifetime. He didn't want Old Charlie to become another victim or cause harm to others.

As he sped toward Haggerty property, he mentally mapped out areas to check. The mischievous bugger liked the ocean and seemed to be drawn to the sound of seagulls. Trouble was, in certain areas, the highway stood in the way.

But so far so good. Kade turned off the highway and drove down a local, less travelled road which led to several properties, including the McCalls and the back of

Haggerty's five acres. With any luck, he'd intercept Old Charlie before the horse found trouble.

Live oak and willow trees dotted the landscape. To the left, behind barbed wire, the terrain splintered to the gulf several miles away. Thanks to a wet spring, the marshes and waterways thrived with birds and ducks, as well as hogs and deer. On most days, it was picturesque. But there wasn't time to enjoy the view.

Still no sign of Old Charlie.

Rounding the bend, he immediately forgot about the horse when he caught sight of a white pickup kissing the side of a tree, smoke rising from the crushed hood. His insides twisted tight. He knew the truck and its owner. The damn designer took over his thoughts most every day.

He parked behind the busted pickup, flung the door open, then rushed to the driver's side, heart pounding heavily in his chest, only to drop to his boots when he found the vehicle empty…with blood on the steering wheel. "Brandi?" He whirled around, searching for signs of the woman.

Christ. Where the hell could she have gone?

He'd just come from the highway, she hadn't headed that way for help. He would've seen her… unless someone had stopped and picked her up. The knot in his stomach twisted. Why hadn't she used her phone? Dispatch would've called. He glanced inside the truck again. Fuck. Her purse and phone sat on the seat.

Turning around, he resurveyed the area. Although mostly flat, there were several dips and bends, as well as large trees that could be obscuring his view of the injured woman. An invisible band tightened across his chest. Visions of the beauty stumbling around with a head injury flashed through his mind.

He sprang into action. Since he already knew she wasn't behind him, he sprinted forward on foot. "Brandi," he called as he searched. "Brandi, where are you?"

Movement, up ahead and to the left, caught his eye. He upped his pace.

"Kade?" Her voice was faint, but he spotted more movement. "Thank God. Hurry!"

Running full out, sweat trickling down his back and face, he didn't ease up until he reached the woman. *What the...?*

He stopped dead.

"Quit gawking and get the horse," she said, pointing to Old Charlie grazing near a tree.

He wasn't gawking. He was stunned. Utterly and completely stunned. "How the hell did you manage to get caught in the fence without a shirt?"

Chapter Four

She wasn't just caught. The woman was practically sprawled out, ripped shirt hanging from the barbed wire fence in one spot while she apparently reattached herself a few feet away as she reached for something on the other side. And, damn, at that angle, she was spilling out of her sexy-as-hell black lace bra.

"That's not important right now," the trapped woman replied. "What's important is the horse and the dog."

Kade blinked, forcing his body to ignore the luscious spillage. "Dog? What dog?"

"The one I'm trying to reach. You get the horse, I'll get the dog," she muttered, struggling to grab something behind her, apparently mindless of the fact she was shirtless and bleeding.

With Old Charlie still happily grazing by the tree, Kade rushed to Brandi. "Hold still," he told her, trying to unhook her jeans from the fence, but she brushed him away.

"No, take care of the horse. I hit him…or he hit me. It happened so fast. I don't know. Just make sure he's okay. I have to get this puppy out of the hole before it fills with water."

Her words rushed through his brain so fast it took a second for his mind to catch up. He glanced at the object of her attention. At first, he saw nothing, then the scraggly pup moved in an attempt to jump up the small ridge, but fell back down to where water from the marsh began to seep in.

Quickly assessing the cut on the designer's temple to be minor, a byproduct of the crash, and the one on her upper arm to need stitches from her fight with the fence, he took over. "I'll get the dog. You stay put," he ordered, yanking her free of the barbed wire, the sound of tearing fabric echoed around them. "Don't move. You may be concussed from the crash."

"No. I'm okay. Just a small headache, but the poor thing is going to drown, and I don't want that horse to wander away. He may not be so lucky next time."

Once again, the woman blew his mind. Here she was, half-naked, dirty, hurt and bleeding, and all she cared about was a scrawny mutt and an old horse that wrecked her truck. He cupped her face, careful of her wound as he spoke calm and clear.

"I'll take care of them." When she blinked, and he could tell she got the message, he released her to take off his shirt. "Are you hurt anywhere else?"

"No." She shook her head and winced. "Just, please, get the dog." Tears began to stream down her face.

Something inside him tightened then burst. He placed his shirt over her shoulders, resisted the urge to pull her close—barely—then turned to the dog. With no time to fetch the canvas tarp from his jeep to drape over the wire, he hit the dirt and belly crawled under the fence to reach down for the dog.

"Come on, Ace, let's get you out of that hole," he said, scooping up the pup. The sting of wire ripped into his shoulder as he backed them under the fence.

Once free, he turned around and sat up. The wet, matted, skinny pup crawled up his chest to lick his face. Kade chuckled. "It's okay, boy. You're safe now."

But she wasn't. Oh, hell no. Brandi blinked. She was in trouble. It felt as if she'd hit that tree all over again. A bigger tree. A gorgeous, gray-eyed Adonis cradling a puppy tree. The sight of the shirtless sheriff sitting on the ground, dirt and sweat clinging to his tanned face and muscled torso while he gently nuzzled the mangy puppy, hit her hard. Real hard.

God, he looked so sweet.

Her pulse raced out of control and heart hurt from staring at them. She rubbed her chest, but the ache didn't lessen. Then he glanced up, gaze warm and friendly.

The world tilted.

Literally tilted without warning.

She stepped back to steady herself. Kade immediately surged to his feet, dog in one hand while he cupped her elbow with the other.

"Easy, there, Brandi. You okay?"

All she could do was nod as the hunk stood, sweet little puppy in his arms.

"Here, you hold him and sit down."

Forcing air into her lungs, she reached for the bundle of fur, doing her best not to reach for the man currently melting her resolve…her heart…her panties. Darn him. Why did he have to be so sweet? And so gorgeous? And so…so…near?

Heat emanated from the bare-chested sheriff as he transferred the rescue into her arms. "Got him?"

"Yes, thank you for rescuing him," she said, tears filling her eyes from out of the blue.

Great. What a picture she must make. Hugging the squirming ball of fur, she tried not to think of her less than appealing appearance. Dirty, bleeding, goose-egg on her forehead, partially naked. Yeah, he must think her an idiot. A bumbling idiot. No, a *fat*, bumbling idiot.

"It's all right," he said.

He rubbed her arm, strong, warm fingers, sending a round of shivers straight down to her toes, then back up.

"Why don't you sit down, while I round up Old Charlie?"

"Who's Old Charlie?" Geez, there was another person here? Her gaze shot around the area. "Shoot, he's seen me without a shirt."

Crud. So did Kade. That realization turned her legs a bit rubbery, so she sank to the ground, with the sheriff's help. He landed on his knees in front of her, hands firmly holding her arms as she clutched the puppy to her chest. Her nearly naked chest. She glanced down. Thank goodness tomorrow was laundry day and all her white, normal, boring bras were in the hamper, forcing her to slip into a lacy black number this morning.

"Relax, honey. Old Charlie's the horse." He chuckled, fixing his shirt back around her shoulders.

The sound sent another round of shivers down to her toes. "Oh."

Releasing her, he sat back, a small smile still tugging his lips. "Brandi?"

"Yeah?"

"How in the world did you get caught on the fence?"

Caught? Felt more like she was skewered. She had no idea how it happened. It just did. Because her life was a comic book and she was the star. *Brandi Wyne, Mayhem Magnet.*

With the cute puppy licking her scratching hand, she took a deep breath. "Well, first, I was hit by a horse. Crashed into a tree. Rushed after said horse with rope from my truck. Tripped over the rope. Landed in the fence. Heard the puppy. Ripped my shirt clean off trying to get the puppy. Then you showed up, and the rest you know."

Did she leave anything out? Oh, yes, her head was beginning to hurt like a bitch, arm stung, heart ached for the abandoned puppy, and her body? Oh, boy, her body. Need for the man kneeling in front of her rushed through so fast she physically shook. *That's new*. She'd never had that response to anyone before. Ever. Not even with help.

Frankly, it scared the hell out of her.

"…Where's the rope?"

She blinked, trying to focus. He had the most amazing eye color. Several shades of gray. Light and dark, with a kind of chrome rim…

"Brandi?" He brushed her face with the back of his knuckles.

The light touch grabbed her attention. She drew in a deep breath and blinked again. "What?"

"The rope," he repeated. "Where's the rope you said you'd gotten from your truck?"

Her eyes widened as she got a clue. "Oh…yes, please catch the horse. He must be hurt. I don't know if I hit him or he ran into me. It doesn't matter. I'll pay for whatever he needs."

The sheriff's gaze warmed and her throat instantly dried. "Charlie seems just fine," he reassured. "But I'd like to secure him. Where's the rope?"

The rope. Right.

"Over where my shirt's now decorating the fence." Laughter bubbled up her throat. She was beginning to feel a bit giddy and weird. "Maybe I should add that to my portfolio? Fence decorating. Although, I'm a designer. I can move walls. Maybe I should've moved the fence?"

He chuckled, then patted the puppy snuggled in her arms before rising to his feet. "Stay put while I catch Old Charlie."

She *stayed put*, right on her butt, as she watched his with interest. Damn, that uniform hugged the man in a very good way. A way she'd be happy to take over. More laughter escaped, but evaporated just as quickly when her appreciative gaze rose to his back. She sat up straight, hugging the puppy tighter.

Kade was hurt. Blood trickled down his back from a gash in his left shoulder blade.

And it was all her fault.

"The barbed wire cut him," she told the puppy as she watched the sheriff secure the horse to the tree with her rope.

The pounding in her head increased as the reality of what happened hit her full force. Chills wracked her body, and she began to shake. Brandi knew it was shock setting in and that there wasn't much she could do to stop it. At least the dog was okay, and the horse was okay. Too bad Kade had to get hurt in the process. Kade. Wasn't he just a sweetheart today?

"It's all right. Everything is fine." His voice was low and warm, and his warmth seeped into her.

No, wait, that was the blanket wrapped around her, and when had he bandaged her arm? She was about to ask when he sat down behind her, then drew her against his hard, muscled chest. *Heaven.* She just found a little bit of heaven. She always knew heaven was in Harland County. Snuggling closer, she sighed and closed her eyes. Yes, he felt too damn good for her to worry about if it was wrong or right. Hell, the man was bleeding for her.

Bleeding...

"Wait. You're hurt." She twisted to face him. "We need to fix your cut."

He smiled and shook his head. "Don't worry about me. I'll live."

But she did worry about him. "I…thanks, Kade."

Tears filled her eyes and slid down her face. Dammit. And she'd tried so hard to keep them in. He must think her weak. And stupid. More chills and shakes decided to join the pity party.

"Hey, come here," he said, gently drawing her against him again.

Mmm…he was nice and warm and hard. Before common sense had a chance to flicker, she flipped her legs over his right thigh, and the puppy thought it was a game. He reached up to lick the tears from her face, then the sheriff's jaw. She laughed despite how awful she felt. "Thank you, Ace."

"Ace? Is that me, or the dog?" Kade asked, amusement coating his tone.

She smiled. "Both."

"Is that right?"

"Yeah," she replied, snuggling closer, her smile widening as those strong arms of his tightened their hold, yet somehow avoided her wound. "You called the dog Ace when you were rescuing him from that hole."

"So I did."

She nodded, loving the feel of his steady heartbeat against her ear, and firm jaw resting on her head. "And, well, you are certainly an ace today. I really appreciate your help with the animals…and me." Her mind raced the fast pace of her heart. "And, please don't say it's your duty, because I just might have to hit you for ruining my fantasy."

He stilled. "You have a fantasy about me?"

Hell yeah. Several. But those were too private…and hot. And just delicious enough to make her quiver. "Yes." He wasn't getting any more out of her. *Nosiree.* She'd already said too much.

"Well now, I'd love to hear it."

A giggle escaped her dried throat. "I bet you would. But it's not happening, sheriff...cowboy...soldier...whatever you are."

He shifted their position so quick, she found herself lying back in his arms, staring straight up into his mischievous gaze.

"That sounded like a dare, and you should never dare me, honey."

"Oh yeah?"

Shoot. Why'd she say that?

"Yeah," he replied, warm breath hitting her face. "I bet I can make you tell me."

He could make her do a lot of things. Hell, her body was already humming his name. And if it weren't for Ace licking the sexy man's chin and nose, she probably would've taken the guy serious. And maybe just taken the guy. But with puppy slobber and fur on his skin, all she could do was laugh.

"Oh, you think it's funny?"

She nodded, reaching up to pick a piece of white fur from his chin. "Yep. I do. I really do."

"We'll see about that, honey. One day soon, when there's no blood or skinny puppies running blocker, we are going to pick up this discussion."

Promise?

A slow smile claimed his lips. "Promise."

Shoot...did she say that out loud? Her heart rocked in her chest. The man was seriously flirting with her. But why?

"Uhum."

The sound of someone clearing their throat had them both turning to investigate.

"Don't you two look cute?" A familiar looking paramedic with black hair and blue eyes stood a few feet away, lopsided grin on his handsome face. "I hate to break things up, but you called for assistance?"

In the blink of an eye, Kade was on his feet, holding her in his arms, all traces of heat gone from his expression. "What are you doing here, Jace? I called for a paramedic."

"Yeah, and you got me instead. They're short staffed so I volunteered." The newcomer's attention shifted to her. "Hi, Brandi. What happened? You didn't like the tree so you tried to take it out?"

She laughed, recognizing the general practitioner she'd met when she'd first moved to Harland County. The cute physician had recommended an endocrinologist to continue her thyroid treatment. "Hi, Doctor Turner. And, no. I liked the tree just fine. I needed a new truck."

"Well, that's a dangerous way to go about it," he replied, warm fingers gently brushing her hair aside. "Looks like you hit your head in the process. Since Top has you…"

Top? Ah…Kade. First Sergeant. Handsome sheriff holding her against his yummy chest.

"…and doesn't seem like he's ready to relinquish his hold, he can carry you over to the ambulance so I can take a look."

With a curt nod, her rescuer followed the doctor, carrying her to the vehicle parked near a fire truck. *When the heck had they all arrived?* Must've been the bump to her head, or the thump of her heart because she had no recollection of the fire department arriving. Or the pickup with a horse trailer that parked near the tree where Old Charlie continued to graze.

"I hope the horse is okay," she said. "He had to hurt something. He'd come out of nowhere and clipped the corner of my truck. That's when I swerved away to avoid him and hit the tree." Okay, she'd sort of already told him, but at least now the doctor knew how she'd gotten the bump.

As Kade set her down on the back of the opened medic mobile, she grabbed his arm and stared up at him. "Thanks, but don't go. You need to get your back checked."

"I'll be fine," he said, breaking her hold to grab the puppy from her arms.

"What's wrong with his back?" Doctor Turner clamped a hand on Kade's shoulder when he made to leave. "Hang on there, Top. You may be the First Sergeant and sheriff, but you bleed just like the rest of us. Let me have a quick look."

That confirmed her suspicions. She glanced from one alpha to another. Yep, they were definitely in the Guard together.

"I'm fine, Jace." He shook the doctor off. "Just take care of Ms. Wyne."

Ms. Wyne? When had she gone from Brandi to Ms. Wyne?

The doctor smiled broadly. "Sure, I'll take good care of Brandi."

Kade's eyes narrowed and he glanced from her to the physician before he nodded. "Good. Doc Kirkland just pulled up. I need to take this little guy over and talk to the vet about Charlie, too." He twisted around, puppy in arm, and walked away.

"Now that was very interesting," Doctor Turner said, standing in front of her, shining a flashlight in her eyes.

The pain in her head increased enough to make her grimace. "Oh...how so?" She pulled the blanket tighter around her shoulders and tried not to glance at the sheriff, the dog or the horse.

He just smiled and shook his head. "I've known Kade Dalton a long, long time and I've never seen him act that way around a woman. You, *Ms. Wyne*, are very good for him."

She smirked. "Yeah, about as good as an abscessed tooth."

"Oh, I can assure you, you're nothing like that to him." The cutie held up a finger, asked her about her vision, her stomach, to rate the pain in her head. "You don't appear to have a concussion, but just in case, keep the drinking and partying to a minimum."

"Will do, Doc." She laughed, then closed her eyes against the pain.

"You may want to avoid sudden movements," he said, touching her shoulder. "Sorry, hun, I know it hurts."

She opened her eyes and nodded. Then winced.

Empathy filled his blue eyes. "What did I tell you about sudden movements?"

"Didn't think nodding fit that category."

"'Fraid so. And it wouldn't hurt to avoid sleeping for the next few hours," Handsome said, turning his attention to her arm. "Now, what's this I hear about you fighting with the barbed wire fence?"

"Yeah, and I lost...my shirt," she added, dropping the blanket, and digging deep to find the courage to drop Kade's shirt, too. "I even left some skin for good measure."

The doctor smiled as he removed the bandage Kade had applied, then quietly assessed her wound before he checked the rest of her for cuts and scrapes. She only blushed a little. Her head and arm hurt too damn much to care about her nakedness. A nakedness no man had seen in years.

At this point, she'd show him the full monty if he could stop the pounding in her head. He placed the blanket back over her unharmed shoulder and pulled it around and under her injured arm so she could cover her chest.

What a sweetheart. Seemed Texas was full of them.

"When was the last time you had a tetanus shot?"

Before deployment, part of the Guard's required regiments of shots, but thanks to the pounding in her head, she couldn't quite remember the year. "I'm not sure exactly. A couple years ago," she answered without conviction. It was getting harder to think.

If the doctor thought her answer was odd, he didn't show it. He just nodded, then opened a few boxes and produced a vial and syringe.

"Allow me to reacquaint you two."

Then the little devil smiled as he sterilized then stuck her arm. Smiled? If the bugger wasn't so cute and sweet she might've had a few choice words.

"Okay, now for the unpleasant part."

Unpleasant? She blinked at him. "Trust me, that wasn't all that enjoyable."

He shook his head, a rueful smile on his face. "Then you're going to hate this, because I have to stitch you. But you have a choice. I can do it here or at the hospital."

"Here." She had no desire to see the inside of a hospital again. Ever.

Doc Handsome chuckled. "Okay. Just so you know, a few shots are required to numb the area so I can clean and stitch you. Your arm's going to be sore for a little while."

Lovely. At least it was no longer required for her livelihood. Her musical livelihood. But now that she was a designer, she could manage to work on the Masters' patio without using her arm for a few days. "Just do what you have to, then when you're done, look at Kade's back. I don't care how much he complains."

Another smile tugged the cutie's lips. "Yes, ma'am. See? You are good for Top. The man always takes care of others. No one ever takes care of him, not since his aunt died, and even then, he more than likely insisted he was fine."

And while the good doctor picked, poked, prodded and stitched, she thought about those sad words, and recalled Kevin's words, and the image of a young boy with big gray eyes filled her mind.

Now Brandi's heart ached, along with her arm and head.

It'd been a long and trying day, but Kade couldn't quite constitute calling it bad. Once they'd determined Brandi and her truck had received more damage than Old Charlie, the vet had carted the horse back to Haggerty's ranch, and he'd taken responsibility of the woman. No vehicle. No family. Someone had to help her. But even as he'd slipped into a spare Army T-shirt stored in his jeep, he'd known it all boiled down to the fact he just hadn't been ready to leave the designer.

Then there was the puppy. With no chip, a mass of fleas, in need of a good bath and several meals, Ace had been given a clean bill of health…and to Kade.

It was either that or a shelter. He was having none of that. He didn't abandon. Ever. Even if he technically hadn't been the one to find the dog.

His glance settled on the woman curled up against him as he sat watching the evening news at her house. Pangs of some foreign emotion battered and poked until he shifted. He really should go. This was crazy. What was he doing here? *Christ*. He was too messed up to play house, no matter how good the woman felt in his arms.

"You okay?" Big, brown eyes looked up at him, all sleepy and warm.

That warmth settled inside him and squashed the urge to run. He brushed a piece of caramel colored hair behind her ear and smiled.

"Yeah, I'm good. How about you? Doc gave me your pain meds. It's been several hours since your shot. You want one?"

"No." She shook her head and winced. "Okay, yeah, maybe."

Gently wriggling out from behind her, he wondered just how the woman kept ending up in his arms today, as he got to his feet to fetch water and pills from her kitchen. She'd given him the grand tour when they'd first arrived. The quaint little seaside cottage done in whites and blues, although small, had a big, warm feel. The designer claimed it suited her and her cat just fine.

Ace had certainly approved, rushing in and out of all five rooms in record time. Her big, fluffy, orange cat Mozart hadn't appreciated the rescue's curiosity and promptly retreated to the sanctuary of the window seat the dog couldn't reach. No matter how many times he tried. And he tried many.

Kade didn't blame the poor cat, though. Ace was most definitely hyper, even more since Brandi had insisted they bathe and treat the bedraggled pup for fleas in a basin out back two hours ago.

He glanced down at the dog following closely at his feet. Who knew there was a cute white puppy underneath all the dirt and dust that had matted his fur? Now he could see the poor dog was minus a few too many meals. Something Kade would rectify without trouble at Shadow Rock. In the meantime, Brandi had insisted he stop to buy kibble for the pup on their way to her house, so now the little guy was cleaned and fed. Which was more than could be said for him. But his needs could wait until Brandi's were met.

"Okay, here you go." He handed the pretty designer the bottle of pills and a glass of water. "You sure I can't get you something more to eat?"

"No." She shook her head, and then winced as she sat on the couch. "Kerri and Jordan are bringing food over when they leave work in an hour. Besides, you already made me some killer grilled cheese. But, please, if you're hungry, go ahead and fix yourself something."

"I'm good," he said, part of him relieved to know he only had to keep an eye on her for another hour, while other parts of him protested. The woman was too tempting. And he'd seen more of her luscious body than he should. Thank God she'd put on one of her own shirts and a pair of jeans that weren't ripped when they'd arrived. He was only human. "You only had half of the sandwich, though. Surely you're still hungry? That was over three hours ago."

Brandi took her medicine and smiled. "I'm fine." Then she frowned at the clock above the stone fireplace. "I feel so bad. You've been babysitting me for a good five hours, Kade. Go home. The girls will be here soon."

"Nope." He smiled and retook his seat on the couch. "You're not getting rid of me that easily." Ace promptly jumped up and settled on his lap. "Looks like it's unanimous."

She scooted closer to scratch the pup behind his ears. The white bundle of fur let out a sound of acquiescence and rolled over for a full belly rub. Lucky dog. Brandi laughed, the light sound going straight through Kade as he fought the urge to touch the woman's soft skin.

"I'm glad he's a nice dog."

Grateful for the subject change, he latched onto it like a vice. "Me, too. You do know it's not smart to try to catch a stray dog though, right?"

The thought of her getting bit, especially by something rabid stopped his heart. She turned and hit him with an open brown stare. More open than she'd ever allowed him to see.

"No," she said simply. "If I can help, I help. And I somehow got the impression you were the same."

It was the strangest feeling to have a piece of his heart click into place. Hell, he hadn't even known it was out of place. But it was, and now, as he stared into the smiling woman's warm brown eyes, he realized she wasn't as hard and shallow as he'd originally thought.

Damn.

Keeping his distance was a damn sight easier when he saw the sexy woman as superficial.

Now what the hell did he do?

"You didn't seem to waste any time grabbing the stray, and you got cut in the process. Sorry about that, by the way. But I'm glad you didn't need stitches. Or we'd both be taking the happy pills." She paused, a frown creasing her brow. "Then who would be watching us? Ace?" She giggled. "No, Mozart. Yeah, my money's on Mozart."

"The cat?" He smiled, deciding he really liked the laid back Brandi.

"Of course, silly." She punched his arm. "Oh, sorry. Didn't mean to hit your booboo."

His smile widened. "Brandi, you're the one with a cut on the arm."

"Oh, yeah, right." She giggled some more. "Yours is on the back. Sorry about that."

"I know. You told me," he replied. "It's okay."

"If you say so, Ace. Oh, wait, that's the dog, right?"

"Yes." He frowned, narrowing his gaze. Something was wrong. "Are you okay?"

"Yes, sir." She saluted him and giggled. "I'm feeling okie dokie, Top." Then she crooked a finger at him, glancing back and forth before placing the finger to her mouth. "Shhh…I probably should've only taken one pill."

He stilled, then grabbed her face. *Shit*. Her pupils were slightly dilated as her gaze darted around. "How many did you take?"

"Only two, but it's okay." She waved at him. "Don't worry. I just won't take any next time."

He put the dog on the floor, sprang from the couch, then turned to stare her down. "Stay put."

Damn woman saluted him again.

He made a quick call to Jace and was relieved when the doctor told him Brandi would be a bit loopy, but otherwise okay as long as someone was with her until it wore off.

"Well?" She rose to her feet. "What's the verdict, Top, Topper, Toppest? Am I going to live?"

"Yes." He bit back a smile. She was just too cute, hands on her hips, smile on her lips, eyes bright. Heaven help him, the woman was really going to be hard to resist, now. "You just may feel a little drunk."

"Okay. Cool." She twirled around and stumbled. "Is this what drunk feels like?"

He lurched forward, grabbed her uninjured arm and steadied her with his body. "You've never been drunk?"

"Nope. N. O. Nope."

"Why doesn't that surprise me?"

"Because you think I'm a stuffy poopyhead." Her pout turned into a wicked-ass grin as she patted his chest. "But I'm not."

Damn, she was irresistible. Lifting his free hand, he pushed the hair out of her face and chuckled. "What am I going to do with you?"

"I have a few suggestions," she said with a wink. "And they all involve getting naked!"

His heart slammed into his ribs before beating at a faster pace. *Son-of-a-bitch*, he must've heard wrong. "What?"

"Oh dear, did I say that out loud?" She scrunched her nose. "Just forget what you heard. You heard nothing." The adorable designer waved a hand back and forth in front of his face. "You are getting very sleepy. Oh, wait…that's me." She giggled. "But sleeping is bad, so let's dance."

Before he could respond, she pressed her gorgeous curves into him and slipped her hands around his neck, tempting the hell out of him.

"Brandi, there's no music."

"It's okay," she said, without releasing him. "I have it in my head."

Enticement kicked up a notch when she began to move against him. *Ah hell*. He jerked back, untangling himself from her arms in the process.

"Bad idea," he said. "Bad idea." The second time was for him, because, damn, he wanted very much to *dance* with the sexy woman. He was hard, hot, and in big, big trouble.

"But why?" Her gaze clouded, happy expression completely turned upside down. "It's because I'm fat. Isn't it?"

"What?" He reeled back. "No. And you're not fat."

"Yes, I am." She dropped onto the couch with a bounce, her bottom lip protruding out in a pout. "Ed told me so. That's why he stopped sleeping with me."

Shit. She should not be telling him this. And if what she'd just said was true, then her ex-boyfriend was more than an ass. He was a bastard, and if the man had lived in Harland County, Kade was so mad right now, he'd hunt the prick down and introduce him to his fist. Several times.

"Brandi, honey, listen to me." He sat next to her, grabbed her hand and squeezed until she made eye contact.

Her expression brightened. "Did you change your mind? Do you want to sleep with me?"

Before he could blink, the woman pushed him back and climbed up his body, her soft curves rubbing him in ways only his wildest dreams dared to hope. But, *son-of-a-bitch*. This was not good. How could he be the responsible one when his body was already ready to burst?

"No," he told her, gripping the cushions to keep from cupping her luscious curves.

A cold, wet nose brushed his knuckles in an attempt to gain attention. But he had to ignore the dog, because if he even thought of removing his grip on the couch…it wasn't the puppy he'd touch.

"No?" She stilled, then drew back. "See? It *is* because I'm fat."

"*Jesus*, you're not fat. Okay?" He followed her into a sitting position. "Your ex was a jackass."

"True dat. But I did gain over forty pounds while I was dating Ed. That's a lot to ask from a guy, even though I had no control over it because my thyroid died an unexpected death. Wait!" Her eyes widened to an unblinking stare. "Maybe it was murdered…"

"Just stop for minute." He placed his finger on her lips and waited until she stilled, then released the tempting woman. "Listen to me. You're gorgeous as you are, and you deserve someone better than your ex. If he cared about you, your weight gain shouldn't have mattered one damn *pound*."

"Are you serious?" She leaned forward and squinted into his face. "Forty friggin' pounds wouldn't have mattered to you?"

"No," he replied truthfully. "It would not have mattered." A woman's waist size never made a difference to him. Compassion and a sense of humor were more important. And eyes. A woman's eyes were always the first thing to draw him in.

Like now.

Damn.

His heart rocked in his chest at the look of hunger and need darkening her gaze to resemble the incredible color of vintage brandy.

"And you still would've had sex with me?"

A *hell-fuckin'-yeah* response throbbed through his groin. "Of course."

She leaned closer. "Then why don't you want to have sex now?"

Christ. This conversation was going from bad to worse. He drew in a deep breath and steadied his pulse. "Because, you're not in your right mind at the moment, and I prefer to have sex without drugs involved."

Her mouth curved into another wicked-ass grin. "What if I don't remember?"

Now he blinked, truly at a loss.

"Shh…we just won't tell me." She giggled, running her hand down his chest to his abs, then further south.

Breathing was suddenly a problem. A big problem. And he needed air to clear the fog from his brain before he did something stupid. Like give in to need.

Grabbing her wandering hand, he placed it on her lap. "Stop."

"It's okay," she whispered. "We aren't telling me, remember?"

What he couldn't remember was when his control had ever been stretched this thin by a woman. A sweet, poorly treated, sexy, drugged woman who deserved his restraint. And respect.

He cupped her face and brushed her cheek with his thumb. "The thing is, I *want* you to know, Brandi. I *want* your mind clear. Your body naked. And for you to know exactly what is taking place."

She blinked, her big brown eyes warming as some sort of realization hit her. "So you do find me attractive?"

"Yes. Hell, yes."

"Even though I'm fat?"

Chapter Five

Jesus. Kade released her and his knuckles cracked into fists. Why was she so damn thickheaded? "For the last time, you're not fat."

"Sure I am, look." She lifted her shirt, grabbed his hand, uncurled his fist and jammed his fingers on her hip. "See? You can pinch an inch."

Heaven help him, her warm, supple flesh was too much. Just too damn much. The day had been long and trying, and the woman was hot and trying and willing. He was done. No more fighting the need.

"I can *also* do this," he said, tracing her waist, watching her eyes round as he skimmed his hand across her stomach in slow, small strokes. "I'd love to strip you naked and kiss every last *inch* of you, Brandi."

"Y-you would?"

"Oh yeah." He continued to caress the designer's soft skin, brushing her ribcage on his way to that damn, sexy black bra that had tormented his mind all day. "And you know what?"

"W-what?"

He brushed a thumb over the rounded flesh just under the lace, his body tightening with each tremor that shook through her mouthwatering curves. "When I finished…I'd do it all again."

She let out a strangled whimper, the sound ripped through him with savage force.

"Do it now," she pleaded, cupping his face, pulling him close. "I don't care what mind I'm in. This is my body and I want you now. Do you hear me, Kade? I want you in me now. Please."

Son-of-a-bitch. Air funneled into his lungs. That was it. He'd reached his limit. The sound of his control snapping echoed through his head...which was weird, because it sounded like a doorbell.

Shit. It *was* the doorbell.

He vaulted to his feet and sucked in a lungful of air, closed his eyes, and released it in a long, slow gush. Damn, that was close.

He opened his eyes in time to see Brandi answer the door. Holy shit, the woman recovered quickly.

"Hi, Kerri! Hi, Jordan." The designer smiled and moved back to allow the sisters in. "Good thing you came when you did, because I didn't."

She giggled, and he had to fight the urge to slap a hand on his face.

Kerri frowned, but Jordan took one look at him and bit her lip. Damn woman was too shrewd for him to do anything but shake his head.

"Well, hello. Who are you?" Taking pity on him, the brunette let the comment slide and bent down to pick up the pup jumping at her feet.

For a foolish second, he thought maybe he'd get out of there before the subject of Brandi and sex arose again.

"I have good news, girls," the damn designer said. "Kade doesn't mind that I'm fat."

"You're not fat," he said in unison with the sisters.

Brandi smiled. "I know. Kade told me. He also told me what he wanted to do to me." She lowered her voice. "We were about to make out on the couch."

He wondered how long it would take to scoop up the dog and get out the door before it closed.

"I think you need to stop talking now," Kerri said, placing a brown bag full of take-out on the counter; her apologetic gaze meeting his as she unloaded supper.

"But I didn't get a chance to tell him what I wanted to do to him." Brandi pouted, dividing her attention between both sisters. "Maybe I should before he leaves."

Jordan set the dog on the floor, draped an arm around the loose-lipped woman and guided her to the couch. "Honey, you took more than one pain pill, didn't you?"

"Yes. This is me drunk."

"Well then, let's sit down and you can tell us all about your day while we eat." The clever woman glanced at him and smiled. "You joining us, sheriff?"

"No. I think you can handle things from here. If you need help, call Doc Turner. Goodnight."

With a nod to all three women, he grabbed Ace and got the hell out of Dodge.

Good news. Her truck was salvageable.

Bad news. Her dignity was not.

Brandi couldn't believe some of the things she'd said and done while under the influence of pain medicine a few days ago. *Note to self: Don't ever get drunk.* As if coming onto the guy wasn't bad enough, she'd told him about her stupid ex refusing to have sex. *Cripes*, it had been humiliating when Ed turned down her naked body, but this…this was worse. Baring her mortifying secret to the sexy sheriff was much worse. That whole afternoon was a little fuzzy. Just what the hell else had she revealed? Or done? She was proud of her ability to laugh at herself. But this was stretching it a bit. A big bit.

Parking her little blue rental car behind the project foreman at the Masters property, she got out and thanked her lucky stars she didn't have to worry about running into the sheriff here. The last thing she needed was to see Kade Dalton. In fact, she'd avoided him quite efficiently the past three days. Guilt hung heavy in her gut at neglecting her horse, but she couldn't take the chance on bumping into the man on his ranch. Mainly because she didn't know what road she'd take. The high road. Low road…

The *avoid-at-all-cost* road.

The last one held the most appeal. Then she wouldn't have to choose a course of action.

Embarrassment.

Pretence.

Apology.

See? None of them appealed to her. Yeah. She liked avoidance best. Then she could *pretend* she wasn't *embarrassed* and didn't have to *apologize*. She really was tired of having to apologize to that man. It was getting old. And annoying as hell. If only her brain cells would function around the handsome sheriff.

But her deficiency wasn't just because of his looks. No. She had no trouble functioning around Connor or Cole McCall, and those two men were gorgeous. And what about Kevin Dalton? Gorgeous with a capital G, yet she functioned just fine around him. Then there was Jace Turner. Drop dead gorgeous, *and* a friggin' doctor. Trouble? No. All systems were a go around the guy.

Enter one gray-eyed sheriff, Guardsman, rancher, whatever the heck he was, and her brain immediately took a hike, closed up shop, hit the road. It's a wonder she didn't walk into walls. Yeah, when that guy was around, she was a hazard to herself and others.

The best thing for her to do was concentrate on work. Safe, reliable work. A world she was comfortable in. A world where she was in control. Her own element.

She walked to the back of the house and smiled when chaos met her gaze. Holes and trenches dotted the landscape where the underground electricity and sprinkler system lay ready for tomorrow's scheduled inspection. After a quick word with her foreman confirming they were indeed ready for the city to come in and inspect the setup before they could proceed with cement, sod, pavers and landscaping, Brandi went in search of Mrs. Masters to see how the woman was holding up with all the chaos in her back yard.

Spotting the pretty, older woman handing out glasses of iced tea to the workers, she picked her way around the maze of projects.

"Brandi, hi," her client said on her approach, a genuine smile lighting her face. "Please join me for a glass."

And before she could decline, her friend's mother grabbed her hand and tugged her to a nearby table and chairs, the only untouched area out back.

"Thank you," she said, having no choice but to sit and drink. The woman really was good at that.

"How are you doing, dear?" Mrs. Masters pointed to Brandi's bandage. "I heard about your accident. I'm glad Old Charlie didn't hurt you too bad."

She rubbed her temple and smiled. "Yeah, it's just a small bump. The stitches in the arm weren't his fault. I did that trying to get Ace out of the hole."

"I heard that, too. You're such a sweetheart." A slight breeze blew a strand of silver-streaked brown hair in her client's face as she leaned forward to pat her hand.

"And I'm glad Kade came by to help. He's a sweetheart, too."

At the mention of the sheriff's name, Brandi's mind went on alert. She was well aware of the matchmaking efforts the woman deployed to hook up her daughters with the McCall brothers. And because those tactics worked, the older Masters and McCalls where no doubt looking for new prey.

Well, it wasn't going to work. She was more than happy to be 'married' to her career.

She sipped her drink and nodded. "Yes, he is good at his job."

"Oh, honey, from what I hear, you're more than a job to him."

Brandi's heart sank while her face heated. Shoot. She'd hoped her lack of sense hadn't reached the older generation just yet. Unsure just exactly what Mrs. Master had heard, she knew better than to give the woman any ammunition.

"You probably heard wrong, then. We're just friends, and he was just doing his job." She nodded toward the workers building a stone wall. "Speaking of jobs, how are you faring with all this going on? You still have a good ten more days of the chaos to go."

The smiling lady sat back in her chair and nodded. "It's all good. And we can't wait for the final reveal. In fact, my husband and I are throwing a party two weeks from now and you must be here. It is your design, after all, and we'd really love to show it, and you, off. We're quite certain the get-together will bring in more work for your business."

"Thank you." Touched, she reached for her client's hand and squeezed. "I don't know what to say."

"Just say you'll be here."

"I'll be here." She smiled, really understanding where Kerri and Jordan got their warmth and compassion.

"Good." Sitting back, her friends' mother reached for her tea. "Will your stitches be out by then? I'd hate to see you get them wet in the hot tub."

Hot tub?

Oh, hell no. No way in hell she was going in a hot tub...especially with others around. That required a bathing suit. Of which she owned none. She hadn't been in one in over five years—when she was younger, thinner and a lot less self conscious.

But she knew it was best to keep that to herself. "Yes. I have an appointment with Doctor Turner on Thursday," she said, and deliberately kept quiet about the hot tub. There would no doubt be plenty of guests more than happy to use the water feature.

Steering the conversation back to the project, Brandi gave her client a quick breakdown of the week's upcoming work schedule, finished her drink and stood. "Well, if you'll excuse me, I should get going. Jen and Brock are dropping Cody off at my house while they run to visit his grandmother in the hospital."

"See? You are a sweetheart."

Sweet had nothing to do with it. She was lonely. "Nah. Cody reminds me of my nephew, Tyler, back in Pennsylvania."

He had been the hardest one to leave. She Skyped with the four-year-old every chance she got, as well as her brothers, but it wasn't the same as holding him or sitting on the floor playing Legos.

Mrs. Masters slipped an arm around her as they walked through the house toward the front door. "You miss him, huh?"

"Yeah. My brother, Ethan's, wife died three years ago while he was on deployment." Her heart still lurched whenever she recalled that horrible time. She'd stepped in to help, despite her personal struggles and complaints from Ed that she was spending more time with the child than him. And considering he didn't do anything to her but put her down, she had no idea why he complained.

"How awful. I'm sure they both are missing you pretty good right now, too," her client said. "Is your brother still in the Guard?"

"Yeah. All four of my brothers are."

"Oh, my." Stopping at the door, the pretty lady turned to her and frowned. "How do you manage to stay sane? The worry must eat you alive."

"It does, and I've never claimed to be sane," she joked, both of them laughing as they stepped onto the front porch.

"Is Ethan deployed now, or did he come back in February like Kade?"

"They were actually back last September." And as soon as the power of attorney and custody for Tyler reverted back to Ethan, Brandi summoned the courage to pack up and head for Texas.

Mrs. Masters nodded. "Well, at least they're stateside now, and *you* can worry about *you*."

Brandi smiled. "True. That's exactly what my brother told me."

Although, she never stopped worrying.

Leeann McCall sat on her front porch enjoying a cold glass of lemonade as she watched several horses grazing in the far pasture. A light breeze helped to ease some of the heat from the late June day.

"I thought I might find you here." Her husband kissed her quick on the cheek before dropping into the Adirondack chair next to her.

She smiled and poured him a drink. "Yes, I thought I'd sit out here while I waited for Hannah to call. It's so pretty this time of the day."

Alex nodded, and they both sipped their drinks, watching the horses in a companionable silence. This was exactly what she wished for her boys. All her boys. Not just her sons, but the Dalton cousins, too. Kade and Kevin had been a part of her heart for as long as she could remember. If they wanted to be single, that was okay. She just didn't want them to be lonely. Her heart ached at the thought. And after she and Hannah had both witnessed envy in the cousins' eyes whenever Cole and Jordan or Connor and Kerri were around, she and her friend had vowed to help fate find happiness for all their boys.

As if fate heard her thoughts, the phone rang with Hannah's name appearing on the screen.

She glanced at her husband as she answered the call. "Hi. So...what's the verdict? Is Brandi going to be there?"

"Yes, and I didn't even have to prod," her friend said.

"Well, that's a first." Leeann gave her husband a thumbs up and he smile.

"I know. She seemed happy at the prospect of gaining more clients, which I'm sure she will, but we both know that's not the real reason for the party."

"True," she replied. "Kade has already confirmed he isn't on duty that day, and that it's not a drill weekend, so he's agreed to attend."

"Super. He thinks it's to celebrate my new back yard, too?"

She sat back in her chair and smiled. "Yep."

"Okay, then I guess our work is done," Hannah said, and Leeann could almost see her friend nod through the phone. "We won't push. Just get those two together in a relaxed atmosphere and let nature do the rest."

"And don't forget about fate." She clinked her glass with her husband's as she continued to talk. "You've seen them together."

"I most certainly have. They're fated, and you can't escape fate."

"True." Over the past year, she'd watched both her sons give it a go to no avail. "Cole tried, but he proved it's impossible, so we just need to toss Kade and Brandi together every once in a while and let fate do its thing."

"Agreed. Starting with my party."

Her friend's voice came through the phone loud enough to make Alex smile.

"Yes." She nodded with a grin. "I'm excited. I have a feeling it's going to open doors for our Pennsylvania transplant…and not just in a business aspect."

Walking out of the meeting he'd called with his platoon leaders just before final formation, Kade was pleased to hear each MOS, Military Occupational Specialty, had accomplished their goals that weekend. Scheduled and planned weeks in advance, the training had gone without incident, injury or anyone AWOL.

All and all, it had been a good drill.

"First Sergeant Dalton," his superior, Captain Hernandez called from behind.

He swiveled around. "Yes, sir?"

"Just wanted to make sure I can count on you to attend the meeting with the full-timers this Wednesday at oh-nine-hundred to discuss last minute issues before annual training next month."

"Of course, sir," he replied.

"Good." The captain slapped his shoulder and they fell into step together. "Now, let's call final formation and send these soldiers home."

"Yes, sir."

Twenty minutes later, Kade walked through the nearly deserted armory, mentally cataloging information he'd need to bring to the full-timer's meeting that week, when he passed the collage of photos on the bulletin board by the door. The one of Sergeant Bobby Nylan never ceased to pull the breath from his lungs. He stopped to silently pay homage to the fallen soldier.

"It's not your fault, you know," Lieutenant Turner said, appearing by his side out of nowhere.

Kade turned to Jace. "Not your fault, either."

"I was the first medic on the scene."

"And we both know he'd lost too much blood…and body parts to be saved."

The doc sucked in a breath, and then let it out slow as he nodded. "Doesn't make it any easier."

Kade turned back to the photo of the soldier who'd been his responsibility for such a short time. "No, it doesn't."

He'd let the man down.

The overwhelming urge to hit something shook through Kade, shooting a wave of heat up his body that burned his scalp.

"You did your job," Turner said, still staring at the photo. "We all did."

"Yes, we did."

Too bad it wasn't enough.

"So…" Jace twisted to face him, subject change apparent in his steady gaze. "How's your back?"

"Fine."

"And Brandi's arm?"

"I've no idea."

And he hadn't thought of the woman for oh, a good half hour now. The doc just had to go and bring up the sexy designer. Now the memory of how soft, hot and responsive she was would haunt him for the rest of the day. Great.

"So, you haven't seen her since Thursday?"

"Nope." A whole three days had gone by since the woman begged him to be insider her. If it weren't for drill, Kade probably would've come up with a reason to accidentally run into her.

Bad idea.

Very bad idea.

Instinct told him the connection he'd felt when she'd shoved his hand on her hip was not going to go away just because he willed it.

A familiar knot began to form in his stomach. The more he saw her, the stronger the feeling got, so keeping his distance was a smart maneuver…and a necessary one.

"I'm seeing her on Thursday," Jace stated, smug smile on his lips.

Funny how the knot in Kade's stomach morphed to the size of a watermelon. He clenched his jaw to keep from asking something stupid, or saying what he most certainly did not want to hear.

"Yeah, I'm taking her stitches out at two," the doctor clarified with a big grin splitting his damn face. "Oh, buddy. You should see your expression." Jace snickered, hand cupping Kade's shoulder. "You don't know it yet, but you, my friend, are snagged."

Then the idiot released him and laughed as he walked away. *Laughed.* There was nothing funny about the foreign emotion shaking him up from the inside out. Turner was just lucky they were still in the armory, and in uniform, or the merry doctor would be stitching Kade's hand after plucking his missing teeth from the wound.

"It's called disgust," he said, and would've been happy to elaborate to the doctor's retreating back when his phone started to ring. Thrilled with the interruption, he fished the cell from his pocket and frowned. His cousin usually never called when he had drill. "Jen, is everything okay?"

"Yes, sorry to bother you, Kade." she said. "But they're running more tests on Brock's grandmother and we'd like to stay. Could you pick Cody up from Brandi's? Kevin is still in Dallas on business."

Brandi's? Shit. Why couldn't it be Kerri or Jordan watching his nephew? Well, not technically his nephew, but close enough. The little boy called him uncle, so he treated the little rascal as such.

"Sure," he said, cursing his luck as he pivoted on his heel and headed to the locker room to change into his civilian clothes. Heaven forbid he should show up at the designer's door in his fatigues. "Take as long as you need."

His cousin's sigh echoed through the phone. "Thank you so much, Kade. We really appreciate it."

Now he felt like shit. He knew how much Brock's grandmother meant to them both, and how worried Jen had been when the woman had been admitted with chest pains last night.

By the time he pulled up to the cottage, he had his emotions under control and hoped to God he could say the same about his body. A few good, solid inhales on his way to her door helped to firm his resolve. He was not, under any circumstances, going to throw her on the couch and pick up where they'd left off on Thursday. He was not.

Knocking a little louder than necessary, he stood back and waited.

The sexy designer opened the door, and her eyes widened while color rushed to her face. "Kade?"

The blush deepened the brown of her mesmerizing gaze, and his gut took an invisible blow.

"I…what…" She drew in a breath. "Why are you here?"

Apparently she didn't get the memo. "Jen's tied up at the hospital. She called me at drill and asked if I could fetch Cody."

"Oh. I hope everything is okay."

He shrugged. "More tests."

She stepped back to let him in. "Cody's asleep on my bed. We had a great day on the beach. He's tuckered out. Do you want me to wake him?"

Once his brain caught up to her questions, he shook his head. "No. Unless you'd like me to leave." He had no idea why he was acting and feeling so strange around her.

Probably *because* he wanted to throw her on the couch and pick up where they'd left off last Thursday.

She shook her head, the pretty blush deepening as she turned and began to pick plastic dinosaurs up off the floor. "No, of course not. Why would I want you to do that?" Dropping the toys onto the coffee table, she avoided his gaze and bent to pick up some more. "I mean, it's not like I have anything to be embarrassed about. Oh, wait...yeah...yeah, I do."

A strange giggle-hiccup followed her words along with inaudible mumbles and head shaking. He wondered briefly if she was having some sort of seizure until she stood and brushed past him to shove a box of crackers from the coffee table into a kitchen cupboard.

"And the award for biggest *poopyhead* goes to...yours truly." She slapped a hand over her chest and laughed.

God, she was adorable. He knew he should stop her, but he honestly couldn't get enough of the ruffled *unrufflable* woman.

She swiped the salt shaker from the table and cradled it to her chest with both hands. "I'd like to thank the academy, and a stupid ex-boyfriend for making me the idiot I am today."

"Okay, enough." He sprang into action, removing the shaker from her hand and cornering her against the fridge when she stepped back. "Hey...hey. It's all right. Calm down."

She shook her head and closed her eyes. "God, I'm so embarrassed, Kade. And so, *so* sorry for what I said...and did to you..."

"Brandi, look at me."

She opened one eye.

"Both eyes, Brandi," he said, a smile tugging at his mouth.

The other eye opened.

"That's better. Now, listen to me. You have nothing to be embarrassed about."

The snort that left her throat caused her head to jerk back and hit the refrigerator. "Yes, I do. A good number of things. But I am really sor—"

He pressed a finger to her lips, intending to stop her apology, but...*ah hell*, he hadn't expected the instant awareness that spread through his body, heating his spine. She must've felt it too, because her brown eyes widened, and she trembled against him.

That's all it took to send him to the same state he was in last Thursday on the couch. Just one touch. That was it. One miniscule touch. He had no defense. He was done. His brain shut down and need, fierce and consuming, took over.

Cupping her face, he closed the distance between them and covered her mouth with his.

Damn, he knew it.

He knew those tempting lips of hers would feel soft and supple...and hot.

When she let out a breath of acceptance and slid her hands up around his neck, he discovered heaven. There was no other word for the feeling of completeness that came over him. Everything about the woman in his arms was right. Her touch, her curves, her lips. *Christ*, her lips. She kissed him with a matching wild abandon, lips drinking and drinking like she'd been thirsting for him, and only him. And if they hadn't needed air, no way in hell would he have stopped.

With a reluctance he'd never known, Kade broke the kiss and set his forehead against hers, careful not to touch the bruise on her temple. Spurts of warm air hit his neck, signaling she too was having trouble getting her breathing under control.

"Wow," she said with a gush. "That...was..."

"Wow," he finished for her, and she laughed.

"Yeah, like firecracker wow."

He drew back to frown down at her. "Just firecracker?"

She smiled. "Okay, maybe an M80."

"*Unkewl* Kade..." Cody appeared out of nowhere, standing next to them, rubbing his eyes. "What's an M and M 80?"

They broke apart, and the sound of Brandi's head smacking the refrigerator went unnoticed by his nephew who blinked up at him.

Jesus. How much had the little guy seen?

"Is it *wike chocwit*?"

Completely at a loss as to what the right thing was to do—ask the four-year-old if he'd seen the kiss, and if so, address the kiss, ignore the kiss...ask Brandi for another kiss. No...no...that would be bad. At least, not in front of his nephew.

"Cuz I *wike chocwit*." The little boy continued to talk, apparently oblivious to the battle going on in his uncle's thick head. *Heads.*

Knowing he needed to respond, Kade swooped up the sleepy child and went for the fail-safe maneuver; he tickled his tummy. "No, an M80 is like a firecracker, but bigger," he said, looking pointedly at the silent designer.

She smiled, and his heart actually rocked in his chest. Rocked. That wasn't good. Movement. Damn. No. That was not good. He didn't need a woman making him *feel* his heart. *Causing* his heart to move. Life was much easier without that complication. Hell, he'd managed just fine without that complication for over thirty-two years.

Suddenly, he didn't feel so good.

Time to go.

He transferred his gaze to the little boy in his arms. "What do you say? You ready, buddy?"

"I guess. Can we get some *ice cweam*? *Bwandi* said I could get *chocwit ice cweam fwom Fostews aftew* my nap. And I napped. Isn't that *wight, Bwandi*?"

"Yes, you did," she said, stepping close to ruffle his nephew's hair. "I'm sure your uncle will get you some ice cream."

Two small hands grabbed his jaw and turned his face. "Can we, *Unkewl* Kade?"

He grinned. "Sure. Go gather your stuff," he replied, setting the child down. "We'll stop for it on our way home."

"Yippee!"

He chanced a glance at the silent woman, but couldn't tell what she was thinking or feeling. Was she sad? Mad? Relieved? He had no idea. He only knew he had to leave.

"Come on. I want *chocwit*." Cody tugged his hand. When he didn't budge, his nephew glanced up. "Come on, *Unkewl* Kade."

"Don't you have something to say to Brandi?"

Big blue eyes blinked up at him. "Oh. Yeah. I *fowgot*." He turned to his babysitter. "Do you want some *ice cweam*, too?"

Damn. That wasn't what he'd meant. His heart stopped for a full beat. A full beat. *Shit*. More movement. Once again, the sexy woman interfered with the beating of his heart. Not good.

"Awe, thanks, sweetheart, but no," she replied, kneeling down, staring at his nephew eye-level. "You two go ahead. Enjoy."

"We will. Thanks for *pwaying* with me today," Cody said, body slamming her with a hug.

She laughed and hugged back. "Anytime."

"Okay, Cody. Let's go." He set a hand on the boy's shoulder, really needing to get out of the small cottage. Breathing was becoming a chore. "I think someone could use some alone time."

The pretty designer's smile turned sad. "Yeah. I think someone could."

Now he felt like an ass. He knew she was self conscious and confused. No doubt trying to figure out what the hell just happened in her kitchen. But he had no answers. He was at a loss, too. He needed to regroup, and that wasn't going to happen in her presence. So, rude or not, yeah, he was kissing then running.

The alternative was feeling, and hell no, he was *not* having any of that.

For a Monday, the day didn't actually suck. Brandi had half expected the sky to fall or a horse to run into her car or a handsome sheriff to kiss her like she was his last breath then leave her high and dry. Oh wait, that last part happened yesterday.

Though, she shouldn't be so hard on the sheriff. Heck, after their incredible kiss, she'd had the urge to run, too. He just beat her to it. The man made her feel too much, that was the problem. And the last thing she needed was to feel with her heart. But, damn, if there was a way to keep her heart out of it, she wanted more of his delicious kisses.

Shaking her head to rid her mind of the Kade-induced fog that had clung to her ever since their lips met, Brandi gathered her purse, and what was left of her wits, and exited her rental car for her meeting with Jordan at the restaurant.

Based on their requests and the measurements she'd gathered at the McCall's last week, Brandi was confident the master suite plans on her tablet were going to please her friends. Especially their standup shower.

Smile tugging her lip, she entered the quiet restaurant and stood just inside the door to allow her eyes to adjust.

"Hello," she called, slowly making her way toward the kitchen.

Incredible smells of fresh garlic, butter and onions filled the air, and Brandi's stomach promptly growled, reminding her it was time for a snack. She fished a cereal bar out of her purse and knocked on the swinging kitchen door as she pushed inside.

"Hello?"

"Hi, Brandi." Kerri smiled at her from in front of the stove where the incredible smells percolated. "Jordan is upstairs in the apartment. She said to tell you to go on up when you got here. So, go on up."

"Okay," she replied, readjusting the strap on her shoulder before she bit into her bar.

Kerri stepped forward, smile twitching her lip. "Wait... Don't you have something to tell me?"

"No." She frowned and shook her head. "I don't think so. Why?"

Her friend's smile widened. "Connor and I noticed Kade's truck outside your house last night..."

Cereal bars didn't taste so good when you choked on them.

She coughed and shook her head again. "He was just picking Cody up for Jen."

"Uh, huh." The cook folded her arms across her chest and regarded her closely.

Damn, she looked like her sister.

"Then why the sudden need to choke?"

"Because...because..." She glanced at the door. "I really should get to my meeting."

Kerri chuckled. "Okay, I get it. Believe me. You're wearing the same look I lived in last year, thanks to a very confusing cowboy."

Not knowing what to say or how to respond without incriminating herself, Brandi just nodded. Best to not even open her mouth. Her friend stepped close and squeezed her free hand.

"If you ever need to talk, I'm here. Okay?"

She nodded again. "Okay. Thanks. But I'm good…and should go."

"You do that." Kerri released her with a laugh. "I'll see you in a bit."

Happy to make her escape, she turned and shot out the door in one point two seconds. A new record. Personal best. She was still congratulating herself as she knocked on the apartment upstairs.

Jordan opened the door and smiled. "Hi, Brandi. Come on in. I'm excited to see the plans."

"I'm excited to show you." And she refrained from blowing out a breath in relief. Another bullet dodged. She'd half expected her client to take one look at her and ask her about kissing Kade. After all, Jordan was nothing if not astute.

Following the woman into the open kitchen, she forced her mind into business mode. "I've incorporated all your wish list items into the master bedroom footprint."

"Sweet!" The beautiful brunette rubbed her hands together. "I can't wait to see."

A smile tugged Brandi's lips as she pulled her tablet out of her bag, fired it up and set it on the counter between them. "Here you go." She called up the plans and waited and watched as her client's brown eyes widened.

"Oh my God, Brandi. This is fantastic."

"Thank you. But you haven't even seen the 3-D rendering."

Jordan grabbed both her arms and squeezed. "You have it in 3-D?"

She laughed. "Yep. It's on my laptop. Call me old fashioned, but I prefer to use the software on the computer, not the tablet."

"Sweet," her client said again, releasing her arms.

Smiling, Brandi removed the computer from her bag and set it on the other side of the counter. "And I found these great glass tiles for your shower in the colors you wanted," she informed as her laptop booted up.

"Cole is going to freak."

That visual caused Brandi to laugh. She highly doubted the CEO of McCall Enterprises ever *freaked* over anything in his life. "Speaking of Cole, please tell him thanks. I absolutely love this rendering software his company puts out. So much easier to maneuver than the old program I used to use."

"Thank your boyfriend's cousin."

Brandi glanced up from her computer and frowned. "What?"

"Kevin," Jordan replied as if that clarified everything.

"What about him? And I don't have a boyfriend."

Her client smirked. "Sure you do. You're just in denial. It's okay. My sister and I went through the same phase. It'll pass," the woman stated with a wave of her hand. "And Kevin is the one who created this rendering program."

Information overload. Brandi didn't know what to address first. Jordan's misconception that she had a boyfriend, or the fact that the good-looking, flirtatious, blue-eyed cowboy was a genius.

The ding alerting her of a Skype message saved her from answering. "Sorry, it's one of my brothers. I'll just let him know I'm busy."

"No, don't do that. Take the call. I'll be here drooling over my soon-to-be master suite," Jordan said, staring at the tablet.

"Okay, I won't be long." She clicked the window and her brother's face appeared. "Hi, Ben. Is something wrong?" Her second oldest brother rarely Skyped and was the reason she bothered to answer in the first place. Anyone else and she would've ignored the window and waited until later to call back.

"You tell me, Brandi," he said, green gaze regarding her with a shrewdness she could feel even through the screen. "I've had this feeling something was wrong for several days now. What gives?"

Darn him and his sixth sense. Ever since she'd known her step-brother, Ben had had this weird ability to clue into people when they were injured or in trouble. She knew better than to deny it—that would only put his ass on a plane, and he'd be knocking on her door in a matter of hours. Besides, it was no big deal.

"Oh, sorry." She shrugged, doing her best to play off the accident as minor. It was to her. "You're probably referring to last Thursday. I swerved to miss a horse and clipped a tree."

"What?" He sat up and moved closer to the screen. "Are you all right?"

This was the reason she hadn't told anyone back home. It was no big deal, but they'd treat it otherwise.

"Yes, just a little bump on the head and a few stitches in my arm." Okay, the cut wasn't from the accident, but he did *not* need to know about her fence incident. She'd had enough embarrassment for one week.

"All right." He blew out a breath. "As long as you're okay," he said, settling back in his chair, arms crossed over his broad chest.

All four of her good-looking brothers were tall, ripped, and blessed with gorgeous dark hair, but Ben was the only one who didn't inherit his dad's brown eyes. Apparently, he had his mother's green eyes.

"I am," she reassured with a smile.

A knowing gleam came into those eyes, and he cocked his head. "So then, who's the guy?"

Chapter Six

Great. Brandi resisted another forehead palming and played dumb, instead. "Excuse me? What guy?"

"That's what I'd like to know," he replied, eyebrow raised. "The one responsible for the sparkle in your eyes."

"His name is Kade." Jordan spoke up.

Brandi jumped, having forgotten the woman was there. Shoot. Now her client got up and came around to her stool.

"He's the local sheriff, First Sergeant in the Guard, and co-owner of a horse ranch here in Harland County."

Her eyelids fluttered a few times. Really? How in the world did they know? Did she have a sign on her face saying Kade Dalton kissed her to within an inch of her life and now she was confused as hell? And what was with her client spouting Kade's resume?

"Well, hello there." Ben sat up, arms dropping to his sides as he stared open-mouthed at Jordan.

"Hi, yourself." Her friend smiled.

Brandi snickered and waved a finger at her brother. "Don't even think about it, Casanova. Jordan's married."

His face fell. "Why is it all the good ones are taken?"

"And why is it they're the only ones you look for," she countered. It would truly be wonderful if her brother stopped avoiding meaningful relationships. "Could it be you're too afraid of commitment?"

"Oh, look at the time." He pretended to glance at an invisible watch on his wrist. "Got to go. Nice meeting you, Jordan. Good talking to you, Brandi. First Sergeant, huh? Wow. Glad to hear you're willing to take a chance with another soldier. Good for you. Oh, and give Dad a call. I know he'd love to hear from you. Bye."

The screen went dead.

Brandi smiled. Worked every time. One mention of commitment and her brothers ran away like little girls.

"Oh, you're good." Her friend snickered, holding her hand up for a high-five. "Nicely played."

"Thanks." She smacked Jordan's hand. "I had to learn a trick or two over the years to survive."

"How many siblings do you have?"

"Four older brothers."

Her friend's eyes widened as she dropped back onto her stool. "Oh, hun. That had to be brutal during your teenage years."

Brandi nodded. "You've no idea."

Kade was damn happy to be busy. It was late Wednesday, and between his duties at work and the Guard, he'd hardly even thought about the designer and her talented lips, hot taste, soft, supple curves, need-quivering body…

Bullshit. He hadn't stopped thinking about Brandi all week. Whoever coined the phrase 'out of sight, out of mind' never met the Yankee bombshell.

"Sorry to be such a burden, Mr. Sheriff, sir?"

Donny's voice snapped Kade's mind back to the present and the call he'd received that sent him to assist the kid. He glanced from the deputy, holding his hat in his hand, to the rear end of the squad car somehow hung up on a section of guardrail. "So, tell me again exactly how this happened?"

The deputy cleared his throat, hat practically spiraling out of his fingers. "Well, Sheriff Dalton, sir, it...it's not my fault."

Of course not.

"I'd just picked up our supper from the Texas-Pub that Ms. Masters was kind enough to make, and was backing out of the parking lot when a pig came out of nowhere."

"Pig?"

"Yeah, well, wild hog, sir."

He nodded. Although rare, the critters did tend to show up in town once in a while. "Still doesn't explain how your rear end contacted the guardrail...in the adjacent lot."

"Oh, well that was because of the cat, sir."

Kade glanced around the deserted lot. "Cat? What cat?"

"The one chasing the wild hog."

Scrubbing a palm over his face did little to clarify the situation, but just to be sure, Kade did it twice.

"You look like you could use some help, buddy."

Connor's amused drawl hit his ears, and he turned to see his friend ambling over from the restaurant parking lot, a lop-sided grin on his face.

"Do I want to know how this happened, Skippy?" His friend stared at the squad car, confusion clouding his gaze.

"It's Donny," the deputy corrected. "And all I did was swerve to miss the wild hog."

Connor's brow rose.

"Don't forget about the cat," Kade reminded.

Now both his friend's brows disappeared behind his Stetson. "Cat?"

"Yeah." He nodded. "The one chasing the hog."

Connor's jaw worked as he blinked. "I'm beginning to understand your face palm."

"Thought you might." Kade knelt down to inspect under the car. Not as bad as he'd thought. He rose, brushing his hands on his pants, his heart doing that stupid rib-kicking when he noticed a certain designer getting out of her car at the restaurant.

"Look, Kade," Connor said. "There's your girlfriend."

The cowboy waved to the woman, giving Kade no choice but to do the same.

"I didn't know Brandi was your girlfriend," Donny said, joining in on the waving.

She smiled, a little hesitant, but lifted a hand and waved back. He wondered if anyone would notice if he strangled his friend in broad daylight. Then the designer turned and walked into the pub and all thoughts of strangling fled from his mind.

Damn, she sure filled out a pair of jeans.

"You're a lucky man, sir," his deputy said. "Brandi's nice. I run into her at the creamery. We sometimes talk as we eat our ice cream. I have to tell you, the guys are always checking her out."

Guys? What guys? He opened his mouth to ask, then caught site of Connor biting back a snicker, and decided the questions could wait.

"Well, *Moose*, looks like you and I can take care of this."

His friend nodded and headed for the other side of the car as Kade turned to his deputy.

"Donny, you climb in, put the car in neutral and don't do anything else. Got it?"

The boy's face brightened. "Yes, sir. We don't need a tow truck."

No, but he could use a stiff drink. He glanced across the back of the trunk to his friend. "On the count of three. One. Two. *Three*."

Gripping the bumper, he and Connor lifted the heavy car enough to free the rear end from the rail. Once they set it down, the kid had the good sense to hit the brake and put the car in park.

Donny got out and smiled. "Thanks, boss. You want your supper here?"

Kade shook his head, his appetite strangely nonexistent. "No, go on and take it to the station. And, Donny?"

"Yeah, Sheriff Dalton?"

"Fill out an incident report."

"Ah, shoot." Deep lines creased the kid's forehead. "Do I have to, sir?"

"Yes, you have to," he said.

The kid sighed as he climbed back into the car, then drove away.

Connor walked over and clamped a hand on his shoulder. "You look like you could use a beer, buddy."

Kade help up two fingers.

"Oh, boy, something tells me it's more than the deputy fueling that thirst."

He snorted, but kept his mouth shut as he twisted around and headed for his jeep. Thank God he was off duty for a few days, starting tomorrow. After the week he'd had, he sure as hell needed the break.

"Well, at least you get to spend time with me and some horses at the auction the next couple of days." Connor slapped his shoulder again, falling into step with him. "That should take your mind off of things...but it won't help with Brandi."

He stumbled just a little, but enough to cause his buddy to laugh. Damn giant thought because he had a good thing going with Kerri he knew everything. Just because his friend had screwed up royally—several times—and managed to fix things, and redeem himself, and get the girl… *Shit*. Okay, maybe his buddy *did* know something. The thing was, Kade didn't need help. He was fine. Just. Fine.

"Whatever it is you just thought…you're wrong," Connor said. "And if you think you don't need her, you're wrong." They came to a stop by his vehicle, a huge smile on his buddy's face. "And the big one, my friend. Take it from me, if you think, for one minute you're in control of the situation…you are completely and utterly fucked."

Wrong. He shook his head. "This isn't like what you have with Kerri."

Connor threw his head back and laughed. *Laughed.* Kade didn't see any humor in his words. Just the truth. "It's not the same, asshole. It was just a kiss."

His buddy's laughter increased to the point where the cowboy had to lean against the side of the jeep for support, large body shaking with a merriment lost on Kade.

"Come on, Connor." He frowned, waiting for the guy to stop. "Don't you think that's overkill?"

The giant finally sobered enough to meet his gaze. "No. I think it was spot on. With the right woman, a kiss is *never* just a kiss. Sadly, you have a lot to learn, and you're going to learn whether you want to or not."

More laughter shook through his friend's large frame.

Kade folded his arms across his chest and stared. "You're enjoying this, aren't you?"

Connor nodded. "Only a lot."

If he hadn't been in uniform, in a parking lot, in plain view of the public, he would've given his buddy the finger.

"You just mentally flipped me off, didn't you?" the smirking cowboy asked.

"Yep." A grin tugged his own mouth.

"Well, I'm going to take pity on you and go inside. I'm supposed to be having dinner with my fiancée." He straightened up from the vehicle then cocked his head. "Would you like me to stop by Brandi's table and tell her you said hello?"

"Would you like my fist to tell your teeth goodbye?"

Connor's chuckle echoed around them. "In your dreams, Dalton." He adjusted his Stetson and nodded. "I'll pick you up around six am so we can get an early start for the auction."

"Sounds good," he said. "Thanks for your help, buddy. You'd better get inside. You've kept your fiancée waiting long enough."

"True, and you'd better get back to the station to babysit Skippy."

Kade nodded. Sadly, it was becoming a full time job.

S unday afternoon, Brandi was at Shadow Rock Ranch watching little Cody so Jen and Brock could visit his grandmother, who had undergone open-heart surgery two days earlier. She enjoyed her time with the little boy; he reminded her so much of her nephew.

A sharp pang of regret sliced through her insides. Even after several months, it still hurt to think about Tyler. She'd practically helped raise the little boy since before his second birthday, and had had sole custody of him while her brother was deployed last year. Giving him up had been tough, but inevitable. And now, thanks to her time with her nephew, watching the rambunctious four-year-old heir to the Dalton dynasty was a piece of cake.

Chocowit cake…with a topping of extra energy.

The little cutie was a lot like his uncles. He had blue eyes like Kevin, although his mama had them, too. But Jen wasn't a prankster, and Brandi could already see that trait in Cody. The way he'd constantly moved her drink today when she wasn't looking was a dead giveaway. Pure Uncle Kevin, there.

"No. That's bad," he said now, reprimanding the kittens in the barn when the runt tried to nurse on mama cat but the others wouldn't move.

Brandi watched in awe as the little boy gently but firmly adjusted the kittens so they all had room. Now *that* was pure Uncle Kade. Cody definitely inherited his uncle's kind and helpful traits.

"Nice job, Cody," she told him, patting his head, holding in tears of pride she knew the little boy wouldn't understand. A treat was in order. And she knew just what to do. One of his favorite activities. "Now, who's ready for a piggy-back ride?"

"Me," he hollered, excitement lighting his face as he rushed to climb on her back.

Kind of reminded her of Ace when Cody played on the floor. The little dog had been quarantined to the inside of the ranch when Kade wasn't around. Apparently, the mischievous pup needed lots of supervision near the horses.

"Okay, hold on tight." Brandi rose to her feet and galloped through the barn with the giggling toddler clinging to her back.

They were rounding the corner, heading outside,

when two horse trailers pulled up and several cowboys hopped out. She stopped dead, but her pulse continued to gallop. Darn. She'd hoped to be gone before Kade returned from the three-day auction.

With the exception of that *across-the-parking-lot* meeting last Wednesday, she hadn't seen the guy since their *kiss-'n'-run* a whole week ago. Dealing with her mixed-up, crazy feelings was a hell of a lot easier when the guy wasn't around. Now, her gaze was immediately pulled to the soldier. Sure, he was dressed like the other cowboys—boots, jeans, Stetson—but none walked with the lethal grace, or the deliberate, controlled movements of a man ready for any situation.

He took her breath away. And she was already winded.

"There's *Unkewl* Kade," Cody yelled. "Let's ride to *Unkewl* Kade." The little guy bounced on her back.

She'd rather retreat into the barn and *ride* in the opposite direction. Her chest tightened in anticipation. For what, she had no idea. Given the way he'd rushed from her house the last time they were together, there was a good chance he'd avoid her now. But she wasn't there for him. She wasn't there for her. She was there for Cody. So, doing as her little charge asked, she ordered her face not to turn red and galloped to his uncle.

Brandi could feel the man's gaze and didn't even want to contemplate what he thought about her trotting display. Yes, she had some north and south action going on, despite her expensive bra. It couldn't be helped. She pushed away her embarrassment. Entertaining Cody was her job, so that's what she was doing. And the little boy was enjoying the ride very much. His giggles filled the air with a wonderful, heartwarming sound. And his laughter was contagious. Even the cowboys were smiling. She glanced over her shoulder at him and grinned at the toddler's wide smile and sparkling blue eyes.

He was having fun, and that's what mattered.

Swinging her gaze around, she chanced a glance at Kade, and her heart rocked against her ribs. He was standing next to Connor, looking at her with such longing and need that, when she tried to inhale, the air clogged her throat. Not exactly ideal while in the middle of physical exertion. Then something unrecognizable passed through his gaze and he looked almost…pained.

"*Unkewl* Kade, look at me," Cody said. "I'm riding a piggy-back."

He set his shoulders and strode toward them. "I can see that." A genuine smile eased the lingering shadows from his face. "Do I get a hug?"

"Yeah!" Cody nearly leapt off her back into Kade's arms.

Brandi straightened and stretched to work the kinks out between her shoulder blades. "Cody was keeping an eye on things in the barn."

"Yeah," the little boy said again. "Like you *aksed*."

"I appreciate that, Cody. Thanks. I knew I could count on you," Kade told him, expression earnest as he held his nephew's gaze. "What do you say you hang out with Brandi for a bit longer while the guys and I unload the new horses?"

"Can I watch?"

"Sure, but from out of the way. Okay?" he asked, handing the little boy back.

Cody nodded. "'Kay."

Kade's attention finally turned to her. "Hi." He smiled, gray eyes twinkling like liquid silver. "Getting a workout, are you?"

She laughed. "A bit."

With a nod and a touch to his hat, he walked away, and she found she could slowly breathe again.

Snapping out of her fog, she headed for a safe spot near the corral where the horses were being unloaded. And as Cody watched the animals, Brandi watched the sexy cowboy who'd been a constant companion to her thoughts and the subject of her delectable dreams the past week.

Strong and sure, Kade moved about with an easy grace. Jacket off, sleeves rolled up on his black shirt, he worked alongside Connor and the men from both ranches. Muscles rippled in his arms as he helped guide several beautiful horses down the chute and into the corral.

"I like that one," Cody said, pointing to the last one the men unloaded. A gorgeous white and brown painted horse.

Brandi nodded. "What a beauty."

When the gates were closed and the animals were ushered to their respected corrals, Connor turned and ambled toward them.

"Here comes, *Connow*." Cody wiggled forward. "Hi, *Connow*!"

"Hey, buddy." Dimple glaring, he hopped the fence with ease and nodded. "Hi, Brandi."

"Hi," she replied, but didn't have the opportunity to say more because Cody lunged for the cowboy.

Connor caught him, then tossed the giggling toddler in the air a few times, before handing him to Kade who joined them. The handsome man in black lifted the little boy by his ankle and turned to the other cowboys.

"Any of you seen Cody?" he asked, and all the men smiled but shook their heads.

"I'm *wight hewe,*" the four-year-old insisted between cackles.

Kade twisted around, pretending to look for the little boy. "Who said that?"

"I did. It's me, Cody."

Still holding the boy by his ankle, Kade lifted him up until they were face to face. "Oh, there you are," he said, righting the giggling toddler. "Why didn't you say something?"

"I did."

Brandi rubbed at the ache in her chest as she smiled and watched the exchange. The sheriff would make a great father. For some reason, the ache increased, but she refused to dissect the meaning, blaming it on the double thick peanut butter and jelly sandwich followed by pizza she and Cody had had for supper. Okay, she'd only had a little of both, but the combination was still lethal.

"All right, champ." Connor stepped forward and grabbed the boy from his friend. "What do you say we go get a drink for the guys?"

"Sure," Cody said, leading the tall cowboy.

A second later, she was alone with Kade. Her pulse immediately increased. She leaned back against the fence, hoping to look calm and cool, when she really did it for support. Something was wrong with her damn legs. They were shaky.

Kade turned to face her fully and smiled. "Hi, again."

She smiled back. "Hi." Then cleared her throat. "I guess I don't have to ask how the auction went. Looks like it went well."

"Yes, ma'am. We picked up quite a few horses trainable for stock as well as a magnificent stallion."

"The paint?"

He nodded. "Connor got one, too." He motioned toward the horse still in the trailer. Agitated snorts grew louder. "He's going to have to get him home soon."

She nodded. "Yeah, it's not good to let him stand in a trailer too long."

Brow lifted in surprise, he studied her. "No, it's not."

Something shifted in his expression. His whole demeanor changed. And because she wasn't confused enough, he moved closer to trail a finger up her bare arm, smiling at the goosebumps he created.

"You look great."

She stared at him, trying to figure out Kade Dalton. His actions, his words, they surprised her speechless. The last time they'd talked, he'd run like a little girl from her touch, and now...now *he* was initiating contact.

His gaze moved to her face, while his finger continued to brush over her skin. "I take it you're babysitting Cody?"

"Yeah," she replied a little throaty.

His gaze darkened at her tone. "For how long?"

"Until your cousin gets back from the hospital."

He studied her closely. "You can leave now, if you want. I'll watch him."

She didn't want to leave, but he confused her. "Do you want me to go?

"No," he replied, his gaze heating as he stared at her lips. "I was really looking forward to tasting you."

And just like that, she went damp.

Her whole body tightened at his admission. "I—you did?"

"Oh, yeah. I do." He nodded, his attention still glued to her mouth.

For as wet as she was down south, her throat and all

things north were bone dry. She swallowed and licked her lips in an attempt to alleviate the situation.

His sexy growl drifted between them, and he opened his mouth to respond just as the agitated stallion grew louder. Blowing out a breath instead, he released her and stepped back. "I'd better go find Connor."

"No need," his friend said, ambling toward them, a smiling Cody perched high on his shoulders. "I'm here. What do you need? Some pointers on how to—"

"No," Kade cut off the cowboy. "You'd better get that paint home. He's stomping and chomping at the bit in there. If you don't go soon, he might injure himself."

Connor transferred the giggling toddler to Kade's shoulders. "Yeah. I'm leaving. You two have fun. As I understand from Cody here, you have two Disney DVDs to watch tonight."

Brandi nodded, and picking up the teasing vibe, she joined in the fun. "Yes, and one even involves princesses."

A scowl skittered across Kade's features while Connor's smile broadened to beaming proportions.

The tall cowboy slapped his frowning friend on the back. "Enjoy your movies, buddy. Just don't forget to leave your *Man Card* at the door."

She bit her lip to keep her reaction inside.

"At least I have one," Kade called to the chuckling cowboy's back.

Connor raised a hand before sliding into the truck with the rest of his men, and then disappeared down the dirt drive.

"*Unkewl* Kade?" Cody frowned down at his uncle's head. "What's a *Mancawd*?"

Gray eyes blinked at her, and she watched a smile spread across the handsome man's face. "It's an imaginary piece of paper not all grown men earn."

"Oh." Now the little boy blinked. "So, *Connow* doesn't have one, but you do?"

"Exactly." A firm nod and smug smile met her gaze.

The little boy pointed to himself. "I'm going to get one when I *gwow* up."

"I believe you will, Cody. I believe you will. But right now," Kade said, pulling his nephew off his shoulders to hold him in front. "I believe it's bath time." His gaze shifted to her. "Isn't that right, Brandi?"

Shoot. Her throat instantly dried again. "Yes."

The little boy smiled at her. "*Awe* you getting one, too, *Bwandi*?"

"No." She cleared her throat, refusing to meet Kade's gaze. "I'll get one when I go home, later."

Cody shrugged. "Okay. When us guys *awe* done, we can all eat *popcown* and watch movies."

Nearly two hours later, she was on the floor with a snoring Cody nestled comfortably between her and Kade. And a snoozing Ace sleeping against the little boy's legs.

She glanced over at the silent man, not surprised to find his gaze on her. He'd been watching her most of the evening, making it hard for her to breathe, let alone swallow. Popcorn had been limited.

And she loved popcorn.

Barefoot, in jeans and gray T-shirt, the sexy sheriff had played havoc with her senses, smelling of soap and so…so male. Her mind had barely kept up with the animation on the screen. But she did know it was the second DVD because he'd gotten up to change movies a half hour ago, giving her the perfect view of the well-worn denim sitting low on his lean hips.

Without a sound, he sat up and reached for his nephew. "I'm going to take him to his room."

Tail wagging, the dog followed him to his feet.

"I'll be right back. Don't move."

The heat in his gaze caused her heart to slam into her ribs. Hard. What should she do? Clean up and leave? Lie there on the floor and wait? Neither of them were ready to start anything, and yet…here they were.

By the time the sexy man returned, without his nephew or the dog, she'd barely gotten her pulse rate down to the earth's atmosphere and her mind to this side of functioning.

He smiled a killer smile and dropped down next to her. "You're still here."

The intent look in his eyes as he rested on an elbow and stared down at her sent what little sense she'd gathered right out the window.

"Yeah," she replied, dragging air into her lungs. "Ace staying with Cody?"

"Yep. He does every night." Using a thumb, he lightly traced her cheek. "I'm glad you didn't leave."

His touch was too much for her needy body. She trembled, and his gaze immediately darkened to a gorgeous smoky hue.

"Brandi," he said, voice low and rough as his face slowly lowered close.

All thought, logic, and any little iota of alarm or warning left in her foggy brain disappeared with her breath. Lips parted in anticipation, she lay there waiting for his kiss, heart hammering out of control, butterflies flapping furiously in her stomach as his thumb brushed her lower lip. Needing to feel him, to touch him, she lifted a hand and cupped his face, palm rubbing the delicious stubble covering his jaw. What she wouldn't give to feel that sensation on other sensitive parts of her body.

With their breath mingling and gazes locked, his mouth hovered, driving her crazy before he finally lowered and their lips touched. A needy sound escaped her throat, but she didn't care. Her eyes fluttered closed, and she gave herself over to the sensations shooting through her body.

He tasted of butter and popcorn, and very hot. And oh boy could the guy kiss. Over and over, he nipped and drank, treating her to slow, deep, drugging, wonderful kisses that drew her out of herself, sending her to a new and wondrous plane. Where in the world had this come from and why the hell had he held back last week? She slid a hand up his chest, loving the feel of hard strength under her palm. Kade Dalton was slowly driving her out of her mind.

Releasing her mouth, he drew in air and initiated a new directive. "I've thought about this all week," he said against her skin, placing open mouth kisses down her cheek and neck, while his hand snaked under her shirt to caress her flesh.

She turned her head, giving his lips better access, then clung to him as he happily obliged. Round after round of chills raced down her body and her good parts tingled as their chests brushed and his fingers stroked.

"Where is everyo—oh, sorry," Kevin said, coming to a halt just inside the doorway.

With lightening speed, Kade rolled to her other side and shielded her from his cousin's view. Even under libido-trying circumstances, the man's valor shined through. He rose to his feet then held a hand down to help her up.

"Well, that's a new one, cuz," the business suited cowboy said, blue gaze bouncing from the television to them. "I never thought of using Disney to set the mood."

She laughed, despite the heat rising in her cheeks. "You might want to try it. Just make sure there's a princess in it."

Kevin's chuckle filled the room. "Duly noted."

"But you have to leave your *Man Card* at the door," she added.

Kade snickered. "Forget it. He doesn't have one."

"Hey, I do so." His cousin frowned in the doorway. "You're just jealous 'cause it's bigger than yours."

Before anyone could reply, Kade's cell phone when off.

"Great, what has Skippy done this time?" Kevin shook his head.

Blame it on the Kade-induced fog, but she was at a complete loss. "Who's Skippy?"

"That's the nickname the McCalls gave Deputy Donny," the blue-eyed cowboy replied as Kade answered his phone.

"Oh, Donny." She nodded, picking up the pillows from the floor and tossing them on the couch. "Boy, can that kid sketch."

She'd run into the young man several times at Foster's Creamery just down the street from her cottage. The last time, the kid had pulled out his sketch pad and showed her his drawings. Why he was at the Harland County Sheriff Department instead of in art school boggled her mind. He had serious talent.

"Okay. I'll be right there," Kade said, hanging up with a sigh. "Old Charlie's loose again." He sent her an apologetic gaze. "I have to go."

"Of course," she said, bending to pick the blanket up off the floor. "Since Kevin's here and can keep an eye on Cody, I need to head home. I have an early start in the morning."

This week was a crazy one. The Masters' project was scheduled for completion and Jordan's was starting tomorrow. Brandi was running two teams and two projects at the same time. Nerve-wracking, but doable.

Kind of like Kade.

One of the moments Brandi had been dreading for days finally happened. The invite to go dress shopping for Kerri's wedding.

She was happy for her friend, she really was, but ever since her thyroid problems began, trying on clothes sucked. They either made her look fat or didn't fit because she was in between sizes. All and all not fun, and something she'd avoided like the plague.

But there was no avoiding this, and in retrospect, she felt bad. This was her friend's big day, and Kerri had been through a lot. The woman was a sweetheart and deserved to be happy. Shame on her for thinking about herself.

"I know it's short notice, but can you meet us at the restaurant at noon? We'll all drive together," Kerri was saying on the other end of the phone, a note of excitement in her voice.

"Sure. I can make it," she replied, mentally juggling a few things. "I just have to finish planting one of the flowerbeds here at your mother's, then I'll go home and shower before meeting you and the girls."

"Great. Thanks. We'll see you then."

Brandi hung up, a knot already starting to form in her gut. Hopefully, the bride-to-be would find a style she wanted for her bridesmaids fairly early. She had no preferences and would be fine with whatever Kerri, Jordan and Jen wanted. No doubt she'd look fat no matter what was chosen.

"Was that my daughter?" Mrs. Masters appeared out of nowhere, a happy expression lighting her face as she set a big box on the outside table.

"Yes," she replied, putting on her brightest smile. "We're going dress shopping for the wedding. Are you going, too?"

Her client shook her head. "No, dear. I was with Kerri when she picked out her gown. We also checked out a few designs for you girls to try on. I'm sure you'll all be happy with whatever you pick."

Doubtful. "Okay, then once I'm finished with the verbena, I'll leave the rest of the planting to my foreman." She pointed to the box. "Is that something for the backyard, too?"

"No," Mrs. Masters said. "It's for—"

"Me," Kade finished, coming around the side of the house, sexy as sin in jeans, cowboy boots, and soft blue T-shirt.

Her heart rocked in her chest. She hadn't seen or heard from the guy in three days. Hadn't even run into him on her early morning visits to Shadow Rock to ride her horse. Yeah, they were both busy, but still, no word, no sightings…nothing. Not since they'd made out on his living room floor. Hungry and hunk-deprived, her gaze devoured the man. He looked good. Damn him. She was immediately conscious of the dirt coating her clothes and arms. Probably her face, too.

"Kade, hi." The older woman smiled, patting the box. "Thanks for coming to pick up these extra stockings. I know the holidays are months away, but I was rearranging stuff in the garage, getting ready for Sunday's party when I came across the box."

"No problem, Mrs. Masters. The FSG is already getting donations for this year's holiday party. The cowboy boot stockings were a big hit overseas last year, and they'll be just as big a hit with the kids this year. Thank you so much," he said, giving the woman a big hug.

Brandi's heart cracked open watching the two embrace. She rubbed her chest and fought back tears she didn't understand. The Family Support Group, she understood. Donations, she understood, but the ache in her chest made no damn sense. She inhaled and steadied her pulse while the man had his back to her and couldn't witness her weakness.

Ed had despised her bouts of weakness. Browbeat her over her *silly* tendencies, so she'd learned to curb them. But, since being around this handsome, sweetheart of a Texan with haunted, yet mesmerizing gray eyes, her flaws had resurfaced.

Kade released the older woman and stepped back.

"Let me get you some iced tea," her client said and disappeared into the house before the man had a chance to reply.

Turning around, he hit Brandi with a steady gaze. Her pulse hiccupped on cue.

"Hi," she said, not exactly sure where they stood, but not one to be ignorant either.

He walked over to her, a hint of a smile tugging those sexy lips of his. "Hi," he replied, lifting his hand to brush a thumb across her cheek. "You got a little something there."

Heat rushed to her face, and other parts she ignored. "Thanks, but it was probably for naught since I'm not through planting and will no doubt replace what you just wiped off."

He chuckled, the deep sound tingling her neck and tips of those other parts she was still ignoring. The man was too damn potent.

Thank goodness his phone rang. She was on the verge of melting at his feet.

"Sorry," he said, fishing the cell from his jean pocket.

Glancing at the screen, he stiffened and all of the sparkle left his eyes. Alarm immediately shot down her spine.

"Hello? Yes, this is him." He pivoted on his heel and strode toward the house. "No, I'm glad you called. Sure, I can meet you."

Grabbing the box with one hand, he nodded to her and Mrs. Masters, who came out of the house with a tray of drinks, then turned and disappeared the way he had come.

Her client looked at her and frowned. "Who was that, my dear?"

Brandi shrugged. "I've no idea."

An hour later, showered, changed and headed to meet Kerri, Jordan and Jen at the restaurant, she was still pondering that question. Kade had seemed leery at the caller, and perhaps surprised, but not angry or upset.

And as she drove past Foster's on her way to the Texas-Pub, Brandi understood exactly why the guy had taken off in such a hurry. Why wouldn't he? His haste made a whole hell of a lot of sense when she caught a glimpse of him eating ice cream and laughing with a very pretty redhead.

Chapter Seven

Shock.

Surprise.

Both emotions had shot through Kade and stiffened his spine the second he'd received the call from Shayla Ryan. He never expected to hear from her again.

Last spring, without anyone's knowledge, he'd made a trip up north to visit Sergeant Nylan's fiancée, just to make sure she and her baby were doing okay. The woman had thanked him for his open offer to help should something arise, but insisted they were fine and politely showed him the door.

Now, she was in Harland County, with her year-old daughter, in need of protection from her abusive, ex-con father. And he sure as shit was going to give it to her.

"I'm sorry to be such a burden," the pretty redhead said, ire sparkling in her blue eyes. "Believe me, Sergeant Dalton, if it were just me I had to worry about, there's no way I'd be here."

"It's all right," he reassured as they sat at a corner picnic table drinking milk shakes, the location of her daughter and sister still a mystery. All he knew was they were somewhere nearby. With only one hotel in town, he was pretty sure the mystery was solved. "I'm glad you called. I can help."

"Thank you. Like I said, I don't know if he'll find us." She rubbed her arms as she stared out over the ocean. "Maybe I'm being overly cautious."

"No such thing."

She nodded and returned her attention to her

milkshake. The woman was tough. He got the sense she'd been through hell. His stomach clenched. And the latest was his fault. Her dead fiancé.

"Anyway. I wasn't sure what else to do. My sister is twenty-three and finally in her first year of college. I don't want her to drop out. That man has ruined our lives enough."

It stopped now. Shoulders set, he stared at the woman, determined to help. "Moving here is smart. Your sister will be able to stay in school and commute from Harland County. And if he bother's to track you down, I'm a phone call away."

She nodded again, some of the tension leaving her shoulders.

"And I know of the perfect place for you to stay."

Her gaze grew weary. "Where? And don't say on your ranch, because I refuse to bring my problems to your door. Bad enough I'm invading your town."

Kade smiled. He liked her gumption. Sort of reminded him of a redheaded Jordan. "No, it's actually right down the road. A nice two-bedroom apartment above a restaurant owned by some friends of mine." He pointed to the Texas-Republic and added, "Female friends. One's a former L.A. cop."

Shayla's chin lifted, showing her interest.

"Her name's Jordan McCall. The other is her sister Kerri Masters. She's a world renowned chef."

"And they just happened to have an apartment available?"

Okay, still skeptical.

"Yes. Kerri used to live there, but recently got engaged and moved out." He stood to throw his empty cup in the garbage, then turned to the frowning woman. "We can go talk to them now, if you want."

She slowly rose to her feet, reluctance ruling her movements. "I don't know. I don't want charity, and it looks like there's a bar. I'm not sure that's the best place for us."

"There's a separate entrance out back. As a matter of fact, you have to go through two doors to get to the apartment. It's pretty secure," he said, mentally running scenarios through his head. "Why don't we go check it out and you can judge for yourself. Choice is yours."

"I don't like people knowing my business."

He held up a hand. "Not a problem. I'm not saying a word. Just making the introductions. You'll take it from there."

The more he thought about it, the more comfortable he felt. Yes, the place was a good fit for the women. Apparently she thought so, too, because Shayla got in her own car and followed him to the restaurant. Now, he just hoped the girls were back from their dress shopping.

When he opened the door and she stepped inside, he could hear laughter emanating from the kitchen. Looked like they were in luck.

"The place doesn't open until four in the afternoon," he explained on their way through the darkened restaurant.

Pushing the swinging kitchen door open, he waited for Shayla to enter then followed her into the room.

"Hi, Kade."

"Cuz."

"Sheriff."

Three out of four women shouted greetings. The only one he had a special greeting for, remained silent, a pinched look about her face as if she was in pain. He wondered briefly if the designer's arm or head was still giving her problems, but then her expression cleared and she smiled.

"Ladies." He nodded. "This is Shayla. Shayla, this is Kerri, Jordan, Jen, and Brandi." He pointed to each woman as he introduced them. "Shayla is looking for a place to stay, and I know you're looking to rent the apartment."

"Yes." Kerri smiled.

"Absolutely. Come on. We'll give you the tour," Jordan said, ushering Kerri and Shayla out the back in a matter of seconds.

Jen walked over to him and gave him a hug. "Nice to see you, hun." She released him and turned to the silent woman. "Bye, Brandi."

Opportunity knocked. Hell yeah. He was happy for the chance to give the beauty a special, *personal* greeting.

Brandi swiped her purse from the counter and rushed forward. "Hang on, Jen. I'll leave with you. I have to get back to work."

And just like that, Kade was alone.
What the hell?

The prospect of finding new clients gave Brandi the push she needed to attend the Masters' party. She knew they were excited about their renovated backyard and wanted to show it off, but for some reason, the luster of, well, anything just kind of disappeared lately. Why? Complete mystery. No idea.

Just like the bathing suit she let the girls talk her into buying on their shopping excursion earlier in the week. Along with a few other items. She was such a pushover. Why had she allowed them to persuade her to purchase a brown two-piece? She hadn't worn a bikini in almost ten years. And she wasn't going to wear one now. No way.

That's why she'd *accidentally* left the bag in the store. *Ah, what a shame. No hot tub for her today.*

Brandi smiled as she parked the truck—newly released from the repair shop that morning—behind the long line of cars in the driveway. She'd just have to make do with networking and socializing, since the Masters were sweet enough to set the get-together up.

Following a crowd of newcomers into the house, Brandi was amazed at the turnout she spied out back through the floor-to-ceiling windows in the great room. People mingled, drinks in one hand, plate of food in the other, loaded with entrées and mouthwatering pastries from a table set up along the house.

"There you are."

She turned to find Kerri, where else, but in the kitchen.

"You look great," the cook continued. "I'm glad you decided to go with the orange and white sundress. It's perfect."

God, she hoped so. She'd only modeled several last night for Kerri and Jordan when they'd dropped by, thanks to her panicked *help-I-don't-have-anything-to-wear-tomorrow* phone call.

"Thanks. It smells like heaven in here," she said, heading into the aroma zone. Garlic, butter, BBQ…hot sauce? As usual, her friend cooked up a storm. Fruits and vegetables lined the counter, begging to be touched. So, she did, procuring a grape. "Need any help?"

Kerri shook her head. "Nope. You've done your work. Go reap the rewards." The grinning brunette pointed outside. "Your fans await."

Brandi laughed. "I don't know about that," she said, popping the grape into her mouth, gaze falling to the crowd of people outside.

"I do. Everyone's raving about the yard, wanting to talk to you about ponds and gardens and water features." Kerri smiled. "And a certain sheriff is here, too."

Her stomach instantly knotted. Damn. Okay. She knew the guy would probably show up. He was very good friends with the Masters. She just wasn't sure she was up to seeing him laughing and having fun with another girl. Even though they only kissed a few times…really, really good kisses, mind boggling kisses…they never staked a claim. Heck, she didn't *want* to stake a claim, so she had no right to feel whatever the hell she was feeling about Kade and that redhead. It was stupid, and she was going to put it behind her right now and mingle.

"There's my girl," Mrs. Masters said, rushing in from the patio. "Come on. Everyone's asking about you. I have a ton of people to introduce you to."

Four hours later, Brandi congratulated herself for a job well done. Not only had she gotten several possible jobs, she'd networked, discovering a wonderful local artist who fired handmade tile, a welder, furniture maker and a glass blower. Plus, she avoided the hot tub and any mention of bathing suits.

Then there was Kade.

Hotness personified. In jeans and white button-down shirt with the sleeves rolled up, the man made her mouth water. Still, she managed to not embarrass herself in front of him. Small miracle. He was there—minus the redhead—laughing, talking, looking sexy and at ease. Maybe he was meeting the woman later. In their love nest. Above the restaurant.

She needed a drink.

No she didn't. Stopping mid-stride toward the outdoor bar, she turned to find Jordan staring thoughtfully at her. Ah hell. Not good. Bulldog McCall was on alert.

Maybe she needed that drink after all.

"Okay, Brandi. It's time," Jordan said, walking toward her with two glasses filled with red liquid and mouth-watering lemon, lime and strawberry slices.

Time? She frowned. "For what?"

"For getting in that hot tub," the woman replied, handing her one of the refreshments. "The guests have gone, the tub is empty. Time to enjoy the fruits of your labor."

She laughed and sipped her drink. Mmm…sangria. Kerri's sangria. "No can do," she said, thrilled to have a legitimate excuse. "I don't have a suit. I must've left it at the store or something."

Her friend's smile broadened. "You did, but not to worry, they called Kerri."

"Kerri? B-but why?" Her frown returned.

"She has an account there, and they remembered us telling you how much you looked like Marilyn in that bikini."

More sangria slid down her throat. *Just shoot me now.*

"So, you see? It's all good. The three of us can slip into our suits, then the hot tub, and enjoy our sangrias."

Brandi had to admit, that sounded like heaven. She glanced around, noting the older McCalls and Masters sitting near a small grove of trees in the far corner of the yard, watching Cole, Connor, Kade and Kevin playing horseshoes in the pit she'd specially designed.

Jordan slid an arm around her shoulders and guided her into the house. "Your suit's in Kerri's old room, you know the way. We'll meet you in the tub."

Run. Complain of a headache, stomach ache, which

technically, they both did…ache, but she was never good at running. Besides, that hot tub had called to her all week. Beckoned and teased from a backyard that turned out incredible.

The huge patio had an outdoor fireplace near a wrought iron seating area topped with decadent red cushions, and the hot tub steamed in the corner where she'd installed a retractable awning. Pavers dotted the yard, leading to different sections—a grassy area, koi pond, flower garden, vegetable garden. The team did a great job. She did a great job, and *dammit*, she deserved to relax in that tub with her friends. The remainder of her sangria slid coolly down her throat. Yes. It would be wonderful to soak all the hard work of bending, lifting, planting, out of her sore bones.

Five minutes later, courage wrapped around her like a blanket, Brandi walked out onto the patio in nothing but her brown bikini.

And her refreshed glass of sangria.

Kade was hot.

And bothered.

And *son-of-a-bitch*, he couldn't feel his tongue. Must be somewhere near his feet since his jaw hit the hardwood floor the second a certain sexy designer stepped onto the patio in a mouthwatering display of curves and cleavage. *Bombshell*. Exactly what the woman was, because she certainly blasted his libido into overdrive.

He stopped dead, unsure whether to give his position away or retreat as the three oblivious bikini-clad women slipped into the bubbling water. They must've been upstairs changing when he'd stepped inside to use the bathroom. Now, he was in a bit of a bind.

"See? You look just fine, Brandi," Kerri proclaimed, waving a hand at the woman sliding neck deep into the water.

Better than fine. She was damn fine. She was downright mouthwatering.

Jordan smiled. "You'd give Marilyn a run for her money in that bikini."

"If you say so." The designer shrugged, sounding far from convinced.

"Okay, spill." The cook folded her arms across her chest and stared pointedly at the woman. "Who was he?"

Brandi blinked. "Who was who?"

"The guy who did a number on your self esteem," Kerri replied. "And don't say no one, because I've been there."

The bombshell sipped her drink, brown eyes widening. "You have?"

"Yes." Her friend nodded.

Kade thought about retreating again, and possibly going out the front door, then around the side of the house. This conversation was not meant for his ears.

"My former husband," Kerri replied. "I thought he was cheating on me because I'd done something wrong. Turns out it wasn't me at all."

"Oh, mine is different." The designer laughed without mirth. "I'm pretty sure it was me."

He stilled, his gut clenching at the sound of self-loathing in her tone.

"How can you be sure?" Jordan questioned.

"Because he said, and I quote, '*I don't find you attractive anymore, Brandi. You're too fat.*'"

"That prick!"

"What a bastard!"

Shock rushed through Kade in a heated frenzy and

his fists shook in silent rage. She'd said something about her ex the other day, but he thought it had been the painkillers talking. *Christ.* The sisters were both right. Brandi's ex was a no-good, prick bastard who didn't deserve the designer's sweetness. Or any woman.

"Oh, hun, I'm so sorry," Kerri reached out to take Brandi's hand. "I hope you know that he was a big jerk. If he cared about you, your size should *not* have mattered."

A small smile tugged the beauty's lips. "That's what Kade said."

"And he's right." Jordan nodded before downing the rest of her drink.

Damn straight.

He was also done. Kade had heard enough. Made him sick to think he and that fucker wore the same uniform. It was time to show the woman just how attractive he found her lush body. He wasn't looking for a commitment. He wasn't looking for a relationship, but he sure as shit could treat the woman how she deserved to be treated.

"Not so sure Kade still thinks it." She sighed and looked down at her hands.

Kerri frowned? "Why not?"

"Well…if he did…then why…what was he doing with the redhead?"

Ah hell. She thought… He blew out a breath. *It probably did seem odd.*

"Shayla?" Jordan's brow rose. "Trust me. Kade would never get involved with her."

"Why not? She's stunning and thin…and stunning."

Really? The designer really didn't know how beautiful she was?

"*And* the fiancée of the soldier who died," his

friend's wife stated.

Brandi's inhaled breath reached his ears. "Oh..."

"Yeah, so trust me," Jordan said. "Kade is not interested in her that way. But you...oh yeah."

He nodded with a smile. Exactly. And it was time he made his attraction to her perfectly clear.

The guys and their game of horseshoes forgotten, Kade strode to his truck to retrieve the swim suit on his front seat, only one thought in his mind...

Showing Brandi Wyne how a real man appreciated a woman with curves.

The hot tub was a good idea. For the first time in days, Brandi was relaxed and enjoying some *me* time...after they got off the subject of her and onto discussing the upcoming wedding. All it took was one question asked on her part, and boom, subject changed. Still, she was glad the girls had talked her into buying the suit. Glad they talked her into the tub, too. The bubbling water soothed her troubles away with a warm, encompassing hug. Just what the doctor ordered. Her eyes fluttered closed, and she sighed.

It had been a crazy week of work, annual blood tests and throat ultrasound for her upcoming thyroid checkup, dress shopping, incredible, mind-blowing kisses...

"Got room for more?"

No. Her gaze shot open, heart rocking into her ribs, sending the butterflies in her stomach into a frenzy. Four lean, muscled, nearly naked cowboys smiled as they neared. *Oh, Lordy.* The tub fit four comfortably. Seven would be snug. Very snug.

And the urge to snuggle into the very fit, approaching sheriff trembled through her. Damn, the ripped man made her scalp sweat, and body quiver with a need to taste and explore his delicious, broad, muscular terrain with her mouth. And tongue. There wasn't an ounce of fat on him.

Too bad she harbored enough for them both.

"Absolutely."

Of course, Jordan would be the first to answer. And even stood to make more room. What did the former cop care? The smiling woman was trim and curvy and gorgeous.

Her stomach knotted. She should've gotten out while she had the chance. *Oh, lovely*. Now her other friend was standing. And why not? Kerri was tight and…and…perfect.

No way in hell was she getting up. No way. They could all just squeeze in. She was not moving, except…maybe to slink further into the water.

"Well now, ain't this cozy?" Connor smiled as everyone settled into the water.

Crazy was a better description for being sandwiched between the virile cowboy and hunky sheriff. She glanced at the bubbles, grateful the swirling water hid her body from view. It didn't, however, hide her body from touch. And with the cramped quarters, touch was impossible to avoid.

Funny how a simple brush here and there with Connor was just that. Simple.

Kade, on the other hand… That man made her right side tingle and body heat on contact. And she was already hot from the spa.

"But…hey." Kevin frowned as he sat between his cousin and the stairs. "I'm the odd one out."

"No." Cole laughed. "You're just odd."

Brandi laughed with the others, not just because it was funny, but because of the pout on the gorgeous, blue-eyed Adonis' face.

Kevin leaned back and grinned. "You're just jealous."

"Of what?" Cole shifted Jordan until she sat across his lap, arm slung around his neck.

The cowboy's smile faded. "Never mind."

Again, everyone laughed, and Brandi tried to relax. None of the guys looked at her with disgust in their gazes. They were friendly and warm. Except for Kade. Every time she snuck a glance, the sheriff glanced right back, his mesmerizing gaze hot...and interested.

Her whole body was tingling under his scrutiny. And the damn bubbles weren't helping. They tickled her tingling good parts, enhancing her body's reaction to the man. The man whose deliciously calloused hand was now tracing light circles on her thigh. God, she could scarcely breathe.

"Brandi, this yard looks fantastic," Cole was saying. "I'm excited to have you finish our master suite, and think maybe we might contract you to do our back yard, if you can pencil us in."

Her mind had formulated plenty of scenarios for their backyard having stared down at the barren area while working in their house this past week. And she would've been happy to relate that information, except she still couldn't find her breath. She nodded instead.

A big, warm, wonderful hand lightly squeezed her knee. "How'd you make out today? Any prospects?"

She turned her head, and Kade's open, smiling, hopeful gaze made her dizzy. And confused. Was he seeing that redhead? If so, why was he flirting with her? He didn't seem the type to toy with two women at the same time. But, maybe she was just blinded by lust and couldn't see the real man.

"Brandi?"

Her inability to breathe was now affecting her sight. Great. Can you say loser? She finally found a hunky guy who wasn't repelled by her body and she couldn't even communicate. Or breathe. That was going to be a problem. Damn, it was hot. And they were shaded by the retractable awning they'd opened.

"Brandi," Kade repeated, his tone a little more urgent.

The next thing she knew, he lifted her out of the water and carried her dripping, jiggling body to a nearby chaise.

Mmm...he felt good, all hot and hard and wet.

"Brandi?"

She blinked, and drew in a breath. If it weren't so embarrassing, this moment would almost be perfect.

"Jordan, Kerri, are there any sports drinks here?" he asked.

She closed her eyes against the spinning sky. A second later, she felt the soft cushions of the chaise beneath her as someone shoved a bottle in her hand and helped her drink. It was blessedly cool and quite tasty. Raspberry. She liked raspberries.

"That's it. Keep drinking," Kade encouraged in a tone both soothing and commanding.

Is that how he sounded to the horses? At this point, she'd do anything he asked. Run around a pasture. Hop a fence. Jump him... A few more gulps and colors and shapes came into view.

"There you are," he said, gentle hand feeling her forehead.

His touch was like heaven, chocolate heaven—all warm and delicious...wait...

She inhaled then blew out the breath. "How many

calories was that?"

He chuckled, amusement chasing the worry from his gaze. "Yep, you're back."

She glanced at the other concerned faces, noting the older couples had joined in the vigil. Oh, goodie. Heat surged into her cheeks. *If you're going to make a fool out of yourself, might as well do it in front of everyone.* "I'm good."

"You sure?" Kerri frowned over her. "You're awfully red still."

Brandi nodded. "Not to worry, this shade is brought to you courtesy of embarrassment."

"Nothing to be embarrassed about," Jordan said. "It's a hot day, in a hot tub. Add in the sangria and it was the perfect cocktail for dehydration."

"Yeah," Kade agreed, smiling down at her. "It could've happened to any one of us."

She forgot to mention his nearness, unwavering interest, mouthwatering muscles. Then there were his hands. Cripes, her knees hadn't had that much attention from anyone or anything except maybe a razor for years. One touch and every cell in her body had clamored and yearned for more.

"Well, as long as everything is okay, we're going to go," Mrs. McCall said. "There's an outdoor concert in Galveston."

"Yeah, we want to get good seats." Mrs. Masters nodded. "You all stay and have fun."

Galveston. She envied them. Over the past several months, she'd visited the pretty, gulf city to attend a few of their wonderful outdoor concerts. Alone. She wanted to enjoy the symphonies without explaining her acquaintance to some of the musicians she ran into that, once-upon-a-time, she used to accompany. It was such a joy to be anonymous, and a patron on the opposite side of the coin.

"Have you ridden your horse yet today?"

She blinked at Kade, surprised by the question. "N-no."

"Want to get out of here?" His voice was low and incredibly sexy.

So sexy, her body began to hum.

"I… Okay."

Twenty minutes later, stuffed back into her sundress, Brandi chewed her lower lip as she drove to Shadow Rock, wondering if she was out of her ever loving mind.

Kade decided to follow rather than lead the bombshell to his ranch. He wasn't stupid. Sure, the woman was attracted to him, but Brandi was also leery and battling low self-esteem. He intended to nullify both concerns. Today.

When she parked near the stables instead of the ranch, he knew he was going to have to tread carefully. Despite the hunger he'd seen in her gaze, the designer was nervous. He'd take it slow, let her have the lead. He would never force her into doing something she didn't want to do.

Parking next to her, he got out, smiling to himself when she remained in her truck. At least she'd cut the engine. She was too cute. If the poor woman was really that nervous, he was fine with just riding horses.

Now, if only he could get his body on the same page. The image of her falling out of that sexy-as-hell bathing suit was still wrecking havoc with his groin.

He opened her door and held out a hand. The combination of heat and anxiety darkening her gaze hit him with the force of a physical blow. His grip tightened on the truck.

"Come with me," he said, pleased when she took his hand without hesitation. And because he couldn't resist, he added, "I want to show you something in the barn."

Bypassing the boarding stables and the hustle of activity at the training arena, Kade led Brandi to the quiet barn set off to the side. Without a word, the woman walked with him, hand in hand, no indication she wanted to tug free. He held tight, relishing the feel of their entwined fingers. She was a vision in her white and orange dress, caramel waves falling past her shoulders, skin glowing from her time in the sun, emphasizing those big, brown eyes. The woman took his breath, and he was glad she agreed to come with him.

"Have you been in here lately?" he asked as they walked inside the quiet stable.

She glanced at him and shook her head, small smile playing about those sweet lips of hers. "No. Not since our...incident, which I really am sorry about."

"I know," he said, squeezing her hand. "And I think you might be surprised."

He stopped in front of the stall where the image of her bent over flashed through his mind, as it had every damn day since their *incident*. Her sweet, blue jean clad ass had fueled many late night fantasies.

"Oh, Kade..."

It took him a moment to realize the breathless endearment had been real and not one of his fantasies. She squeezed his hand before releasing to step up to the stall door and peer closer.

"She looks so much better." Glancing over her shoulder, the woman hit him with an over-bright brown gaze full of emotion. "You certainly have a healing touch."

He shrugged, and leaned next to her against the stall. "Nah. She just needed care and respect."

A single tear rolled down her face as the beauty turned to him and nodded. "Guess all creatures do."

Gut tightening as if punched, he felt his heart snag in a rare occurrence. There was just something special about this woman. He lifted a finger to wipe away the tear.

"We all need healing," he said softly.

She stepped closer, brushing her lips across his palm poised near her face. "Even you."

"Me? I'm fine." No way was he delving into that darkness. Brandi and her gorgeous body were much more appealing. Made him feel alive. He trailed his finger across her cheek. "In fact, I'm feeling pretty good right about now."

She smiled. "Me, too."

"Good." He twirled a piece of hair around his finger and tugged her closer. "Let's see if we can improve on that."

With his heart knocking a hell of a beat against his ribs, he covered her mouth with his and found what he hadn't known he was missing. Satisfaction. Completion. Something sappy and sentimental, but he didn't care. Her lips drew a response from him like no other, fulfilling more than just a physical need. He probably would've run like hell if he hadn't been so caught up in the embrace.

Warm hands slid up his chest to settle at the base of his head as she leaned into the kiss, fingers lightly brushing his neck in a back and forth motion. Killing him. He groaned and dropped his hands to her luscious ass. Her curves felt good in his palms, amazing, even better than he'd fantasized. She moaned, and *sweet Jesus*, rocked against him, stretching his erection to full tilt.

He broke for air, brushing his lips down the curve of her neck. "Damn, you feel good. I want to be inside you."

She shook in his arms. "Y-you drive me crazy."

"Ditto." He smiled, holding her ass while he pressed against her.

She drew back to stare at him, eyes dark and heated, making him just a little nuts.

"I...before this goes any further, I think we need to talk."

Ah hell. The *talk*. Damn, he hoped to God she didn't bring up the 'r' word, because he didn't do relationships. But, if that was what she was expecting, it was best he heard now and set her straight.

He loosened his hold, but couldn't bring himself to release her fine ass. "Okay."

She inhaled. "I guess I just need to know what we're doing."

"Well now, I think that's obvious." He chuckled, pressing their lower halves together.

She inhaled again. "No...I know that." A small laugh broke from her throat. "I mean you and me."

Shit.

"Look, I don't want to hurt your feelings or anything, Kade," she rushed to say. "But I'm not looking for a relationship. And I don't think you are either. I just started a new job. You just started a new job. There is no room for a relationship. That's a complication I can do without right now, and I think the same goes for you."

He blinked, happily surprised by her words. "Yes, I completely agree."

"Good." This time she released a breath, and played with the front of his shirt. "But I've never just had sex. I don't know. I mean, can we just do that…have sex…without a relationship?"

A smile tugged his lips. God, she was adorable. "Yes, as long as we both know that's all it is upfront. Then no one gets hurt. I want you, Brandi, very much so. And unless I'm reading you wrong, you want me, too. So, now that we both know neither of us is looking for a commitment, we'll be fine."

She cocked her head as if thinking, then nodded. "I guess you're right. We can have it this one time. No one will get hurt. And no one else has to know."

"If that's how you want it, no one has to know. Both my cousins are away for the night. Kevin got a call as we were leaving the party. He was meeting some flight attendant he knows at his apartment in Houston." He brought his hands to her hips and bent at the knee to peer into her eyes. "But, honey, let me assure you, we will be *'having it'* more than once today."

"W-we will?"

"Hell yeah," he said and, unable to resist, he leaned in to spread kisses against her collarbone. "Starting right now."

"H-here? B-but someone will see…" She clutched his shirt and moaned.

He continued to kiss her neck, nipping at the soft spot behind her ear. "No one comes into this barn but me and Brock. He's at his grandmother's with Jen and Cody this weekend."

She trembled against him, her hands under his shirt now, stroking his back. He loved the feel of her flesh against his, and longed to get them both naked. But not yet. Not here. He somehow didn't think she was comfortable enough with her body to expose it in a semi-public place…in the daylight.

But he would make damn sure she'd remember the barn.

Placing kisses on her jaw, he made his way back to her mouth and upped the heat of their embrace. She sighed into him, and the touch of her tongue kicked his pulse clear out of Harland County. Damn, the woman was potent. He groaned and dragged her body close, exploring her mouth, plunging deep and long, enjoying her equally thorough response.

She was hot and soft and shaking in his arms, and heaven help him, he needed more. Backing them up to a stack of hay bales in an empty stall, he continued to kiss and caress the trembling woman until air became a necessity.

He drew back and stared down at the panting woman. "I need to touch you, Brandi."

Brown eyes, hazed with desire, blinked at him. "I—I don't know about here." She bit her lower lip and glanced around.

He gently grabbed her chin and turned her to face him. "It's okay. You don't have to get naked if you don't want."

"I'd rather not…but how…"

He smiled and pulled her close. "Much better to show than tell."

Capturing her mouth, he enjoyed her eager response as she drank him in, sucking on his lower lip, driving him beyond nuts and straight to psycho. He groaned and ran his hands over the front of her dress, cupping both breasts, brushing his thumbs back and forth across her peaked nipples until she moaned and shook in his hands.

Oh, hell, yeah.

He wanted to do that for so long, and only wished he could taste them, but it would have to wait until later.

Right now, he had a mission. Releasing her, he took her hand and sat back on a stack of hay, three feet off the ground.

"Turn around," he said, gripping her hips to help her sit on his lap. "Now, just relax. I've got you." Once he started to kiss her neck, he felt her back relax against his chest and she sighed.

"But I can't touch you."

He glanced down over her shoulder and watched as he reached around to cup her gorgeous chest. Heat skittered down his spine. Damn, she was stacked and hot. "Trust me, honey, you are," he said, brushing his thumbs over the peaks demanding attention.

She let out an unintelligible sound and pressed back against him, giving him better access to her throat—which he took—and her breasts—which he also took. Slipping a hand inside the opening of her top, he cupped her generous, soft flesh and pinched her peak, fighting the rush of need heating his body. This was not about him. This was about Brandi, and he intended to take care of the woman.

While sliding his free hand down her hip and thigh, he transferred his kisses to her other shoulder and began to bunch up her skirt. She stiffened.

"Shh… Relax. Close your eyes," he soothed.

After a moment's hesitation, she did, her hands reaching behind her to grip his hips. Taking that as a green light, he snuck his hand under her skirt and caressed her hot, trembling thigh, nearly coming undone when he slid a finger under her panties and found her wet.

"You're soaked."

She nodded against his shoulder. "Kade, I—I need…"

"I know," he reassured, and at his first stroke, she jerked back, nearly setting him off.

Eyes closed, he counted to ten backwards, then slipped his finger inside her slick warmth. Her moan shook through him all the way to his boots. She felt good. So damn good. In and out, he slid his finger in slow, sure strokes. She opened wider and, releasing her breast, he took advantage of the silent invitation. Bringing his other hand to her thighs, he relished the heat emanating from within and added a finger.

"Kade…" She jerked back again. "I can't…"

"Don't hold on. Come for me, Brandi," he urged, his voice hoarse with need from the beautiful, responsive woman thrusting against his hands.

And a second later, with two fingers sliding in and out of her heat, he brushed his thumb over her center and she burst, his name flowing from her lips in a drawn out, sensual moan.

God, he'd never heard or felt anything so incredible.

Letting her down easy, he slowed his strokes, then pulled out to hold her gently against him. And as she worked to get her breathing under control, he used the time to talk his body out of exploding. *Hell*, he wanted release inside her body, not in his damn jeans.

Chapter Eight

When her vision returned and she came back down to herself, Brandi twisted to stare at Kade. Her pulse hiccupped. The man stole her breath. Heat smoldered in his gaze, giving him a rakish, dangerous appearance. He was damn hot. It was a miracle the bales they sat on didn't burst into flames.

"I'm speechless…and legless." She glanced down at her body. "Are they still there? Because I can't feel them."

He chuckled. "Oh, they're here," he said, reaching down to stroke her thighs.

Her heart thudded in her chest at the thought of what he was going to do to her next, and at what she wanted to do to him. But not here. She slapped away his tempting hand then fixed her panties before she stood. Good, she didn't fall. Enough strength returned to hold her upright.

Positioning herself between his legs, she trailed her hands up his thighs and leaned in to kiss him full on the lips. He needed little encouragement because he took over, crushing her close and deepening the kiss to mind-drugging proportions. And oh, look at that, she couldn't feel her legs again.

He drew back without warning, and rested his forehead to hers. "Okay, we…" He cleared his throat. "We're going to have to save that thought until we're inside the ranch."

She nodded, unable to speak. Inside the ranch was good. Inside her was even better, but inside her inside the ranch worked best.

Warm fingers entwined with hers as they walked to the house, whinnies and neighs echoing in the distance along with an occasional command from one of the ranch hands. The late afternoon air was hot with little to no breeze, and she was immediately grateful for the climate controlled barn they'd just vacated.

"Thirsty?" he asked as they entered the ranch, central air humming in the background.

"Yeah."

She was parched. The guy had dried her throat ever since he'd stepped into the hot tub, all those muscles and ridges begging for attention. And now, praise be, she was about to get the chance.

Still holding her hand, he led them into the kitchen she'd always admired while visiting and babysitting. Open and big, with a swinging door, state of the art appliances, a cute breakfast nook, large butcher-block island, it held so much charm she could see a family grow up happy there. Young Cody was lucky.

"What would you like?" He held the refrigerator open for her perusal.

Her first instinct was *him*, but she caught herself. Ed hadn't liked that stuff and, although she was trying not to compare Kade to the jerk, she just didn't want to presume his likes, either.

"Water, please."

He swiped two from the shelf, passed one to her, then downed his bottle while he watched her drink. It boggled the mind how her throat could be dry during the act of drinking. She lowered and capped her water, and forced air into her lungs. His gaze was deliciously dark and heated.

"You're not going to drink the whole thing now, are you?"

She shook her head. Voice low and full of need, the damn man robbed her of speech again.

"Good, because I'm dying here, hun. I'd never last."

With that, he grabbed her water, set it on the counter...then tossed her over his shoulder and strode out of the kitchen.

"Kade? What are you doing?"

"*You*, in a few minutes."

"I'm too heavy. Put me down. I'll hurt you."

He laughed. "Bullshit, honey. What you are, and what you *think* you are, are way off base." Then he slapped her ass.

"Hey!"

His laughter increased. "Keep putting yourself down and I'll keep smacking your ass."

"You're crazy." She laughed, a carefree, reckless feeling taking over. "What if I like it?"

That stopped him in his tracks. "Then heaven help us both," he said, before he continued to carry her down the hall and into a room blissfully dark, until he flicked on the light.

Dammit.

Kicking the door shut behind him, he slid her down his very hot, very hard body. By the time her feet hit the floor, Brandi was sweating in places that didn't sweat.

"Finally," he breathed into her mouth, cupping her face and kissing her crazy mad.

She shuddered and pressed into him against the door. He was hard. Deliciously hard. Every inch. Slipping her hands under his shirt, she reveled in the fact his stomach quivered under her touch. And she touched, *oh, hell yeah*, she touched, stroking the ridges in his flat stomach, feeling slightly guilty because hers was not.

But then he broke the kiss. She wasted no time

pushing his shirt up, and leaned in to lick his collarbone.

"Son-of-a..."

He yanked the confining T-shirt off and she inhaled at the sight. He was glorious...and hers. But when she made to step closer to continue her lick fest, he grabbed her upper arms and held her back.

"Oh, no. It's my turn."

Without warning, he grasped the hem of her skirt and ripped the dress up and over her head, leaving her standing there in bra and panties.

In broad daylight.

Under the gorgeous, magnificently ripped man's scrutiny.

She glanced down, slightly relieved her intimate apparel matched. Too bad it was all white. And too bad she spilled over in spots.

He inhaled and blew out the breath. "You are so beautiful."

Before his comment registered, he hauled her over his shoulder again. A startled breath whooshed out of her lungs as the strong, sexy man strode to the bed and dropped her on the mattress.

Standing at the foot of the bed, he stared down at her, gaze smoldering, breathing ragged. Her good parts tingled and beckoned.

As if he knew, he crawled over her, a sexy smile spreading across his face. "You've got great bounce," he said, before kissing her to within an inch of insanity.

Then he released her mouth to zero in on the spot behind her ear that made her clutch his back and moan. Damn, he knew her well. Normally, she would've wondered how but, right now, it didn't matter. Nothing mattered but this incredible man who didn't seem to care about her jiggling. In fact, he appeared to embrace her curves. And a second later, he did.

"This has to go," he said, kissing her shoulder as he slid her lacey straps down her arms. "Lift up."

When she did, he unhooked the back and tugged the bra free, tossing it onto the floor. Unable to hold that position, Brandi lay back on the bed, mesmerized at the hunger heating his gaze as he watched her breasts bounce. And bounce.

"Gorgeous," he breathed, leaning on one arm, tracing light circles over her cleavage, around her nipples, driving her crazy.

Her breasts felt achy and heavy, and if he didn't grab them soon she was sure to die.

"Kade." She hated the need in her voice, but hated the ache even more.

Finally, a big, warm hand covered a breast while his mouth found the other. She cried out, but didn't care. He touched and kissed and worshipped both with equal fervor, and by the time he left them, she was wet and hot and just a bit shaky.

"I told you I was going to kiss you all over," he reminded, smoldering gaze dark with blatant need. "Twice."

He kissed a path down her chest, and when he got to her stomach, she squirmed, kind of hoping he'd skip that area. But he paid it just as much attention, caressing and kissing, slipping his tongue into her belly button. She wriggled.

"Easy, honey." His large hand covered her belly, thumb nudging under the band of her panties. "I meant *every* gorgeous inch of you."

She stilled. *He thinks my stomach is gorgeous?* Brandi lifted up to watch, shocked to find he was indeed enjoying her body. And though she knew she should probably lie back down, she didn't. Couldn't. Her gaze refused to leave the man loving her curves.

He placed hot, open-mouthed kisses across her abs to nestle and nip where her hip and waist met. Then he continued down her legs, dragging her panties with his fingers until they joined her bra on the floor. Straightening, the hunky man stood at the edge of the bed and gazed down at her completely bare and unhindered body.

He swallowed hard. And she watched in amazement as his chest heaved as if he had trouble breathing, sweat glistening on his skin, covering those gorgeous muscles with a sexy sheen.

"You, Brandi Wyne, are the most beautiful woman I've ever seen. Don't ever let me hear you say otherwise." His voice was low but firm. "This is what you and your gorgeous curves do to me."

With that, he shed the rest of his clothes and stood naked before her...gloriously naked and fully erect. *Holy hell.* Her stomach fluttered. She'd never had more than six inches before. Kade Dalton was definitely bigger than six inches.

Her mouth literally watered...and other places closer to the magnificent man. "*You* are beautiful," she told him, sitting up, reaching for him. "I need you inside me."

"Not until you tell me *you're* beautiful."

She snickered. Like *that* was going to happen.

"I'm serious," he stated and grabbed her hand to tug her off the bed and into his bathroom. "Now look."

He twisted her around to face the vanity...and mirror. Really? He wanted to bring a mirror into this right now?

"Look at yourself, Brandi." He stood behind her, running his hands down her sides until they rested on her hips. "Look at how you go in and curve out. A guy wants something to hold onto. Something soft and warm."

After she talked her stomach into settling down, she tried to see what he was seeing. Yes, she had curves. Yes, she went in at the waist. Yes, she was soft…because she never made the time to work out.

But then she noticed his fingers and how they splayed her hips…and how she *saw* his hips behind her, and his chest and shoulders. And she realized, if she could see him, that meant…she wasn't as wide as she thought.

Her gaze met his in the mirror. "Go on, Brandi. Say it."

"I-I'm not as fat as I thought."

His eyes closed and jaw clenched before his gaze found hers again. "Good, but that's not what I said." He traced a hand up over her stomach, then ribs, brushing the swell of her breast with his thumb. "How does that look to you?"

The contrast of her curves and smooth skin against his hard, tanned ridges was…

"Beautiful." She swayed into him, body quivering at the feel of his erection poking her ass and back.

He cupped her breast with one hand and slid the other hand between her legs. "And this?"

"Beautiful." Her voice shook.

She grabbed his hips and pressed back, reveling in his muttered curse. In a blink of an eye, he twisted her around and set her on the counter. She squeaked when her heated skin met the cold surface. Taking advantage of her opened mouth, he kissed her deep, and frantic and oh so hot, his tongue pressing against hers. And his hands, those talented hands skimmed down her body and legs, then lingered between her thighs to stroke until she quivered.

"I'm done," he said, fishing a condom out of a drawer, only to curse when she helped him slowly roll it on. "You're killing me."

She smiled. "I know the feeling."

Positioning himself between her legs, he grasped her hips and slowly entered the tip. *Oh, damn*, he felt good. So gloriously good. Their mutual sound of approval echoed around them. And after her body had a chance to adjust to his size, he pressed the rest of the way in.

"*Hell*…yeah…you feel incredible," he murmured, chin up, eyes closed, skin tight across his face as his expression held somewhere between ecstasy and pain.

She hugged his hips with her thighs, her body quivering around him as she laced her ankles behind his fine ass and drew him in further. His eyes snapped open and a wicked smile crossed his face.

Lordy, she nearly came undone just looking at him.

"You want more, do you?"

She nodded, unable to speak.

"Lean back a little." He bent to kiss a path up her throat, slowly thrusting in and out. "Hold onto the counter. I'm not going to last long. You feel too damn perfect."

Doing as she was told, Brandi gripped the edge and fought to hang on. The position allowed for a better angle and heat gathered inside at a crazy speed.

"So damn perfect," he said silkily, one hand squeezing her hip and ass, while the other cupped her breast.

Empowerment rushed through her body. The man made her feel like a size two supermodel—admired and accepted—when on a good day, she was lucky if she fit in a single digit dress. She was beginning to realize her perception of her weight and dress size might be *off.* Perhaps it was all right *not* to be in the single digits after all. The sexy, gorgeous guy currently enjoying her non-petite body would seem to concur. Enthusiastically.

He took her mouth in a hungry, demanding kiss that left her hot and shaking. Yeah, he was definitely enjoying this every bit as much as she was. And his stamina? *Damn*, she couldn't get over his endurance. She couldn't get over his talented hands and lips and incredibly, delicious, thrusting parts.

On the brink, she never felt so alive and on fire, and wished it could last forever. But she was close. Too damn close. So when he skimmed a hand down her chest and pinched her nipple, she broke the kiss and cried out. And as she burst for the second time that hour, she transferred her grip to his shoulders and held tight. Kade let out a low, sexy sound, thrust one last, deep, thrust and followed her over that edge.

Several hours and *sexcapades* later, Brandi opened her eyes to see dawn creeping in through the curtains with a slice of light hitting the floor. She stretched and felt the warmth of the sleeping man next to her, and what seemed like *every* muscle in her body. Chances were, she wasn't going to walk straight, but she didn't care. A smile tugged her lips as she recalled their raid on the kitchen and how *Sheriff Stamina* took her on the window seat in the bay window. She'd briefly worried about being seen, but the stables were all on the side and front of the property. And frankly, the man made her feel too damn good to care.

Then their fun moved to the game room before ending up back in Kade's bedroom, where they had sex in the shower. Jordan was right. A bench seat, a certain height off the ground, would've been ideal last night.

And since she'd never just had *sex* before, she let things get a little wild and crazy, discovering she didn't care to be shackled, and didn't really like handcuffing him, either. She enjoyed his hands touching, ravishing her body.

Glancing at the clock, she swallowed a groan and slid out of bed, careful not to wake the sexy guy who more than earned his slumber. What would he think about the night? Had the sex really been as good as she thought? Now that the light of day had arrived, trepidation began to show its ugly head. What if she had only imagined his enjoyment?

Her gaze fell on the naked man, half on, half under the covers. Long and lean, ridges she kissed and licked until he cursed and buried himself deep inside her trembling curves. God, he was gorgeous, and perfect. She turned her attention to her naked body. Not gorgeous, not perfect, but attractive enough to turn the hot sheriff's head, and make him call out her name several times.

Yeah, he enjoyed their night.

Feeling pretty good, she gathered her clothes and wondered if maybe they could do this sex thing again. But then she reached for her shoe, which had somehow gotten stuck under his duffle bag.

His *Army* duffle bag.

The liquid heat flowing through her veins cooled in an instant. He was a soldier. Their world revolved around discipline and rules, and carried strict expectations. She was not getting caught up in that again. Been there, done that, too many times. She was supposed to find and date a guy who was *not* in the military.

As great as the man made her feel, Kade was disqualified.

No matter. He'd told her he didn't want a relationship, either. And even if he hadn't, she'd seen it in his eyes. No. Last night was just sex. And only for last night. She'd leave it at that and store away the good memories.

"Now there's a sight for sore eyes."

Brandi squeaked, and turned around, clutching her things. Leaning back against the pillows, arms tucked behind his head, the handsome man watched her with a lazy smile.

Her face heated, and yes, dammit, other parts, too.

"Kade, sorry. Didn't mean to wake you."

"You trying to sneak out?"

"N-not really. Just time to go."

Ah the hell with it. She dropped her clothes on the bed and began to get dressed. Butterflies swarmed her stomach at the sound of his intake of breath. She didn't dare glance at him or her no second date, no military rules would fly out the window.

"You sure you don't want to hang around for breakfast?"

Her pulse hiccupped. "Actually, I do. That's the problem. This was supposed to be just one night of sex. If I stay, that makes it two…and is liable to change things. And we both want to stay away from the 'r' thing."

The light started to fade from his eyes. "True." He sat up. "How about we have an actual breakfast, then?"

"Thanks, but no," she said, slipping her shoes on before she stood. "I'm just going to check on my horse, then get home and change before I'm due at Jordan's for work."

"I'll walk you out."

"No," she rushed to say. "I—I think we should just

leave it here."

Being near him would...well, it wouldn't be safe. For whom? She wasn't sure.

He frowned, and for a scary moment, she thought he was going to protest, his chivalry too deeply engrained. But his expression cleared and he nodded. "Okay. Suit yourself."

She rushed to the door, then stopped and turned around. "Thanks for...uh..."

Words failed her at the moment. Seemed wrong to leave without thanking the man for making her feel good about her curves, and well, just satiated and so completely damn satisfied.

"The sex," he replied, small smile tugging his talented lips.

She smiled back. "Yeah, the sex."

"Any time, hun." He winked. "You weren't the only one who enjoyed it."

She nodded, feeling a little bit great.

"You ever feel the need for more, you know where to find me."

Yeah, like that was going to happen.

She left the smiling, naked, sexy-as-sin man and headed to her horse's boarding stall. *Smart one, Wyne.* You just walked away from a morning of wild, satisfying sex with a hot as hell sheriff. She really needed her head examined. And was contemplating that very thing as she stepped into the stable and ran smack into another hot-as-hell Dalton.

"Careful, darlin'."

"Sorry, Kevin," she said. "I—I...what are you doing here?"

"Yeah, see that's the funny part. I live here."

She curbed the urge to smack him, but gave in to the

pull of his fun nature and smiled back. "I know that, silly. But I thought you were in Houston with some flight attendant."

He wasn't supposed to be at Shadow Rock, catching her with Kade.

"I was. The night is over. She's on her next flight and I have the day off, so there was no need to stay in Houston."

Okay, so he technically didn't catch her with his cousin…or did he?

Her mind raced through the events of last night. *Dear Lord*, Kevin hadn't been home when they…

"Relax, darlin'. I didn't see anything you and my cousin did."

She sighed inwardly. At least that was something. Bad enough he knew. She stiffened. Wait. Wasn't he the one they said gossiped like a little girl? Shoot. Great. Now everyone was going to know.

"And I didn't hear…much." His blue eyes sparkled, and she had no idea if he was teasing or telling the truth, until he pointed to her dress. "You wore it yesterday. Doesn't take a genius…"

Ah, crud. She glanced at her outfit. *Idiot*. "Yeah."

He chuckled. "Don't sweat it, darlin'. I think it's great that you and Kade are together."

"We're not together." She shook her head. "It's nothing like that. We just…it was just…"

"Sex?" He chuckled. "Sure it was. Call it whatever you want, but you, Brandi, are good for my cousin."

Okay, she didn't think she wanted to hear this.

"Actually, you're great for him. He needs someone strong yet understanding. He hasn't been right since that last deployment."

Yeah, she definitely didn't want to hear this. Her

mind was already working on scenarios. She didn't want to care. And drawing *concern* into the mix was just too dangerous. Besides, they didn't have a damn relationship.

"We all know it. He took the death of that soldier pretty bad," Kevin continued, his words knotting her stomach. "He won't talk to anyone. Even Connor couldn't get through to him. So, I'm happy you're here for the stubborn jerk."

So, that's what put the haunted look in the sheriff's eyes when his guard was down. Her heart squeezed tight. Brandi knew Kevin meant well, but she was not the answer to Kade's problems. He needed time and professional help. She'd seen a lot of soldiers going through the same thing back home. Back *east*. This was now home.

She shook her head and expelled a breath. "Look, Kevin. There's nothing going on between me and your cousin."

"Right."

"If he's having problems, then he needs better help than anything I could give."

"Right," he repeated.

"I'm serious."

"So am I." The blue-eyed cowboy grabbed her face and kissed the top of her head. "You're perfect for him. Don't change."

And with that, he left. Disappeared. Was no longer in the stable. She blew out another breath, glanced around and realized they'd just held a personal conversation out in public. Thank God the nearest person was clear across the stable.

Since the Casanova cowboy was kind enough to point out she was wearing yesterday's clothes, Brandi decided to head home and change before she ran into someone else. It wasn't like she was going to ride her horse in a dress, anyway.

Fighting a smile, she slipped into her truck and immediately noticed her purse sitting on the seat with the windows down. Jeez. The damn, sexy sheriff had her so off balance yesterday, she'd left it here all night. A quick glance at the contents set her fears to rest. Nothing missing. She grabbed her phone and checked for calls, hoping none of her family decided to pick last night to check up on her.

One missed call. One voice message.

Her heart hit her ribs as she clicked the screen. Her thyroid doctor.

She breathed a little easier. He most likely called about last week's routine ultra sound and blood test results. She clicked on the message.

"Hi, Ms. Wyne, it's Doctor Chang. I've gotten your results back. You're levels are good, and the ultra sound shows no change in the size of your goiters. But I think it's time to do the biopsies we discussed."

Biopsies.

Brandi knew the word inside and out. She'd spent too much time in hospitals when her mom had undergone all kinds of tests and procedures. Nothing worked. Catherine Wynne had still died from cancer.

The knot in her stomach tightened. Yeah, she knew biopsies. Just never had one done on her. Since the goiters—little nodules on her thyroid—had shrunk from the medication, she'd hoped that was enough. Swallowing was no longer an issue. But the doctor was right, they had discussed the possibility—well, *probability*—of having the procedure done. She'd just foolishly hoped that by not thinking about it, the inevitable wouldn't happen.

After jotting down the appointment time and information for pre-registration, she shoved the paper and phone in her purse, and sat back. Well, that sucked. What a rotten way to end a pretty amazing night.

The sun was rising in the sky, peeking through the trees, casting shadows through the fence in a serene display of nature. A half-dozen horses trotted in a green pasture to her right, already

seeking out the shade on the beautiful warm summer morning. Her gaze turned to the rescue barn and the lone mare grazing in a special pasture. Shadow Rock was so peaceful and tranquil. The perfect place to heal. She hoped to God it helped its owner. The mare certainly seemed to be doing well.

She stilled. Wait. How did the horse get out? Brock wasn't home yet.

"Everything okay?" Out of nowhere, Kade appeared at the side of her truck.

She jumped, hand flying to her chest as if that would keep her thudding heart inside. So that's how the horse got out.

"Oh, yeah," she lied, doing her best not to look the man in the eyes. He was too damn astute. And she was fine, or would be as soon as she had some time to herself. And made sense out of the reason she'd had the sudden overwhelming urge to cry when he appeared. "I just got…" Her gaze shot to her phone and she drew in a breath.

No. She was not bringing him or anyone else into that vortex. She'd gone through it with her mother. No way would she put Kade or any of her friends through that kind of not-knowing hell.

Besides, they weren't anything more than friends,

and chances were she was fine.

She set her shoulders, lifted her chin and turned to him. "I'm good. I just got sidetracked. But now I'm late. Have a good day."

And with that, Brandi reversed out of the spot and didn't look back, her body on autopilot as she drove home.

If you considered Sunday the beginning of the week as printed on all calendars, like the one Kade stared at now on the feed store wall, then his week had started off fantastic. Too bad it'd gone downhill ever since.

When he'd woken up Monday morning exhausted and spent from an incredible all-nighter with a very sexy, adventurous, giving woman, he'd had hopes of continuing the fantastic streak. Especially when the first thing his gaze fell on when he'd opened his eyes was one sweet-as-sin ass as the naked, hot, curvy woman bent to pick up her clothes. He should've known the streak was shot when he'd tried to get her back in his bed, but she'd refused, tripping over her feet to get away as fast as possible.

And he'd even offered breakfast.
Breakfast.
What the hell had he been thinking? A Kade Dalton first.

Paying for the purchases already loaded in his truck, he strode out the door, his mind still on the designer. Things had gotten worse once she'd rushed from his room. He'd found her sitting in her truck in his driveway where she'd lied to his face, telling him things were fine when he could clearly see by the damn sheen of tears in her eyes they were not fine.

Women. He'd never understand them. Not for lack of

trying. At least, with this one.

He got in his truck, slammed the door then drove to meet Connor at the only restaurant in town opened for lunch. A hopping little Mom-'n'-Pop diner near Foster's called The Port Hole. With its ship motif, outdoor deck and tables set up for the summer months, the restaurant did a good business.

Parking next to Connor's truck, Kade checked the time. He wasn't late. In fact, his friend was early. A rarity, especially with Kerri's business just down the street. He thought for sure his buddy would've been sidetracked.

As he walked to the deck area around the back, his gaze was pulled to the designer's little cottage a few doors down. Her white truck sat in the driveway. Odd. He knew she was knee deep in Cole and Jordan's renovation. Ah hell, it was no concern of his what she did. And yet, he couldn't stop thinking about her sitting in that damn truck in his driveway several days ago…or her expression as she'd driven away.

Something in Brandi's brown gaze had called to him, spoke to the consummate helper inside. He hadn't gotten the sense it was something he'd done, or hadn't done. No. They'd agreed to a no-strings-attached night of sex, and that's what they'd had, and even though she'd rushed from his room, it was with a thank you on her lips and a smile on her face. No. He didn't think the wounded look in her eyes was because she'd changed her mind and wanted a relationship. The emotion darkening her gaze to resemble rich coffee hadn't been hurt, it had been more like…fear.

Christ. His heart dropped to his ribs. What the hell happened between his room and her truck? He swiped the ball cap from his head and thrust a hand through his hair before shoving the hat back on. Why should he care? They were not in a relationship. That was what the whole talk had been about. But, son-of-a-bitch, it hadn't stopped him from wondering about her expression all damn week.

That was four days ago.

"Over here," Connor called, gaining his attention.

He turned to find his large friend waiving to him from a corner table where a very pretty cook sat at his side. And that explained why the cowboy wasn't late. He'd brought his woman with him.

"Hi, Kerri," he said, kissing her cheek before he sat down. "Your fiancé decide to spring for lunch and give you a break?"

She laughed, amusement and affection twinkling in her brown eyes as she glanced up at the grinning cowboy at her side. "Something like that."

"Hey!" Connor slapped a hand to his chest and brought a pathetic, wounded expression to his face. "I give you lots of breaks. I'm the king of breaks."

"Oh, man. Way to lay it on thick." Kade chuckled, dark mood beginning to lift thanks to his goofy-ass friend.

Kerri patted her fiancé's cheek. "Yes, but I'm not talking about the platter or shot glass you dropped on the floor."

As Connor's mouth opened and brows rose to disappear under his brown Stetson, Kade's laughter increased. Although the woman wasn't brawny by any means, she sure as shit could take his buddy down in two-point-three seconds.

"Now, darlin'. You know that wasn't my fault," his friend fumbled through an explanation, wounded look appearing earnest.

As he watched the interaction between his friends, Kade noted strong bonds of trust and love evident in their voice, gaze, touch, smile, an underlying, unbreakable connection he'd seen before—in Cole and Jordan. The couples enjoyed a strong relationship foreign to the likes of him.

A slice of envy shot through his body, and he rubbed at his chest, confused as to why envy hit him now.

He was still contemplating that after the waitress left with their orders.

"So, I don't know if you know this, but Shayla is working for us now," Kerri said.

"No, I didn't," he told her. "That's good."

"Her daughter is a little doll, isn't she, Connor?"

A knot instantly gripped his stomach and twisted, while the band around his chest tightened. He hadn't seen Sergeant Nylan's daughter since his trip up north three months ago. That had been tough enough. It seemed wrong—and fucking unfair—that he'd gotten to see the little girl when her own father never had the joy.

"Yeah," his friend answered. "A little darlin'."

"Excuse me." He shot to his feet, needing air—even though they were already outside. "I have to check in with the station. I'll be back."

Without waiting for a reply, he weaved around the tables and retraced his steps to the parking lot. Dammit. He inhaled and exhaled in controlled counts a therapist once suggested. It didn't help with the tightness, but the suffocated feeling and need for air eased. He walked to his truck and considered getting the hell out of there. But nixed the notion. He didn't run.

Gripping the roof, he leaned his head onto his forearm and inhaled a few more times. Weeks had passed since he'd had an '*episode.*' He thought he'd made progress. At least the nightmares had stopped.

A pair of large, dusty boots came into view. Great. *Moose*.

"Still running, I see." Connor's tone, although teasing, held a firm edge.

He twisted around to lean against the truck, mimicking the cowboy. "I don't run."

"Bullshit."

"I just needed air."

His friend's sigh echoed around them. "We're already outside. You can't get any more than that, buddy."

Kade laughed. "True." Feeling better, he began to walk back toward the restaurant.

"So, that's it?" Connor asked, falling into step. "You push it aside and move on."

"Yep."

"That's not healthy."

Biting back a curse, he stopped dead. "Just drop it, all right? I'm fine."

"Bullshit. If you need air when you're already outside, you're not *fine*."

He was about to respond when the expression on Connor's face had him twisting around to see what had captured his friend's attention.

Brandi. In the passenger seat of Jace's silver SUV.

"I'm sure it's nothing," Connor said, cupping his shoulder as the vehicle drove by.

The knot returned to his stomach…and brought a friend. "Whatever."

She was free to see whoever she wanted. They weren't a couple. Guess the giant next to him hadn't gotten that memo. Or the knots in his stomach, which increased to the size of boulders when the doctor parked in front of her cottage, draped an arm around the smiling woman and disappeared inside the house.

"So...I'm guessing that doesn't bother you?"

He shrugged, overlooking the strange tightness in his chest. "Nope. Let's go eat. Food should be ready by now." And, ignoring his friend's sadistic chuckles, he made his way back to the bastard's sweet fiancée, talking his fists out of connecting with anything tall and dumb named Connor.

Chapter Nine

And so it begins.

The wait.

It was the day after Brandi's biopsies and she hadn't heard a word. She knew it could take several days to hear, but after her initiation into biopsy horror with her mom, she had no patience. And in her experience, the outcome had always been bad. Very bad.

"Now, I don't want you worrying yourself sick," Doctor Turner had said when he'd driven her home yesterday.

The sweetheart had rescheduled his afternoon appointments after discovering she'd arrived at the hospital for the procedure by herself. He'd even arranged to get her truck home. What a nice man. Of course, she'd made him promise not to tell anyone. His handsome face had frowned in protest, but he'd eventually agreed.

"You know this is just routine, right?" He'd settled her on the couch, doting on her like a child, tossing a quilt over her after flipping on the air conditioning. Mozart had immediately settled on top of the blanket, happily kneading while the doctor added, "Just because your mother had cancer does not mean you do."

She knew this. She really did, but as the hours wore on, her doubts increased. Flopping onto her mattress, she stared at the ceiling. Painted a soft blue, it was quite different from the ceiling she'd stared at yesterday at this time.

Told to lay still and not swallow while the endocrinologist shoved a needle into her throat to gather cells from her goiters, she'd counted the ruts in the ceiling blocks above her head. Six times. Each biopsy had only lasted a minute, but seemed a lot longer when told not to swallow. As the doctor pumped the skinny needle in and out at a rapid pace, she'd imagined her fingers on the neck of her violin, playing the intricate chords of one of her favorite and toughest songs. She'd heard the music. Felt the indenture of the strings under her fingers and found her happy place. The image of a sexy sheriff with smoldering gray eyes and magical hands had also made an appearance. Yes, Kade was definitely a happy place. And as she forced herself to remain still on the hospital bed, she'd made a promise to herself to visit those places again in reality.

Now, twenty-four hours later, Brandi had the perfect opportunity to cross one off her list.

She rolled off the mattress, got on her hands and knees and stared at the lone case sitting under her bed. All as Mozart watched through a lazy gaze.

"Come on, Wyne. Just do it," she said out loud and grabbed the handle to pull the case close. "You need to practice for the upcoming Guard dinner, anyhow."

Why the hell had she agreed to that? Oh, yeah, right. Her father had asked her…okay, more like *told* the committee she'd be happy to perform at an upcoming dinner in Houston in a few weeks. Brandi looked forward to seeing her father and brother, Ben, at the dinner, just not the *playing*—still a few too many dark memories attached to performing. Sighing, she lifted the case to her bed, and once again, stared at the small black container she'd recently nicknamed Pandora.

The heavy, suppressive weight she'd felt whenever near the case the past year was much lighter. Maybe Pandora was on a diet. She chuckled, noting her throat was not as sore as yesterday. And despite the discomfort of a scratchy throat, her voice remained fairly unaffected, with only a miniscule deepening of her tone. Thank God for small miracles. At least she wouldn't draw attention to herself.

"Okay, you can do this."

On an indrawn breath, she opened the lid, expecting the weight in her chest to increase, but it remained the same. She blew out the breath and gingerly lifted her violin out of the velvet indenture.

Intense feelings, some good and some bad, rushed through her from head to toe, settling in her tight chest. She swallowed a few times, blinked a few more and the tightness lessened. Placing the violin on the bed, she glanced at the cat and shook her head.

"You know the drill."

Sniffing, she unlatched the bow and rosin and prepared the neglected hair. She was doing this. This was going to happen. Now. One song. She'd get through one song. Baby steps. Bow completely rosined, she placed the violin on her shoulder, put her chin in the chin rest, and before she could think another thought, played the first song that came to mind.

Beethoven's "5th."

As her fingers slid across the strings, hitting the chords, bow connecting to create the sound she'd fallen in love with at an early age, she relaxed and gave herself over to the music. Sweet, soft, hard and passionate, the violin encompassed it all. Every time her mother had undergone a biopsy or procedure, Brandi had played and played until her fingers bled. Music was her out. The violin was an extension of herself, one she realized she'd missed. Why the hell had she hidden it away all these months?

Oh, right. It also reminded her of suppression, and duty, and control, and she'd packed it away, along with the bad memories that took the joy out of playing.

Until today.

She'd left Ed, resigned her position with the Philharmonic—a position she once coveted, until he made her hate every single minute—and went back to designing, something she'd always found as a good, creative outlet.

And she was happy for the first time in a long time. She enjoyed designing. Couldn't imagine not designing. But now that she'd caressed the neck of her old friend, the reunion was sweet. The instrument would no longer remain packed away, collecting dust under her bed. No. She'd figure something out. But, she still had to work through the negative feelings. Playing for fun was easier than playing for commitment. She needed to go slow.

"My goodness!"

"Holy shit, girl!"

Brandi stiffened, the bow screeching across the strings in a sharp stop. She twisted around to find Kerri and Jordan standing in her bedroom blinking.

"I-I didn't hear you come in," she stammered, trying to ignore the fact she stood there gripping a violin and bow in her hands.

"Wow..." Kerri rushed forward. "That was *incredible*."

"Yes, I had no idea you played," Jordan said, stepping further into the room. "Do you do anything like Apocalyptica?"

She loved the band and their interpretation of rock with her beloved string instruments. "Yes. Some." In fact, she did a lot of different musical genres, having always loved the challenge.

Jordan sank onto the bed and cocked her head. "Are you getting sick?"

Really? She should've known better. "No. Throat's just a little dry."

"Oh." The shrewd beauty nodded, then smiled. "So, can you play some Apocalyptica?"

"Yeah, they're great," Kerri agreed, fussing with her phone.

Tightness returned to Brandi's chest. "I...I don't know."

She placed her violin and bow back in the case, then closed the lid, wanting to close the lid on the whole subject. But Bulldog McCall and her sister had caught her scent. She was screwed.

Mozart stood and stretched, then purred and rubbed against Jordan who scratched under the feline's collar.

"You'd played for the Philharmonic?" Kerri asked. "Why didn't you say?"

How the hell did she...

"That was way too good for a closet player. I had to look you up on the net." Her friend held up her smart phone with a photo of Brandi and the rest of the orchestra in some sort of photo op last year.

The band across her chest tightened. She pushed past the woman and strode into the living room as if the subject would remain in the bedroom with Pandora.

"Brandi, hey." Kerri caught up with her, took her hand and pulled her to the couch where they sat down. "Hun, you don't just *get* a job with an orchestra. You have to be great."

She stared at her hand. "I auditioned."

"Exactly."

Great, now Jordan sat in the chair next to them.

"Says here, you had to audition and interview."

Kerri pointed to her phone.

Brandi sighed. "Yeah, there was a process. So?"

"So, you're better than good. You had to be great. Committed."

Yeah, she was certifiable right about now. She laughed. "Probably should be."

Jordan smiled, but Kerri frowned.

"Why did you leave?"

"Yeah." The older sister leaned forward. "Not that I'm not thrilled you're designing, but, why leave a music career like that? You had to love music and playing in order to achieve what you did."

Fighting tears, Brandi blew out a breath and nodded. "I did. Do," she corrected.

Kerri squeezed the hand she still held and waited for her to glance up. "What happened?"

Blame it on the stress and worry of the past twenty-four hours, or the exhaustion of keeping her past a bit of secret, Brandi sighed and told them the whole story about Ed. About how he loved the limelight her position with the orchestra gave him. How he wouldn't let her miss any venue or show, and made sure she practiced daily. How he took something she loved and killed it.

"At first, I thought it was so great that he understood how much music meant to me, even at the expense of time spent together." She laughed without mirth. "Boy, was I wrong. He only wanted the spotlight my little bit of fame afforded him. He didn't give a damn about me."

"Oh, hun, I'm so glad you told him good-bye." Kerri hugged her close.

"I hope you kicked his ass," Jordan said, her hands balling into fists. "Because if not, I'd be more than happy to fly up there and do it for you."

This time, genuine laughter bubbled up her throat.

"That would be great to see, but he's not worth it."

It may have taken her months to realize that, but at least she had, then packed up and left him. Taking her fat and violin with her, leaving him free to find someone else to boss around and control.

She sat back and wiped her face. "I'm sorry to have kept it from you. It's just that it's still a bit raw."

Like her throat, but she wasn't going to burden them with her latest problem.

"Well, I hope, when you're ready, you'll play whatever you want at the pub," Jordan said, leaning forward to squeeze her knee. "People here will love it. Classical, rock, country. You know how they pack in every Tuesday for amateur night. They'd be thrilled to hear someone of your caliber. Trust me."

"I-I'm not ready for that, Jordan. I just couldn't yet." Bad enough she had to do this Guard thing in a few weeks.

The woman squeezed one last time, then sat back. "When you're ready, hun. Just think about it."

Brandi nodded, hoping it got them to drop the subject. "So…" She cleared her throat, and tried to cover the wince in reaction. "What are you doing here?"

"We actually came to take you to the pub. There's a great band playing tonight, and you haven't been doing anything but work."

"Yes, we're here to make sure you come and have some fun for a few hours."

Her stomached knotted. She didn't want to laugh and pretend to have fun. Not with the big 'C' hanging over her head. And yet, she was tired of sitting and waiting for the phone to ring with results.

"I don't know. I have some plans to go over."

"No." Jordan stood. "You have some *plans* to have

fun. Starting now. Go get changed. Put on a killer shirt and tight pair of jeans."

All her jeans were tight.

"And don't forget boots. Guys love boots."

"Wait, guys? No one said anything about guys." She sat back down.

Kerri and Jordan exchanged a determined look, then each grabbed an arm and escorted her into her room. Mozart glanced at them and yawned. Lot of help he was…the traitor.

She grasped the violin case and pushed it back under the bed, hoping when she stood, they'd be gone. They weren't. And they were in her closet.

"Here."

Jordan shoved a solid burgundy, scoop-necked T-shirt at her the girls had insisted she buy during their recent shopping trip. She'd had no intention of wearing the form-fitting shirt. Heck, the tags were still on it. And she'd shoved it way into the back of the closet.

"And these."

Kerri slapped a pair of jeans on the bed Brandi had purchased at the same time.

"And your Ariat's. I love those boots."

With both sisters staring from her to the clothes on the bed, Brandi had no choice. "Fine." They weren't moving. Apparently they didn't trust her. Double fine. She stripped and was about to shrug into the outfit when Jordan held up a hand.

"Wait. The underwear, too."

"What? Why?" Crap, she was just not up for this.

Kerri touched her arm. "Sexy underwear always makes us feel better. And we know you have some. We were there when you bought it, remember?"

Remember? How could she forget? They'd

practically thrust the pink lacy thong and matching bra in her arms, and because the store actually had her size, she'd let them, figuring she could at least wear the outfit under clothes to make her feel better.

Shoot. She just proved their point.

"Fine." Grumbling, she grabbed the lace from a drawer, and when she turned around the sisters were gone and door was shut. She glanced at Mozart curled up on her jeans, staring at her. "A little too late, buddy."

And because she wouldn't put it past the Masters sisters to check, Brandi quickly changed into all the suggested clothing, stepped from the room, and lifted her shirt. "See? It's all on."

Matching pleased expressions lit her friends' faces, and they nodded.

"Good. Let's go," Jordan said, heading for the door Kerri held open.

An hour later, Brandi dropped back into the booth they'd commandeered, wondering what was in the water. She'd danced with four different cowboys in the last half hour alone. Although it was fun and kept her mind occupied, she was tired and needed a break.

"Your dance card sure is full tonight, darlin'," Connor said, sliding her water closer.

She drank half the glass then turned to him and smiled. "Thanks, and yes, it's kind of weird."

"Not at all." He shook his head. "Proves cowboy's have good taste."

"Awe, thanks." She leaned in and kissed his cheek, then added, *"Darlin'."*

Jordan and her husband laughed from the other side of the table. Then Cole straightened and nodded toward the door.

"Hey, the Daltons are here. Why don't we move to a

bigger table?"

And before Brandi knew it, she was sandwiched between Connor and Kade, with Kevin, Jordan and Cole on the other side.

"If either of you want to dance with Brandi, you'd better put your request in now," Connor said.

And at that moment, she would've been quite happy to have the floor swallow her whole.

"Yeah." Cole nodded. "She's got them lining up tonight."

Okay, in pieces. Swallow her in pieces. Anything so she didn't have to respond or glance at the silent sheriff.

The blue-eyed Dalton smiled from across the table. "Well now, of course she does. The woman's beautiful, ain't she, cuz?"

Pieces or whole. She wasn't partial. Just let the swallowing commence.

Kade turned to her, and he was seated so close she could feel his breath. "Yep," he said, then added in a low, thong-melting tone only she could hear. "Every inch."

Oh, look at that. Her thong melted.

She reached for her water and sucked down the rest. Damn, the man was hot. Real hot. Her body was on fire. But he didn't ask her to dance, or say anything else. Just sat there staring, gaze unreadable. She got the impression he was almost angry.

"Hi, everyone."

Jace appeared at the table, saving her from…from herself probably.

"Hi, Jace." Kevin slapped the doctor on the back. "Pull up a chair."

The doc smiled, but shook his head. "Thanks, but I came over to ask Brandi to dance."

Oh, thank you, Lord. An escape route. The

sweetheart continued to be a big help this week.

"Love to." She set her empty glass on the table and stood, noting the silent sheriff stiffen.

With a smile, Jace took her hand and led her to the crowded floor where other couples two-stepped to the band playing their heart out on stage.

"Any news?"

"No."

He squeezed the hand he held at his chest. "How are you holding up?"

"Okay."

His gaze narrowed. "You sure? You're awfully warm."

She laughed before she could stop. *Yeah, courtesy of the hotty sheriff.* "Dancing will do that," she said instead.

He studied her a moment then nodded. "Dance with Kade yet?"

Her feet suddenly forgot how to work. She stumbled with elephant-like grace. His grip tightened and he pulled her close.

"You okay?"

"Yeah." Her face heated to fairly mortified.

"So, I'll take that as a *no* to dancing with Kade."

"Yes, I mean, no. I didn't dance with the sheriff," she said. "We're just friends."

The doc tossed his head back and laughed, without missing a step. "Right. That's why he's looking at me like he'd like to demote me."

This time she laughed, her heart dipping at that thought for some reason. "Nah, he probably just had a rough day at work."

"With Donny as his deputy, it's no wonder."

They were still laughing when the song ended and he

walked her back toward the table. "You hang in there, okay? If you need to talk, call me."

With the Daltons and McCalls watching, all she dared do was squeeze the good doctor's hand. "Thanks," she said then released him.

He turned to the table and nodded, then walked back into the crowd.

Before she could sit back down, another cowboy approached and asked her to dance. This went on for a whole half hour. Finally, she told the next one *thank you, but no* and made her way back to her chair, noting Kade was now sitting at the bar with Connor.

She'd passed the sheriff on the floor a few times, but other than a nod, he never said a word. Neither had she. What was there to say? They'd had their night of sex. Were keeping it simple. So, why was it *Kade's* chest she wanted to bury her face against? Why was it *his* arms she wanted wrapped around her tight as he told her everything was going to be fine? She dropped into her chair and refilled her glass from the water pitcher, happy to have the table to herself.

"You look like you could use something stronger." Kevin smiled as he joined her after dancing just about every dance since he'd arrived. All with different women.

She snorted, very unladylike, before drinking her water. "Truer words."

He cocked his head. "Would you like me to order you something?"

"No, that's okay." It was getting late, and she was getting tired of playing the dance-check-the-phone-game. "I'm going to leave soon."

"Well now, you can't leave without dancing with Kade." Kevin sat back in his chair, arms folded across his chest. "The two of you have been circling each other all night. What's the problem?"

"Problem? There's no problem." She sipped her drink and shrugged, hoping to appear nonchalant.

"Good to hear. So, go ask him to dance."

The water in her mouth went down the wrong way. She choked like a dog on a bone. Yeah, graceful. Now her already sore throat hurt worse. "No," she managed before taking another drink.

"Why not?"

"Jeez, what's with you tonight? Don't you have a groupie to dance with?"

He threw his head back and laughed. "Nice try, but we're not changing the subject."

"There is no subject. I'm going home."

"You are just as stubborn as my cousin. And here I thought you had more sense."

"What's that supposed to mean?"

"What it means, darlin', is simple." He leaned forward to tap the table with his finger. "You both want to dance with each other, but neither will ask. What's the big deal? So what if you've already had sex? No law says you can't dance with each other, too. Go ask him. It doesn't mean marriage. It's just a dance."

Her gaze drifted to the sexy man in the charcoal shirt. God, he looked good, boots crossed at the ankles as he leaned a hip against the bar and laughed at something Connor said.

Lifting the drink to his mouth, he caught her watching.

Damn. Busted.

He stilled and stared over his glass at her, smoky gaze still unreadable.

Kevin was right. She wanted to dance with Kade,

but until that moment, she hadn't realized how much or why. She really, really needed to have his arms around her, needed to experience that safe feeling his embrace had evoked.

"Go ask him," the blue-eyed devil urged.

Before she could think—or talk herself out of it—Brandi got up and walked straight to the gorgeous man, who set his drink down without dropping her gaze. As she approached, he straightened, and Connor turned, his quizzical expression disappearing under a lop-sided grin.

Go ask him.

Kevin's words rang through her mind, and she hoped he wasn't wrong when she stopped in front of his cousin, wishing she could come up with something witty.

Keep it simple.

Staring into those gray eyes, she fought the sudden influx of emotion she'd kept at bay the past several days. The need to feel his strong arms around her, to feel safe—to just plain *feel*—shook through her and gave her the courage to place a hand on his arm. "Would you like to dance?"

For a heart-stopping moment Brandi thought he was going to refuse. That unexplained anger she'd seen earlier tightened his face for a split second, but something in her eyes must've relayed her need or sincerity. Whatever it was, she was grateful because he nodded, grabbed her hand and led her to the dance floor. Luck was on her side, because the band started to play a slow Tim McGraw song and he pulled her in close.

Needing no encouragement, she sank into his wonderful, hard, welcoming chest, squeezing her eyes shut as she held tight, reveling in his strength and warmth as his strong arms closed around her. A few tears escaped before she could stop them but, thankfully, went unnoticed. By the middle of the song, she composed herself enough to loosen her hold, but not too much. He felt so damn good. Her need for the man turned into an entirely different category. Soon all the brushing and friction from their touching bodies stoked a familiar fire. Her body remembered his, remembered the muscles, ridges, the strength and his ability to take her right out of herself. She needed that tonight. *God*, how she needed that tonight.

But what if tonight wasn't enough?

That question reverberated through her head as the song came to an end. There was no tonight. Just this dance. And it was ending. It had to end. Best if it ended.

Then why was she still holding him?

Because she was weak and the man made her feel strong. He made her feel wanted, and good about herself. But they'd had their night. And even if he'd wanted more, which he'd said he didn't, the guy didn't deserved to be with someone uncertain about her health.

She knew without a shadow of a doubt Kade Dalton would stand by her, but she was unwilling to drag him down that road. He had issues of his own to deal with, and she refused to add to them. His heart was too big; he'd never walk away from the needy. So she needed to suck it up. She could do this on her own. And she would. Starting now.

Releasing him, she stepped back, immediately missing his warmth. Muttering a *thank you* to his Adams apple, because there was no way in hell she'd risk looking into his eyes—those warm and accepting, mesmerizing gray eyes—she turned and walked right out of the pub.

What the hell?

Kade glanced at the faces of those nearby, as if they'd have the answer. No one paid any attention, just danced as if nothing had happened. But *dammit,* something did happen.

"You should go after her."

He turned to find Jace standing next to him, arms behind his back, serious gaze trained on the door Brandi had exited. A foreign emotion squeezed Kade's chest and heated his blood. Why the hell would Jace tell him to go after the girl? Wasn't his friend seeing Brandi?

His spine stiffened. "Why don't you?" he asked before heading back to the bar and the drink he should've stayed to finish.

"Sarge, wait. *Top*, would you wait," the doctor implored, clamping a hand around Kade's upper arm.

Because he was sheriff, and *only* because he was the sheriff, Kade didn't carry out the urge to knock the doc to the floor. Even though he was off duty, he still respected the uniform. Both uniforms. And it was because thoughts of using violence on a friend were so foreign and so far from what he was about, yet becoming more damn frequent, Kade stilled to listen to the man.

"Look," Jace began, wisely removing his hand. "I'm getting the impression you think there's something going on between me and Brandi. But there isn't."

Jesus, did the guy think he was stupid?

"Don't bullshit me, Turner. I've seen you with her."

The guy reeled back. "What? Here? When I came to your table to ask her to dance?"

The deep frown didn't fool him. Folding his arms across his chest, Kade stared the man down. "Yes, *and* yesterday in your car. So cut the crap."

Turner blew out a breath, glanced around, then grabbed Kade's arm again and pulled him to a quiet corner.

He was impressed. The doc's blue gaze held just enough concern to go with his conflicted expression that he was almost prepared to believe whatever was about to come out of the guy's mouth. Almost.

"You need to go to her."

He yanked free. "Not going to happen."

"Look, I only drove her home yesterday because she…" Turner paused, exhaled a curse, then continued, "…because she needed one. Okay? And that dance tonight was just to check on her."

Right… Wait…

His heart rocked hard in his chest when the words sunk in. "What do you mean *check* on her?" He grabbed the guy's arm. "What's wrong? Is she okay?"

The doc gave him one of those damn patient looks. "You'll have to ask her."

"*Jesus*, Jace. I'm asking you."

His mind worked overtime. If Brandi and Jace hadn't been together yesterday in a friendly manner, then it meant professional. And since he knew the designer was only working on Jordan's project right now, that meant…

"I promised her I wouldn't say anything, so I'm not saying anything," the doctor stated, freeing his arm to cup Kade's shoulder and stare him right in the eyes. "Go to her. She needs you."

The knot forming in his stomach tripled in size. *Shit*.

Without a word, he pivoted on his heel and strode out of the pub, making the two minute drive to the designer's cottage in less than one.

Go to her. She needs you…

What the fuck was going on?

Chest tight for reasons he didn't understand or care

at the moment, he knocked on the door, half afraid she wouldn't answer even though her truck sat a few feet away in the driveway. Her odd behavior this past week, and her death-grip on his ribs during their dance, battered his mind.

Why the hell hadn't he realized something was wrong sooner?

He knocked again, louder, longer, then thrust his hand through his hair and squeezed the back of his neck. Christ. She'd even looked at him different tonight, needy—almost desperate—but he'd mistaken it for lust. Somewhere in the back of his mind he'd noticed, but was too damn blinded by…ah hell, he didn't know, he just didn't catch on.

Dumb ass.

Lifting his hand for the third time, he stilled when the door finally opened and Brandi stood there in a pink robe, staring up at him, eyes red and watery. His stomach bunched as if physically punched.

"Brandi, what's going on? What the hell is wrong?"

She shook her head, tears filling her eyes and spilling down her face.

Ah hell.

The invisible band squeezing his chest tightened until he couldn't breathe, cracking something open deep inside. "Come here," he ground out, stepping closer to pull her in tight and close the door. "It's okay. Whatever it is, it's okay. I've got you," he soothed, leaning back against the door as she burrowed into him.

Unsure how to help when he didn't know what the hell was actually wrong, he remained where he was and just held the woman, whispering words of encouragement and kissing the top of her head while she silently cried.

After a few minutes, her tears subsided and her hold on him suddenly changed. Hands that had been gripping, squeezing, now ran down his torso, and before he realized, she had his shirt completely unbuttoned, and her hands and lips on his skin.

Shit.

"Brandi?" He grasped her arms and held her away. "What are you doing?"

A sinful grin claimed her lips as she stared up at him through a heated gaze. "Well now, Sheriff, I would think that was obvious."

And before he could blink, she stepped back, untied her robe and let it slip to the floor.

Son-of-a-bitch...

He inhaled and swallowed. Audibly. The gorgeous woman had on the sexiest damn pink-laced bra and thong. A fucking thong.

He was screwed.

Somehow he put his tongue back in his mouth and cleared a bit of the fog from his brain. But she was pressing her soft, hot curves into him in a surprise counterattack. Damn, she felt good. Real good. He was having a hard time remaining unaffected. Wicked fingers unbuckled his jeans while she placed open-mouth kisses across his chest, driving him out of his mind. Then she licked his nipple.

Uttering a curse, he jerked back, smacking his head off the door. "Brandi, stop," he demanded, and twisted their positions, manacling her hands above her head.

Body trembling, chest heaving, spilling out of her damn, sexy lace. *Holy shit*, she was hot. His groin tightened with a painful throb, and he had to talk himself out of pressing against her and sinking into her willing warmth.

"Why? We're good together," she uttered, leaning forward, mouth hovering near his lips. "You know we're good together."

He did. Heaven help him, he did, but something was wrong to cause the independent beauty to cry and cling just a few moments ago. Something even his hazy brain knew couldn't be overlooked.

"Brandi," he said again, his voice as strained as his zipper. "We need to talk. Why were you at the hospital? And before you say anything, *no,* Jace didn't tell me. I figured it out."

The bleakness returned to dull her eyes, her shoulders hunched and gaze fell to the floor.

"Please, Kade. I-I don't want to talk. And I don't want to think. *God*, I don't want to think." She broke free to burrow close. "I know we were only supposed to have one night. But…I need another. Take me out of myself. You're so good at taking me out of myself," she stated, mouth brushing his skin while her hand trailed down his chest and torso to stroke his abs. "I don't want to think tonight. Just take me out of myself."

And that was when he lost it. Her pleading. Her stroking hands. The need in her voice. Sweet, soft, curvy body, pressing into him. The answering need heating him from head to toe, throbbing through his groin. They all became too much.

"I don't want to talk. Don't want to think. I just want to feel you," she said. "Can you do that, Kade? Take me out of myself? Make me feel you?"

He crooked a finger under her chin and waited for her gaze to lift. "If you're sure."

A wicked smile curved her lips as her fingers slid down his body to unzip his jeans. "I'm *very* sure."

He was so wound up, so ready, her assurance was all

he needed to hear. "Then, hell yeah, honey, I can make you *feel* a lot of things."

In a swift move, he pressed her against the door, and when she let out a startled sound, he captured her opened mouth and kissed her over and over until she was the one to break for air. God, she was incredible, and tasted sweet like maybe she'd been eating chocolate before he'd arrived. He turned his attention to her throat and the curve of her neck, lingering until she moaned and trembled against him.

Heat skittered down his spine. She was so damn responsive.

He drew back slightly to watch as he traced the pink lace of her bra with his finger. "Very nice," he said, and brushed his thumbs across her tight nipples peeking through the lace.

She inhaled and gripped his hips. He brushed her again. And again. Each time she held tighter and moaned louder. Then he hooked a finger under her straps and pulled the lace down her arms, his mouth watering as she sprang free and bounced.

She really did have great bounce.

Unable to hold back, he cupped each breast and brushed her gorgeous, unhindered peaks until she squirmed.

"Kade," she said in a drawn out breath.

He needed no more encouragement and brought his mouth down on the beauties, taking turns suckling and pulling until they were a half-inch long. She clutched his head and shoved more of her glorious flesh into his mouth. His arousal pulsed and ached, but he wasn't ready. Not yet.

Rolling her nipple between his tongue and the roof of his mouth, he slid a hand down her heated body and followed the strip of thong between her legs. *Hot damn*, her lace was wet. She moaned, and her knees began to buckle.

Bracing her with his body, he continued to twirl his tongue around her peak and slip his finger inside her wet folds. She sucked in a breath and gripped his shoulders, and his arousal pulsed and ached, but he still wasn't ready. Not yet.

He released her breast, pulled out of her warmth and watched as she opened her eyes and blinked.

"Turn around," he ordered, gently twisting until her back faced him. He kissed her neck and ran his hands down her arms to grab her wrists. "Trust me." Placing them high above her head against the door, he squeezed to let her know to keep her arms up.

She wanted to feel, he'd make her feel.

Chapter Ten

Kade stepped back to gaze at Brandi's beautiful body and lacy thong barely covering the middle of her sweet ass. His mouth watered and erection throbbed behind his half unzipped pants.

Needing to touch her, he started at her neck, kissing each shoulder, slipping his hands around the front to cup her beautiful breasts and tweak from behind. She moaned and ground that gorgeous ass into him. Sucking in a breath, he forced the fog from his brain. There were still things he needed to do to the woman. He tweaked the tight buds once more, then released them to reach up and gently bring her arms down to her sides.

"Stay there," he said, caressing every curve on the way down to her thong. Hitting his knees, he grabbed two handfuls of cheeks and squeezed. "Gorgeous," he said against her soft skin, his finger now tracing the lace thong to where it disappeared between her legs.

"Kade," she said, body shaking.

"I know, honey. You wanted to feel. I'm making you feel."

Tracing her wet thong with his finger, he kissed her thigh and tugged the lace in an upward motion.

"Kade," she repeated, this time in a whisper.

He tugged again then hooked his fingers around the top and slowly pulled the lace down her trembling legs. Knowing she was very close to losing control, he twisted her back around and sucked in another breath as he stared up at her luscious curves. God, she was perfect. Absolutely perfect. He swallowed hard and counted to ten to keep from busting. Hell no. He had plans for her *and* his erection.

"Spread your legs," he told her, voice low and hoarse with need.

"But—

"Shh…" he interrupted, helping her by pushing her legs apart, then holding her there with his hands. "Just feel."

And hell, he needed to taste the glistening pink staring him in the face.

When he placed his mouth on her, she jerked back, but settled into a good rhythm by the third pass of his tongue. So sweet. She tasted so sweet, and hot, and he couldn't get enough. Using his fingers, he spread her apart, giving him better access to her heat.

Her legs began to shake.

"Kade…I can't stand…" she said between pants.

"It's okay, I've got you."

"But are…you sure…you can hold me?"

"Absolutely." He didn't understand why she insisted she was so heavy. Brushing a finger over her center, he made sure to get her attention. "Let yourself go."

And she did, relaxing against him, letting him control it all. Shouldering her weight, he put his mouth back on her, and in less than a minute, had her panting and bucking.

"I'm…mmm," she moaned.

He was dying. She was killing him. Her actions and reactions were so hot he was about to disintegrate. Not yet. He was determined to finish the mission. *Operation Brandi Feel-Good*. But, glancing up without breaking contact, he nearly lost it. Eyes closed, bottom lip pulled between her teeth, she was so sexy, so damn gorgeous he could barely breathe. Needing to send her over the edge, to make her *feel* good, he slid a finger inside her, and when she cried out, he adopted the rhythm he'd discovered at the ranch. The one she liked best.

"Yes...K-Kade..."

With his name on her lips, she lost control on *his* lips, and he did his damndest to draw out her climax for as long as possible, watching the ecstasy on her face the whole time.

Beautiful.

Stunning.

And her taste? *Damn*, she tasted incredible. Scorching and sweet. A taste he was not likely to ever forget.

Slowing his motions, he removed his finger and lapped one last time before drawing back. As he let her slide down to the floor, she met his gaze and smiled.

"Wow...I...that was...amazing."

He traced her cheek with a finger, brushing a strand of hair off her face to hook it behind her ear. "Yes, you were." He pulled a packet from his pocket and held it up. "But we're not done."

"You got that right, cowboy," she drawled, reaching for the packet.

He moved it out of her reach. "Oh, hell no, honey. If you touched me right now, we won't need this. And I'm not done with you."

She laughed, her gaze playful and happy. No trace of sadness or fear in sight. In record time, he removed the rest of his clothes, sheathed himself, and helped her to stand.

"God, you're beautiful," he told her, his body shaking with the need to be inside her sweet curves. Pulling her close, he captured her mouth and groaned when she pressed her tongue to his and swept the inside of his mouth.

He wasn't going to last. Hands full of her soft curves, he left her mouth to kiss a path down her neck, inhaling her delicious scent. Yeah, he wasn't going to last.

"This is going to be fast. Sorry. But I'm dying here," he said against her throat before he drew back, grabbed her hips and lifted her up.

Needing no direction, she gripped his shoulders, wrapped her soft thighs around him, and then moaned the sexiest damn moan he'd ever heard as he thrust deep inside.

Ah, fuck...yeah. She felt incredible. So damn incredible, her warm, silky heat gripping him tight. Then she moved. Christ. He was about to explode. Liquid fire melted his spine, and leaning forward, he kissed her wild and deep as he pumped in and out of her warm, wet center. Her nails dug into his shoulders, nipples scraped his chest, thighs tightened around him. He broke the kiss, gripped her ass, and adjusted the angle.

"Ohh…"

Her eyes were closed again, head back as far as the door would allow, breasts bouncing a frenetic beat as he upped the pace. Erotic. Sexy-as-hell. A real life fantasy. He was done. So was she. Brandi cried out, her softness tightening around his aching arousal, pulling Kade out of himself as she milked the hell out of his throbbing erection, bringing him to his knees by the time he was sweaty and spent.

He pulled out, but continued to hold her as he flipped them so he sat against the door and she snuggled into his chest. Asking her how she felt would have to wait since talking required breath and, right now, he didn't have any to spare, thanks to the incredible woman panting in his arms. Hot air gushed over his heated skin and cooled when she inhaled.

Damn woman even breathed sexily.

She shifted in his arms and stared up at him, lifting a hand to slowly trace his jaw. "Tell me, Sheriff, did you get the license number of that bus?"

He laughed and gathered her close. "No, I was too busy trying to remember my own damn name."

Her chuckle rippled through him as her lips brushed his neck. "It's Mr. *Yurgood*. Damn Yurgood."

"Yeah?" He drew back and smiled when she nodded. "Then you're Ms. *Thanhell*. Hotter Thanhell."

Brown eyes blinked up at him, a sheen of tears glistening in their depts. "I am?"

"Oh, *hell* yeah, honey," he replied, tracing a line from her throat, over her rounded flesh to circle just outside the hardened tip, which he slowly leaned down to kiss.

As her warm curves shuddered against him, he blew on her wet skin.

She inhaled and clutched his arm. "I'll give you all night to stop."

Trailing a finger over her other breast, he watched her eyes darken and breath hitch in her throat. "What do you know," he said, circling her tightening nipple. "I happen to have all night."

And as luck would have it, Kade did end up spending the whole night. Miraculously, there were no sheriff calls yanking him from *Ms. Thanhell's* bed. Between the second and third *feel-good* session, he sent a quick text to Kevin, letting his cousin know he was with Brandi and wouldn't be home, and ignored the *''bout damn time you got some sense'* reply.

Waking up with the bombshell's ass under his palm

after another marathon night of incredible sex was a little bit of all right. As the memories of the night washed over him, Kade was surprised he could still move. But he didn't want to budge, hell no. Not with a warm, naked, curvy woman softly snoring on top of him, leg thrown across him as if she was afraid he'd leave. Not a chance. Besides, he couldn't feel his own legs.

After they used the two condoms in his pocket, he'd made a quick trip to the all night drug store ten minutes away, giving their bodies just enough time to recuperate. Upon returning, he'd found the temptress in the tub, and a very incredible and wet round three had commenced.

Round four had nearly killed him.

Still, apparently he'd fulfilled the woman's wish for the night because she'd fallen into a steady sleep ever since. Christ, she hadn't been kidding about the *not thinking* part. And the only talking they'd done had been with their bodies. But he wasn't complaining. Hell no. Except, he wished he knew why she had been at the hospital.

His stomach clenched. If he thought Jace would concede under badgering he'd interrogate the guy, but the doctor took the confidentiality of his profession serious, and Kade would never ask the lieutenant to compromise. Still, damn, he wished he knew what was wrong.

All too soon, Brandi stirred, generous curves testing his rigidity by brushing his skin in a slow, enticing stretch. The friction of her soft curves against his flesh awoke the sleeping giant.

Rigidity confirmed.

Half-expecting the designer to give him his marching papers, since she was prone to heat up the night then do an about-face come morning, he was surprised when she lifted her head and smiled all warm and lazy.

That's a double confirmation on rigidity.

"Morning," she said, setting her chin on her hands splayed on his chest. "Sleep well?"

He smiled back, lightly caressing the curvy cheek under his palm, while trailing the other hand up her spine. "Like the dead."

Smile fading, she stiffened and slid off him.

What the hell did I say?

Grasping her arm to keep her from leaving the bed completely, he rolled on top of the woman and pinned her to the mattress. "Oh no you don't. You're not running away. Talk to me. What's wrong?" He lifted up enough to gaze down at the vexing woman.

"Nothing," she replied, but wouldn't meet his gaze.

"Brandi, come on. Tell me."

"There's nothing to tell, except…"

Christ, she wriggled until they lined up just perfect. So damn perfect. He sucked in a breath. "Except what?" His tone sounded strained because, *hello*…he was.

"Mmm…" Her sigh washed over his neck and chest, and she finally met his gaze. "Damn…I love being under you, cowboy. You feel incredible." Warm hands cupped his ass as the sexy designer wriggled some more. "So incredible."

He tried, really tried not to respond, but heat raced through his body, and he found himself thrusting against her hot curves. "I like you under me, or on me, or just plain around me."

She giggled and opened her mouth to respond, but her phone rang. Fear instantly replaced the light he'd managed to put back into her gaze. *Damn.*

"I need to get that," she said, pushing him off to sit up and grab her phone from the nightstand.

Laying on his side, elbow bent, head resting in his hand, he watched her stiffened form as she answered the call.

"Hello? Yes, this is her."

Unable to explain the sudden need to touch her, to convey support, he reached out and lightly rubbed her back.

"It did? Uh-huh."

He felt her sigh and watched as her body visibly relaxed.

"Yeah. Okay. Good. I will. Thanks," she said, then hung up and set the phone back on the nightstand.

Pushing a clump of hair over her shoulder, he tugged a strand. "Good news?"

She stood, then turned around, big smile on her face, tears glistening in her eyes. "Yes, I don't have cancer."

"What?" *Jesus! Cancer?* His heart literally rocked in his chest. "That's great, Brandi, but what the hell?" He shot to his feet. "Why didn't you tell me you'd had tests done?"

She shrugged, dropping her gaze to her clasped hands. "I-I didn't want to worry anyone unnecessarily."

"*Christ, s*o you went through this on your own?" He wrapped his arms around her and crushed the brave, but foolish woman close. Now it all started to make sense.

She nodded against his throat. "Well, not exactly. Jace found out and waited while I had the biopsies on the goiters in my throat, then took me home."

Foreign emotions, strong and fierce seized his chest. *He* should've been the one there for her, not Jace. *He* was the one sharing the woman's bed, not Turner. But he couldn't get mad at the doctor. The guy had helped Brandi through what must've been a horrific day.

And apparently, Kade had helped her through one of

the nights. Guess he was good enough to share bodies, just not life's trials.

Maybe she was right. He'd certainly let Shayla and her baby down in a big way.

Feelings of inadequacy and failure seized his body with a ferocity that crushed the air from his lungs. Breathing was becoming a chore. He released her and began to dress.

"Do you have to go?" She ran a hand down his back.

"Yeah, I have to be at the station in less than an hour."

Not exactly true. He had two hours, but because he'd just told her that, he'd be there in less than one. It would bother him now if he didn't. He zipped his jeans then sat on her bed. Keeping his word had never been a problem, until this last damn deployment. But hey, when he fucked up, he really fucked up.

Jamming his feet into his boots, he bit back a curse and pushed as much of those dire thoughts away as his oxygen deprived mind would allow, then stood.

"Kade, are you all right?" she asked, stepping in front of him to slowly button his shirt. "I'm sorry. It's just, I've been through the waiting and it sucks. I refused to do that to you."

His heart squeezed at her pinched expression. "Hey," he stilled her hands and held them to his chest. "You don't have to explain or apologize. I'm just glad you're okay, and sorry you had to face that on your own. You should be celebrating."

One of her hands slid inside his now buttoned shirt to lightly stroke his skin. "I was kind of hoping you'd help me with that…"

One hell of an invitation.

It was there in her spoken words, saucy gaze,

tempting touch…incredible naked body pressing into him. And yet, those feelings of inadequacy still rolling inside him won out.

Holding her gaze, he brought her hands to his lips and kissed her fingers. "That's quite an invitation, honey, but unfortunately, I have to go." Needed to go. His head was beginning to pound with unrelenting force. He placed a kiss to her temple. "I'm glad you're okay."

Too bad he wasn't.

The very fact he released the gorgeous, willing, naked woman and walked away from her invitation to a morning of hot sex proved he was a damn sight far from okay.

Four days later, Brandi was supervising the installation of tile in the McCall's bathroom and couldn't resist touching the smooth, beautiful glass. Since she was touching, it made sense to help install. She'd just set a square in place on the third row from the bottom of the shower when Jordan walked in.

"This is looking all kinds of fantastic, Brandi," her friend said, standing back with folded fingers to her mouth as she stared, small smile tugging her lips. "I can't wait to use this room."

She laughed. *I bet*. Even she had visions of *using* the shower…with a certain sheriff. In fact, images and memories of the magnificent man had plagued her all week.

"But, right now, I came up here to fetch you. It's time for a break." The smiling woman gently pushed her toward the hall. "You've been working nonstop for days."

She laughed and moved out of the way to allow one of the other workers to take over. "It's my job," she said, falling into step alongside her friend.

"And jobs have lunch breaks," Jordan stated, leading them downstairs to the kitchen where Kerri was setting out dishes of chicken Caesar salads with dressing on the side.

Her stomach dutifully growled. "Yeah, okay. Lunch is a good idea."

All three of them laughed as they sat. The unexpected break and lunch with friends was just what she'd needed. Jordan was right. She had been working a lot. Since the Masters' party, business had picked up. She'd signed up two more projects, worked on two proposals this week and had another still yet to finish.

"Are you all right, Brandi? You look kind of tired," Kerri said, pouring all the dressing from her packet onto her salad.

Lucky shit. "Yeah, just busy." She drizzled half of her Caesar dressing and set the packet aside. Better to use up her daily allotted calories on food than condiments.

Jordan nodded. "Work picking up since mom's party?"

"Yes, scheduling and keeping more than two jobs going at the same time is going to be a problem."

"Can you afford to hire some help?" Kerri asked.

Brandi stilled, forkful of salad poised mid air. "I...I don't know." She chewed on a cucumber, and thought. A helper. Maybe. Then she could schedule more than two jobs, and have others lined up when one finished.

"Seems to me you could benefit greatly by hiring an organized individual with a good eye for design," her client suggested.

"Oh, absolutely. Do you have one hidden away," she joked, stabbing a tomato.

Jordan glanced up and pointed at her with her fork.

"As a matter of fact I do. Well, my sister and I do. And you've met her."

She set her fork down and stared at the girls. "I have?"

"Yes, Shayla, the woman renting the apartment above our restaurant."

Oh, great, the thin, gorgeous redhead.

"You're right," Kerri said, eyes-widening with approval. "She's been helping us out. Her attention to detail is great."

Jordan nodded. "Our storage room is so organized now, we have all this extra room we can hold meetings upstairs if we wanted."

"And she used the Dewey decimal system on my recipes. It's amazing," Kerri gushed.

Jordan finished the last of her salad and sat back. "You should drop by the restaurant and talk with her. Shayla's a hard worker and smart. And I think she could use the job. She has a darling one-year-old daughter, and her younger sister will be moving in with her when she stops dorming at a local college over the holiday break at the end of the year."

Brandi chewed and thought. "I could use the help," she said, pushing her empty plate away. If the woman was as organized as they said, and could multi-task, then her skills were worth checking out. "I'll drop by sometime this week. Thanks."

"Good," Kerri said. "Because Connor and I were talking, and we'd like to hire you, too."

Her head snapped up. "What? Me? But Wild Creek is perfect. What did you want to do?"

A big smile crossed the pretty cook's face. "We've decided to stay there, but want a place within the place."

"I don't follow."

"We want to section some of the upstairs off as kind of our own suite of rooms," her friend replied. "Complete with a state of the art gourmet kitchen, of course."

"Of course."

Already her mind was working on scenarios and possibilities. It would be a big job, but certainly doable. Excitement raced through her veins. "You wouldn't touch the outside?"

"Nope." Kerri shook her head. "We'd need to partition some of the upstairs, and we have a door to the outside if we incorporate the balcony entrance."

"True. Bullet and I used the balcony and stairs to the driveway all the time on his walks," Jordan said, and at the mention of his name, the gorgeous retired police dog ambled over, from his bed in the corner. "Didn't we, boy?"

The German Sheppard's tail wagged so fast his back end moved.

Brandi joined the sisters in a lighthearted laugh. The dog was really so sweet. But, it was time to get off her butt.

"Well, I have to get back to work. Thanks for the tip."

"Hang on."

"Yeah, don't you have something to tell us?" Jordan asked, small smirk on her client's lips.

Her heart shifted in her chest. Were they talking about her biopsy? No. Only two men knew about it, and neither would talk. What else could they mean?

Crud.

Kade.

She decided to play stupid. "Ah, no. I don't think so."

"Really? Nothing?" Jordan stared at her with those

damn, dark, all-seeing eyes.

Brandi sighed. "Look, Kade and I are just friends." With a whole lot of benefits. Great ones. Really great ones. Big ones. Shoot. She reached for her water. Funny how hot it was getting, despite the central air.

Bulldog McCall smiled broadly and leaned back in her chair. "Interesting. I wasn't talking about Kade, but now that you've mentioned him, I think maybe we should."

"No, no…we shouldn't. We really shouldn't."

Lovely. Now Kerri was smiling.

"A double denial," the cook stated with a nod. "We definitely should."

Jordan's brow rose. "I suppose you're going to claim his truck was parked outside your house all night on Thursday because he ran out of gas?"

"Oh, hell no. That guy would never run out of gas. Not with his stamina."

Kerri's indrawn breath and pink cheeks were the first indication Brandi had spoken her thoughts out loud. Dammit. And if that wasn't clear enough, then Jordan's chuckling was confirmation.

She shot from her chair. "Oh, look at the time. I'd better get back to work."

"Oh no you don't," her client insisted, hand snaking out to clamp around her wrist.

Kerri shook her head. "Not after a statement like that."

The sisters were too much. Looking all hopeful.

Smiling, she shook free and held up her hands. "Forget it. I don't kiss and tell."

"So, there was kissing involved." Kerri beamed.

Jordan snorted. "I'd say a whole hell of a lot more for Brandi to make a statement like that. But we'll leave it right there. I just want to say I think it's great. You and Kade. You're perfect for each other."

Why did people keep saying that?

Putting her hands on her hips, she frowned at the sisters. "Hold on. There is no me and Kade. It was just…just…"

"Sex," Kerri answered, cheeks turning pink again.

"Actually, it was great sex," she felt obligated to say. The sheriff had outdone any man she'd ever known, which technically wasn't many, but he'd also bested her fantasies, and well, she did have a fantastic imagination. She had it in writing from her seventh grade English teacher.

"Yeah, I'm guessing that would tie into the stamina statement." Her client grinned.

Instead of embarrassment, she felt the warmth of satisfaction flow all the way to her toes and couldn't help but smile.

"Must be something in the Harland County water," Kerri remarked, then slapped a hand over her mouth as her blush turned crimson.

Apparently the speaking out loud syndrome was contagious.

"Amen to that," Jordan chimed in. "And not that this isn't a fascinating subject, because let me tell you, Cole put the *'S'* in stamina, but I'd like to get back to my original question, Brandi. Don't you have something to tell us about your *violin*?"

Ah, so that was what the woman was getting at. Her past. She'd rather talk about sex with Kade.

Even though playing dumb hadn't worked before, she thought maybe she'd have better luck this time. "Like?"

"Like, when will you tell everyone what you used to

do? And can we hear you play again? And will you please play at the pub sometime?"

A heavy weight settled over her shoulders. She sat down and sighed under the pressure. "I don't think anyone would be all that interested in hearing about my prior job."

"Wrong."

"And as for playing again," she went on as if Jordan hadn't spoken. "I'm not really up to it yet. It's just associated with too many dark memories."

"But I'm sure there are lots of good memories, too. And maybe now, here in Texas, you can make some new ones." Kerri stared at her, brown eyes big and earnest.

The woman had a point. And her cell was a Godsend because it began to ring. "Sorry," she told the girls as she fished the phone blaring David Garrett's version of "Thunderstruck" from her pocket. Her heart dipped a little at the fleeting thought it might be Kade, although, she'd never given him her number.

Glancing at the caller ID, she held back a sigh. A different military man. "Hi, Dad."

"Hi, sweetheart. You are going to the dinner, aren't you?"

Right to the point as always.

"Yes. I'll be there."

"Good. Are you going to sit with your old man and your brother, Ben?"

"Of course." She smiled. "It'll be nice to see you both again. I miss you." The words fell from her mouth before she could stop herself, and she was surprised to realize she meant every word. She did miss them both.

"Miss you too, sweetheart. When you coming back home?"

Another sigh left her lips. Not that again. "I am

home, Dad."

He grunted. "We'll discuss it when I see you. Uh, got to go, hun. There's a Battalion meeting in less than five. See you Saturday."

And just like that, he was gone. Nothing new there. Higher ups said jump, he asked how high. Of course, Major Wyne was just as good at doling it out. And as for *discussing*, his idea of a discussion was a 'this is how it should be done, now do it' mentality.

Guilt squeezed her insides. That wasn't fair. He was actually very patient and caring. Dennis Wyne had been an angel when her mother had needed one, taking her to and from treatments and appointments. She knew the man could very well have turned his back on the sick woman and her daughter, allowed others to take care of his wife, but he hadn't. No. He'd nursed her and attended to her needs right up until the end. He'd gained Brandi's love and respect and had had it ever since. He'd been Catherine Wyne's rock and strength. And although Brandi had been ten when her mother married the man, he'd never treated her any different than his four sons. He even adopted her and gave her his last name. And when her mother died two years later, he'd never wavered in that love.

"Your family must miss you," Kerri said, bringing Brandi's mind back to the present.

Shrugging, she shoved the phone back in her pocket. At times, she missed them a lot. Like this past week. She really could've used her big brothers and their caring and kidding and all things *brother* to keep her mind occupied. Their constant banter and teasing always made her feel safe and loved. Then there was her little nephew. God, her arms ached to crush Tyler close and hold him tight.

Instead, she'd held onto an entirely different kind of

male. Her good parts instantly tingled at the memories.

"Did you tell them about Kade?"

She reeled back and blinked at Kerri. "What? No. What for?"

"Well, you've been having sex with him, and most women tell at least one person in their family about a guy they have sex with," the cook stated matter-of-factly.

"What?"

"You told your brother, Ben, about Kade, remember? In the apartment when we were going over plans."

"No, I didn't. *You* did," Brandi reminded the former cop. "Yeah, thanks for that, by the way." Then a slight problem dawned on her, and she groaned. "Oh, great."

"Ben's coming to Texas with your dad, isn't he? That's what that phone call was about." Jordan's smile was practically too big for her pretty face.

"Yeah, for a Dining Out dinner for anyone who served in one of the joint task forces in an overseas operation. They've been involved in several. I don't remember which one this is for, but it's being held in Houston this year."

"That's wonderful," Kerri gushed.

"Yeah, until my dad volunteered me to play at the dinner." She would rather attend out of respect than a command.

"But you're so good. Why is it a problem?"

She sighed. "It's not that. I-I stopped playing when I was told what to play and when to play. This just brings it all back. But, I'd do anything for the troops, so of course, I haven't declined."

"Have you picked up the violin since Sunday?"

"Yeah, several times."

"Your asshole ex-boyfriend isn't going to be there,

is he?"

Brandi blinked...in unison with Jordan as they stared at Kerri, the sweet cook. She'd never heard her friend say a bad word about anyone.

"Kerri," Jordan said. "I can't believe you called Brandi's ex that."

"Sorry, but he is."

"No." Jordan shook her head. "An asshole serves a purpose."

Brandi snickered. "True. And no, Ed is not going to be there. Just my dad and brother, and a few others from the PA Guard. And, of course, other soldiers from across the county."

"Oh, well, what about for Texas? Will Kade be there representing the Texas Guard?"

"No." Thank heavens. She'd checked that straight out. Called in a marker to a friend in the Guard and had them look up the list. Despite the size and number of soldiers in the Texas Guard, Brandi wouldn't put it past her bad luck to have the First Sergeant on the list. But he wasn't. "A Colonel Dwyer, and a few more are representing the local regiment."

Jordan scrunched her nose. "That's too bad. Kade would've loved to hear you play. I'm sure of it. He loves a good fiddle."

"Well, it wouldn't matter anyway." She shrugged. "They have me down to play some Beethoven and Bach." Although, she did plan to throw in some good ole Texas fiddle. Seemed fitting considering the dinner was hosted *in* Texas.

Her client nodded while scratching Bullet's neck. "So, will your father and brother come back to Harland County with you when it's over?"

Brandi blinked. "I-I don't know. They didn't say.

Probably not. Dad's always on a tight schedule. Probably just stay the night at the hotel where the dinner is being held, and fly out the next morning."

Which worked for her. There wasn't enough room in her little cottage for all three of them.

"That's too bad," Jordan claimed. "I would've liked to have known what he thought of Kade."

"What is it with you and Kade?" she asked, head beginning to ache.

"No, it's *you* and Kade."

Oh, for the love of... "There is no me and Kade."

And in walked Cole...and Kade.

When her mind finally caught up with her mouth, and all the heat rushed to her face, Brandi noted the sheriff didn't appear to be angry. Just stared, one eyebrow slightly raised. Besides, the guy had nothing to be angry about anyway. *He* was the one who'd left while she was stark friggin' naked...and had invited him to stay.

Okay, she'd offered him sex. A morning romp, but he'd clamed up and left for work.

If he hadn't been so attentive during the night before, or taken such pleasure in her body, then she would've been offended. But deep down, she knew that wasn't the case. She'd seen the look before. The tensing of muscles, irregular breathing, dilated pupils. He was having a 'moment.' A pretty strong one at that if he was passing up sex, because she got the impression from their time together he liked having sex with her...a lot.

The feeling was mutual. Dammit.

Deciding this was one of those roll with the punches moments, she nodded to the men. "Hi, Cole. Kade, you're just in time. Maybe you can convince the sisters here that we're not in a relationship."

He stared right at the girls. "We're not in a relationship."

Jordan laughed, Kerri smiled and Cole closed his eyes and shook his head. She had no idea what that meant, but was more than ready to get back to work. All this talk about non-relationships was one thing when she said it, but a completely different feeling in her gut when the man who melted her from the inside out with just one look spoke the words.

Maybe the chicken was bad in the salad. Yeah, that was probably why her stomach felt like lead.

"Not in a relationship, right," Jordan scoffed. "Even though you've spent the night at her place."

Cole shot forward and cupped Kade's shoulder. "Okay, going to have to intervene here. Keep your mouth shut, buddy. Trust me." The CEO cowboy glanced around at everyone and nodded. "If you'll excuse us. Kade came over to check out the horses I got at the auction yesterday."

And just like that, both men nodded, then left through the back door.

She was going to give that tactic a try. "Well, if you'll excuse me, I really do need to get back to work. Thanks for lunch."

Setting her dishes in the sink, she held her breath, waiting for a retort. None came. Breathing a little easier, she headed for the hall, thinking she was home free.

"You two are in relationship denial," Jordan smirked. "It'll go easier if you just admit it and give in."

Kerri nodded. "Yeah, admitting it is your first step to a happily-ever-after."

Snickering commenced throughout the kitchen.

"You two are so full of shit." Brandi swiped a cherry tomato off the counter and threw it in the girls' direction.

She had no idea why this relationship discussion had started. But she was not in one with Kade. Yes, she liked having sex with the guy. Okay, she *loved* having sex with the guy. He didn't mind her curves. Heck, he loved her curves. Embraced her curves. He'd practically worshipped her curves.

And now she was getting hot again.

Still, great sex did not a relationship make.

Cripes, now she sounded like one of those doctors on television. Not that she was knocking great sex. Hell no. It certainly made her feel good. And that was all she was looking for right now. There was no need to introduce her family to the guy she'd had great sex with the past week.

Playing the violin at the Dining Out was enough of a stress maker. Thank goodness Kade was not attending the dinner. That would be just a wee bit awkward.

Chapter Eleven

Although sharp, Dress Blues were not Kade's favorite uniform of choice—he'd much prefer the comfort of the Army Combat Uniform or ACU's. Too bad a Dining Out dinner required more formal attire. Tonight, he'd donned the blue uniform with gold stripe down the side of the pants, double-checked his medals, stripes and insignia to make sure they were all up to date on his jacket—all while silently cursing his luck that a family emergency had forced Colonel Dwyer to call him to take his place at the last minute.

So, here he was, driving up to Houston with barely ten minutes to spare. Had he known ahead of time, he would've scheduled it in, and made plans to commute with a few of the other guys attending from the unit.

Not to mention, leaving Harland County in the hands of Skippy didn't sit well with his stomach. He hoped to God nothing major arose. The kid barely handled a skunk intrusion, speeding tickets, lunch…and Kade didn't even want to think about the *cat-in-the-tree* call the other day. Thanks to the deputy's stellar response, the department now had a hefty vet bill. Poor cat would be stuck in a cast for another two weeks.

Donny wasn't allowed anywhere near Ace. Make that Shadow Rock. He shuddered to think of the havoc the kid could inflict on livestock. Not good.

Pulling up at the venue held in a popular hotel and convention center, Kade put the deputy out of his mind and parked. It was only for a few hours. The county would be fine. He hoped. Right now, he had to switch hats. Literally. Sliding out of the truck, he swiped his beret off the seat and straightened.

"Hey, *Top*. Didn't know you were coming," one of his lieutenants said, stopping by the truck with a pretty blonde on his arm.

"Neither did I. Colonel had an emergency." He donned his beret, shut the door then turned as the lieutenant introduced his girlfriend.

Some soldiers brought a date to the Dining Out and some didn't, he observed as they walked inside. If he'd had more notice maybe he would've...what? Asked Brandi? Probably not. According to the designer, they weren't *in a relationship*. Which was true. He'd more than made that clear when he'd walked away from her naked, willing body the other morning. So why he was a bit put out by her public admission of their non-relationship status at Cole's a few days back was puzzling.

Maybe he actually wanted a relationship?

His chest squeezed tight. *That would be a negatory, Sergeant*. He shut that train of thought down fast. No relationship. No date. No hassles. Tonight was a night to reunite with old comrades. Men and women from across the country who'd participated in one of the operations a few years ago. Even though he hadn't originally planned to attend, he was there now and would enjoy the evening's events.

Removing his cover, he tucked the beret in his belt and joined some of the familiar faces gathered near the cash bar.

A good twenty-minutes had passed and he was enjoying the conversation, nursing his seven and seven, when one of the men let out a low whistle.

"Damn, how the hell did Ben land someone like

that?" one of the guys questioned.

Kade turned with the others, and his heart literally rocked in his chest.

Brandi?

Wearing a knee-length, black dress with sheer sleeves, she was elegantly dressed, and even though her neckline wasn't low cut, just enough of her luscious curves showed to raise his temperature.

Then his gaze travelled down her gorgeous legs to her shoes. Black, high and strappy, with her toes peeking through. Ah hell. She'd painted them a pale pink. They reminded him of her…

He cleared his throat and sipped his drink. He wasn't going there. Wasn't thinking about how her *do-me-shoes* made him want to do just that…right now…in one of the rooms upstairs…with just those damn shoes on.

He downed the rest of his drink. Didn't help. He was now sporting a raging hard-on, in the middle of a Dining Out, thanks to those damn shoes.

"Yeah, she's hot," someone else exclaimed.

Since the men hadn't said anything derogatory, he deduced the anger heating his blood must have something to do with the woman who wasn't crazy about soldiers showing up *with* a soldier. One he didn't know.

He cleared his throat. "Who's she with?" he asked in his best matter-of-fact tone.

"One of the PA soldiers," the guy replied.

Jesus. He hoped to God it wasn't that stupid ex of hers. Surely she was smarter than to hook up with the jerk again.

Flexing his shoulders to alleviate a sudden tightness, he told himself he had no reason to be jealous of the dark-haired, green-eyed guy who had an arm slung around her waist. But, dammit, he was.

"Yeah, that's Ben. You remember, *Top*. He's the supply guy who performed miracles and saved our asses several times when he helped fill our shortages," the lieutenant informed.

And his fuzzy brain got a clue. He nodded. "Right, Sergeant Wyne."

Wait...*Wyne*? Was Ben one of her four National Guard brothers? It occurred to him he didn't really know much about the designer's family, and what little he did know, he'd learned from Mrs. Masters.

She never mentioned anything about her brother coming down.

Did you give her a chance to?

No. He'd pretty much avoided the woman all week. The way they seemed to fall into bed lately, he figured it was better for them both if he kept some distance. Last thing either of them needed was to become dependent on each other. That was a fast track to a relationship...which they didn't want. Or need.

"Hey, Ben, over here," the lieutenant called out.

The guy smiled and headed over, Brandi in tow. She nodded at the others, smile sweet and unsure, until her gaze fell on him, and her warm brown eyes widened. Yeah, imagine seeing him at a Guard function. Did she think he wouldn't find out? And what did it matter, anyway? It really was no big deal, his brain reminded.

"Hello, Brandi," he said, rather enjoying the pink tint creeping into her face.

"You two know each other?" Her brother's gaze bounced between them before skittering to Kade's chest. A slow smile spread across the man's face as he lifted his gaze and held out a hand. "You must be Kade. Nice to meet you, Sheriff. I'm Ben, Brandi's brother. I heard so much about you."

Now it was his turn to raise a brow. Ignoring the looks from his men, he shook hands, and knew by the grip, he was getting that *watch-your-step* brotherly warning. And judging by the gleam in the green eyes, the guy was somehow teasing his sister in the process.

Never one to turn down a tease, he played along. "Hopefully, it's all good. Brandi's a sweetheart."

Her blush deepened, but she remained quiet. He decided to give her a break and talk shop.

"It's nice to meet you in person, though, Sergeant," he said, releasing the man's hand. "Good to have this opportunity to thank you. Any supplies my men needed back then that I couldn't get, you came through. It was much appreciated."

Ben shrugged. "No thanks necessary, First Sergeant. It was my job. Soldiers always come first."

"Unfortunately, not everyone has that attitude, so thank you."

Brandi stepped closer to her brother. "Ben has always taken that attitude. And now that he's the Battalion S4, more people will benefit."

Kade's brows rose again. "Battalion supply? Good for you."

A big grin split the man's face. He nodded and turned to his sister. "Nice try, Brandi. But you're not going to change the subject. I'd love to hear more about you and Sergeant Dalton." The green gaze returned to him, a serious glint present underneath the twinkle. "Why is it you didn't ask her to come with you tonight, First Sergeant?"

Brandi's indrawn breath echoed around them. Kade immediately liked the guy. He cocked his head. "I wasn't supposed to be here. I'm a last minute fill in for Colonel Dwyer."

"I see," Ben said, still holding on to the woman gazing longingly toward the hall. "Then you won't mind sitting at our table? I'm sure my dad would love to meet you."

Her dad? Okay, this wasn't so funny anymore. But, he'd made his bed. *Damn.* Poor choice of words.

"Oh, that's not necessary," Brandi spoke up. "I'm sure Kade...I mean, Sergeant Dalton would like to sit with his men."

"*Top* sees us all the time. It's okay." The damn lieutenant decided to speak up. "You sit with Brandi's family, sir."

And before he could reply, his men walked away. Deserted him.

Bastards.

Calling on his reserve manners, he turned to the Wynes and smiled. "Looks like you're stuck with me. Lead the way."

"First..." Ben took Brandi's hand and placed it on Kade's arm. "That's more like it. Brandi can guide you to our table up front. If you'll excuse me, I see some more guys I wanted to say hello to."

And with a nod, the man was gone, leaving him alone with a red-faced designer. She tried to pull her hand away, but he covered it with his free one.

"Hold on there, honey. Where are you going?"

"Look, Kade. I'm so, so sorry. And so embarrassed. You go on and sit with your unit. It's okay. You don't need to sit with me just because my brother said so."

He turned to face her. "Hey, make no mistake. I'm sitting with you because I want to."

"Oh..." Big brown eyes blinked at him. "Y-you do?" She was nearly eye level, thanks to those sexy shoes.

His insides warmed, and he rode out the tide. "Yes," he replied, smile tugging his lips. "You look incredible tonight."

She blinked again, pink returning to her cheeks. "I do?"

He nodded and leaned closer. "Good enough to eat."

Her lips parted and blush deepened as she swayed into him.

"Now, that's what I like to see. A happy expression on my daughter's face," an older man said as he approached, arms behind his back. His crisp stance and sharp gaze commanded attention.

"Oh, Dad." She jumped back and pointed to him. "This is Kade Dalton. Sergeant Dalton. First Sergeant Dalton," she corrected twice.

Her father smiled and held out a hand. "Nice to meet you, son." He covered Kade's hand with his other and continued to shake. "Hell of a job you did over there, son. Hell of a job."

Her father was Major Wyne? *Tough but fair* Major Wyne? Of course he was… *Idiot*. Why the hell the praise hit deep, Kade didn't know. Fighting unexpected emotions, he pushed aside the ghosts, held himself erect and met the man's gaze. "Thank you, sir."

"I was prepared to come down here to talk my daughter out of her silly notion of staying in Texas, but now I'm not so sure."

He met Brandi's startled gaze. She no doubt had her hands full butting heads with the Major, but the woman possessed the backbone necessary to stand her ground. She could certainly be stubborn.

"Your daughter's nothing if not tenacious, sir," he remarked. And when she deployed that tendency during sex, damn, he was a lucky man.

And this was exactly the wrong time to have those thoughts.

"That she is, First Sergeant. That she is," the major said, slapping Kade's shoulder. "What do you say we all take our seats? I believe this shindig is about to get started."

Seated between her and a corporal, Kade had just finished his appetizer when her brother looked up from his plate and stared at him from across the table. "So, Sheriff, when did you and my sister first hook up?"

"Really, Ben? Give it a rest, will you?" Brandi shook her head and stabbed at a cherry tomato which promptly flew off her salad and landed on his empty plate.

"Actually," the major glanced at him. "I'd like to know that, too."

Great. Tag-team interrogation.

He plucked the tomato from his plate and set it back on her salad, then glanced into her apprehensive gaze. "A few weeks back." In the barn, on a hay bale. He kept that last part to himself, but knew she'd caught his thought by the heat entering her gaze.

"Well, I'm glad, son. It's good to know my daughter has someone down here she can count on. That *I* can count on," her father corrected with a smile, then set his attention back to his plate.

With the subject dropped and their entrées in place, Kade concentrated on his prime rib and listened as the others chatted.

That she can count on...

The words echoed in his head, bouncing back and forth like a ball in a pinball machine. He wasn't the best person for her to count on. Hell, he was no longer blemish free.

And now the delicious steak tasted like dirt.

Swallowing the last mouthful with a sip of water, he set his fork down and tried to regroup. Now was not the time to give into the feelings of inadequacy suddenly tightening his chest, and her father was no doubt waiting for a response. Glancing at the man, he nodded, but didn't offer anything more. Like a promise. That would be stupid.

"I heard some good things through the scuttlebutt about you, son."

"Thank you, sir. I've heard the same about you. You have a reputation for getting the job done." Which was true. No matter how tough, Major Wyne delivered. Some people complained, usually the slackers, because the man rode their asses and forced them to do their jobs, and others praised the ethics.

"Why thank you, First Sergeant, I appreciate that," the man said, his direct gaze serious. "I'm sorry you had a loss. It's tough to lose a soldier. It's happened too many times in this damn war. From what I hear, you handled it well, kept the men going, and to borrow your phrasing, got the job done."

Got the job done…

Well, wasn't that just swell? An invisible vice squeezed his chest tight. Too bad he couldn't have gotten the job done without Sergeant Nylan dying. Then it would've been a good job. Hell, it would've been fucking great. Everyone could have really sung his praises then.

Warm fingers tugged his fist open at his side and wrapped around his hand. It took him a full minute to realize Brandi had not only unclenched his fingers she'd taken over the conversation, asking questions about her brothers back home.

Her grace, her warmth...her unwavering calm seeped into him, and he slowly regained the ability to breath, and his body eventually relaxed enough to hear the exchange.

"...then he turned to me and said, Uncle Ben, when can I be Batman?"

Brandi's laughter was sweet and genuine, and warmed the last of the chill from his bones. He even sensed a slight longing in the tone, and guessed the conversation was about her nephew. Sitting back, fingers still entwined—apparently he wasn't the only one reluctant to let go—he listened to the banter between siblings, and couldn't help but think of his cousins and their dinner table discussions while growing up.

The talk eventually turned to shop and he threw in his two cents when required, but his attention was drawn to the woman by his side. She began to fidget, and he thought maybe it was because she wasn't crazy about the dessert. It wasn't chocolate. But she ate her sorbet. So it couldn't be the dessert. She was getting more apprehensive by the minute. Her whole body was tensing up. At first, he thought maybe he had missed something in her conversation with her brother because she seemed to be watching Ben intently. But then he realized her attention was just past him, on the band setting up in the far corner.

Why in the world was she so apprehensive about the band? Did she know someone in it?

Her fingers began to tighten around his, and they squeezed so hard his knuckles cracked. What the hell? He turned to her and placed his other hand over their entwined fingers.

"Hey, are you okay?"

She blinked and transferred her attention to him.

"What?"

"I said, are you okay?"

"Oh…yeah." She nodded, but her gaze was far too troubled for her words to be believed.

"You'll be fine, sis," Ben said. "It's like riding a bike."

What was that supposed to mean? What was like riding a bike?

Her father leaned close to pat her shoulder. "It's time you got back to doing what you love."

"But I am doing what I love, Dad."

Kade wanted to ask what they were talking about, but one of the Colonels took the podium again.

"Well, tonight we're very lucky. One of our own is going to play a few songs from her time with the Pennsylvania Philharmonic, as well as a few requests. Put your hands together for Ms. Brandi Wyne."

One of our own? Philharmonic?

As his brain wrapped around the introduction, his mind backpedaled to keep up. Brandi had been with an orchestra? When did she find time to study design? And what did *one of our own* mean?

He stared at her, like a complete idiot.

Her mouth opened but only a sigh came out. Then she inhaled, squeezed his hand and leaned close. "Don't leave. Okay? Promise me you'll stay."

He frowned. "I'll be here."

The woman he thought he knew nodded her thanks then tugged free and stood. "I can do this," she said under her breath as she walked toward the makeshift stage area.

The major leaned close and winked. "You're in for a real treat, son. My daughter is fantastic. It's about time she stopped running from the things she loves. The violin was a great stress reliever when her mom was sick."

His heart ached for the little girl and the tough childhood she must've had. "How old was she?"

"Eleven when her mom was first diagnosed with cancer," the major replied. "Twelve when she died."

So young. Too young. He'd been nearly the same age when his mom, well, left him…then died. His chest squeezed tight at the thought.

"Yeah, for a while, she was never separated from the violin," Ben said. "She even carried it to school. The music teacher used to let her use the music room to practice during lunch and recess."

Once again, Kade's brain and mind played catch up. And while they were goofing off, Brandi stepped up to the microphone with a violin in her hand.

"Thank you for the invitation. It's an honor to be here to play for you tonight," she said. "There have been several requests sent in. We'll try to get to them before our time is up." She turned and introduced the other four musicians. "We're going to start with the two hardest and get them out of the way. This first one's called "Asturias" and goes out to my brother, Ben."

"Sweet." Her brother placed two fingers in his mouth and whistled loudly as others clapped. "Nothing like jumping into the fire, sis."

Kade had no idea what the song was, but had the impression he was not likely to ever forget it.

He watched her take a breath, place the violin under her chin then nod to the band. Good thing he was seated. With the first four notes played, the woman's talent and love for music was obvious. Her fingers flew and bow moved so fast he couldn't keep up. Loud, strong, passionate, the music filled the room and blew him away. He never heard music played like that before. Never *felt* music before, but she made him feel. Every pull of the bow, every chord, had meaning.

When the song finished, the crowd stood and clapped.

Her father turned to him and smiled. "See?"

"I sure do, sir." He inhaled then blew out the breath. "I feel like I've run ten miles."

The major laughed and slapped his shoulder. "Just wait. She's only warming up."

Ben nodded. "Yeah. Guarantee she's going to make you feel the gamut of emotions, and usually more than we expect."

"Thank you," she said as everyone sat. "Now, we're going to do "Adagio for Strings." And it's tough for other reasons."

She took another deep breath and...*shit*...started to walk toward the Fallen Soldier table. A table set up at all functions symbolizing those who could no longer attend. At this Dining Out, the small table was in the front of the room with a single place setting, tapered candle, single rose in vase, inverted wine glass, chair set against the table representing missing comrades. He'd avoided that side of the room for a reason. *Christ*, what was she doing? Air became thick and heavy. He couldn't stay here for this. But, damn, he'd promised her he would. Had she planned this? *Son-of-a-bitch.* Did she do this on purpose? His heart rocked into his ribs then thudded so fast he lost his breath.

Get out, his mind screamed, but he remained seated, legs frozen. Completely immobile.

"This is for our fallen soldiers."

With the first strings played, his erratic heart beats slowed and flowed, snagged with the mellow start, building, moving with emotional precision. Something within him cracked, and it was as if she saw inside and put it to music. Clued into the deep emotion, wrapped it around the bow and played his soul. All of it.

She found the pain, the grief, the guilt, the unfairness, the loss, and twisted them together, turning it all into a real thread of feeling, reaching for hope, a hope always just out of his grasp, making him feel like maybe this time he'd prevail.

When it ended, there was silence. No jumping up and clapping. There was also not a single dry eye in the place. And hell, he hadn't even realized his face was wet until he blinked. The tight stranglehold around his heart had eased a bit, and he was able to draw in a few breaths, as did those around him. Then the clapping started and everyone rose to their feet once more, including him, since he miraculously found his legs again.

"Okay," she said, stepping back to the microphone and swiping her face. "Phew, that was the toughest. Now, I'd like to move on to some fun selections. This one goes out to Kade."

His head jerked back. She was playing a song for him?

"Good for you, man," Ben said. "You must mean something to my sister for her to dedicate a song."

He didn't know about that, but his heart was pounding a loud, crazy-ass beat. Damned if he knew why. And the almost sexy smile she sent him ensured his pulse stayed at erratic. When she first started the rock symphony version of "Thunderstruck," he smiled. He was not likely to forget this one either.

She was good. Once again her fingers and bow flew across the strings, spewing the perfect notes with the perfect rhythm. The woman continued to play rock, Beethoven and even Celtic.

A few songs later, the crowd went wild as she began to play "Zorba's Dance" for her dad. The soldiers from the Pennsylvania Guard cheered loudest. He got the impression it was some kind of tradition. Her father and brother stood, took off their jackets and started to dance the traditional Greek dance. As far as he knew, they weren't Greek, but didn't seem to care. The faster she played, the faster they danced. Soon Kade found himself clapping and smiling with the rest of the room, cheering the Wynes on, his earlier distress forgotten as he got caught up in the lighthearted fun.

After the song ended and she hugged her family, Brandi took the stage one more time. "Seems only fitting to end with this song since we're in Texas. This one goes out to the Texas Guard and anyone else who happens to like a little something called "Orange Blossom Special.""

His brows rose. *No way. Fiddle?* He smiled, sat back and enjoyed the final song from the very talented musician. And that's what she was, a musician. An accomplished one. No one played like that if it was just a hobby. The woman no doubt had slept with the instrument under her pillow in her youth. Her talent was an eat-breathe-and-sleep talent.

A virtuoso.

What the hell was she doing designing rooms? Not that she wasn't great at that, but…damn. It was a sin to let all the talent, practice, blood, sweat—the tears go to waste.

When the last strings died and the country band took the stage, it was a good ten minutes before Brandi reached the table. Every few steps someone stopped her, to shake her hand or give her a hug. Kade made sure to have a fresh glass of water ready and the chair pulled back.

After hugging her father and brother, she dropped into her seat and reached for her water. "Thank you," she said.

He settled into his chair and watched as she downed half the glass before she set it on the table and turned to him.

"You stayed." She reached for his hand and squeezed. "Thank you."

Cocking his head, he narrowed his gaze and studied the woman. "Did you make me promise to stay so I wouldn't leave during your second song?" He couldn't bring himself to say "Fallen Soldier" out loud. But he needed to know. He didn't appreciate being manipulated, even if the song somehow released a bit of the constant pressure from his chest.

A frown wrinkled her brow and she shifted closer. "No. I asked you to stay because…I…because you make me feel strong. Like I can do anything. And going up there was tough tonight. I haven't played since I left the Philharmonic."

Ah hell. He squeezed her hand and lifted his other to touch her face, uncaring that her father and brother were watching. He'd more than likely panic later. Right now, his concern for her won out. "You are strong, Brandi. You don't need me or anyone. All you need is you."

She inhaled as tears filled her eyes. Damn. He hadn't meant to make her cry.

"Well said, son." Her father stood and smacked her brother's shoulder. "Let's mingle and give these two some privacy to talk."

With that, all the other soldiers at the table stood, and soon he was alone with Brandi.

"Your dad doesn't pull any punches, does he?"

She laughed and sniffed. "No. Not hardly."

"I like him. He's a good man," he said, wiping a stray tear from her face with his thumb. "I'm glad he was there for you."

She nodded. "Me, too. I know I was lucky." Her hand tightened around his. "Are you okay?"

His insides froze, as they always did whenever the *are-you-okay* subject came up. "Yeah, I'm good." And the thumb she used to brush the underside of his wrist made him feel even better. His insides went from frozen to stirred. He needed to fight it for another minute. "Brandi, what did the Colonel mean during your introduction about you being one of our own? Did he mean a Wyne or…"

"I joined the Guard when I was eighteen."

She was former military? *Son-of-a-bitch*. Taking the news like a slap to the face, he released her hands and sat back. "You have any more secrets?"

She blinked. "It wasn't a secret. It's just not something that comes up." Sighing, she dropped her gaze and fumbled with her fingers on her lap. "I loved the Guard, but left when my weight started to interfere with my performance. I was worried I'd fail the PT test, and not only embarrass myself, but my dad."

Understanding instantly cancelled his mistrust. He reached for her knotted hands and gently pried them apart. "I'm sorry."

She nodded.

He wanted to ask if she'd been overseas, but the thought of her seeing the things he'd seen, experiencing the horrors…did something unpleasant to his insides. And given the way she'd played that song. The emotions she'd tapped into…he knew… *Yes*, she had been deployed.

"You want to dance?" he asked, because otherwise

he was going to give into the urge to kiss her right there in public, in front of his peers, her family...his men. He needed to lead by example. Show restraint.

"Yes," she replied.

For a moment, he stilled, not sure if she meant the dance or the kiss.

"Both." A slow smile spread across her lips as he led her to the dance floor.

She was killing him. Mindful of her father and brother in the room, he forced himself to hold her luscious curves at a respectable distance. "And how do you know what I'm thinking?" he asked, unable to resist the teasing gleam in her eyes.

Her hands slid up his chest to hook around his neck. "Because it's exactly what I'm thinking," she replied, brushing that damn thumb across the back of his neck, sending shivers straight down his spine.

Then she stepped in close—decimating that respectable distance—to inhale near his neck, and this time shivers shot down the front of him, then back up when she puffed a soft, sexy little moan near his ear.

"Oh... I might have to wear these shoes more often. All our good parts are lined up," she observed, deliberately brushing against him.

He sucked in a breath and stilled. "*Jesus*, Brandi. You have to stop that. Your father and brother are here. And my men."

"Sorry." She sighed. "I can't help it. My body has a mind of its own where you're concerned."

"I know what you mean," he admitted close to her ear, fighting the urge to nibble. "But you are right about your shoes. You do need to wear them more often...and without clothes."

She let out a strangled moan.

He smiled. "What are you thinking?"

"That…that you look so good in your uniform, but…I really want to drag you up to my room and take you out of it."

Even though all the blood rushed south, his brain managed to hang onto two important facts. One, she actually said something positive about him in a uniform, and two…

"You have a room?"

He could feel her smile against his neck. "Yes. I drove up last night to meet my father and brother."

Ah hell. He'd forgotten about them. His shoulders slumped. "Oh."

"They have their own rooms," she informed, thumb brushing circles on the back of his neck again. "And Dad doesn't usually stay at these gatherings 'til the end."

And after three more songs, as if to prove the woman right, the major met them back at the table.

"It was nice meeting you, Sergeant Dalton," her father said, shaking his hand. "I can't tell you how relieved I am to know my baby is in good hands."

He wasn't sure what gave the man the impression he and Brandi were in a relationship, but was to the point he didn't care anymore. "Nice meeting you, too, sir," he replied, deciding to remain quiet on the *in good hands* subject.

"Will I see you both for breakfast?"

If a herd of tap-dancing elephants danced across eggshells without breaking them, Kade wouldn't have been more surprised. And judging by the deer-in-the-headlights expression Brandi had going on, she was just as shocked.

"What? You think your old man ain't hip?" The major grinned. "Just make sure you use protection."

If Donny came in dragging two brawling bikers Kade wouldn't have been more surprised. Damn. The major was two for two. And Brandi looked so incredibly cute with her face all red.

"Dad! Really?" She slapped her hands over her ears.

Ben joined them at that moment and smiled. "Ah, Dad gave you the old *use protection* line, didn't he?"

"Hey, responsibility is key." Her father shrugged. "And you haven't given me an answer. Will I see you both at breakfast?"

Kade shook his head. "Sorry, sir. I'm on duty at oh-six-hundred. I have to drive back to Harland County tonight."

"Then I'd best say my goodbyes now." They shook hands again, and the major squeezed tight. "Just remember, son, it isn't a sign of weakness if you admit you need help."

Unsure what he had to do with that statement, he nodded anyway since her father seemed to expect a response. The major released him to turn to his daughter and kiss her cheek.

"You did great tonight, kiddo. I knew you would," her father stated. "I'll see you in the morning. Goodnight." Then the man pivoted on his heel and strode for the door.

"It was nice meeting you, Kade." Ben held out his hand. "Don't hurt my baby sister. You do not want the Wyne brothers down here, trust me."

He nodded.

Her brother released his hand and smiled. "Now, if you two will excuse me, I'm going to go ask the pretty blonde server to dance."

And like the wind, the man was gone.

"I'm sorry about that, Kade," Brandi said, face still a

deep shade of red.

He smiled. "Don't be. Just goes to show how much your family loves you. Kevin and I put Brock through the same treatment with Jen."

"Oh, boy. I suddenly feel very sorry for her."

His smile broadened. "As you know, everything worked out just fine."

"True." She fell silent.

"What's wrong?"

"I…well..." Her cautious gaze held a glint of hope. "It feels as if our non-relationship status changed tonight. Am I right?"

He studied her a moment, not sure where she was going with the statement and question. Something *had* changed, though. He felt it, too.

"Yes." Somehow, whether due to her music, their dancing, touching…he wasn't certain of the cause, he just *knew* he felt an unidentifiable bond to the beauty. "Just be gentle with me," he said, pulling her in close. "I've never been in anything other than a *non-*relationship before."

A sinful smile curved her full lips. "I'll be whatever you want, Sheriff."

Her unexpected statement sent his heart into his ribs and growing erection into his unforgiving zipper. He leaned close to whisper in her ear, "I want you to be naked…except for your shoes."

Chapter Twelve

How could the past two weeks have been any more perfect?

Oh, wait, they couldn't.

Brandi smiled as she shut her cottage door. For the first time in a long time, her insides were as sunny as the day outside. Heat surrounded her and the sun blared overhead as she walked down the sidewalk toward Foster's. Kerri and Jordan had asked her to join them for some frozen yogurt, and to introduce her to Shayla.

Not even the thought of being in the stunning redhead's presence, or the other two beautiful women's for that matter, could dispel Brandi's good disposition. Kade had set the mood this morning, leaving her bed only after they were both...happy.

He'd been real good at that lately. So far, their non non-relationship was working out great. She'd been to the ranch a few times, but never stayed the whole night. She didn't want to confuse Cody. And Kade had stayed at her place a couple nights. The sheriff/cowboy/soldier was the perfect boyfriend. He showed just enough interest in her day not to be nosey, and he wasn't demanding...except in bed, which was okay with her because...well, she was kind of demanding there, too.

Her insides fluttered at the memory of their night at the hotel. He'd driven her crazy, slowly stripping her naked—except for her shoes—and she'd made him wear his beret. Then he took her on the table. Twice.

She was still smiling as she met up with the girls outside the ice cream shop.

"Okay, I know that smile. That's the smile of a satisfied woman," Jordan said, pulling her into a hug.

"Well, believe it or not, for once, you're not going to get an argument from me."

"It's good to see you happy."

"Thanks. I am happy."

"Okay, then Happy, meet Shayla. Shayla, meet Happy," Jordan joked, then smiled at the beautiful little girl in the redhead's arms, the spitting image of her mama. Red hair that curled slightly at the neck and big, blue eyes. "And this cutie pie is Amelia."

"Hi, Shayla, Amelia," she said, bending slightly at the knee to look the baby in the eyes. "I'm Brandi."

Jordan waved a hand at the ice cream shop. "Would you two like to talk first, or eat?"

She glanced at Shayla. "It's up to you."

"Talk first would be good if you don't mind. It's getting close to Amelia's nap time."

She nodded. "No problem."

"Okay, then why don't you leave Amelia with us and you two can go have your talk." Kerri held out her hands and the baby went right for her.

The redhead hesitated, a frown creasing her brow as she stared at her daughter in the cook's arms. "You sure?"

"Absolutely. She'll be fine. Now go." Jordan gave them a small shove.

As they walked to a little picnic area between the beach and the sidewalk, she expressed her condolences on the loss of the woman's fiancé, then went on to outline the jobs she had going and what she needed. "I don't expect you to design. What I need is someone to order supplies, schedule deliveries, keep track of them, keep track of the workers, make sure they have the supplies they need, and so on. In other words, your organizational skills."

"Well, that I have."

The redhead smiled for the first time since she met her, and if Brandi thought her gorgeous before, now the woman was breathtaking. Choosing a picnic table in the shade of a big oak tree, Shayla informed her of her work history, and explained her duties at the pub, all while keeping an eye on her daughter.

She got the sense the woman was extremely protective of her child and allowing someone else to watch the little one was a bit tough. Which brought up a point. "Some of the job sites are too dangerous for a child, so what will you do with Amelia?"

Shayla blew out a breath. "Mrs. McCall and Mrs. Masters volunteered to watch her until my sister moves in after her semester is done in a few months."

"That's right, you're not from around here, either."

A brow arched over an intent blue gaze. "Aren't you?"

She smiled. "Oh, my no. I'm from Pennsylvania."

"Wow." The woman's shoulders appeared to relax a little more. "I'm not the only newbie, then."

"Nope." She laughed. "I'm still getting used to the county, but for the most part, everyone seems pretty nice. A good place for your daughter to grow up."

The redhead blew out a breath and nodded, her gaze once again on her baby happily bouncing on Kerri's knee. She'd heard all she needed to, and wanted to let mother and daughter get back together.

Rising to her feet, she held out her hand. "The job's yours if you want it."

"Really?" The woman stood, her gaze widening. "Just like that?"

"Yes. Jordan and Kerri sing your praises, and from what you've told me, you'll be a great fit. That's all good enough for me."

"Wow, thank you, Ms. Wyne, I won't let you down," Shayla said, shaking her hand.

"Please, call me Brandi," she corrected. "And I know you won't. I'll have you work with me for a while before I let you handle other sites on your own."

The woman nodded as they fell into step. By the time they reached the sisters, she'd ironed out the salary, a start date, and was a little alarmed to hear the redhead only had healthcare through the Guard on her daughter, and only for another month, which was the anniversary of her fiancé's death. Calling around and gathering information on healthcare was the first task she'd give her new hire. And even though she got the impression the woman was secretive and a little untrusting, Brandi still felt really good about hiring Shayla Ryan.

"So, I take it by the smiles that all is good?" Jordan's gaze bounced between them as Shayla gathered her daughter and held her close.

Brandi nodded. "Yes. Shayla will start on Thursday when we begin your job, Kerri."

"Sweet." The cook smiled. "Let's celebrate. My treat."

A little while later, they were seated outside at an umbrella table eating their ice cream when Cole and Kevin pulled up and got out. Since the cowboys were still wearing their business suits, Brandi figured Jordan must've told them to stop by on their way home. Seated next to her, but across from Kerri and Shayla, Brandi watched the sharp-dressed men turn heads as they ambled near.

Kevin approached, warm gaze trained on the baby

looking over her mother's shoulder. "Who's the cu—"

And like a ton of blue-eyed bricks, the dreamboat fell to his knees, taken down by an elbow to the groin from a swift acting, startled redhead.

"Kevin, are you all right?" Kerri untangled herself from the bench so Cole could help the doubled-over Kevin sit in her vacant spot.

The grimacing man held up a finger while working to catch his breath. Brandi still couldn't believe how quick Shayla had moved. She'd seen a look of panic cross the woman's face, but had no time to stop her or warn the poor guy.

"I will be later," he said, color starting to return to his handsome face. "Once the fellas drop. Right now, they're folded in on themselves trying to get away from the redheaded shrew." He frowned at the mother hugging her daughter close. "What the hell, lady?"

She shrugged. "You're wearing a suit."

Kevin's mouth dropped open, along with everyone else's. Not exactly the response they'd all expected. "A suit? Really? *Christ*, I'd hate to see what would've happened if I were a biker."

"Look, I'm sorry. It was reflex. You shouldn't sneak up on people."

"And you shouldn't be around people. You're dangerous."

Cole's eyes glinted with unreleased humor. "Calm down, buddy," he said, cupping his friend's shoulder. "You're just used to women falling at your feet, not doing the falling."

Kevin grunted. "I didn't *fall* at her feet," he said, as if the woman wasn't there.

Brandi could see Shayla's expression was less than tolerant. She held back a grin. The cowboy had better watch his step.

"No," Jordan said, lifting her cheek for Cole's kiss. "But you were taken down by a woman."

"I was not."

Shayla raised a brow. Kevin scooted further away.

Brandi clenched her jaw. She knew she shouldn't laugh, but it was becoming harder and harder to keep it all in. Even Kerri stood with her bottom lip between her teeth.

"Well, I have to go. Time to put this one down for a nap. Thanks for the ice cream, Kerri," the redhead said, rising to her feet, then glanced to her. "And for the job."

Kevin inhaled and stared at her like she'd grown a second head. "You hired her? For what? A bodyguard? Enforcer? Assassin?"

Shayla turned and stared down at the guy, her blue eyes glinting so cold they sparkled. "No, to keep playboys like you in line."

And with that, her new assistant left with the slack-jawed cowboy staring after her. He shook his head and transferred his gaze to his crotch.

"Okay, fellas," he said. "It's safe. You can come down now. The shrew's gone."

A pink-faced Kerri sat in the vacant spot, hand over her mouth as she shook. "I can't believe that just happened."

"You *can't...*" Kevin reeled back. "Neither can we."

Unable to hold it in anymore, Brandi laughed and was soon joined by the rest of the table, even the disgruntled victim. The day had certainly been eventful, and with plans to head to Galveston with Kade for dinner tonight, she was hopeful the interesting events would continue—

"Stop!"

The urgency in the familiar, young voice rocked her, and she twisted toward the cries. Her heart stopped for a full beat, then rocked hard in her chest again as two big, bald, burly men ran from the sheriff and his deputy. Kade dove at one of them, hitting the guy in the back of the legs, taking him down.

"Stop," the deputy called again, trying the same maneuver, only he was too far away.

Grasping the man's ankle, the skinny kid was holding on for dear life as the guy dragged the deputy across the grassy picnic area she'd been at with Shayla. A second later, a blur in the form of Jordan hopped the table and raced toward the scene. Brandi jumped to her feet along with Cole.

"Jordan, wait," he said, but his wife continued to run toward the commotion as others moved to the side.

"Stop right there! I'm a former cop..." her friend spouted and planted her feet.

"Outta my way, bitch!"

The man took a swing, but Jordan ducked, landed a fist to his gut, and as he doubled over, she clasped her hands together and brought them down hard on his back, sending him to the ground. While he was down, she wasted no time twisting the man's arm behind his back, her knee set on his spine.

"Cuffs." Jordan snapped her fingers at a blinking Donny.

The deputy released the thug's ankle, sat up and fumbled for the handcuffs on his belt. Brandi couldn't believe the poor kid had held on that long. His uniform was full of dirt, blood and grass stains. She watched him hand the cuffs to Jordan who nodded for the deputy to come closer.

"No, this one's yours, kid. Go ahead."

Donny smiled and cuffed the cursing man, then pulled out a paper from his pocket and began to read the guy his rights.

"Jesus, Cole," Kevin said with a shake of his head. "Your wife just brought down that big punk."

"I know."

"That was hot."

"I know," Cole said again. "Excuse me." He walked over to his wife, crushed her close and kissed her in front of the gathering crowd.

"Damn. Where can I get me one of those?" Kevin pouted.

But Brandi was too busy making her way through the people, searching for Kade. Last she had seen of him, he'd been cuffing the other bald man. Not knowing what the suspects had done, she was trying hard not to give in to the scenarios running through her head. He wasn't hurt. At least she didn't think so. Her heart pounded in her ears. The man knew what he was doing. He was fine.

And as she pushed through the crowd and saw him standing with his hand on a suspects elbow, she had all she could do not to run and put a lip-lock on him, not unlike what Cole was still doing to Jordan.

His gaze met hers, and he either sensed her fear or read it in her eyes because he nodded, and sent her a reassuring smile.

Okay, he was good. He was fine. He wasn't hurt. She then proceeded to talk herself out of that lip-lock idea, and let her gaze roam his fine form, making sure she hadn't missed anything.

"Jordan, you're crazy, you know that," Kerri said, coming up behind her with Kevin.

"Yeah, that was really insane and totally nuts." Kevin frowned with disapproval as he folded his arms over his chest. "Can you do that again, but maybe this time in a bathing suit and in slow motion?"

Cole draped his arm around his wife and pulled her in close to his side. "Get your own."

Kade walked over, suspect in tow. "Thanks, Jordan. When can you start?"

Her friend blinked. "Start what?"

"As my new deputy," he replied. "These two are suspected in the rash of burglaries. Thanks for the assist, I—"

"*Halt*," the deputy yelled, cutting him off, glancing from the escaping suspect to his boss. "Mr. Sheriff, sir. He's getting away!"

Kade blew out a breath and stared at the kid. "*Go get him.*"

Everyone watched in disbelief as the scene repeated itself. Donny took a flying leap, but this time he…missed.

Cursing under his breath, Kade thrust his suspect at Jordan, then ran after the cuffed man booking it through the grassy park. They witnessed the sheriff tackle the guy, then right him before escorting his big frame to the nearby cruiser. Face grim, Kade set the man in the back and shut the door. He turned to Donny and crooked a finger.

"Sucks to be Skippy," Kevin muttered.

The deputy rushed to the car and nodded, then stayed put, shoulders drooped as he leaned against the car and watched his boss head back to them.

Once again, Brandi's gaze traveled up and down the man, searching for bruises. He was dirty and grass stained, but she didn't see any blood. Her heartbeats leveled out by the time he neared. Yeah, he was just a little dirtier and sweatier, but still okay.

Gray eyes dull, mouth set in a straight line, he looked tired, and she longed to get him back to her place and dote on him. And, well…as far as tonight, she was more than willing to take top.

"So," he said, retaking possession of his suspect. "You going to help me out, Jordan? I'm begging you. The county can't take much more. *I* can't take much more."

Her heart squeezed.

"You serious? You're offering me a deputy job?" Her friend glanced from Kade to Cole, then back again. "For real?"

"Yes, I'm dead serious," the sheriff replied.

Jordan gazed thoughtfully at the cruiser before her attention turned to Cole. "I'll have to discuss it with my husband."

"Okay." The sheriff nodded. "The job's yours if you want it."

Kevin stepped forward and slapped a hand on Kade's shoulder. "If she doesn't, you may want to offer it to that redhead. You should've been here just a bit sooner. Guarantee you these boys would've cuffed themselves and walked into your station on their own."

How could a week from hell have heavenly moments?

Kade didn't know. Only that it did, like now. He sat with his friends in a booth at the pub, arm around his girlfriend, her warm curves brushing against his side. Funny how the word 'girlfriend' used to scare the shit out of him, but now, with Brandi, it was fitting. Natural. Right. She was his heaven. Plain and simple. Whenever he had a rotten day, and lately, he'd had many, she always made him feel better. Made him feel worthy.

"Whatcha thinking?" Her brown eyes gazed up at

him, warm and just a little bit wicked as her hand ran up his inner leg.

He leaned close and whispered, "That if you don't stop, we aren't even going to make it across the street to your house."

"Oh, but, Sheriff," she said, tipping her head back to whisper in his ear. "Then you'll have to arrest me for indecent exposure. And *cuff* me."

His body went on instant alert and throbbed at the thought. Damn. The woman was potent.

"Okay, enough with the lovey-dovey," Connor said, approaching at a good clip. "I want the scoop." He twisted a chair around and sat down, arms folded across the top. "I'm gone six days. *Six days*...and all hell breaks loose?"

Kade nodded. Boy, did his buddy nail that analogy.

"My sister-in-law takes down a criminal and becomes a deputy," the cowboy stated, pointing to Jordan. "And what about, you, Kevin? You got taken down by a girl, too? Come on. Someone? Anyone?" His buddy's brown gaze bounced to everyone at the table. "Please, tell me, and don't leave out any details."

Jordan shrugged. "Not much to tell. I saw a suspect running away from the sheriff and his deputy so I intervened. End of story."

Connor straightened. "That's it? Come on. I know there were fists involved."

"There were," Kade said. "Jordan landed one to the guy's gut then slammed him on the back and sent him to the ground."

"Damn," Connor said. "That must've been hot."

"It was," Kevin echoed Cole.

"And so now you're the new deputy?" Connor studied his sister-in-law.

She nodded. "Soon. Just waiting for the paperwork to go through."

His buddy transferred his gaze to Kevin and grinned. "So, how'd you managed to get taken down by a girl?"

Brandi's chuckle vibrated through him. He squeezed her closer, enjoying her softness and unyielding warmth. She fit perfectly against him. He kissed her head, catching the sight of several pairs of eyes watching from across the room. The McCalls and Masters. They lifted glasses at him. He smiled. They were good people, and he knew they worried about him sometimes.

"I wasn't taken down by a girl," Kevin insisted, blue gaze narrowed. "It was a shrew. There's a difference. Shrews are mean. And she was mean."

"And pretty," Jordan added.

His cousin shrugged, but Kade could tell the woman's beauty did not go unnoticed by the guy.

"And lethal. She nearly maimed me for life."

"Oh, you're such a girl. She barely elbowed you." Cole frowned and sat back in chair.

"Yeah, but did you see the size of her elbow?" Kevin blinked at them. "It was pointy and…and…lethal."

Cole shook his head. "Forget it, man. You, the mighty Kevin Dalton, was brought to his knees by a pretty redhead and her cute daughter."

Kade's chest tightened. They wouldn't even be having this discussion if he'd done his job. If Shayla's fiancé hadn't died overseas. If the little girl's daddy was still alive.

Why did everything always come back down to those thoughts? Would they ever leave his head? Would they ever leave him the fuck alone?

A small smile tugged his cousin's lips. "The daughter was a cutie. Now she…she could bring me to my knees."

"If there was one thing I learned this past year, Kevin," Connor said, a big grin dimpling his cheeks. "It's that there's nothing wrong with the right woman bringing you to your knees."

"Amen, brother." Cole slapped his brother's hand then kissed Jordan's smiling face.

He didn't know anything about that, but he did know if there was a *right* woman for him, then Brandi was that woman. She got him. Sometimes too well. Like now. He could feel her gaze on him. She made him feel too much, and there were times he held back, closed himself off. He was not ready to relinquish that much of himself to anyone. The last two times he did only brought him pain and disappointment. He wasn't ready to try again. Granted, they were both with father figures, but the pain was intense and deep.

"So, Kade," Connor said, pouring himself a glass of beer. "What are you doing about Skippy? You have two deputies now?"

He shook his head. "Hell no. Donny is enrolling in the art program at the local college. Seems somebody noticed his sketches and encouraged him to give college a try." His gaze shifted to Brandi and she smiled.

"He does have talent," she said.

"Good, because as a deputy, he sucked," Kevin remarked, lifting his glass, then stilled. "Speaking of talent, I hear you're one with a fiddle. When do we all get to hear you play, Brandi?"

Expecting her to stiffen against him, Kade waited but it never happened.

"As a matter of fact," Jordan said, brown eyes twinkling as she glanced at his girl. "Right now. She's part of the next set."

"What?" He turned his gaze on her. "When?"

Over the past few weeks, Jordan and Kerri had tried to get Brandi to join them a few times on stage, but she'd turned them down. And even though he hated to push, and refused to be like her last asshole boyfriend telling her where to perform, he'd encouraged her to play in public. But she would just shrug and say she wasn't ready.

Her warm fingers squeezed his leg as she gazed up at him. "I decided you were right. It's time to enjoy myself. Enjoy playing when I want and where I want. And I want to play tonight, for all of you."

A wave of some kind of positive emotion hit him hard. He cupped her face and kissed her square on the mouth. She kissed him back, and tasted sweet, and happy and full of life, and for nearly a minute he'd forgotten where they were, and that they had an audience.

Until his cousin's voice broke through his haze. "So, I guess once Kade relinquishes his hold, we'll all get to enjoy Brandi's talent. You guys having open mike tomorrow night? 'Cause it might take that long."

He drew back slightly and caught her happy gaze. "Are you sure? I don't want you doing this if you're not ready. I won't be mad."

Tears filled her eyes, but she blinked them away. "Thank you. But yeah, I'm sure. I'm ready and really want to do this."

"Okay," Jordan said. "You heard the woman. And she's not going up alone, isn't that right, Cole?"

Her husband smiled and nodded. "I have the honor."

Kade nodded. "You've no idea." He turned to Brandi. "Has he heard you?" She shook her head and his smile widened. "Then this is going to be real good. What are you playing?"

"Dueling Banjoes."

He laughed. "Oh, man, you're toast, Cole."

Kevin snickered. "Come on. We're talking about Cole, here."

Jordan nodded. "Yes, and Kade's right. My husband is toast." She turned to Cole and patted his open-mouthed face. "Sorry, hun. But I love you anyway."

"Well, I think we need to get this duel started." Cole stood and held his hand out to Brandi. "Shall we?"

"Hang on," Kerri said, rushing in from the kitchen to hug the smiling designer. "Good luck. You're going to bring everyone to their feet."

Kade nodded. The place was not going to be the same again.

As he watched Cole and Brandi take the stage, he settled in his seat, pride and some unknown emotion tightening his chest. The woman never ceased to amaze him. She knew her limitations, pushed through her fears and tackled challenges head on.

"Hello, everyone," Cole said, and the crowd clapped then cheered when they noticed he was holding a banjo and Brandi a fiddle. "For those of you who don't know, this here is Brandi, and the two of us are going to do a little dueling."

The cheering audience picked up a decibel, then settled down when Cole plucked the first string. Excitement and anticipation skittered down Kade's spine, and he watched both performers for different reasons. Brandi, because this was a big step for her, and his heart filled to the point of bursting to see such enjoyment light her face as she played with the audience cheering her on.

And Cole because he was getting his ass handed to him by a girl.

The faster he played—and the guy had skills—the

faster and more complicated the sound Brandi created, all while holding the tune.

"Holy shit," Kevin said, mouth opened as he stared at the stage. "Dude." He elbowed Connor. "You're brother's getting beat by a girl."

His buddy nodded. "I know, ain't it great? Damn, she's good."

When the last string was strung, the crowd whistled and cheered. Cole pulled Brandi in for a hug, then held her hand up, declaring her the easy winner. Kade was on his feet clapping for his girl, noting both Kerri and Jordan had wet faces as they, too, stood and clapped.

"Damn," Kevin said as they all retook their seats. "Why didn't you tell us she could play like that?"

"Oh, trust me," Jordan said. "That isn't anything. She's amazing."

Kade nodded. "That she is." The woman blew him away.

Soon Cole was trading his banjo for a guitar, a few others got on stage with their instruments, and the crowd was treated to some lively Celtic with Brandi leading the way. She was sweet. Everyone adored her. He adored her.

And as that thought settled in his mind, his chest tightened further. What did he do with that? He was at a loss. Watching the woman play her heart out, putting it all on the line, he never felt more like a coward. He could never open up like that…take a chance like that.

When she finished and put away the violin, the crowd complained. He understood. She made you feel, and if she played something upbeat, you felt good. And who didn't want to feel good?

"That was fantastic," Jordan said, pulling Brandi in for a hug as soon as she reached the table.

He waited until everyone congratulated and hugged his girl. Then he drew her in close and held her. Just held her. "I'm proud of you," he said against her temple, and felt her indrawn breath all the way down to his toes. "You okay?"

She nodded and drew back. "Yeah. I'm great."

Cole came over, kissed his wife then cupped Kade's shoulder. "You were right. I was toast." His friend smiled at Brandi. "You're amazing. I hope we get the chance to play together again."

"Absolutely," she said. "I'd like that."

As the night wore on, once again he was sitting at the table with his arm draped around the beauty at his side, joking with Connor when Kevin leaned toward Cole.

"So, tell me, buddy, how does it feel to be married to a deputy?"

Jordan smiled and gave a slight shake to her head. "I'm not one yet."

"True." His cousin nodded. "But close enough, so spill, McCall."

Cole lifted his wife's hand to his lips. "I don't care what she does for a living. I just love her."

"Oh, man, are you trying to make me puke?" Kevin shuddered. "That's not what I was asking."

"I have no problem with Jordan being a deputy. I think she'll make a damn good one."

Kade couldn't agree more. In fact, he was counting on it. The thought of having someone else on the force capable of doing the job set his mind at ease. Especially with his annual training coming up next month. He knew he'd be leaving the county in good hands for those two weeks he'd be away at AT.

Cole turned to him and nodded. "I also know I can

count on you to keep my wife safe."

He stiffened. Ah, hell. Every hair on his body stood up, while all his blood felt as if it turned to cement. Brandi turned and stared at him. He could feel her gaze, but he couldn't bring himself to face the woman.

"Ah, Cole, buddy." Kevin snickered. "You're wife can take care of herself, remember? You saw her bring that big guy down."

Jordan nodded. "I don't need anyone taking care of me."

Now there were more gazes on him. He felt them, too. The tightness in his chest increased until the urge to leave shook through his body. He had to get out. Sweat gathered between his shoulder blades and trickled down his back.

Before he knew it, Brandi tugged him to his feet, slipped an arm around him and addressed the table. "Thanks for tonight, everyone. I appreciate the support. I had a great time." Then she maneuvered them through the crowd and outside into the wonderful night air. "It's okay," she said. "You need to breathe, Kade. Just breathe."

Fuck. He hated feeling weak. Fucking hated it!

He released her, walked to his truck and grasped the tailgate while he dropped his head and dragged air into his lungs. This was ridiculous. These *episodes* had to stop. And if people would stop saying shit like they counted on him, or expected him to do something, then maybe he'd be just fine.

A warm hand slid up his back. "Jeez. You're all wet."

He grunted. "No shit." Then felt bad at the harshness of his voice.

"Come on." Although her hand stilled, it remained

on him. "Let's go to my place."

And because he had every intention of going there, he nodded and opened the passenger door. He even smiled and kissed her hand before he walked around and got in behind the wheel. But he sat for a minute. He still needed another damn minute to regain control. A myriad of thoughts rushed through his head. He counted as he breathed and soon this mind and pulse calmed to a dull roar. The night hadn't gone as he'd planned.

Once safety was no longer an issue, he drove the short distance to her house and parked in her driveway. She was staring at him again, and he couldn't blame her. With nothing to say for himself, he remained quiet as he walked her to her door. He was an ass, and was beginning to realize she deserved better. A whole hell of a lot better.

She unlocked the door, flipped on the lights and tugged his arm, but he didn't budge.

"Not tonight. I'm going to go home," he told her, his heart squeezing at the disappointment clouding her gaze. Lifting his hand, he traced her jaw. "You did great tonight. I'm so proud of you."

Cupping his hand, she pressed his palm to her face. "Then come inside. Please, Kade."

God, he wanted to, he really did, but something felt off, not right. An anger resided in him that wasn't going away.

Usually, after a few minutes of calming down, or method breathing, he'd manage to move forward. But not now. It was getting tougher and tougher as the weeks wore on. Damned if he knew why. This had happened before, not often, but it had happened, and experience taught him it was best if he spent time alone until this mood subsided. He was not up for company, not even hers.

"Sorry, I have to go. I'm not good company. I need to be alone."

She stepped into him and kissed his neck. "Bet I could change your mind."

Any other time, and she would have, but not now. Now, he just wanted solitude. The woman made him feel, and that was exactly what he didn't want.

He grabbed her upper arms and gently but firmly put her away from him. "No." He shook his head. "I need to go. Goodnight."

Pivoting on his heel, he strode to his truck, feeling lower than low at hurting the best thing to ever happen to him. But he knew, deep down, somehow he knew this was for her own good.

Chapter Thirteen

Brandi wasn't sure when things had gone south with Kade, only that they had. The relationship was still on, but something had changed. They still saw each other, had sex, all the stuff they'd done before, but something was off.

It had manifested before he'd gone to annual training, and although she'd hoped when he'd gotten back things would be better, they were actually a little worse. He wasn't as talkative. Almost closed up. She'd missed *him*, missed being with him, riding horses at his ranch, listening to him talk about the horses; they didn't do that anymore.

She pulled up in front of Shadow Rock, thriving with cars and people with the annual end of summer barbeque in full swing. Hopefully, Kade would be less stressed and they'd get to spend time together. Her heart warmed at the thought. If they could just have some quality time together. That should help.

Spotting her friend wearing a similar denim sun dress, she waved to Kerri, pasting a bright smile on her face as she slid out of her truck. Brandi refused to bring the woman down. Her friend was happy and excited about the wedding around the corner, and renovations to the Wild Creek Ranch.

"Hey, you two," she said to the approaching couple holding hands.

Kerri slung her free arm around her shoulder and squeezed. "Ready for some end of the summer fun, Dalton style?"

She laughed. "Boy, am I ever."

"Good," Connor said, every bit the cowboy in his red, button-down shirt and jeans. "'Cause it's good people, good eats, good fun."

"I know you really enjoyed the last one," she said, watching the couple exchange a quick kiss.

"Yep." Connor tipped his hat at her. "I got me the best fiancée during the last one. Maybe you'll get one during this one…"

Brandi's heart hit her ribs. Fiancé? Kade? They weren't anywhere near that. She exhaled and shook her head. "Hold on there, cowboy. We've barely gotten to the actual relationship stage."

Kerri squeezed her shoulder. "Which is great. You work with that. Don't mind my well-meaning-but-clueless cowboy. Take your time."

Standing in the food line, she glanced around for Kade, trying to ignore the nagging feeling of…doom. Which was stupid. Everyone was here. Everyone was laughing, eating, dancing to one of the local bands she'd seen showcased at the Texas-Pub. The sky was clear and bright, so weather wasn't an issue.

"There's my sister," Kerri said, nudging Brandi toward the deputy eating at a table with her husband and Jen, Brock and Cody.

"Hi, everyone." She nodded as she sat. "Hey, Cody."

"Hi," the little boy replied, not bothering to look up from his plate of food.

Kerri sat next to her and smiled at her sister. "Wasn't sure you'd make it."

Jordan returned the grin. "I'd never miss a Dalton barbeque if I could help it. I can be on duty just as easily here as the station." Her friend held up her radio.

She knew from Kade that his new deputy was a

godsend. For several weeks now, Jordan had been on the force, and he'd told Brandi he'd rested easier during annual training knowing the county had been left in capable hands. According to her handsome sheriff, her friend knew law enforcement. Knew how to enforce the law. Knew how to write reports, take down bad guys, shoot, and most importantly, make lunch runs without getting the cruiser hung up on guardrails.

"Damn, Jordan," Kevin said as he approached in a blue shirt and jeans, appearing every bit the local heartthrob. "You look a hell of a lot better in the uniform than Skippy."

She hid a smile as she ate. One never knew what was going to come out of that man's mouth.

"Damn straight," Cole said, slapping his buddy's shoulder when he dropped next to him.

Brandi glanced around the cowboy. No sign of his cousin. Disappointment dulled the taste of the wonderful food.

"He's in the stables." Blue eyes, clear and serious, stared at her from across the table. "Been quiet today. I thought maybe you two had a fight."

She frowned. "No." They'd actually had a decent time on the beach with Cody three days ago. Then ended the night at the ranch, watching another DVD and falling asleep.

"He has been awfully quiet a lot lately," Jen said, her light eyes wearing the same worried expression as her brother's.

What little food she'd eaten turned to lead in her stomach.

"Yeah, he didn't even go with me to the auction yesterday." Connor shook his head as he ate. "Not like him."

Brandi carefully set her chicken leg down and wiped her fingers. Kade didn't go? Her heart dropped to her boots. He'd told her he was going. She hadn't bothered to call or text him. Hadn't wanted to interrupt his time with Connor. She'd hoped some time with his good friend might snap him out of his funk. It usually worked. Connor had a way of bringing a smile to Kade's face.

This wasn't good.

She swallowed and glanced at Kevin. "Where did you say he was?"

"The stables," he replied.

Placing her napkin on her plate, she stood. "Excuse me."

"No he isn't," Cody shook his head. "*Unkewl* Kade went *widing*. I saw him *wide* away."

Jen glanced at her son then lifted her troubled gaze. "But he knew the barbeque was today. He wouldn't do that."

"He did, mom. I saw him," Cody insisted.

Connor stilled. "What's the date?"

Cole cocked his head and frowned. "The tenth, why?"

She watched Connor close his eyes and mutter a curse. Now her whole body was as tense as the strings of her violin. "What is it?" she asked in barely a whisper.

The cowboy opened his eyes and hit her with the most serious brown gaze he'd ever worn. "Three days from now is the anniversary of that soldier's death."

The whole table collectively inhaled and her stomach pitched. She had to find him. God, she couldn't let him face this alone.

"Cody, when did Uncle Kade leave?" Kevin gently prodded his nephew.

"Just before *Connow* and *Kewi* and *Bwandi* got

hewe."

Connor set his plate aside and stood. "I think I know where he went." He turned to her and nodded. "Come on."

Not exactly dressed for riding, she practically raced to keep up with the tall cowboy. But didn't care. She was going to find Kade. Had to find him. At least she had her boots on, her mind reasoned as they strode past an empty stall in the stable.

Connor cursed again. "Yep, if he's on *Itherael*, I know exactly where he went."

Unsure what all that meant, she just nodded and waited as the cowboy quickly saddled one of the faster horses. She'd thought about saddling hers, but didn't want to waste time. Connor seemed to know what he was doing.

Swinging his large frame into the saddle, he wore a look of determination on his face that set her mind at ease. It was going to be okay. Connor knew his friend. Knew where to go. He'd take her to the man she loved and she'd make—

Her heart tripped and rolled in her chest.
The man she loved?
How…when did that happen?
"Give me your hand," Connor said.

In her dazed state, she did as directed and large fingers clamped around her forearm, lifting her like she was a feather, and deposited her behind him in the saddle. Thank goodness her denim dress had a full skirt. Made straddling easier.

"Hold on. We've got a ways to go and we're going fast."

As they galloped over blackbrush, the mesquite and live oaks went by in a blur, Brandi tried to wrap her mind around her revelation.

She loved Kade.

It was true. The gorgeous, sweet, giving man accepted her. Made her feel good about herself. Wanted her to change *nothing* about herself. He was thoughtful and caring, always put himself last…and *God*, yes, she loved the man very much.

She had to help him get past this hurt. Help him feel as good as he made her feel, but she didn't know how. Physically, yes, that she knew, but emotionally? Mentally? She wasn't sure.

They'd been riding hard for over an hour and a half. She couldn't feel anything from the butt down anymore, but didn't care. Finding Kade was all that mattered. Thank God he had such a good friend in Connor McCall. Guilt clawed in her gut. She'd taken him away from his fiancée and the party. But something told her he would've been doing this even if she hadn't been around.

Finally, she felt the horse slowing its pace and Connor called over his shoulder.

"Found him."

She inhaled, then exhaled slowly, forcing her mind to clear. He was probably not going to be happy they'd intruded, but too bad. She was here and wasn't going anywhere.

"Connor, what the hell are you doing here?"

"I could ask you the same thing, buddy," her escort replied. "But I think I know, and we're here to help."

"We're? What do you mean, *we're?*" Kade's tone was steel and full of dread.

He obviously hadn't seen her behind the tall cowboy. Bracing herself, she set her spine, lifted her chin, then used Connor's outstretched hand to steady herself as she slipped off the horse.

"He means me," she stated, facing a very disgruntled cowboy.

Wearing jeans, a charcoal button-down shirt, gorgeous black Stetson and a very deep frown, the man bit back a curse. "Brandi? What are you doing here?"

"Looking for you."

"Right, and now she's found you, my job is done. Have a good night, you two." Connor tipped his hat, turned the horse, and with a slight kick, sent the large creature into motion.

"Connor! *Son-of-a-bitch*. Get back here! Take her with you." Kade raced forward.

His friend didn't listen. Just raised a hand and kept riding away.

Her heart was thudding in her throat as she watched the agitated man slowly turn to face her. Jaw clenching and unclenching, he stared for a few maddening seconds.

"You shouldn't have come."

With crisp, efficient strides, he moved past her to a group of boulders, stopping in front of a large one battered by weather, and what appeared to be marks, as if someone had beaten it with a bat.

"Neither should you," she said. "Your family is throwing the barbeque."

He ripped the hat off his head, thrust a hand through his hair and muttered a few choice words. Twisting around, he set his very fine butt against the boulder and sighed, staring at the hat in his hand.

Since Connor marooned her, and there was only one horse, she felt confident Kade wouldn't leave her, no matter how tough it might be to stay and face whatever problems arose. She walked over to stand in front of him.

She wanted very much to ask him what was wrong. To get him to talk, because she knew he needed to talk, to get everything out in the open and face his demons before he could heal. But by the tight set of his jaw and shoulders, she knew he was still too closed up.

He needed to be loosened.

And she knew exactly how to do that…

Without a word, she took the hat from his hands and set it on the boulder. When he opened his mouth, she put her finger over his lips and shook her head. It wasn't time to talk, yet. It was time to feel.

Getting the impression the spot had meaning, she intended to add to the trend. Whether it was good or bad didn't matter. She planned to add some very good memories to the place. Right now.

Cupping his jaw, she pressed into him, inhaling near his neck. Damn, he smelled good. So male…so Kade. She trailed her lips across his stubble, working her way to his neck where she sank her teeth. His inhale echoed around them, but he didn't touch her, didn't move, just clutched the damn boulder.

"It's okay," she said against his skin. "Let me in, Kade. Feel me."

He shook his head. "No. I'm too broken."

His words and rough, desolate tone slayed her—hit deep—and she had all she could do not to break down in front of him.

"I can't. I won't." He grabbed her arms and tried to pry her away. "Brandi, please. Let go. You deserve better. Someone who isn't tainted."

She tightened her hold. "No. I deserve you. I want you. No one else, Kade. You hear me? No one else."

"But, don't you understand," he said against her temple, his voice hoarse with emotion, sounding raw to the bone. "I'm not whole. I'm a broken man."

She nodded, then kissed his jaw. "Use me, Kade.

I'm your glue."

He inhaled deep, then buried his head in her neck and held her so tight she could barely breathe. But, God, it was worth it. It was so worth it because he let go of his emotions. Let go of everything he'd been holding back. The man finally opened up and let her see his pain. He slid to the ground, but didn't release her.

For several minutes they clung to each other, her straddling his lap, cradling his head to her chest as she reassured this special man she was there for him. Would always be there for him. It was on the tip of her tongue to tell Kade her true feelings, but was worried it might somehow put more pressure on him, and she sure didn't want to do that.

Somewhere between breaths, the embrace began to change. Needs switched and heat started to seep into their touch.

"Brandi," he breathed against her neck, his hands, no longer clutching, now roamed freely over her body. "God, I want you...*need* you."

That was it. She was toast. Soggy toast. She melted into him and gave herself over to the desire he invoked. Her fingers worked the buttons of his shirt while she kissed his neck and shoulder. "I want you, too, Kade," she said, spreading open-mouth kisses to his ear where she closed her teeth around his lobe and tugged.

His body shuddered under her palms and, an instant later, two hands clamped around her, one snaking up to the back of her head, the other sliding down to cup her ass as he crushed her tight.

He tugged on her hair, and when she released his ear, he captured her mouth and devoured her strength. Slow, and with aching precision, the man kissed her to within an inch of her sanity. Again. God, he was so good at that maneuver. He drank, dipping deep, sweeping long until her toes curled in her boots, and she wondered briefly how she was ever going to get them off. Then it no longer mattered. He was dipping her back to trail kisses down her throat and chest, hands sliding up her body, sending heat to every peak and valley she possessed.

"This has to go," he said against her neck.

She drew back and stood. Grasping both sides of her dress, she tugged the snaps open in one swift move.

A slow, hot smile spread across his face as he gazed up at her. "God bless denim," he said, sliding his hands up her legs, brushing his thumbs over her center and groaning. "You're wet."

She smiled down and nodded. "Yep." Then let the dress slowly fall off her shoulders before she set it on one of the boulders.

He sat there, between her legs, his gaze hot and dark as he took in her bra, panties and boots. "Mmm…and God bless cowboy boots." He made to get up, but she pushed him back down.

"No." She reached behind her back and unhooked her bra, watching his gaze darken and throat work in a swallow as her breasts bounced free. They felt heavy and ached when he gazed at them with such hunger. Leaning over him, she set the bra on her dress, then inhaled when his hands snaked up to cup her and brush a thumb over her nipples.

"Gorgeous," he rasped before lifting up to take one in his mouth.

Her legs nearly buckled. Then he was sucking on the other one, and she was holding his head to her chest.

"Wait, not…oh…that feels so good," she said into the quiet sky, the sun casting a golden glow behind his grazing horse.

He released her and spread kisses down her belly, hooking his index fingers in her panties as he slowly drew them down her spread legs. She lifted one to move it closer so he could work the lace over her boot. Then he sat back against the boulder and gazed up at her.

"Mmm...now that's a beautiful view." Warm hands glided up her exposed calves, lightly brushing behind her knees to skim her thighs, all in an assault to test her strength.

She was losing. Fast. Need shook through her legs so bad, she would've fallen if he hadn't steadied her.

"Not yet," he said, tugging her to stand over him.

Her palms hit the boulder. "Oh, Kade, I doubt I can stand. You take my strength," she admitted, staring down into his handsome, desire-ridden gaze.

"Trust me." He smiled, then cupped her ass and guided her knees to his shoulders. "Just hold on," he said before putting his mouth on her.

Brandi inhaled and closed her eyes. Damn the man was good. Within seconds, he had her panting, using just his mouth. His talented, wicked mouth. Heat gathered in all the right places, and when he adjusted the angle and pressed closer, she lost control and burst.

When she finally regained enough of her faculties, he pulled her down on top of him and kissed her long and deep. He was hot and hard and oh so delicious her stomach fluttered. She trailed a hand down his torso, over his jeans to trace the bulge driving her mad.

He grunted and captured her hand, then drew back to stare into her face. "I won't last, honey."

"Then let's get you naked," she said, tugging free to slip his shirt off his shoulders before she leaned down to lick his nipple.

"Hey, minx," he said, grabbing the back of her head and bringing her mouth to his for another of his amazing kisses.

When they broke for air, she fumbled with his jeans, but he grabbed her hands and pulled them away.

"Stand up."

She did, praying she had enough strength to hold her weight while he quickly shed the rest of his clothes. Then he pulled a packet from his jeans, sheathed his glorious erection, and her mouth watered in anticipation. The man sparked a hunger, made her greedy for release, a release only he could provide.

He fixed his clothes and sat on them with his back to the boulder before guiding her over him again. Her pulse hiccupped. Ed hardly ever let her take top, saying she was too heavy. But Kade had let her take top several times, seeming quite happy with the position. Still, this…this was going to be different. He was sitting straight up. They'd be…

"Oh…" Her throaty cry mingled with his groan as she slowly sank onto his erection. "You feel so…perfect."

He nudged her knees out a little further, and she moaned when more of him slid inside.

"Ah, hell yeah," he muttered, voice strained and rough and deliciously hot.

His hand slid up to grip her hips as he leaned forward to capture a nipple in his mouth and tug.

"Kade." Her eyelids fluttered closed, and she clutched his shoulders as she began to move. Had to move. Needed to move. Was going to die if she didn't start to move…

A low, sexy sound resonated from deep in his throat. He released her nipple to spread hot, open-mouthed kisses over her collar bone, and then bit her neck in the spot behind her ear that he knew drove her crazy.

Breath caught in her throat while heat skittered down her spine, chasing the goosebumps that got a head start. She squirmed, her whole body tingling as they brushed, torso to torso. And when he released her neck, she opened her eyes and her pulse leapt.

They were eye level. So close she could feel his heart beating against her own chest. The connection was strong. His gray, smoldering gaze was open and frank, and she saw everything he couldn't say. Felt everything. He held nothing back, showing it all. Her heart soared, and she let him see how she felt about him. Showed him all she had, gave him all of her as they moved, heartbeat to heartbeat, soul to soul…one wounded, healing human to another.

And as the emotions and touches and need became too much, she started to close her eyes…

"No," he said with a shake of his head. "Don't close them. I want to see you. Need to see you."

She nodded, focusing on the need in his eyes, the hunger…the love. And as they rocked together, upping the pace, he brushed a finger over her center and it all became too much. Everything burst.

Brandi cried his name in a drawn out moan, watching the beautiful man as he followed her over the edge, her name on his lips, gaze to gaze, heart to heart.

They were going to be all right. Everything was going to be all right.

Who the hell was he kidding?

Kade sat in his truck, staring at the newspaper he'd picked up along with his coffee that morning. The front page article commemorating Sergeant Nylan's death was enough to suck what little hope he had managed to dredge up the past few days.

He was done.

Brandi deserved better. He'd said it all along. Now, he just had to do something about it. Every time he tried, she managed to get under his skin, take hold and make him feel like there was a light at the end of his dark tunnel. That he could still offer something to the world. Her world.

He crumpled the paper in his fist. Who the hell was he kidding?

As First Sergeant, his soldier had depended on him, counted on him, and he'd let that soldier down. Whipping the paper across the cab, he cursed as it scattered on the floor. He'd let the soldier's family down. The soldier's daughter down. *God*, he didn't want to let Brandi down. Didn't want to be in a position where she needed him and he wasn't there for her. He couldn't deal with that. Could never live with that...

Pressing the balls of his hands against his eyes, he knew what he had to do. Always knew what he had to do. Now he just needed to grow a pair and let the woman go. She'd shared so much, gave so much, there was no way he could give that much back to her. She deserved someone who could. He removed his hands and straightened.

His gift to her was freedom.

"That a new way to read?" Connor appeared outside his door, a damn smirk on his face. "It's easier if your eyes are opened, not smashed into her hands"

"I'm not in the mood, Connor."

"I can see that."

"Did you want something? I have to get to work."

"Seeing as you're sitting outside the station, I'd say

you have the *get to work part* covered, buddy."

Kade let out a long breath. Christ, he didn't need this right now. He opened the door, forcing the tall cowboy to step back. "You're right," he said, grabbing his coffee before he slid from the truck. "Thanks."

As he headed up the sidewalk, he silently cursed when his buddy fell into step and lumbered beside him. Damn McCalls. Stubborn. The whole lot.

"Won't work, you know," Connor stated, following him into the station, nodding to his sister-in-law sitting at her desk, her gaze snapping to them as they walked in.

In his office, he set his cup on the desk and clamped his jaw tight to keep the curse inside, then dropped into his chair. "What won't?"

Connor shut the door and leaned against the filing cabinet. "Ignoring me. I'm a McCall. We're like a bad habit. We don't go away."

"Don't I fuckin' know."

Dumbass stood there and grinned that lop-sided grin. "Someone's all riled up."

"Connor, what the hell do you want?"

"I want to know if you're okay."

Fuck. Not that again. "I'm fine. Just fuckin' fine. Okay? Now go." He made a shooing motion

A brow rose on his friend's face, but the cowboy made no damn movement to go. In fact, the pain-in-the-ass sat down on the bench and stared at him. *Don't sit.* Kade sipped his coffee and held his buddy's stare.

Finally, he shrugged at the tall oaf. "What?"

"You spouted the JFF."

"What?" he repeated, beginning to wonder if he'd had a mini stroke. Some of what his buddy was saying wasn't making sense.

"The JFF—just fucking fine. We don't spout that

shit when we're fine, we spout it when we're not. Got it?"

Kade rubbed his temples and groaned. "No, what I have is a headache. A six-foot-four-inch headache."

"That's only because you're special."

"*Jesus*, Connor! I'm not special." He jumped to his feet and began to pace. "I'm far from special. Okay?"

"No, it's not okay. And neither are you, Kade." Connor was on his feet, grabbing his shoulders before he could blink. "The sooner you realize it and get help, the better. I'm worried about you, man."

Christ. That last sentence got him. He sucked in a deep breath and let it out slow before he met his buddy's gaze. "Sorry, Connor. I didn't mean to worry you. I'm just tired," he said, slapping the man's arm.

"I can see that." He hesitated before releasing him. "I know today's a tough day. If you want to blow it off, get drunk—beat the shit out of boulders. I'm your man."

A smile tugged his lips as a flicker of humor reached his soul. "Thanks. I'll keep it in mind. But I'm fine."

His buddy cocked his head. "As long as you're not *just fucking fine*. Remember, no JFF."

"Right." His smile broadened. "No JFF. Got it."

"So…no beer?" Disappointment skittered through the man's gaze.

He shook his head. "No beer. I'm on duty."

"Damn. Guess I'll have to go rustle up some cattle, then." Connor slapped his shoulder. "Call if you change your mind."

"Will do."

He walked the man to the door, mostly to make sure the guy actually left the building. He really did have one hell of a headache and just wanted to put his head down on his desk for a few minutes without undergoing the third degree. Guilt immediately flooded his gut. He knew Connor only badgered out of concern.

Five minutes later, he lifted his head from his desk to find a pair of shrewd brown eyes studying him. Another damn McCall.

His deputy leaned against the closed door, arms folded across her chest, gaze unyielding. When the hell had she walked in? And closed the door?

Straightening up, he played dumb. "Something wrong? We get a call?"

Her lips twitched. "No. Good try, though." She held her hand up when he opened his mouth. "Save it. I've tried it all, *and* am an authority on masking feelings."

Christ. Not her, too. "I have a headache. That's all."

"Bullshit. That is not all."

Something in her gaze kept the retort from finding his lips. There was no pity in her expression. It was dark and haunting. *Jesus.* The woman *did* understand his pain. But how? She wasn't in the military. Didn't see combat. Didn't lose a soldier...

His head snapped up. But she *did* lose a husband. To a bullet. In front of her.

He rose to his feet, crossed the office and pulled her into a hug. "I'm sorry, Jordan. That had to be so tough."

She was stiff for a moment, then hugged him, patting his back. "You got all that in a glance, huh?"

He nodded. *Once you experience that kind of pain, guilt...it marks you forever.*

"It was tough, but I got through it, and so will you." She drew back to stare into his face. "It won't be easy, but the pain does lessen. Life does go on. The guilt...doesn't go away."

Not what he wanted to hear.

"But it eases. Won't always be as sharp. Won't feel

like you're trying to breathe with a gut full of broken glass."

Yeah, she did know exactly what he felt.

"The key to healing is to *want* to heal, Kade," she said. "Admit to yourself that you need help, then get it."

He didn't *need* help. He needed to not feel that broken glass every damn time he sucked in a breath. Needed everyone to stop telling him he was going to be okay. Needed to stop seeing Sergeant Nylan's face whenever he closed his eyes. Needed to stop seeing the dead man's little girl every fucking time he turned a corner. Needed to stop seeing the dead man's girlfriend every time he saw his own.

Blowing out another breath, he nodded.

With one last pat to his back, Jordan left him to his solitude.

She was right. He needed to do something. In fact, he was going to do just that, starting tonight.

Everything was not all right.

Brandi thought, after what they'd shared, what they'd showed, what they'd done to each other out on Kade's land, everything was going to be okay. That they could get through anything.

She was wrong.

How could the two of them get through tough times if only one wanted to try?

It'd been three days since the barbeque. Three days since Kade Dalton had taken her out of herself and showed her his soul, shared his heart. Three days since she'd seen him.

After making love against the boulder, they'd gotten dressed and took a slow ride back to the ranch. It had been incredible. Riding on the back of a horse with

Connor was not the same as riding on the back of a horse with Kade. She'd clutched him tight, felt his heart pounding under her palm, heard the strong beat against her ear...

And when they reached the ranch, the party was still going on. They'd danced, holding each other, barely moving, the connection so strong others noticed. Kevin had even commented he was staying the hell away from women and horses.

He needn't worry.

She glanced at the clock on her living room wall. It was ten after eight. Kade was supposed to come by for dinner at seven. He was over an hour late. She blew out the two candles and stood. Same thing had happened last night. And the night before. Each time he'd called and said something about working late, or getting an unexpected call. Some were true, some weren't. Tonight he hadn't even bothered to call.

Her mind, her heart, held out hope that he was working and couldn't get to a phone. But, being that his cell was always with him and it only took a few seconds to send a text, she let hope dwindle and faced the sting of reality. He was avoiding her. But why?

They'd connected. They'd opened up. They'd shared more than bodies.

A tear slipped down her cheek. She inhaled and swiped it away. It was the connecting, opening up, sharing that he was running from. She knew it to her soul, but didn't know what to do about it.

Picking up her violin, she gave into her emotions and played until her heart hurt too much to continue. She stopped and pulled in a breath. Kade meant the world to her. She couldn't just give up. There had to be something she could do to help him. To get him to seek the help he needed.

When a knock echoed through her little house, she set the violin and bow on the table and raced to the door. *Please let it be him.* She didn't care that he was late. At least he came.

She opened the door and breathed a sigh of relief. It was him. Dark circles under his eyes, face pale, mouth drawn, he looked exhausted. Her heart ached for the man she loved.

"Kade." She burrowed into him and held tight. "I was worried about you," she said, then noticed he'd stiffened and didn't return the hug. Drawing him into the house, she shut the door and frowned. "What's wrong?"

He moved out of her grasp, glanced at the table and cursed. "I'm sorry, Brandi. You cooked dinner. I forgot."

"It's okay."

"No, it's not." He shoved a hand through his hair, then turned to face her. "And neither are we. That's what I came here to tell you."

Dear God. Her heart rocked hard in her chest. "What? That we aren't okay?"

"Yes."

"You're wrong. You're just scared." She grabbed his arm and squeezed. "It's okay. So am I. What we're feeling—"

"Stop! Okay. Just stop it, Brandi." He shook free. "I'm trying to break up with you. We're done. You deserve better. End of story."

"Are you kidding me?" She grabbed him again. "No way, Kade. I told you already. I deserve you. So, forget it. You're not getting rid of me that easy. Just because you feel something is no reason to run. Whatever's wrong, whatever's going through that head of yours, we'll deal with it together."

"No." He broke free again, then grabbed her by the arms. "Nothing is wrong except *me* for *you*. So let's just cut our losses and move on."

She palmed his chest. "Move on? Kade, I love you. I can't move on. I *won't* move on. Let me help you."

"Ah, *Jesus*, Brandi. No. Just let me go. Quit clinging." He pushed her away, strode to the table and cursed. "You don't need me to be strong. You don't need me at all." He ran a hand over her violin and picked up her bow. "Look what you've accomplished. You are so strong. You've come so far. You don't need me."

"You're wrong. I do need you. I love you and won't let you go that easy. If you just got some counseling I'd go with you—"

"For fuck's sakes, Brandi. Just stop!" He slammed the bow onto the table and a sickening snap resonated around them.

Her sharp inhale was nearly as loud. That had been a present from her mother.

His gaze fell to the broken bow hanging limply in his hand. "Christ, I'm sorry, Brandi. See what I mean? I'm a menace. Dangerous. You're better off without me. Just fucking better off without me. Good bye."

Before she could move, before she could even breathe, he'd set the limp wood on the table and walked out, leaving her as broken as her beloved bow.

Chapter Fourteen

The week of Kerri's wedding arrived in a blur. In fact, the days since Kade had walked away all fell into each other, mostly because Brandi had been working her head off. It was either that or breakdown and cry.

So she'd jumped into her job with both feet, accepting all the work that had come her way in the six weeks that had past. No job was too little or too big. Thank God for Shayla. Boy, her friends weren't kidding when they sang the redhead's praises. The woman's organizational skills and ability to multi-task allowed Brandi the opportunity to go full throttle.

Because of this, Kerri and Connor's project was already halfway done. They had their own wing, own entrance, and construction had already started on their gourmet kitchen, and the master suite Connor had wanted once he'd seen Cole's bathroom.

She smiled. Men. What was it with them and having sex in the shower? Of course, she'd enjoyed every bit of it with Kade…

Her heart clenched tight. Dammit. Once again, she'd forgotten. For a split second, her mind had hiccupped and overlooked the fact the man was no longer hers. Was no longer in the picture. Didn't want to be with her. As much as she hated it, without him willing to even try, what could she do? It was hard to have a relationship when it was all one-sided. He didn't want to fight for them. Didn't want help. Until he did, he'd never let her in.

Tears burned her eyes and throat, but she quickly

blinked them away as she walked across the street to the pub. Today was Kerri's bachelorette party. And Connor's bachelor party. The groom insisted on a combination of the two. She wasn't sure why. Jordan said it had to do with something from his past. Whatever the case, it would be interesting, especially considering Kade was sure to be here. The two of them hadn't told anyone about their split, though it wasn't a secret. They just never said anything. And with the wedding so close, she had agreed to his request when they'd bumped into each other a few weeks back, not to put a damper on their friends' special time. They didn't want Kerri or Connor to have to worry about the two of them standing up together.

She'd only seen Kade alone, one other time. He'd knocked on the door the day after he'd walked out. For a brief, heart stopping minute, she'd thought he'd changed his mind. Was going to get help. Was going to let her stand by him while he got that help. Thought he'd come to his senses. He hadn't. The sweet man had simply handed her a battered violin case.

Instead of replacing the bow, he'd gotten her a beautiful, vintage violin. He didn't have to, she wasn't angry. She knew it hadn't been deliberate, a heat of the moment kind of thing, and told him as much, but he'd insisted and shoved the case in her hand, then turned and walked away. Just staring at the aged instrument, Brandi had felt the history, the affection, the story of everyone who ever owned the beauty, and chills had covered her flesh as a Charlie Daniels song had come to mind, "Talk To Me Fiddle."

The man knew her so well. Knew she wouldn't want a new one. He knew a loved, cherished, treasured violin was more important to her. What he hadn't realized was how much the instrument had symbolized himself. Used, battered, bruised, but oh so loved, priceless and waiting for someone to come along and bring it to life. In the right person's hands, a very precious gift. And *he* was a gift. *God*, why couldn't the man see that?

She'd tuned the beauty and played it every night since.

Would today be tough? Yes. Would the wedding be tougher? Hell yeah. Would she get through it? Damn right, and her friends would be none the wiser.

Stepping inside, she pushed all sadness aside, determined to enjoy time with her friends as she was immediately hit with the delicious aroma of Kerri's cooking. Something with garlic and barbeque and salsa. Her stomach rumbled. It hadn't done that in weeks.

"Hi, Brandi," Mrs. McCall said, coming up to give her a hug. "I understand you're playing something you composed at the wedding. That is so sweet. I can't wait."

She smiled and nodded accordingly. "I hope they like it."

"I'm sure they will, dear." The woman led her toward the others at the bar having drinks. "Where's Kade?"

"I don't know," she answered, as honest as possible. Her body relaxed. He wasn't there yet. She had time to prepare and talk without the threat of tears overtaking her control. "I'm sure he'll be here soon."

Jordan approached, out of uniform, which meant Kade was on duty. Maybe he wasn't going to be there after all.

And just like that, breathing became a little easier.

"Hi, Brandi. Here, let me," her friend said, taking the purple wrapped gift from her arms to place on a nearby table laden with presents. "How've you been? I haven't seen much of you lately."

"Working." She smiled as they walked toward the others. "With Shayla helping out, I've taken on two more projects."

"Good for you," Mrs. McCall said. "She'll be down in a bit. Hannah and I are going to watch all the kids upstairs so everyone can have some fun."

She nodded, already wishing she could head for the door. This was going to be a long afternoon.

The kitchen door opened and Kerri and Connor walked out with another happy couple and Mrs. Masters carrying a cute little boy.

"Oh, come on. Let me introduce you to my friends from California and my sweetheart of a godson." Jordan grabbed her hand and tugged her toward the smiling crowd. "Shawn, Megan, this is Brandi."

She shook their hands then turned to the little boy Jordan was now holding. "Well, hello there."

"This is Eric." Jordan beamed, kissing the little guy's cheek. "He just had his first birthday two weeks ago."

Brandi's heart did some more of that tugging thing. She really missed Tyler. He'd been just a little older when she'd gotten custody. Of course, he didn't have a sprinkling of red hair.

Again, the kitchen door opened, this time Jen and Brock came out, along with Cody, who carried a plate of cookies to the dessert table. Once he set the dish down, he turned to everyone all smiles.

"I got to taste the *fiwst* one," he said. Spotting Brandi, he rushed over. "*Bwandi*! *Whewe* have you been?"

Laughing, she bent down to pick the little guy up. "I've been working. Boy, you're getting big."

He hugged her tight. "Can you *wowk* on something at *ouw wanch* so I can see you?" he asked...just as Kade stepped close.

She bit back a rush of tears. *Shoot. When had he walked in?* Her heart slammed into her ribs.

"Hey, buddy," he said, taking the boy from her, gorgeous, smoky gaze guarded but friendly as he leaned in to kiss her cheek.

She knew it was for show. She really did. Tell that to her jumbled heart—the sucker raced out of control. And her body? Lordy, her body rejoiced at his elusive touch. It was her hot, swollen throat and numb tongue having trouble communicating. But luckily, she was spared from having to say something, or from anyone noticing her silence, when Kevin and Cole walked in carrying a suspicious looking package wrapped in red bandanas.

A smile tugged her lips at the groom's unblinking, wide-eyed stare. Then his gaze shot to all three men.

Kade held his hands up. "Don't look at me. This is all them."

"Damn," Connor grumbled. "That makes me real nervous."

"And so it should," Kevin said, then his face lit up as he walked over to talk to the Californians.

A few minutes later, Shayla walked in and the mothers of the bride and groom took the kids upstairs while everyone else lined up for food.

Apparently, she was going to be spared from having to sit next to Kade as they were gender segregated. Which was good. At least she might have the ability to taste her food today.

Jordan stood and addressed both tables. "Okay, so this is how it's going to go down. We'll each have our own little parties, then we'll get together for some joint fun later."

Brandi's insides twisted to pretty much reflect the weariness in Shayla's blue eyes. Yeah, neither of them were up for joint fun. She knew why she was leery, but was a bit curious as to her employee's apprehension. Granted, like her, the redhead didn't know the couple from California, but they seemed really nice. So, what was the problem? The woman was friends with everyone, well, except for Kevin. Which was odd. The easy-going cowboy loved everyone, and everyone loved him. Except Shayla.

Yeah, okay. So, that was obviously the problem.

Pushing all thoughts aside, she concentrated on the guest of honor, laughing, eating, joking with the others. And if her gaze strayed to the guy's table and lingered on a certain sheriff, then it was just a coincidence, but acceptable since they were still supposed to be a couple. The knot in her stomach tumbled. He looked tired, and haggard, and she longed to touch him and ease the tension from his body. And hers.

Cripes. She was such a Kade whore. But, damn, her body had blossomed under his touch and gone without for far too long. Being in the same room, so close, her good parts tingled to life and need slammed into her, hard. Dammit.

Did he feel it, too?

As if sensing her, his gaze lifted, and for a wonderful moment their connection sizzled, tripping her pulse. But then his expression closed, and she could no longer feel his warmth, just a stark, cold reality. She shivered and rubbed her arms.

An hour and a half later, with food, games and presents all checked off the list, including a bandana wrapped box full of rubber rattlesnakes for Connor,

Brandi made the mistake of thinking the party was over.

She should've known better when there were McCalls involved.

"Okay," Jordan said, rising to her feet once more. "Now it's time for some joint fun. Since there's an even number of guys and girls, we're going to do some fun couples games. Sorry, Kevin and Shayla, yes, this means you'll have to put your differences aside and get along for the next half hour."

They weren't the only ones.

Her gaze met an apprehensive gray one. Yeah, he was thrilled, too.

"*Ah hell.* Can't you give a guy more of warning? I would've brought my cup," Kevin stated, amusement lighting his blue eyes as he grinned at the redhead.

Shayla groaned and stood. "Don't get your panties in a bunch. I need to go check on my daughter anyway."

"Oh no you don't." Kerri jumped to her feet and blocked the exit. "Mom just texted and said all of the children were just fine. So relax. Besides, it's only one game. And it's not even really a game. More of a…" She paused as Jordan bought out a covered tray from the kitchen then lifted the lid to reveal Kerri's famous stuffed strawberries.

No. She couldn't do it. Not a…

"Joint dessert," their host finished.

As everyone oohed and aahed, Brandi and Shayla groaned.

"So, girls, grab your strawberry, and guys, grab your girls and enjoy," Jordan finished with a smile.

"I just remembered," Kevin said. "I'm allergic to strawberries."

The redhead snickered. "Figures."

"What's that supposed to mean?"

"That you've still got your panties in a bunch."

No one moved—or breathed—as everyone watched the exchange, then raised their brows when the cowboy strode to the tray, plucked a strawberry and gently placed it in Shayla's opened mouth.

"I'll show you bunched panties," he stated just before he cupped the woman's face, bit into the strawberry, and kissed her shocked employee, long and thorough and slow.

"*Damn*," someone said.

A second later, people were grabbing strawberries and partners and sharing a very hot *cold* dessert. A stuffed berry was shoved into her hand. *Oh boy.* Her stomach fluttered at the thought of finally sharing the decadent dessert with Kade.

He stood in front of her, staring at the strawberry, then her mouth. Heat flooded her body in a wave of need too big to withstand. She swayed forward, unsure how to proceed. God, she couldn't kiss him. She'd never stop. And she couldn't *not* kiss him, not without tipping their hand.

Heart pounding in her chest so loud she swore they could hear it in the next county, Brandi watched as Kade lifted the dessert to her mouth and slowly leaned in. Heaven help her, she wasn't going to survive.

As the strawberry touched her lips, his radio went off.

He stiffened, dropped the dessert into her hand and stepped back. "Got to go."

Disappointment flittered through his gaze dark with longing, and a pain so fierce it hit her like a physical blow. She sucked in a breath and stumbled slightly, grateful no one had witnessed her lapse.

A moment later, he was gone. That was the second

time a stuffed strawberry went unshared between them.

"I'll tell ya, buddy, I can hardly believe the day is actually here," Connor said, standing in front of a mirror at Wild Creek, doing a piss-poor job of knotting his tie.

Kade watched his friend fumble for another minute before he took pity on the guy. "Come here. Let me do it before you choke yourself."

The groom twisted around and dropped his hands. "Thanks. I'm all thumbs today. I just want everything to go right for Kerri. She deserves a perfect day."

He nodded, making quick work of the knot. "And it will be. My deputy helped plan everything. Trust me. Things will be great."

Connor's chuckle filled the downstairs guest bedroom the groom and his groomsmen were using since the bride and her bridesmaids were upstairs in the couple's new suite. "True, Jordan's certainly whipped my brother into shape."

"Hey." Cole rose from a chair, frown disappearing into a broad smile. "You're right. She did."

Kevin stepped to his boss and slapped his shoulder. "Would that be with, or without, handcuffs?"

As the younger McCall's smile broadened, his cousin's disappeared. Kade snickered along with Connor. Never a dull moment. His buddy slipped into a black suit jacket and turned to check in the mirror.

"*Damn.*" A lop-sided grin tugged the groom's lips. "I don't clean up half-bad."

"Which means you don't clean up half-good, either," Kevin pointed out, to which Connor flipped him the bird. "I've no idea what Kerri sees in you."

His buddy's expression turned serious. "Me either. But I'm one lucky son-of-a-bitch. It just takes the right woman to make you see it. Ain't that right, Kade?"

Heart rolling in his chest, he nodded. The last thing he wanted to do was talk about the *right woman.* He knew he had been lucky to have her, but he also knew Brandi deserved a hell of a lot better. Still, it didn't mean it didn't rip his guts out every time he saw her face.

"So, are you going to be the next one to take the plunge?" His friend smiled.

Now his rolling heart ceased in his chest. *Christ. Would the ache ever stop?* He forced thoughts of pain from his mind and lips into a smile. "Let's just worry about you today, buddy. You got the rings?"

Connor nodded, then patted his pocket, a panicked expression crossing his face as he patted the other one. "The rings! Where are the—"

"Relax, bro. I have them, remember?" Cole came up behind the groom and handed the cowboy his Stetson. "It's all good."

Stiffness melted away and an easy grin crossed his buddy's face. "Okay, then. Let's go get me hitched."

As he stood outside on Wild Creek soil, staring at a make-shift gazebo similar to the one used at Cole's wedding, decorated in white and purple, Kade mentally braced himself for the onslaught of emotions he knew were heading his way.

Brandi.

She was scheduled to play a song during the wedding, but not at the beginning. Right now, the march sounded from the speakers set up around the backyard. Which meant…he had to escort the beauty down the aisle.

Touch her.
Breathe her.
Be near her.

Christ. He just had to get through this day. One day. He could do it. Wouldn't be near as tough as that damn stuffed strawberry at the bachelor party a few days ago. Hell, that had sucked. The temptation of tasting the hot, sweet, incredible woman again had been too much. And, *Jesus*, he'd certainly failed that test.

Thank God Old Charlie had decided to hit the road again.

"Here we go." Kevin twisted around to wink at him as Brock met Jen in the aisle, held his arm out then walked down the white runner leading to the gazebo.

With Cole standing up front with Connor, Kade paused to appreciate the momentous occasion. It had taken a few decades and a couple of missteps, but one of the county's most eligible and beloved bachelors was about to officially be taken off the market. It did his heart good to see his best friend so happy and utterly content. This still left his cousin to hold up the reins, but Kade knew there were several unhappy women crying in their beers today.

"We meet again," his cousin said to a beaming Megan as he held his arm out to the Californian bridesmaid and escorted her down the aisle.

Steeling himself against threatening emotions, Kade set his shoulders and smiled at Brandi as she hooked his offered arm and stared up into his face with those fathomless eyes, brown gaze open and warm and full of all the things he didn't deserve.

God, she was beautiful. In a knee-length dress of deep purple that hugged her ample chest and flared out at the hips, she took his breath. How he got down the aisle he didn't know, only that he did, because they were miraculously in the correct positions when Jordan walked past and everyone stood to catch a glimpse of Mr.

Masters approaching with the bride.

Wearing a white lace dress with purple rose accents, matching white and purple flowers in her hair, and a pair of purple cowboy boots, Kerri positively glowed. Her blissful expression was soft and sweet and exuded so much love for the cowboy waiting for her at the end of the aisle it was nearly tangible enough to touch.

His buddy's indrawn breath had Kade turning to see emotions brighten the cowboy's eyes and puff out his chest as adoration and love emanated from his brown gaze. Bittersweet, the happy emotions warmed his heart, yet intensified the hollowness in his gut. Life would be so much easier if he just didn't feel.

And in front of family and friends, he watched his best friend marry the woman of his dreams in a ceremony he admittedly only half heard, thanks to the pounding in his head.

It had started before he'd walked Brandi down the aisle, then manifested as the beautiful woman played an incredible piece on the violin—the *one* he'd given her to replace the bow he'd broken. He hadn't expected her to use the violin, too, although, when he'd seen the used instrument in the music shop where he'd gone to buy a bow, he knew...he *knew* the violin belonged with Brandi.

And hearing her play, watching her handle and hold the instrument as if it were an actual person she loved and cherished with all her heart, had touched something deep inside him. For a brief, wonderful moment he'd felt warm and good...and whole, as if *he* was the instrument.

Then reality set in when he'd caught a glimpse of Shayla and the fatherless baby sitting in the back row. He'd condemned the innocent child to a life without her father. Sergeant Nylan would never walk Amelia down an aisle. Loved? Fuck no. He didn't deserve to be loved.

Not when the little girl would never know the love of her father.

Thanks to him.

And an hour later, as he stood behind the bride and groom, staring down into Brandi's sweet, accepting face, he told himself he didn't deserve the warmth of her kiss, or the love in her touch he was forced to endure in front of family and friends.

When he drew back, intent on getting away from feeling, she grasped his arms and squeezed.

"Are you okay?"

He was so fucking sick of hearing that damn question.

"I'm fine," he said, pulling free to go to his seat, and repeated the words in his head for most of the evening.

He'd laughed and toasted, danced and smiled, made all the motions necessary for his best friend to have a great celebration without him ruining the night. But now his friend was getting ready to leave on his honeymoon, and Kade was nearly home free.

"You sure you can handle things here while I'm gone?" Connor asked his smiling brother.

Cole nodded. "I'm sure. You just worry about yourself and your pretty bride."

"Will do," the cowboy said, happy gaze turning serious as he glanced from Kevin back to Cole. "You'll take care of that thing we talked about earlier? 'Cause if you need me to—"

"We got it covered. Now go. The jet is fueled up and scheduled to leave in two hours," Cole stated, apparently needing to reassure his pigheaded brother the ranch wouldn't fall apart without him while the two honeymooned in the Caribbean for a week.

Connor turned and shook his hand. "You take care,

and thanks for today."

He laughed, more than confused by his buddy's sudden touchy, feely moment. "No thanks necessary. I'm very happy for you and Kerri."

He meant it. And would be happy when he could leave and get away from such a caring environment, and the woman he loved so close and so willing—

Shit...

His heart crashed into his ribs. *No.* He didn't want to love Brandi Wyne. Didn't want to feel. Didn't want anything to do with the beautiful, giving woman he did not deserve.

"You okay, buddy?" Connor grasped his arm and frowned down at him.

Son-of-a-bitch. The damn question again. He inhaled and forced his jaw to relax.

"I'm fine, but you won't be if you miss that flight."

His buddy's gaze cleared. "You're right." Connor winked, then picked up his squeaking bride, slung her over his shoulder and lumbered from the party.

Downing the last of his cola, Kade mentally relaxed. The bride and groom had gone. He was free to leave now. And, oh hell yeah, he was out of there.

After saying goodbye to the Masters and McCalls, he was almost through the living room when Brandi cornered him.

"Kade, wait," she said. "I haven't had the opportunity to thank you."

He reeled back. "Thank me? For what?"

"My violin."

A sweet smile stole across her lips and interfered with his pulse. He clenched his jaw and shook his head.

"*Jesus*, don't thank me for that. I don't deserve thanks. You shouldn't have needed it. If it weren't for me—"

Warm fingers pressed against his mouth and cut off his words.

"If it weren't for you, I would never have had the opportunity to play something so sweet and beautiful and perfect." Sucking in a breath, she lifted her chin, a sheen of tears evident in her eyes. "So just stop it right there. I don't want to hear it. I know you didn't mean to break the bow, but I'm glad you did. That's all I wanted to say." She released his mouth, and a lone tear streaked down her face. "Except that I love you, and I miss you. And I know you feel the same way."

"Brandi, don't." His voice was low and rough because, hell, he was barely holding it together. "I have to go." Grabbing her arms, he picked her up and moved her out of his way, then strode toward the hall.

Would the nightmare ever end?

"Hey, Kade, there you are," Cole said, walking toward him. "Would you mind coming with me for a minute. There's something I need your help with."

Ah hell.

He let out a breath and nodded. Probably something to do with the ranch. The guy had a billion dollar software company to run. No doubt cattle didn't fall into the scheme of things.

"Sure," he said, walking into Cole's home office.

He was a little surprised to find his cousin leaning against the desk. Maybe it was company business he needed help with? He turned to ask, then stopped dead when the younger McCall leaned against the closed door as if guarding it.

"You might want to sit for this, Kade." Cole motioned to one of the plush leather chairs in front of his desk.

With his head beginning to really pound, he folded his arms across his chest and stared the guy down. "I'll stand. What the hell is this about?"

"You, you idiot," Kevin replied, straightening from the desk. "This is an intervention, cuz."

His arms dropped to swing at his sides. "A what? You've got to be fuckin' kidding me." He strode to the door. "Get out of my way, Cole. *Now*."

The only movement the younger McCall made was a slight lift of his chin. "No. You need to hear your cousin out."

"I don't need to do shit. I'm the sheriff, and still on duty."

"My wife will handle any calls that come in. Now sit down."

Wrong answer. He swung, Cole blocked, but wasn't ready for the right hook that followed.

"*Son-of-a—*"

The guy body checked him, but Kade's training kicked in and he remained upright. Barely. *Jesus*, Cole was strong.

"What the hell? Kade, cut it out," Kevin said, grabbing him from behind, and helping his buddy bring him to the floor.

Kade shook off his cousin, and scrambled to his knees, but McCall knocked him back down.

"Get the fuck off me," he growled.

"Really, Kade? You're not that stupid, are you?" Kevin said. "You think we want to do this? You've left us no choice. You're just lucky Connor isn't here. We had to badger him to get him to leave. But if you keep this up, I'll call him back."

He stilled.

Is that what the cowboy had meant about taking care

of the thing? *Christ.* Was he the *thing*? He hated that his friends were worried about him. Didn't want to be a burden to anyone.

"I'm fine. Why don't you all just give it a rest?"

"You are far from fine," Kevin said, sitting up and resting his back against the nearby couch, gaze intent and dark with worry. "You don't sleep, barely eat…hardly work with the abused horses anymore. Christ. You *love* those horses. You would never abandon them. Ever. For you to do so now means you are so far from okay you're not even on this planet. Brock had to take over the care of that mare. And then there's *this*." His cousin waved a hand at their friend. "You're not violent, Kade. So how the hell do you explain this odd behavior?"

He closed his eyes and sighed, torn between the urge to continue to fist fight his way out of the room, and reassuring his cousin and friend that he was fine.

"Talk to us. What's going on in that head of yours, cuz?"

"I don't eat because I'm not hungry. And yes, I'm tired, but every time I close my eyes I see that damn soldier, or his fatherless kid, or…" He sucked in another breath, not ready to bring Brandi into the conversation.

"Why the hell hasn't Brandi tried to help you?" Kevin asked, accusing tone way too pissy for Kade's liking.

The woman was sweet, warm, loving and caring and didn't deserve the attitude. He opened his eyes and glared. "Leave her out of it. She's tried."

"*Ah hell*, Cole, you were right." His cousin sat back and shook his head. "The idiot *did* break up with her."

How the hell did they figure that out?

Cole nodded, walking to a small bar in the corner to pour out three glasses of scotch. "Several weeks now, by my estimate." The guy handed them out before settling his large frame against the desk, a red mark appearing on his jaw.

A sparkle of remorse trickled through his anger. He shook hit off. With the door no longer blocked, Kade contemplated his chances of escaping.

"Forget it, Dalton. It's locked." McCall held up the key before shoving it in his pants pocket. "So, drink up, and let's talk."

He downed the scotch, got up off the floor, and set the glass on the desk. "Done talking. Drank your damn drink, now let me out, or I'll break down the damn door."

"Kade, look at you." Kevin jumped to his feet and shook his head. "You need help, man. Professional help."

"Oh, for the love of Christ, would everyone just stop fucking saying that?" He began to pace, walls closing in, heat overtaking his body. "What I need is to be left the hell alone. Why won't you all just leave me the hell alone, already?"

"Because we love you, you idiot," Kevin stated. "Everyone is worried. Your family, your friends, Brandi."

He stilled and stared at his cousin.

"Who the hell do you think came to us, asking us to intervene?"

Anger set his already heated blood to boil. Dammit. "Why doesn't that woman leave well enough alone?"

Kevin shrugged. "Like I said, she loves you."

"She needs to stop."

Cole laughed. "It doesn't work that way. Believe me, I tried it once. Women are more fucking stubborn than men."

Kade snorted, not at all amused, but in total agreement. Especially since it was the truth.

"And that woman loves you, so you might as well accept it."

"No way," he protested. "She deserves better. I won't let her."

More laughing. "Listen to you, you idiot."

McCall nodded. "You don't *let* women do anything."

"She needs to move on. I'm not worth it."

"That's fucking bullshit," Kevin said, curling his fists. Anger glistened in his cousin's eyes.

Kevin never curled his fists. He didn't even know his cousin knew how to make one.

"You're letting the guilt win."

He blinked at the guy. "Yes, because I am guilty."

"Of what? Being human?" Cole asked. "Then we're all guilty."

He twisted around and glared again. "It's not the same and you know it."

"You're right. I do." His friend nodded. "So, you're saying it *is* my fault Bess died."

"What?" He tossed his hands in the air, beyond disgusted with the conversation. "No, that's not what I'm saying at all. This has nothing to do with you or your first wife."

"Sure it does. It was my fault Bess was on the road that night, therefore it's my fault she was hit by the truck."

"You know, I don't have to listen to this shit. Let me out of here." He strode to the door.

"Why? Because you're not the only one who lives with guilt and you don't want to hear it?"

He twisted around and glared at his captors. "Are you going to let me out or do I need to take the key from you?"

"*Jesus*, Kade. Calm down," Kevin frowned.

"I am fucking calm. Now let me out."

"No," Cole stated calmly. "If you're guilty of that soldier's death, then I'm guilty of Bess' death. Jordan's guilty of Eric's death."

"And I'm guilty of my dad's death."

Kade reeled back with Cole to stare at Kevin. "What?"

"It was my fault he was in that pasture," his cousin said, tone low and sad. "I was supposed to put those horses out before school that day. I forgot, so Dad did it and…"

"*Christ*, Kevin, you were just a kid." Kade clamped a hand on his cousin's shoulder, heart squeezed tight at the thought of the guy carrying around the unfounded guilt for years. "How were you to know something would spook your dad's horse and he'd hit his head?"

"How were you to know the enemy would open fire on that convoy, in that sector, on that day?" Kevin remarked. "Did you think by doing your job and ordering your men to do theirs, they wouldn't come to any harm? You were in a *war*, for God's sake, Kade."

He shook his head. In fact, his whole body shook. "It's not the same." They just didn't get it.

"It's exactly the fucking same," Kevin barked. "What? Only *you* get dibs on guilt? Hell no. It's like Cole said, we all carry some kind of guilt. Doesn't make us bad. Just makes us human."

His friend pushed from the wall and turned to face him. "You think you deserve to be punished, so by living with the pain, your suffering is justified."

Kade inhaled and nodded. That was exactly what he thought.

"Here." Cole handed him a business card.

"What's this?"

"The name of a therapist."

Son-of-a-bitch... His insides squeezed so tight he swore they were now on the outside.

"She's mine."

He blinked at the serious brown gaze. He hadn't expected that.

"She's good."

Kevin touched his arm. "You need to get help."

"Think about it," Cole urged. "Your family needs you. Your friends need you. Harland County needs you. Brandi needs you. But if you let this guilt eat up anymore of you, then there won't be anything left but bitterness. I know. I was a bastard for months."

"Years," Kevin corrected.

Kade grunted. Cole *had* been really bad. God, was he acting like that?

"Yes." His cousin nodded as if reading his mind. "It's getting to the point where Cody's afraid to ask you a question."

"What?" His heart dropped. "I never realized…" He sank down into the nearest chair.

"You've been worse lately, snapping at everyone." Kevin slipped into the chair at his side. "My guess, about the time you left Brandi."

He sucked in a breath. Hearing it in laymen's terms brought it home a lot harder. "I can't be with her. Can't subject her to my…"

"Bad moods?" Cole nodded. "Then you need to ask yourself a tough question, my friend."

Kade inhaled. Jesus, he didn't want to ask what he knew he had to ask. "What question?"

"Knowing you're causing your family, friends, and the woman who loves you to suffer…" Cole folded his arms across his chest and held Kade's gaze. "You have to ask yourself, who's pain is more important? Yours? Or theirs? Because you can't put an end to theirs, without stopping yours first."

Chapter Fifteen

Brandi stared at her computer screen, watching her brother's mouth move, but only half-hearing what he had to say during their call. It had been two weeks since Kerri's wedding. Two weeks since she'd approached Kevin and the McCall brothers for help. Two weeks since Kade's intervention.

God, she hoped he didn't hate her.

She just hadn't been able to stand by and watch the man she loved deteriorate any more. Her heart sat heavy and broken in her chest. He wouldn't listen. Wouldn't get help. She didn't have a choice. So she approached Connor and Cole and Kevin. Now, she could only wait, and hope it worked.

"Then I told Santa to stop on by your place and take a picture so the aliens on the moon would know what you looked like."

She nodded to Ben. "That's nice."

"Earth to Brandi." Her brother snapped his fingers incessantly in front of the computer. "Hey. Snap out of it. What gives, sis?"

Blinking, she focused on his handsome face, noting concern darkening his gaze. "What do you mean?"

"I mean I've been talking for a good ten minutes and am lucky if you heard ten words."

She smiled and held up her hand. "Five, only five were worth noting."

"Oh?" He arched a brow and sat back in his chair. "And what were they?"

"You coming home for Thanksgiving?"

He grinned. "I don't know, are you?"

"Ha ha, very funny."

"I thought so." He winked. "Clever, too."

"Oh, brother."

"Yes?"

Smiling, she shook her head. Ben always could get her to laugh. No matter how rotten she felt. Like now. Her smile faded.

"All right. Who is it I need to come down there and rough up? Kade?"

Her heart squeezed. Hearing his name out loud brought memories, touches, feelings into the open. God, it hurt. "No. No one."

"You two still seeing each other?"

She shrugged, then shook her head, trying to work past her hot throat. "Not really."

He straightened up and moved closer to the screen. "Then come on home, Brandi. At least for the holiday. A change of scenery will do you good. You know Tyler misses you."

Her strangled heart tightened further. Damn. Ben didn't play fair. "That was low."

"No, it was the truth. And we all miss you. Come on up. Snow will probably be on the ground by then. You might even be able to get some skiing in before you head back to Texas. If you go back."

"No *if's* about it. This is my home now." She could never leave Kade. He needed her. Hell, she needed him. He was her heart.

"Then come to the Poconos for a visit," he said. "At least promise me you'll think about it."

Nodding, she inhaled and let it out slowly. "I'll think about it."

No harm in thinking. Didn't mean she'd be doing.

After ending the call, she walked to the kitchen and stared out the window over the sink. In the distance, whitecaps crashed into the shore as wind whipped the waves into a frenzy.

Boy, could she relate.

A sharp rap on the door brought her attention back inside the house. Maybe it was Kade. She turned and rushed to answer, then did her best to keep the disappoint from her face when she found Kerri, Jordan and Shayla, holding a bundled up Amelia, standing on the porch instead.

"Hey." She moved aside. "This is a surprise. Is something wrong?"

"You tell us," Jordan replied, stepping inside. "You were supposed to meet us for coffee and cake a half-hour ago."

Shoot. "Sorry. I was on Skype with Ben and it slipped my mind."

"No problem, hun. I'll put the coffee on." Her friend smiled then made her way to the kitchen.

"Yep, we brought dessert here." Kerri held up a plate with a mouthwatering chocolate cake begging to be devoured. "And it's only a hundred calories a slice."

"You are a goddess," she said. Shutting the door, she turned to help Shayla remove Amelia's coat. "And you are a sweetheart."

The redhead placed her daughter's coat on the couch. "She couldn't wait to come over to see Mozart."

"Oh, I know. It's all about the cat."

A smile tugged Brandi's lips as she watched him get up from his spot in front of the lit fireplace and stretch before walking toward the little girl. Having been around Tyler, the cat was used to being roughed up, and was surprisingly gentle with the toddler.

"So, how is your cute brother?" Jordan asked.

"Which one?"

Shayla raised a brow. "You have more than one cute brother?"

"Actually, I have four very handsome, very single brothers," she informed.

"Damn." Her assistant sighed.

"Ben is fine. He's trying to get me to go to Pennsylvania for Thanksgiving."

Shayla picked up her daughter and walked into the kitchen. "And you're not?"

"No."

"Why?" Kerri frowned, placing cake on plates. "Your family must miss you."

"Yeah, but I... I don't feel right leaving."

Jordan pulled four mugs out of the cupboard and glanced at her. "Because of Kade?"

She nodded, tears heating her damn throat again.

"Hey, honey, come here." Kerri pulled her in for a hug. "It's okay. He's going to come around. I'm sure of it."

"I'm glad you are, because I just don't know." She sniffed. "It's been weeks since we really talked. I cornered him at your wedding, but I doubt he heard what I had to say."

Her friend squeezed tighter. "I'm sure he did."

"You should go," Jordan said.

She drew back and stared at the woman pouring coffee. "Where? Pennsylvania?"

"Yep. In fact. You *need* to go."

Now Kerri was nodding.

"Yeah," her assistant agreed.

And Brandi just stood there shaking her head, her heart hurting so bad she couldn't find the words. God, she *couldn't* leave. What if Kade needed her? What if he showed up here and she was gone? No. She was staying.

Jordan took her hand and tugged her toward a kitchen chair. "Listen. I know it hurts. Hurts like a son-of-a-bitch. But don't you see? Kade needs to not have you around."

"I haven't been around him."

"It's not the same." The woman shook her head. "You need to be out of Texas. I had to do the same thing last year. And yes, it was very tough, but Cole needed to realize he needed me in his life. He had to come to that conclusion on his own. The same goes for my boss."

Kerri nodded, passing her a plateful of cake that, at the moment, would probably taste like cardboard.

"Yes," the cook said. "Once he realizes you're not here, and he won't run into you at Shadow Rock, or my house, or the pub, reality will set in."

"I-I don't know." She glanced at three eager faces. "If I go, I can only go for a few days. I have too much work started here. I can't leave for more than that."

"Sure you can," Shayla said, settling her daughter on her lap. "I can handle things. Just tell me what needs to be done and by when, and I'll make sure it happens."

"See? Perfect." Jordan nodded. "Now, let's make plans over chocolate."

The day before Thanksgiving, Kade sat in his office, playing solitaire on his phone. Since hiring Jordan, more than half of his workload had disappeared. He swore some days his deputy stared at the phone, wishing someone would commit a crime so she had something to do.

Less of a workload was better these days. Less work, less stress. According to Doc Carrington, the therapist

Cole had recommended and Kade had been seeing for the past six weeks, less stress was a plus for him right now.

After returning stateside earlier this year, he'd seen a round of shrinks, as per protocol, but it had stopped with their mobilization. And hadn't helped. Mainly because he'd need more. Much more, he'd recently realized, but with a backlog of over several hundred thousand soldiers inputted into the system, most were going untreated. Like him.

Having brought that dilemma to Cole's attention, his friend had started a foundation through McCall Enterprises for returning Veterans to seek the help they needed.

The Bobby Nylan Foundation.

Slowly, he was getting back on track. Breathing no longer hurt. The constant knot in his gut had disappeared, and his headaches had lessened. Now, if he could just do something about the damn ache in his chest and unrelenting need for a certain designer, life would rock. But he was determined to stay out of Brandi's life. Give her a chance to meet someone normal. Someone who wasn't broken. Someone who didn't need a damn therapist just to get through the day.

Okay, things were not that bad anymore. In fact, they were rather good. He'd gone from meeting three times a week, to once a week. And sleeping had returned to normal. No more nightmares, just dreams of Brandi and how incredible she'd tasted and felt, and how wonderful she'd made him feel.

Christ... He shut down the game and tossed his phone on the desk. He needed to stop thinking about her if he was to move on, too.

"Sheriff Dalton?"

Head snapping up, he was surprised to find Shayla

standing in his doorway. Then alarm set in and he jumped to his feet. "Are you okay? Did something happen?"

"I'm fine." She sent him a reassuring smile. "I just wanted to talk to you about something."

He nodded and pointed to a chair. Okay, so it wasn't her deadbeat dad. "Sure. Sit down. What can I do for you?" Shutting the door, he noted there were only a few tight bands squeezing his chest in her presence.

Progress. Something to report to the doctor at his next appointment.

"I wanted to talk to you about Bobby."

More bands appeared, and brought their friends. *Shit*. He tried to pull in a few breaths before breathing became a chore. Funny how mentioning her dead boyfriend had increased the stranglehold.

Kade retook his seat and stared across the desk at the woman. "What about him?"

"I'm sorry," she said, twisting the bracelet around her wrist. "I should've told you sooner, but I needed the healthcare for Amelia, and I was worried the truth would've affected her coverage."

Healthcare?

He cocked his head and frowned. That was certainly not what he'd expected the woman to say. "Told me what, exactly?"

She drew in a deep breath and continued to play with the bracelet. "That Bobby was never my boyfriend…or Amelia's father."

He sat back and blinked for a full minute. Sixty seconds of absolute confusion and a jumble of emotions. The man he killed…did not leave a child behind? *The soldier who'd died*, his mind corrected—another breakthrough to tell the doc.

The soldier who'd died did not leave a child behind.
"He wasn't?"

"No." Her red waves rippled as she shook her head. "Bobby and I were friends. We'd been in a few foster homes together growing up. When I found myself in trouble, he told me he could get me healthcare if we pretended he was the father."

And that's when things started to make sense. "The birth was covered, and once she was born, he had Amelia registered in DEERS as his daughter, and she was automatically covered."

"Yes."

"But when he died, coverage only lasted a year."

"Yes. I'm really sorry." Tears filled her guilt-clouded eyes. She blinked them away and drew in a breath. "I had no idea you...I just didn't realize how this all affected you. I'm sorry I was such an idiot. If I didn't have to keep moving, then I would've found a steady job before now, gotten my daughter on my own healthcare plan and come clean about Bobby sooner."

He set his elbows on the arms of his chair and steepled his fingers. *The dead soldier did not leave a daughter behind.* Funny how that *one* thought made such a huge difference. That was what ate at his gut. That he'd taken away the baby's father. He knew what that was like. It had happened to him, twice. First his actual father, when he'd died during the first Gulf War with the Marines. Then, a few years later, his uncle had died, the man who'd selflessly stepped in and up, taking in a cantankerous, hurt, miserable little boy and turned him into a man.

"I'm sorry. You must really hate me," Shayla said, chin tipped at a defiant angle, yet her eyes still held that apologetic expression.

Kade shook his head. "No, I understand. You were worried about your daughter."

She nodded, blinking back a fresh sheen of tears. "Yes."

"It's okay. I can't fault you for caring about your child." He wished to God his own mother had had that attitude.

The woman smiled. "Brandi said you'd understand. I'm going to miss her."

"Miss her? Why? Are you leaving?" He rose to his feet and stared down at her. "I'm not sure that's such a good idea from what you told me about your father."

"Me? No." She shook her head and stood. "*Brandi*. She's gone back to Pennsylvania."

Brandi? His heart rocked so hard in his chest it felt as if someone had ripped it out from clear across town. "She left?"

Without saying goodbye?

Of course, idiot. After all, he'd told her, *insisted* she let him go. That she move on and forget about him. So why the fuck did it hurt so bad?

Because he loved her and didn't want her to move on. He wanted her to love him so much she would never leave. Would never abandon him. Just like his mother had done.

His father.

His uncle.

His aunt.

Christ.

Just like *he'd* done to Brandi.

He shouldn't have given up on them. He should've tried to fight, held on while he sought help.

"Yes, she left a few days ago." Shayla headed for the door, then stopped and turned to face him. "I shouldn't be saying this, but well, I feel bad about keeping you in the dark about Amelia so maybe I can make up for it with Brandi."

His pulse tripped. "What about Brandi?"

"It wasn't her brothers she went up there to see."

Her words sent a sharp pain through his chest. Sharper and more painful than any band or vise. He glanced down to see if the statement had drawn blood.

Ripped open...

Gutted...

Jesus, she wasn't going to go back to Ed? He couldn't bear it if he'd sent her back into the arms of that asshole.

"But I know she cared for you," Shayla continued. "So, if you feel the same, maybe you can go get her and tell her. There might still be time."

With a firm nod, the woman left his office and him in a state somewhere between shock and panic. Blind fucking panic.

Brandi was gone.

He would no longer see her.

What was she doing with her horse? Had she made some sort of arrangements with Brock? Maybe she hadn't planned ahead. Maybe she left on the spur of the moment.

Maybe he should start coming up with answers instead of adding more questions to the already huge pile.

Maybe he needed to think about what he wanted...ah hell, who was he kidding. He *knew* what he wanted.

Brandi.

That was never a question. And he knew what she'd wanted. Him.

Question was, did she still feel that way?

Only one way to find out. But it was not something you did over the phone. He was a man of action, and this required action.

Kade strode from his office to stand in front of Jordan's desk, waiting impatiently until she got off her phone.

"Yes." She held up her index finger and nodded for him to wait. "We'll see. I think so. Absolutely. Yes, tell Emma we'll be there for dinner tomorrow. Maybe have the champagne on standby."

Champagne? What were they celebrating?

"He's right here, I'll ask." She moved the phone from her ear to her shoulder and smiled at him. "Cole's mom wants to know if you're coming for Thanksgiving dinner tomorrow."

He shook his head. "No, thank you. I have other plans." Out of state plans.

"He said no, but thank you. Okay. I'll tell him. All right. See you then. Bye." His deputy hung up the phone then rose to her feet. "She said if you change your mind, you and your family are always welcome to drop by."

He nodded. An open invitation that stood for decades. Some years he took them up on it, others he didn't...this was an *other*.

"Okay, boss." She placed her hands on her hips and stared at him. "What did you need?"

A little stab of guilt poked him. "I hate to do this to you, but I need you to cover down tomorrow."

A wide smile crossed her lips. Odd, he thought maybe she'd be upset.

She stepped forward and grabbed his upper arms. "You're going after her, aren't you?"

A helpless sound, similar to a snort left his throat.

The woman knew everything. *Jesus*, Cole never stood a chance.

"Yes. I need to beg her forgiveness."

"True, and bring her chocolate," she said then pulled him into a hug. "I'm happy for you, Kade."

"Happy? Aren't you jumping the gun there, Jordan? She hasn't forgiven me yet."

"True, but she will. Brandi loves you."

He sucked in a breath and closed his eyes. God, he hoped so. Hoped he hadn't killed her feelings for him by being a bigger ass than Ed. "It's time I find out."

Time he did a lot of things. Like take the therapist's advice and worry about himself. Think about what he wanted. Put himself first.

And *what* Kade wanted was no longer in Texas.

Chapter Sixteen

Thanksgiving morning was always a busy time in the Wyne household. Between turkey, and stuffing, and football games in the back yard with a bunch of Guard buddies, there was barely anytime to think. Exactly what Brandi needed.

Lord, she needed to just not think.

Coming back to the Poconos had been a good idea, but bittersweet.

Sweet because she couldn't imagine Thanksgiving anywhere else but with her family, in their big, old, rambling house full of activity, and laughter and love.

Bitter because she missed Kade. Missed his big, old, rambling ranch full of activity, and laughter and love. Missed his warmth, his acceptance, praise, affection, his hard, hot, sexy body and the way they fit. Perfect. Absolutely perfect.

Would he ever realize it? Did he even know she was gone?

Jordan, Kerri and Shayla told her to just go. Not to say goodbye. They'd take care of it. But, it's not like it was forever. Her two weeks up north would probably go unnoticed by the guy. It wasn't like their paths crossed much anymore.

But, if he did know, did he miss her?

She brushed away the tears burning her eyes, and bent to check on the turkey. Again.

"You know, unless it's re-grown feathers and learned how to fly, old Tom is still in there working on his tan."

A smile tugged her lips. "Hey, Ben." She straightened and turned around expecting to see just her older brother, but found all four of her brothers standing inside the kitchen, arms folded across their chests. "Wow, game over already?"

"Nah," he said on the way to the fridge. "We just came in for a drink."

She shook her head, recognizing the concern in their eyes. "Bull. You came in to check on me. But I'm fine. Really, go ahead and play your game."

"The game can wait," Mason unfolded his arms and drew near. "Scott and the guys can manage without us."

She hated that they were inside worrying about her when they should be outside playing football with their Guard buddies. "Go have fun. Really. I'm okay. I have *Tom* to keep me company." She nodded toward the oven and even managed a smile.

Ethan cocked his head. "Good try, sis."

Her youngest brother, Keiffer, grabbed her hand while Ben took the other and together they led her to the chair Ethan pulled out from the table. *Oh boy.* Lots of testosterone permeated in the air. She knew better than to balk at them when they worked as a collective. Best to go with the flow. Sitting down, she glanced up at a wall of concerned *Wyne*.

"This is an intervention, Brandi," Mason informed. "Talk to us."

Keiffer nodded. "Yes, what's going on?"

She hadn't seen such stern faces since Mason's fiancée had left him.

Ben squatted in front of her and touched her knee. "What happened between you and Kade? Did he hurt you?"

"No." She shook her head at their dark expressions.

They were out for blood. "He didn't hurt me. Not in the way you think. And not intentionally."

Mason's chin lifted. "Then in what way?"

"Yeah." Keiffer curled a hand around his fist. "And where can we find him to have a…chat?"

"Whoa, hold on." She jumped up, nearly knocking Ben over. "They'll be no *chatting*. Kade only left me because he thought I was better off without him. Which of course is wrong. Totally and utterly wrong. I love the idiot. And he loves me. He just needs to realize it, and…and get some help."

Mason stiffened. "Help? What kind of help?"

"Therapy," she said quietly. "He lost a soldier under his command last year."

The posture on all four of her brothers changed. Their stiff, aggressive stances instantly mellowed, and with expelled breathes, they pulled out their chairs and sat down. No one said a word. Unfortunately, being in the Guard, each of her brothers understood what Kade was going through.

"I didn't want to leave him. I want to be there for him, but…" She sniffed, and when Ethan stood and pulled her in for a hug, she set her head on his shoulder. "He won't let me in."

"It's going to take time, Brandi," her oldest brother said, patting her back. "Just don't give up on him."

She nodded. "I won't." Then she drew back and wiped her eyes. "Okay, so…" She cleared her throat. "Now, enough with the faces. You have a game to win. Some friends to crush…yada…yada…"

They smiled and nodded.

"Aunt Brandi?" Tyler came rushing into the kitchen, big brown eyes alight with excitement.

He was so full of life. Happy. Exuberant. It had been

great to visit with her young nephew. She'd hardly left his side since arriving a week ago. He was a breath of fresh air. She squatted down to stare eye level. "What is it, Tyler?"

"You have company." He grinned a toothless grin and pointed toward the doorway.

Company? She'd already met Lea and few of her friends for lunch two days ago. Following his little finger, her gaze slammed into a pair of jeans, and a very male, very familiar crotch. She knew those jeans. Knew that crotch. She'd removed those jeans from that crotch, many times.

Her heart slammed into her chest at the same time she glanced up into the troubled gray eyes of the man she loved, and the momentum of both knocked her on her butt, literally.

"Kade," she said, struggling to right herself.

He was in front of her in a shot, hands clasped on her arms as he helped her to her feet. "You okay?"

She smiled and threw herself into his chest as tears blurred her vision. "I'm fantastic now. You came for me." Squeezing him tight, she buried her face in his neck and inhaled. This wasn't a dream. He was really there, smelling all clean and woodsy and male. Kade was really there.

"Brandi, wait." He drew back and held her at arm's length, all eyes on them. "Hold on. I came here to grovel. And by God, I'm going to grovel. You deserve some groveling."

"Hell yeah." Keiffer nodded.

"I like this guy." Ethan smiled, and Mason murmured in agreement.

"Good to see you again, Kade." Ben nodded, sweeping Tyler into his arms as he headed for the door.

"Come on, kiddo. Nothing to see here."

"But I want to talk to Aunt Brandi's company."

"You can talk to him later," Ethan said, falling into step, mussing his son's hair. "They need some privacy."

"But…"

"You heard your dad, Tyler, time to go." Her father stood by the door, ushering everyone out, then glanced at them when the room cleared. "Let the groveling commence, son." With a nod, he pivoted on his heel and strode from the room.

Her attention returned to the man still holding her arms. Her heart ached and rejoiced at the same time. Face not as hollow, dark circles not as prevalent, he still appeared tired and haggard. She reached up to touch his cheek. "I don't want groveling. I just want you."

He shook his head and backed her up until her legs hit the chair she'd vacated earlier, and gently pushed her down. "Sit. You're getting both. So please, just listen. Can you do that?" Bending at the knee, he stared at her until she nodded. "Good," he said, then let go and stood.

It took all the strength she could muster not to jump to her feet and hug him again. To pull him close, and melt into those warm, magnificent, beckoning muscles and never ever let go.

She just couldn't believe he was there, standing nervous in her kitchen, all gorgeous in a black coat, gray Henley, jeans and cowboy boots. Jordan and Kerri were right. They said he'd come for her. And he did. He actually came to Pennsylvania. For her.

He shrugged out of his coat and set it over one of the other chairs, then blew out a breath and turned to her. "I'm sorry, Brandi. Sorry I was such a damn jerk."

Reassuring words sprang to her lips, but he shook his and she closed her mouth. Once again, she recognized the merit to doing what she was told. The sooner he got this off his chest, the sooner she could burrow into that chest.

He began to pace. "I know you tried to help, but I was too stupid to recognize it. You also tried to open my eyes to the fact I was in trouble and in need of professional help. Again, I was too stupid." His steps halted and he glanced at her. "Thanks for having Kevin and Cole intervene, by the way. I started going to Cole's therapist."

Tears slid down her face. She couldn't stop them. Happiness, relief—it was all too much and the emotions built until they overflowed. "I'm glad."

He nodded and his gaze softened. "I realize now some of my guilt was unfounded, and the rest I'll find a way to live with. But *Christ*, I've been such an ass. In my infinite wisdom, I thought you were better off without me. Better off finding someone who could love you like you deserved to be loved. But now I realize, now I see that I was wrong." He dropped to his knees in front of her, grasped her hands and squeezed. "*I* am that person, Brandi. *I* can love you how you deserve to be loved. Hell, I already do. More than life."

That was it. She was done staying still. Done staying quiet. No more.

She slid to the floor and hugged him tight. "I love you so much, Kade."

Strong arms wrapped around her and he buried his face in her neck, crushing her close. "I'm so lucky, Brandi. Don't think I don't know how damn lucky I am to have you. How lucky I am that you love my sorry ass." He inhaled and shook against her. "I promise I'll never leave you again. And I sure as hell am going to love you like you deserve to be loved."

She increased her hold and nodded against his chest, her whole being warmed by the strength of his words, the two arms holding her tight, the steady heart beating under her ear. This time, they really were going to be okay. He wanted help. He got help. Now he was there for her. He wanted her.

He got her.

"I love you, Brandi," Kade said, bringing them both to their feet. Cupping her face, he stared into her eyes, his gaze sure and strong. "Come back to Harland County with me. I know it's asking a lot, you leaving your family again. And whoever it was you came up here to see." His eyes closed briefly. "God, I hope it wasn't Ed. But whoever it was, I swear to you, I'll love you more."

Her mouth dropped open, and Brandi was sure her expression had to be better than priceless. "Of course I'll go back. I only came up for a two-week visit." She lifted her shoulders. "And I can assure you, Ed had nothing to do with it."

"Shayla said you returned to the Poconos for someone other than your brothers…"

Now he was the one blinking.

"Yes, to visit my nephew." She caressed his face, pulse kicking up as her palm came in contact with the rough stubble on his chin. Her body remembered the sensation all too well. Missed it. Missed him. "But I wasn't staying here. My place is with you. I'd never leave you, never desert you, Kade. Ever."

Emotions darkened his eyes and he clenched his jaw as he nodded.

"I love you," she told him again, holding his gaze, his face, making sure there would never be any doubt. "We're going to get through whatever you need to get through, together."

His exhale washed over her. "God, I love you," he said, lowering his face, brushing her tears away with his lips, moving across her cheek until his mouth finally covered hers in a kiss that never tasted so good. So right. So perfect. Full of hope and love and heat, so much heat her knees buckled and her whole body trembled for the man who wore many uniforms, many hats, and all of them part of the cowboy she loved with all of her Yankee heart.

Epilogue

Another year, another Christmas party, but this year, *this* party was very special. Leeann McCall smiled and basked in the warmth engulfing her heart. This year had seen the weddings of both of her sons. Cole and Connor had married the loves of their lives. She stood in the corner of her gathering room festively decorated in reds and greens while she watched the crowd. Her boys danced with their wives. Kade and Brandi were out there, too, but barely moved, just held onto each other. So sweet.

Doctor Turner was there and some of the other Guardsmen. So nice to have them home safe and sound. And Shayla was in the corner with her cute little girl, and her younger sister who'd just arrived in Harland County earlier this week. A quiet beauty with brown hair and blue eyes.

"What are you thinking, sweetheart?" Alex asked, stepping behind her and pulling her back against his chest. "About our boys?"

She nodded, wrapping her arms around his. "It was a good year."

"Indeed it was. A very good year."

"Two marriages and one engagement," she said.

Her husband bent to glance at her from the side, dark eyes alight with joy. "Engagement? Kade asked Brandi?"

"Yep." She nodded with a smile. "Last night, I believe." She motioned to the couple holding each other on the dance floor.

"Then it's time to bring out the champagne," her

husband said.

"Already ahead of you there, my friend." Nate and his wife appeared with four glasses of bubbly. After handing them out, her friend's husband lifted his drink in a toast. "To Kade and Brandi."

"Yes, may they be as happy together as our children," Hannah added, to which they clinked and drank. "But don't expect a quick wedding. Kerri said Brandi wants Kade to concentrate on his therapy."

"Smart woman." Leeann nodded, tears blurring her vision. It did her heart good to know his aunt and uncle would have been so pleased with Brandi. "I bet Hal and Sarah are smiling down."

Her friend wiped her face as she nodded.

"And Kade's father, Raylan, too," Nate said, and her husband agreed.

"Now, there's only one left." Alex tipped his glass toward the blue-eyed cowboy wearing a black Stetson with mistletoe fringe and a blonde under each arm. "And something tells me he's going to be the toughest one of all."

"Oh boy," Cole said, arm around his smiling wife as they approached. "I know that look."

Jordan arched a brow. "You aren't seriously going to try to take on Kevin?"

"Who's taking on my cousin?" Kade asked, stopping by with his arm around a beaming Brandi.

"Never mind him. Congratulations! I'm so happy for you."

Leeann pulled them both in for a hug, then Hannah joined in, and soon everyone had a glass of champagne in their hands and were toasting the happy couple.

"Hey, where's my glass?" Kevin appeared without his entourage. "I'd like to toast my cousin and his better half, too."

Brandi lifted on tiptoe and kissed the cowboy's cheek. "Thank you, that's sweet."

"Well, I'm just a sweet kind of guy, darlin'."

"Yeah, sweet on himself," Shalya said, her cute baby girl in her arms, dressed in green velvet like her pretty mom. "We didn't mean to interrupt. Just wanted to congratulate you two." The redhead hugged the couple then stepped back.

Kevin grunted. "You're just jealous because *you're* not."

"Not what? Sweet?" The redhead smirked. "Oh, I can be plenty sweet, cowboy. I just choose not to be toward you."

One eyebrow raised, the younger Dalton leaned closer to the woman and sent her his trademark winning grin. "You were plenty sweet to me when we shared that strawberry at the pub."

She'd heard about that. Apparently, Kerri's stuffed strawberries were a big hit.

"I wasn't being sweet, you idiot," Shayla said. "I was eating the strawberry."

Leeann exchanged a glance with Hannah and held back a grin. Oh, they just found their contender. And if the sparks shooting between the cowboy and redhead were anything to go by, this coming year was going to be very interesting.

As if unable to resist, the little girl reached for the fringe on Kevin's hat. He backed up, smile still on his face as he captured the little girl's hand.

"No no, sweetheart. Mistletoe is not good for you."

"Neither are Casanova cowboys," the redhead muttered.

Once again, Leeann had to fight to hold back a grin.

"Oh no, don't call him that." Cole grimaced. "That'll go to his head."

"Too late." Kevin winked, brushing his lips across the little girl's hand.

Shayla stepped back, removing her daughter from the cowboy's grasp as she turned to face Leeann. "I'm going to go sit with my sister. Thank you for inviting us." Her gaze bounced to Brandi and Kade. "Congratulations, again."

And, hugging her daughter close, Harland County's newest resident made her way to her quiet sibling still sitting in the window seat. There was a bit of a haunted expression on the pretty girl's face. Leeann couldn't help but wonder what put it there, and why it sometimes crossed Shayla's face, too.

"It's so great to see you both happy," Jordan was saying to the engaged couple. "If there's anything you two want for an engagement gift, please let me know."

"Actually, I have a question for you, Jordan," Kade said, arm still draped around Brandi as he glanced at the other couple.

"Me?" Her daughter-in-law blinked, slipping her arm around Cole. "What?"

Kade smiled. "Ever think of becoming sheriff?"

The immediate area stilled in silence as the question hung in the air.

Kevin laughed. "Did you feel that?"

Her son glanced at his wife then frowned at his friend. "What?"

Oh, boy. Devilment danced behind those killer blue eyes.

"The crime rate just dropped across the lower half of this state." The cowboy smirked.

Leeann smiled and could feel her husband's chuckle

against her back. There weren't many that would mess with her son's brave wife.

"Well, while you all ponder the *Jordan for President*, I mean *Jordan for Sheriff* thing, I'm going to go exercise my mistletoe rights."

And with a tip of his hat, *Casanova Dalton* sauntered off, turning many pretty heads on his way to the food table. Within seconds, the two blondes appeared out of nowhere to take up residence at his side again. That boy led too wild a life. It was high time he settled down.

Her gaze traveled across the room to the pretty redhead smiling into her sweet baby girl's face. The cowboy liked pairs. She had a sneaky suspicion she knew just the two to bring him to his knees.

**♥*
***

Fallen Soldier Table

The table is small, set for one- symbolizing the frailty of one soldier alone against his enemies.

The table cloth is white- symbolizing the purity of the soldier's intentions to respond to their country's call to arms.

The single red rose symbolizes remembrance. It is displayed in a vase, reminding us of the families and loved ones of our comrades in arms who keep their memories alive, lest we forget.

The red ribbon tied prominently on the vase is a reminder of the blood they shed protecting the liberty so loved by our country.

A slice of lemon sits on the bread plate to remind us of the bitterness of their fate.

The plate is covered in salt- symbolic of their family's tears.

The glass is inverted, for they cannot toast with us tonight.

The chair is empty, for they can sit with us no longer.

In remembrance of all the fallen soldiers.

♥

**♥*

Shayla fled to Harland County, Texas with her baby girl and college student sister, hoping to stay a step ahead of their deadbeat dad. Tired of running, she wanted to settle down into a normal life. A safe life.
A solid, forever life.
Too bad her body insisted on responding to the local heartthrob,
the drop-dead gorgeous Casanova cowboy.

♥

Please turn the page
for a preview of

Her Forever Cowboy

Available Spring 2014

Chapter One – Her Forever Cowboy

Come to the pub, they said.

It'll be fun, they said.

"Fun my ass," Kevin Dalton grumbled, none too happy his friends failed to mention the sexy, redheaded she-devil would be at the Texas Republic with her killer lips and elbow to match.

Swallowing a few choice words, and they were juicy, he slumped further into the booth at the restaurant/bar owned by the Masters sisters. Or would that be McCall sisters? After all, Jordan and Kerri had married the McCall brothers this past year.

"What's with the face," his best friend Cole McCall asked from across the table, brown gaze twinkling with undisguised joy. "Forget to wear your cup?"

Bastard. Make that ex-best friend.

"Very funny." He didn't laugh, but he did groan as his friend's brother decided to settle into the booth with him.

"Nah, he probably forgot to put on his big-boy underwear. Ain't that right, Dalton?" A lop-sided grin accompanied Connor McCall's jab to the ribs. "Quit being such a girl."

"Up yours, *Moose*." He didn't bother with the finger. A guy that big required a verbal reprimand if there was any hope of it sinking into the giant's thick skull.

"Come on, guys. Give my cousin a break," Kade Dalton said, sitting next to Cole, gray eyes full of compassion and...*ah shit*, mirth. "You know Kevin doesn't have his *Man Card* yet."

"Bite me," he replied, tone sounding more aggravated than he actually felt. No, he was thrilled to see his cousin so upbeat and positive.

God, for a while there, Kade had been just the opposite. His older cousin had needed an intervention to seek professional help regarding issues from a recent deployment with the Texas National Guard. It was truly great to see the guy happy. Of course, Kevin knew the transformation wasn't all attributed to therapy. Hell no, most of the credit went to his cousin's angel of a fiancé, Brandi Wyne. Too damn bad the beautiful designer from the north didn't have a sister.

Or two.

"Yeah, you're right." Connor nodded. "He needs to earn it. Maybe once he takes off the girlie pants."

Kevin forced his lips to curve into a smile, and even managed a chuckle. "You're just jealous cause I'm better looking."

The cowboy's head jerked back with his smirk. "Yeah, right."

"Actually, guys," his buddy spoke up, lifting his beer. "We have to give 'ole blue eyes credit for those triplets I told you about from our Japan trip last year."

Oh, yeah. The Nakamura sisters. Satisfaction spread warmth throughout his body and a matching smile across his lips. Triplets. Japanese triplets. Two items he'd crossed off his bucket list.

Kade nodded. "True."

"Yeah, I have to admit, that was very ambitious. Don't know how you managed that one, Kevin." Connor shook his head, small smile tugging a dimple to life.

"Nearly killed me," he admitted. Truth be told, he'd pulled a muscle in his groin. But hot damn, it had been so worth it. "Cowboys everywhere were relying on me to deliver. So I did."

"Three times?" Connor raised a brow.

"Yes." He nodded. "I made damn sure each girl was satisfied before I crawled back to my room and passed out." With an icepack on his abused…muscle.

Laughter filled their booth and lightened the mood.

Kade lifted his beer and smiled. "To Kevin. Looks like he *did* earn that *Man Card*, after all."

The three laughing bastards clinked mugs, but he didn't care. Hell no. Because *he* had the memory *and* the satisfaction of knowing he'd actually pleased the amorous sisters. A genuine smile crossed his lips and he sat a little taller. Yeah, he'd represented real well.

"So, what seems to be the trouble with this one?" Cole nodded toward the line dancers tearing up the floor.

Trouble? He frowned. "With what one?"

"You know *exactly* which one."

Yeah, he knew. They were referring to spitfire with long auburn waves, bouncing down her back as she kicked up her booted heels alongside Brandi. He'd come to blows with the beauty a few times. Sure, he'd felt a connection, a damn strong connection, but he'd also felt her wrath. No thank you. Plenty of willing females out there. He did not need nor want to coax.

He took a pull on his beer, then nodded to the dancers. "Let's just say I know better than to bark at a dead tree."

Dark brows rose as his buddy turned to face the crowd. "She doesn't look all that dead to me. In fact, I'd say she looks quite…energetic."

She'd tasted even better.

Damn her.

"You've been avoiding her like the plague," his friend stated.

His head jerked back. "I have not. Jeez, you're such an exaggerator, McCall."

"Bull." Cole laughed. "You've avoided her here. Around town. My mom's Christmas party. Seriously, Kevin. What gives?"

A grinning Connor leaned close. "He's got an aversion to her elbow."

Kevin readily agreed with a nod. "Can you blame me? An elbow to the groin is not exactly a wonderful first meet."

He still couldn't believe she'd poled him. *Poled him*. And for no reason.

He'd been innocently walking toward Cole's wife Jordan, her sister Kerri and Brandi. The women were sitting at a picnic table eating ice cream at The Creamery, along with a redhead who was holding the cutest little baby girl he'd ever seen, when wham! The spitfire had elbowed his favorite body part and dropped him like a sack of cement.

"Sure left an impression, though." Cole snickered.

"Hell, yeah," he said. "The fellas about-face when that woman's around. They cower and run for safety."

"You didn't seem all that put out when you two were strawberry sharing a few weeks back."

"Damn, man." Connor nodded, dimple still glaring. "I thought the pub was going to catch fire."

Kade scratched the bridge of his nose, a small smile tugging his lips. "Yeah, cuz. You were kind of burning the place up."

The place?

Hell, he'd been ready to self combust. Burst into flames. Explode. One touch, one taste, and *bam*...his hunger for the prickly beauty intensified full throttle. What the hell? He'd pulled her close, and with their bodies lined up in perfect symmetry, which only intensified the damn heat, he'd proceeded to share the dessert and one hell of a memorable kiss. Delicious. Succulent. And it had nothing to do with the fruit. Absolutely nothing.

No. Sweet, juicy...hot, it was all her.

All Shayla Ryan.

***
For announcements about upcoming releases and exclusive contests:
Join Donna's Newsletter
Visit me at: www.donnamichaelsauthor.com
***

Harland County Series
Book One: *Her Fated Cowboy*

L.A. cop Jordan Masters Ryan has a problem. Her normal method of meeting a crisis head-on and taking it down won't work. Not this time. Not when fate is her adversary. Having kept her from the man she thought she'd always marry, the same fickle fate took away the man she eventually did. Thrown back into the path of her first love, she finds hers is not the only heart fate has damaged.

Widower and software CEO, Cole McCall fills his days with computer codes and his free time working the family's cattle ranch. Blaming himself for his wife's death, he's become hard and bitter. When his visiting former neighbor sets out to delete the firewall around his heart, he discovers there's no protection against the Jordan virus. Though she understands his pain and reawakens his soul, will it be enough for Cole to overcome his past and embrace their fated hearts?

***

Harland County Series

Visit my **Harland County Series Page** at my website www.donnamichaelsauthor.com for release information and updates!

Book One: Her Fated Cowboy
Book Two: Her Unbridled Cowboy
Book Three: Her Uniform Cowboy
Book Four: Her Forever Cowboy

Become a *Cowboy Tamer!*

Drop me a line at donna_michaels@msn.com and request some Cowboy-Tamer swag!

***
She Does Know Jack
A Romantic Comedy Suspense
by Donna Michaels

Releasing July 2013

Former Army Ranger Capt. Jack 'Dodger' Anderson would rather run naked through a minefield in the Afghan desert than participate in a reality television show, but when his brother Matthew begins to receive threats, Jack quickly becomes Matthew's shadow. As if the investigation isn't baffling enough, he has to contend with the addition of a beautiful and vaguely familiar new contestant.

Security specialist, Brielle Chapman reluctantly agrees to help her uncle by going undercover as a contestant on the *Meet Your Mate* reality show. Having nearly failed on a similar assignment, she wants to prove she still has a future in this business. But when the brother of the *groom* turns out to be Dodger, the only one-nighter she ever had—while in disguise from a prior undercover case—her job becomes harder. Does he recognize her? And how can she investigate with their sizzling attraction fogging her brain? Determined to finish the job, she brings the case to a surprising climax, uncovers the culprit and *meets* her own *mate*.

***
Thanks for reading!

Made in the USA
Lexington, KY
26 February 2016